THE
FOREST
OF
DESPAIR

THE FOREST OF DESPAIR

RYAN HOYT

Machete & Quill Press

To Natalie and Daisy—
May you always be the heroes of your own stories.

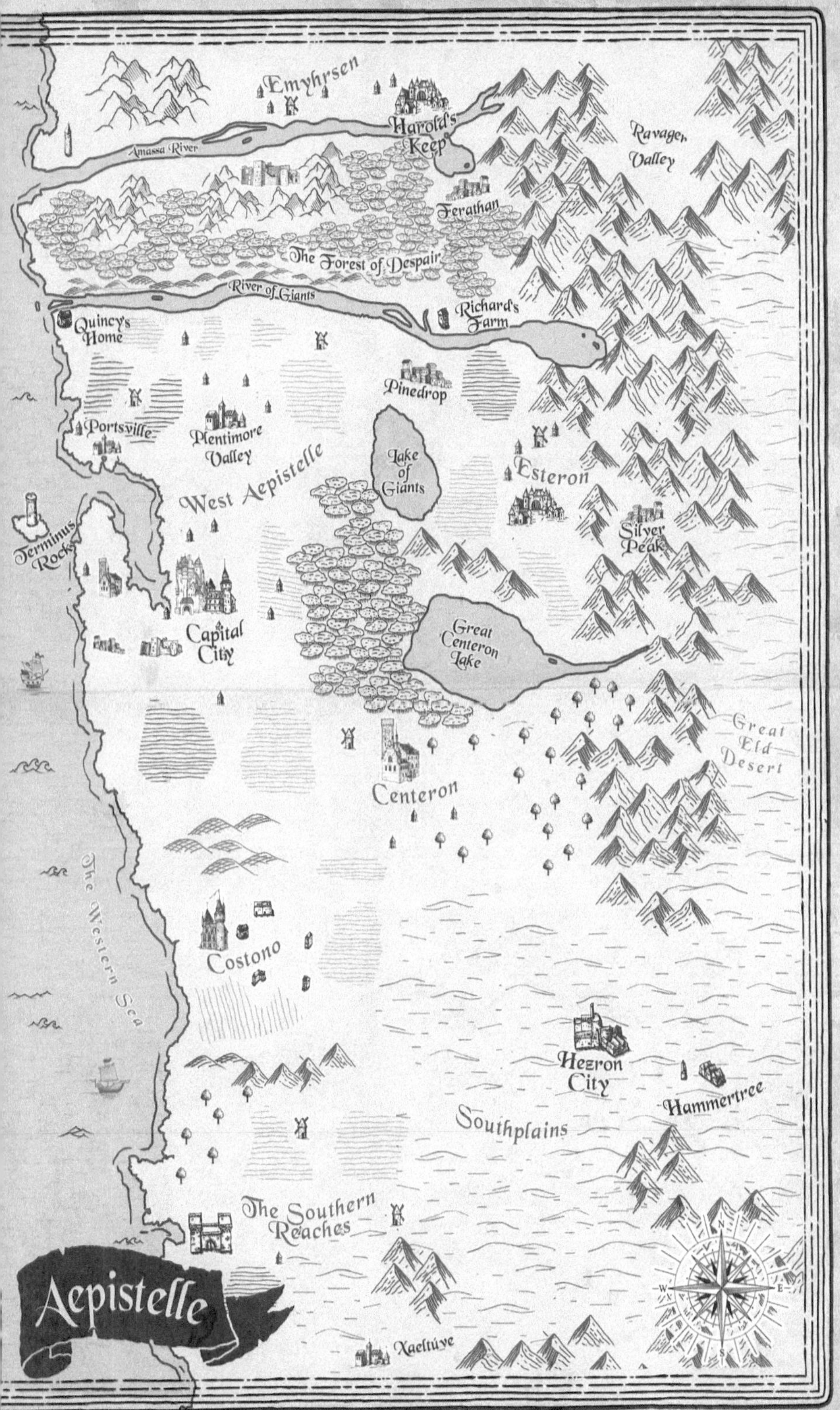

Emyhrsen
Harold's Keep
Ravage Valley
Amassa River
Ferathan
The Forest of Despair
River of Giants
Quincy's Home
Richard's Farm
Pinedrop
Portsville
Plentimore Valley
Lake of Giants
Esteron
West Aepistelle
Silver Peak
Terminus Rocks
Capital City
Great Centeron Lake
Great Eld Desert
Centeron
The Western Sea
Costono
Hezron City
Hammertree
Southplains
The Southern Reaches
Aepistelle
Xaeltúye

PART I
TRAINS

CHAPTER 1

TELMAN ABERNATH

It wasn't as if Gemma Calvertson were some sort of *chosen one* foretold by the prophets. Nor did she have any particularly special skills that Abernath knew of, even if she was academically and emotionally intelligent. It was just that she was going to be in the right place at the right time.

Oh, and that wasn't by chance, either.

Abernath had arranged the assignment in secret with Gemma's boss, Garrod Hannon. Sometimes, even evil men can sprout consciences, hoping they bear fruit that make up for their insidious past choices. Abernath and Hannon were two of these men looking for redemption. The girl was a tool for making that happen, even if she didn't know it yet.

Telman Abernath peered over the bannister of the fifth floor of the library, his usual perch as the head of the institution. Unlike many aged libraries, which were dark and dusty affairs, the Royal Library of Aepistelle was a grand place with many windows, including the glass-domed rooftop. There was an open, vaulted space between the mezzanine and the dome above the center of the fifth floor. Thus, natural light could shine upon all corners of the building, especially on the rows of tables that sat on the bottom floor.

That was where the girl, Gemma, sat nearly every afternoon as she engaged in her research. It was where she pored over massive tomes about the taxation rates under one king or another or compared historical accounts of the crown's responses to famines and floods. Maybe the girl did have some kind of superpower after all if she was able to stay awake through all that. Her boss, Hannon, even said that Ms. Calvertson had it in her to become one of the great historians. That is, as long as she stayed within the narrow lanes afforded to her by the latest laws set by King Davin and his Royal Mystic Committee. So much was off-limits these days. So many books burned, so many lies sold as truths, and Abernath himself was regrettably part of it all.

Down below, one of Abernath's assistants handed a note to Gemma. She startled at the interruption, read the note, and turned to look up at Abernath on the fifth floor. Within a minute, the girl had made her way effortlessly to the top of the winding staircase. Abernath opened the half gate that barred unauthorized entry to the library's special collections floor. Up here, there were a number of books that barely made it past the restrictions placed on the Kingdom of Aepistelle over the last twenty-five years, restrictions just older than the girl herself. Some of these books contained limited information on the history and geography of the lands to the north; others were religious texts of some of the less dangerous faiths that had once been practiced in Aepistelle. Even these books had been carefully examined; all had passages redacted, and some were missing entire chapters. Abernath's own hands were responsible for much of it.

"I was told you wanted to see me, Mr. Abernath," Gemma

said. She had been up to the fifth floor many times since she had started working for the University Press. It took a request from someone such as Hannon to even be granted access, let alone browse even partially unsupervised. "I don't believe I need anything from the restricted archives today, but thank you."

"Ah, yes, I know, Miss Calvertson. I'll only take a moment of your time." Abernath reached into his deep robe pocket and fiddled with the scroll hidden there. He pulled it halfway out and saw Gemma glance down at it. "I understand you are setting off on a big assignment for Mr. Hannon."

"That's right," Gemma said. "I leave this afternoon."

"Yes, well, my good friend Hannon is very excited about the work you will be undertaking."

Something caught Abernath's eye across the corridor and one floor down. A woman stood at a shelf near the fourth-floor balcony with a book pulled halfway out of place, but she was obviously focusing her attention elsewhere, even if her eyes weren't pointed up at Abernath and Gemma.

What a fool I am, standing here in the open while I incriminate the girl, Abernath thought. *They're already on to me—and on to her—and I haven't even given her the scroll.*

"Is there something wrong, Mr. Abernath?" Gemma asked.

Abernath shook off his thoughts, but the expression on his face was grave. He tried to force a smile as he shoved the scroll back down into his pocket, then wiped his brow with his empty hand.

"Uh, no, I'm sorry. An old man's mind isn't always the sharpest, even when surrounded by a lifetime of books. I just wanted to wish you good luck on your journey, and we look forward to seeing you take up your favorite seat in the study room when you're back."

"Oh, okay, thanks, Mr. Abernath. I should be seeing you again in a couple of weeks. Take care!"

The girl flashed a genuine smile at the old librarian, then went back through the gate and down the stairs to where her books awaited her.

Abernath looked back down to the fourth floor, but the strange woman was gone, and the book she'd been touching was still halfway out of its place on the shelf. The slight creak of the gate sounded, and Abernath turned toward it.

"I'm looking for the section on treason against the crown," the woman said.

Abernath was taken aback. *How could the Royal Mystic Committee know about the plan?*

"I'm sorry, but you must have a referral to be up here," Abernath said. Despite his years as the head of the library, he had never developed a voice of authority.

"I think you know of my commander, don't you, Mr. Abernath?" The woman walked slowly toward the librarian as he stepped backward. "I believe you know of Sir Marin Allemon and the Royal Mystic Committee. Is that enough of a referral?"

"There must be a mistake. We do not have any books of interest to you here."

Abernath's hand crept back into his robe pocket as he backed into the bannister. He could just make out Gemma down below, gathering her materials and preparing to leave.

"I didn't say anything about a book, you fool. It's a scroll I'm looking for."

The woman reached under her coat and pulled out a throwing dagger. At the same time, Abernath pulled his hand out of his robe. The scroll in his possession wielded much more power than the woman's weapon.

He reached over the railing and dropped it at the same

moment the woman released the dagger. Abernath slumped down against the banister, blade protruding from his left eye, as the scroll plummeted down through the sunlit rotunda. With his one remaining eye, Abernath watched as the rolled-up parchment landed on the marble floor just behind Gemma Calvertson.

The girl did not seem to notice.

Abernath's mission appeared to have failed.

The heavy double doors on the first floor flew open. An unnatural gust of wind stormed the library. Books flew off shelves, papers scattered from the study tables, and patrons jumped to their feet in surprise. Abernath noticed that his attacker seemed to forget about him, and he managed to push away from her to get a better look.

He heard the sounds before he saw what made them. From the front door, from the unlit fireplaces throughout the building, and crashing through the domed windows above, thousands of pigeons swooped in and circled the library frantically. Abernath could just make out a figure emerging from among birds at the front entrance. It was a strikingly tall man.

"What sorcery is this, Abernath?" The woman from the Committee slammed her boot down onto the librarian's left kneecap.

Abernath cried out in pain. His attacker lifted her foot and was about to hammer it down on the same spot once again when she was pushed off balance by a swarm of pigeons. She screamed as she fell on the floor next to Abernath and flailed her arms and legs at the birds.

Abernath looked back down to where Gemma was collecting her scattered papers from the floor. In the pile, unbeknownst to the girl, was the scroll. Abernath watched as Gemma hastily shoved everything into her bag. As she rose, ready to flee, the mysterious tall man set his hand on

Gemma's shoulder and appeared to speak a few words. The girl froze for a moment before walking calmly out the front doors of the library.

The blood was overtaking Abernath's vision when he spotted the tall man again, now just a few feet away at the top of the stairs. Up close, Abernath could clearly see his features and chuckled, perhaps too joyously for a man in the last moments of his life. The newcomer was hairless but for the comically large handlebar mustache protruding from his face. He was dressed in a fine suit. He was, Abernath recognized, a priest of Solendaron. And if a clergyman of one of the long-outlawed religions was making such a bold attack in Capital City, then perhaps redemption truly was close.

Abernath's remaining eye closed for good, but his other senses still worked for a few more moments. He heard the woman screaming, felt the wind created by the birds flying all around, and then the screams again, seemingly descending through the air to the marble floor below. He felt a warm hand on his shoulder, and a man's voice spoke softly to him.

"The girl will succeed," the priest of Solendaron said to Abernath as the librarian took his final breath. "You may rest now, my friend, for the girl *will* succeed."

CHAPTER 2
GEMMA CALVERTSON

Gemma found herself standing in her bedroom, snapping out of a daze. She could remember being in the library. There was that odd meeting with the librarian, Mr. Abernath. It had seemed as if he'd wanted to give her something from his pocket but had changed his mind. What had happened after that? She'd heard a crash from the front door of the library... and then she was here. Perhaps the stress of leaving home for her latest assignment was impacting her more than she had expected.

Gemma looked around her bedroom, feeling strangely as if this was the last time she would see it. She was twenty-three years old, but the contents of the room hadn't changed much since she was a young girl. That is, other than the shelves full of books she now studied, books with much less wonder than the ones about adventures and heroes that she'd pored over as a child.

On her bed, Gemma laid out two bags. One was filled with the research materials she had hastily managed to gather from the library, which she hoped to brush up on during what were sure to be uneventful evenings in Pinedrop. The other bag contained her clothes and toiletries, a smaller knapsack to take on strolls, and her notebooks and pens. *I'll be lucky to fill even one of these notebooks*, she thought to herself. *I'll be lucky if Richard the Elusive even speaks to me at all.*

"You're sure this is what you want to do?"

Gemma turned toward the doorway, where her brother stood. He held one of his kittens in the crook of his left arm, but it pounced away when George spoke again. "You're sure you trust this guy? You know what war can do to a person. Just look at Dad."

"Yes, George. You don't have to remind me what happened to Dad in the war. And I don't think Richard the Elusive is as bad as the rumors say."

Gemma couldn't believe he was trying to use their father's mental illness as an excuse to hold her back. She knew George loved their family, but he still constantly shirked the responsibilities of taking care of their father.

George had never really cared for school, and he'd never made it to college. Instead, he'd gone straight to work as an apprentice blacksmith. He had eventually gained enough skills to become a farrier, shoeing horses throughout Capital City. Business was down lately with more people riding the train, so he was more on edge than ever. He knew education was important to Gemma, but *he* was earning to support the family, along with their mother, who worked as a maidservant in King Davin's castle. That left nobody to keep their father company, and his mind had become quite useless in the quarter of a century since the war.

As for Gemma, her days as a student were over. Capital University's publishing arm had hired her as a researcher. This was her big chance to use her history and writing skills. She wasn't about to let her family hold her back, especially since the advance she'd been paid was more money than her brother was likely to earn in a month.

"If you're so worried, you could always come with me," Gemma said. They looked at each other for a moment, and the tension broke. They both laughed.

"What, and leave my kittens? I wouldn't dream of such a thing!" George had in fact never left Capital City. Gemma had taken the train south once, but George had never stepped foot on one of the machines.

"Is that all you're concerned with in life? Your cats?"

"Well," George said as he glanced down the hall, "there's Wellyn, I suppose." Wellyn and George had been together off and on since George was only fifteen years old, but they weren't exactly romantic. They supported each other's endeavors, but they never seemed happy in any way. George didn't like to be pressed about it.

Gemma latched her bags tightly and pulled them off her bed. Her brother reached out to take one for her, but Gemma walked past him with a wink.

"Wait up!" George shouted as she headed down the stairs. George, with his stocky legs, struggled to keep up with his tall, slender sister. Other than their figures, it was quite clear that the pair was related. Their olive-brown skin and dark hair set them apart from many in Aepistelle, traits passed down from their paternal grandparents from the Ferromin Islands.

Gemma walked into the living room, where her father had sat nearly all day for as long as Gemma could remember. Like George, the older man was heavily built, but where George's muscles had grown from his job, Geoffrey Calvertson had atrophied over the years. Geoffrey didn't look either of his children in the eyes as they approached him. He just stared at the wall as if watching some invisible battle in another realm.

"Dad, I'm leaving now," Gemma said hesitantly. "Wellyn will be in to check on you when Mom and George are at work. I'm going north to Pinedrop to interview Richard the Elusive. Do you remember? You met him years ago."

"N–North? R–Richard?" Geoffrey stirred a bit. Gemma stepped into the line of his vision, hoping her father would see her. "Richard. Don't know Richard. I remember the north. I re–remember the f–fire. The forest. The…"

"It's okay, Dad. I just wanted to say goodbye. I love you." Gemma leaned in and kissed her father's forehead. She tried one final time to look into his eyes. For a moment, she saw a flash of recognition as she caught his gaze. He muttered her name and gave a slight smile, but it quickly faded. It had been like that for most of Gemma's life—bouts of delusion, moments of clarity, and explosions of anger or fear—but Gemma knew that trapped inside the troubled facade, deep behind those glazed and troubled eyes, was a hero who loved her.

———

A TRAIN WHISTLE BLEW, ACCOMPANIED BY AN EXPANDING cloud of black. The station was bustling with people, most of whom covered their noses or coughed out the polluted air as the train rolled to a stop in front of them. This was all still new to most of them—these massive carts on tracks of steel, propelled not by horses but by the burning of coal. Many people in the crowd were about to ride on a train for the first time; ticket prices had finally fallen so that train travel was no longer just a tool of convenience for the wealthy.

"Final boarding call! All aboard!"

Gemma rushed through the crowd of people on the platform, quickly apologizing as her bags bumped into knees and elbows. Perhaps she *had* packed too many books. After much effort, she located an attendant outside the train. She handed over her ticket. He stamped it, handed it back, and said, "You may walk through to the first-class dining car, ma'am, after you've checked into your private room. Have a wonderful ride."

Gemma was shocked. She looked down at the ticket, and sure enough, the university had provided a first-class one. She stepped aboard the car, a crowded passenger car that she had originally assumed she would sit in. This was the kind of car in which she'd ridden down to the Southern Reaches, and it *almost* felt odd to ride anywhere else.

Almost.

Gemma smirked with a kind of satisfaction she didn't expect from herself as she walked past the rows packed full of people.

She pulled open the door to the next car, a sleeper car full of bunks that were separated only by thin curtains. She pushed her way past men and women who were tossing their bags onto the bunks. Gemma was pleasantly surprised that she wouldn't be sleeping there tonight. She went through another set of doors, this time into the first-class car. Here, she was greeted by a porter, who glanced at the information on her ticket and then led her to room 3B.

"Here you are, ma'am," the porter said. Gemma could tell he was putting on a faux accent, as servants of the wealthy often do. She noticed her mother doing it sometimes when she got home from work, as if she were still serving the royal family and honored guests of King Davin. Hearing this trick used on her felt wrong, but this was a new experience all the way around, so she accepted it. "We will collect your luggage prior to our arrival and have it waiting for you when you exit the train. After you get settled here, I can guide you to the dining car for luncheon and beverages. Do enjoy your stay with us."

———

GEMMA SAT IN THE DINING CAR, ADMIRING THE AUTHENTIC silver and decorative porcelain that was used to serve her three-course meal—and this was just lunch. She had seen such fine tableware only a couple of times when her mother had brought home old chipped plates or teacups from King Davin's castle, saving them from being thrown in the trash. However, even those didn't stay in the cottage for long, as her mother always ended up selling them when money was tight.

"Anything else for you, ma'am?" her server asked.

"Oh, I really couldn't eat anything more, thank you. May I have the bill now?"

The server looked at Gemma, chuckled, and responded, "It's all included, ma'am. Dinner will be served at six, but feel free to sit here as long as you'd like."

Gemma noticed that the server dropped his faux accent as he spoke to her, as if he realized she was a fraud. She suddenly felt even more foolish than before. This luxurious treatment was new for her and something she knew not to expect again. Looking around the first-class dining car, she also felt under-dressed. These were the kinds of people King Davin invited to his court for royal banquets, the kinds of people her mother served during those nights when she stayed late and came home feeling a little less dignified than before. Gemma always imagined that those people looked at her mother with contempt for her low status. She imagined now that they were looking at her in just the same way.

She was so lost in her thoughts as she sipped the last drops of tea out of her too-fancy cup that she didn't even notice the man sitting down on the chair next to her at the otherwise-empty table. Startled, she turned her head when she felt a hand touch hers.

"Easy, Gemma," the man said.

In her sudden fright, she dropped her empty teacup. Its rim chipped when it struck the edge of the table. Had she noticed, she would have wondered if the server would take this cup home to his own family. Perhaps it would be the fanciest item adorning their pantry until it was pawned the next time a bill was due.

Her eyes and mind refocused as she recognized the handsome but cocky man sitting next to her.

"Walker? What are you doing here?" she asked. "Don't tell me—"

"The Committee sent me, Gemma. They tasked me with protecting you." Walker talked in a hushed voice and looked around uneasily, as if he was afraid of being heard. "How are you enjoying your luxury so far?"

She couldn't believe it. "Protect me from what? Does Hannon think I'm just some helpless little girl who can't take care of herself?"

"Don't draw attention, Gemma. You must have known from the first-class ticket that there's more going on here. The university wouldn't have paid for this. Hannon is protective of your family after all the time he spent serving with your father in the war. And I don't blame him. Not even the Royal Mystic Committee knows what Richard will be like or if he is as crazy as the rumors say. People call him Richard the *Reclusive* for a reason. Hannon knows as well as you do what the war did to the people involved."

"Wow, did you and my brother plan this?" Gemma asked. "George said pretty much the same thing. If I could put up with my father these last few years, I can handle Richard the

Elusive without your help. It's been twenty-five years since he came home from the Great Journey. If he were going to crack and murder someone, he would have done it by now."

"All right, all right, I'm only doing my job. I'll keep my distance, but I need to be close enough to pull you out if a situation goes sideways. I have some other things to take care of in the northeast anyways, so I won't be in your hair much. Whatever you do, don't let Richard know I'm there. It's important that he thinks you're only there for his story."

"I *am* only here for his story. I have no other motives." Gemma's anger was boiling over now, but she didn't want to ask any more questions. She already felt the snooty eyes of her fellow first-class passengers boring into her, this time maybe not as imagined as before. She had been living a lie this past hour, and she wanted no part of it anymore. She stood up abruptly.

"As long as you're convinced of that, Richard will be, too," she heard Walker say. She turned away from him and hurried back to her room in the next car.

CHAPTER 3
DENNY OF ESTERON

At the same time, hundreds of miles to the east, a different train pulled into Esteron Station and ground to a halt.

Thousands of pounds struggled to transition from forward motion to a standstill. The squeal of the brakes caused all the people on the platform to cover their ears. Babies cried out suddenly, mothers reached out for their children to soothe them, and fathers grimaced and rolled their eyes. Many were there to greet their loved ones traveling in from other parts of Aepistelle. Others were waiting to depart on their own trips to visit family or friends across the country or to go on business ventures away from this backwater town.

But not Denny.

The fifteen-year-old boy was perched on top of one of the station buildings, crouched on a flat stretch between several slopes of roofing Denny called home. He wasn't interested in the passengers coming off their train or the families waiting for their arrival. Instead, he was observing the cargo train parked on a parallel track. Men had been hard at work for the better part of the morning, unloading goods and wares from the train and stacking them onto horse-drawn carts. Normally, Denny would be creeping closer to these cars, ready to grab what he could while the crew members were busy chatting with each other. This time, however, something else had caught his attention.

Denny slid down the small slope to the center of the roof. He crawled under the canvas tarp that served as his own rooftop, rummaged through his few belongings, and found what he was looking for. He pulled out a dirty, leather-bound book with the words *Journey of Perils, Heroes of Men: A Memoir by Jestan the Just* embossed on the spine. The book wasn't quite old enough to justify its worn and decrepit condition, but it had been well read by Denny and had miraculously survived the elements to which it was exposed in the alleys and rooftops that Denny called home.

Denny climbed back up to the peak that overlooked the tracks, book in hand. He crouched low to avoid the notice of the nearly nonexistent security in the station. He lay down on his belly with his head extending over the edge, then opened the book. His fingers knew exactly which page he was looking for. They ignored the opening sections about bravery and vigilance. They passed over the history of magic on the Aepistelle continent—a section conspicuously omitted in later editions. They flipped past the chapters about Jestan's humble beginnings. They skipped the shorter section about Richard. They stopped with precision at the chapter introducing two fellows from the lush vineyard territory a day's ride north of Capital City.

Denny finally looked down at the book, knowing he was on the correct page. He caught sight of the illustration of two young men, short and cherubic, much too jolly-looking to ever be thought of as great warriors or heroes and apparently only a few years older than Denny was now.

He looked back up, but he couldn't find what he was looking for in the distance. Some of the carts started to pull away, cargo from the train piled high, but a few still remained. Denny realized he would need a closer look.

With the book in one hand, Denny slid down the roof again, crossed the crevice he called home, and climbed up the other side. He carefully made his way over the loose tiles he'd learned to avoid, clambered to the edge, made sure nobody was around to see him, and jumped down into the large waste receptacle below.

CRASH!

Normally, the landing was softer, more graceful. This time, however, Denny failed to realize until it was too late that the rubbish bin was full of glass bottles. Mercifully, they weren't yet broken when he landed on them, or else he'd really be in a situation, though he could feel that those he'd shattered were already finding their way into his skin below the knees. Perhaps worse, the noise had surely been heard by the station staff, as he was just outside their break room. He sank down low, further enveloped by the newly broken bottles, as the back door of the station office opened.

"Get out of here, you mangy mutt," he heard a station worker yell. The door slammed shut again. Denny waited a few seconds more until he was sure he was alone again, then climbed out of the pile of glass.

He regretted dropping down onto the ground, as a shard of glass pushed farther into his foot. As quickly as he was able, he pulled off his boot and surveyed the damage. He winced as he dislodged the bloody glass from his heel, emptied the broken shards out of the boot, and quickly slipped his foot back in. He didn't have time to wallow in pain and self-pity if he wanted to catch a closer glimpse of what he was sure he'd seen.

He reached up into the bin and grabbed his book, miraculously still in one piece, and then made his way across the platform. It was clogged with passengers and their families, grazing like cows in a crowded field as they embraced each other, gathered luggage, and chattered about their journeys. They took no notice of the grungy, bleeding boy slipping past them, and he took no notice this time of the pocketbooks jutting slightly out of rear pants pockets or unattended handbags that would be simple enough to slip under his shirt and make off with.

"Tsechev," he said to himself under his breath. He didn't know what it meant, but it was something he had started saying in the past few days. A nervous tick, perhaps. "Tsechev ni-fellen."

Denny raced up the platform and crossed in front of the engine of the parked passenger train. He could smell the burning of the brakes and the fumes of the coal that still lingered. His eyes burned from it, but that made no difference right now. On the other side of that track was the cargo train, where workers bustled to fill the last remaining carts. Denny crept past them, but they were too busy to notice him. He stooped behind a large crate in the middle of the cargo platform and peered around it. He opened his book to the same page as before, studied the illustration, looked back up at a tired middle-aged man hopping aboard one of the carts, and looked back down again.

The caption under the young man in the illustration read "Arnem the Loyal."

CHAPTER 4
ARNEM THE LOYAL

There was nothing enigmatic about the Enigmatic Esteron Tavern; it was the same as all taverns, east, west, or wherever. Arnem would know. He had visited quite a few of them over the years. More than Selah would like, and surely more than she knew about. *Who am I kidding*, he thought. *It shows from my bulging gut to my fat, rosy face.*

Arnem wasn't all that physically different from most of his kinsmen from Plentimore Valley, the lush lands he called his home. They tended to be on the short and stout side, and they also tended to drink a good deal of ale while bottling up the wines they mostly shipped off to other parts of Aepistelle. But Arnem always told himself that he should amount to much more than his peers. He'd seen more, done more, lived more in his lifetime than any of them. His name was known across the lands. Then again, his image—well, at least the depiction of whichever artist Jestan had hired to illustrate his books—was out there for all to see. And unfortunately, that image was of a fat little man who, along with his pal and childhood neighbor Maachel, was dwarfed by the tall, muscular Jestan and the seemingly oafish but hulking Richard. Sure, the pictures were quite exaggerated, but Jestan's books were the defining sources about their merry little band from all those years ago.

As he sat, sipping on his ale, Arnem couldn't help but feel that his life was already defined by those texts and illustrations. He'd been barely twenty years old when it had all begun, and it had all been downhill from there.

A fight broke out behind him, but Arnem hardly noticed. A mug sailed just inches over his head and exploded against the wall behind the bar, but Arnem couldn't be shaken from his thoughts. His wife and daughters had noted with increasing regularity that Arnem spent more time in his own head than he did in reality. He knew they meant well and were worried about him, and he often got angry at himself for being so emotionally distant, but as hard as he tried, he couldn't quite figure out how to be present all the time. It wasn't only the memories of what had happened, but also what could have been. What if he had made that final journey into the unknown with Maachel and the Vheisenia, or the Ancient Ones, as most of Aepistelle knew them? What if he'd spun tales about their quest and entertained people while traveling in luxury the way Jestan had? What if...

Well, I suppose I could be worse off. I could be all alone, like Richard the Reclu—

Arnem stopped himself. He knew that Richard had sacrificed so much more than the rest of them to receive the same hero title they had all gotten.

"Hey, aren't you that one guy?" said a voice, suddenly pulling Arnem back into the present. Arnem looked up at the face that went with the voice. It belonged to a man dressed much too nicely for such a place. Arnem realized instantly that he must be a fellow traveler.

"Wynstone from Wynstone and Sons Farming Supply Company," Arnem responded. At least Jestan had left family names out of the texts, so most people didn't know his full name.

"Oh, but you're—"

"So you've heard of our little operation, eh? We do supply farmers all the way from the Southern Reaches up to the outskirts of the Forest of Despair! And I can see you're a fellow traveling man yourself, huh?" Arnem deflected questions as often as he could, even when he knew people could see right through him.

The man looked embarrassed, so perhaps he hadn't seen through Arnem. "Sorry, I thought you were someone else," he said. "Yes, I'm traveling from Capital City, representing the Royal Tax Board. Everyone's favorite person to see this time of year. What brings you to Esteron?"

No need to deflect here. Arnem wasn't concerned about boring another person out of a conversation simply by telling the truth about his business. "It may be tax season, but it's also prime planting season out here. I like to personally oversee the larger shipments of goods, give that little extra touch that farmers appreciate from Wynstone and Sons."

"Why not just have one of your sons do it?" the taxman asked.

"Oh, it's..." This was a sore spot for Arnem. "No sons; my brothers and I inherited the business from my father. We were the 'and sons,' but now it's just me and whatever help I can hire."

"Sorry, my friend. It's a lonely life without children. I have four of them myself."

"I do have two daughters, just no sons," Arnem

responded. Selah had tried for years to get Arnem to change the name to Wynstone and Family. He had refused, first because he'd held out hope of having a son and then, when he'd realized that having daughters was his lot in life, because he was too stubborn. Not that he was disappointed in his girls, really, but he didn't feel that he could put them to work or rely on them to take over the business when they were older. They pitched in as much as they could—definitely as much as any boys their age could, if not more—but he was too hardheaded to admit it.

Arnem shifted his weight to reach for his pocketbook. He had half a glass left, but he wasn't in the mood for any more conversation. Besides, the train was leaving the station soon, and he didn't like traveling while tipsy.

The taxman didn't seem to take the hint. "Well, sounds like you should marry off those girls and put their husbands to work! I always tell people I—"

"Hey, you can't be in here!" the bartender yelled as he was collecting Arnem's cash. Arnem and the taxman turned their heads to see who the bartender was yelling at. "You dirty little thief, I'll have them lock you up this time!"

Arnem looked on as two patrons grabbed an awkward, gangly boy by the arms and quickly hauled him out. One of the men, a tall and chunky bald man that Arnem recalled seeing unloading cars at the train station, yelled out to the bartender. "We'll take him to the lockup, Hester, just have a cold one waiting for us when we return!"

The teenage boy was filthy, with unkempt hair, ill-fitting clothes that may have once been a light khaki color but were now stained all shades of dark, and boots that were torn open in several places, barely hanging on to the soles by the few remaining threads. As the men dragged the boy out, Arnem locked eyes with him. His gaze seemed to be a knowing one, as if he recognized Arnem.

Arnem used the commotion to leave the conversation with the traveling taxman and head for the exit. He almost tripped over something in the doorway. He looked down to find a familiar book. *One of Jestan's many curses*, he thought to himself. He could feel the taxman looking his way as Arnem stood there holding the book that revealed some of the truth about who he really was. He quickly exited the tavern before there were any more questions.

Once outside, Arnem realized that the book must have been open when it was dropped. The already worn-out pages had been newly bent when the book had fallen, and Arnem instinctively knew which section it had been turned to. It was the picture of two young, plump, innocent-looking lads. Best friends, neighbors, and not yet heroes. Maachel and Arnem, a couple of kids about to take on the world together. But now there was a different kid here, one who had apparently put himself in harm's way just to see Arnem, one who needed help. *If you want to be a hero still, then act like one*, his wife always told him.

Well, I suppose now is the time, he thought.

"Stop!" Arnem yelled to the men. When they turned around, he noticed that they had murder in their eyes. He swallowed down his fear and walked toward them.

"Yeah, and what are you going to do, fat man?" the bald one asked. "You want to take this little thief home for your sick pleasures?" The men looked at each other and laughed, then turned back to Arnem. Baldy then asked, "What's that you're holding?"

Before Arnem could answer, the boy responded for him. "It's a book, you daft idiot," he said. "I bet you goons can't even read, though, so what did I expect?"

The bald man loosened his grip on the boy and grabbed the book from Arnem's hands. He studied the page it was still open to, looked at Arnem, then back at the page. He glanced nervously at his companion, who let go of the boy.

"We're sorry, Mr. Arnem, won't happen again," Baldy said as he put the book into the kid's hands. He and his friend walked back toward the Enigmatic Esteron Tavern without glancing back.

The boy looked up at Arnem. His eyes opened wide, and his jaw dropped. And then Denny spoke.

"It *is* you. Arnem the Loyal." He paused, apparently trying to figure out how to phrase his thoughts for Arnem. "I know how this will sound, but you've got to listen to me. Something terrible is about to happen. We need to hurry if you want to save your friend!"

CHAPTER 5

GEMMA

Gemma was famished.

After the confrontation with Walker on the train, Gemma had spent the rest of the train ride, nearly a full twenty-eight hours, in her room. The porter had brought her beverages and a few light snacks when she'd told him she felt sick, but nothing substantial to make up for skipping the three-course dinner or breakfast. It helped, then, that Gemma's first stop after the Pinedrop rail station was the weekend farmers market at the heart of town. She didn't quite have time to check into a local inn and drop her bags off, so she lugged them around with her.

The weekend market in Pinedrop was the one place that townsfolk reported seeing Richard the Elusive on a regular basis. He set up a stall each week to sell goods from his farm, which was located a morning's walk north of town. Reportedly, Richard harvested huckleberries, blueberries, and cabbage from the terraced hills behind his home. It was said Richard stopped in at a supply shop and occasionally a pub on his way out of town, then was never seen again until the following weekend's market.

Gemma's ticket had been timed to allow her to catch the beginning of the market when she got into Pinedrop. However, a five-hour delay in the farmlands north of the royal vineyards had pushed her arrival to the end of the market. Her hunger led her to stop first at a meat pie stand, which served the most substantial prepared foods she could see. Many stands were already emptying of goods, and some vendors were loading up their carts with empty crates and tables.

"Sweet sun-ripened berries! Just in from the river ferries!" a vendor called out. "Sweet, sweet berries here! Hey, girl, try one of these, on the house."

"Huh?" Gemma turned toward the vendor.

"Yeah, you, have a sample. These are from the eastern borders, just shy of the Great Eld Desert."

"Oh, uh, thank you," Gemma said as she took the sample. She ate the berry. "Thank you, it's very delicious. I—"

"You're looking for something in particular," he interrupted. "I can tell."

"Some*one* in particular, yes, but I don't think he's here anymore."

"Probably that gentleman over there. He's been watching you this whole time."

"What?" Gemma turned to follow the vendor's gaze and realized he was referring to Walker. He was half turned away from Gemma but was side-eyeing her obviously enough that even the vendor could tell. Gemma's anger started to rise again, and she felt her cheeks turn red and fiery. "Oh, excuse me."

Gemma stormed over to Walker, momentarily forgetting

her luggage, which she had set down in front of the vendor's stall.

"Walker, what are you doing? I thought you were going to keep your distance," she said in a huff.

Walker turned to face her. "I was until you walked over here," he rebuked. "Now, stop blowing my cover."

If heat was rising in Gemma before, now it boiled over. "That merchant could tell you were watching me. You aren't doing a very good job of being subtle," she shot back. "Just leave me alone already!"

Walker raised his hands gently in an apparent attempt to diffuse the situation. "Listen, while you're here, I spotted him. He was already packing up his booth and heading out. He was walking north from the veranda."

"Oh no, I can't lose him," Gemma said. "I'm going to follow him, but don't tail me this time!" She ran off in the direction of the veranda and headed up the north sidewalk. She stopped after a few short steps.

"Your luggage," she heard Walker say, but she passed him without even a glance. She picked up her luggage at the fruit vendor's stall, then stormed silently past Walker.

"You're welcome," he said under his breath. He received no reply.

Unlike her hometown of Capital City, which was a chaotic maze within a maze and was constantly being built upon, Pinedrop was a relatively straightforward town, laid out like a grid. The train station was on the southern edge, the town square and marketplace quite centered, and the main streets roughly followed north-south and west-east directions. Gemma figured it was safe to assume that Richard was heading north up Main Street to the river. From what she'd seen on the map she had studied before her trip, there were only two bridges that crossed the River of Giants, and only one was still in use these days. She knew that if she crossed that bridge, she would find only a few farms still in use. Richard's was the farthest north and the only one still inhabited. The other farmers crossed the bridge in the morning, worked their land, and crossed back into town in the evenings.

Gemma looked up the street and saw a man in the distance, about a block and a half away, pulling something behind him. She picked up her pace but tried to keep enough distance between them to avoid making the same mistake Walker had. However, neither of them were spies, and it showed. She got near enough to the man to see the cart he was pulling. It was wooden with two wheels and two handles, filled with near-empty crates. It looked like he had almost sold out of the goods he'd brought to the market. Gemma was surprised to find herself filled with happiness for him.

That's weird—I don't even know him, she thought, *but if people were comfortable enough to stop at his stall and buy his goods, he must not be all that intimidating.*

Without realizing it, she sped up—or perhaps he slowed down—and his physical features became clear as she got closer. Gemma first noticed that he was much older than he was in the illustrations from Jestan's books. *Well, yeah, that was twenty-five years ago*, she reminded herself. He was a large man, really hulking in size. He had a crooked gait, possibly because of the awkward way he pulled the cart behind him, but also likely because of the spinal issues that unusually tall men often had in middle age. It wasn't until he stopped in his tracks and turned around that Gemma really saw what Richard the Elusive had become.

She started when he turned his head to face her.

"Good evening," he said with a voice that was somehow both gruff and gentle.

Gemma caught her breath. "Oh, um, good evening to you, too."

"You look new to town. Are you seeking anything in particular? The Frontiersman Inn is just around that last corner," Richard said as he nodded in the direction Gemma had just come from, glancing down at her luggage.

"Oh, yeah, sorry," Gemma replied. "I wanted to stay at that one near the train station, but there were no vacancies. This one is a lot farther, I guess."

There was an awkward silence. She had fully intended to be forthcoming with Richard when she met him, but she felt a kind of awe that she was unfamiliar with, and she couldn't think clearly. Gemma had never been the hero-worship type. She respected Richard and his compatriots, but she had never idolized them by any means. Now that she stood face-to-face with him, though, a deep respect and admiration washed over her that was almost crippling. She didn't want to look like a bumbling journalist on her first big assignment, even if that was close to what she was, so she decided this wasn't the right time to introduce herself.

"It's just down that last street there and to the right," Richard said, breaking the silence at last. "If you're just out for a leisurely stroll, though, you probably don't want to go farther than the river up ahead. You know what they say about the woods beyond the river."

"Yes, I, uh... well, thank you, sir. Have a pleasant evening."

"And you as well," Richard said as he turned and continued up the street toward the river.

***

GEMMA ARRIVED AT THE FRONTIERSMAN INN MINUTES later. It had clearly seen better days; perhaps it had once been a rest stop for travelers on their way to the north country and King Harold's Keep beyond the forest. The Pinedrop Suites and Inn near the rail station was far more luxurious and far more expensive. This place, on the other hand, was wedged between two pubs and was likely a frequent destination for tipsy men and their hired escorts.

After she checked in and entered her room—the less said about its cleanliness and decor, the better—Gemma took a notebook and fountain pen out of her knapsack. Her assignment was to write a more scholarly piece on the Great Journey from the perspective of Richard the Elusive and others involved, rather than the tall tales that Jestan's writings seemed to be. But for now, she just had to put down her thoughts from her first meeting with Richard.

It's like when you read a book and imagine what a character would look like. It's based on your preconceived notions of what a hero of legend must be, she wrote. *Well, Richard was massive, tough, cunning, yet gentle. And there was something else there, too. I don't know why I didn't expect it, but there it was. The look in his eyes. It was... despair. Sadness.*

And what else did I expect? This is a man who marched with his friends to the edge of the world, forced to fight off creatures of pure evil and the humans who sided with them. Put to the test of the sword, of fire, and even of sorcery. What those eyes must have seen— the things nightmares are made of.

She continued to write out her thoughts as she processed them.

And his body, clearly once full of muscles and stamina, was now bent and hunched, almost broken. Despite his speed, I recognized pain in every step. Every atrophied muscle must have been on fire as he pulled his cart behind him. I felt a sadness of my own as he walked away. I felt like this world was lost.

I also couldn't help but see my father in Richard the Elusive. It was the same war that broke them both, though their paths crossed only briefly. I told myself when I set out on this assignment that it was solely to learn about the history of Aepistelle. But perhaps this is really about better understanding my father... and better understanding myself. After what Walker revealed about this being some setup for the benefit of the Royal Mystic Committee, thoughts of giving up crossed my mind. Now, however, I think I need to pursue this more than I've needed anything before.

Gemma wrapped the band around her notebook and shoved it into her smaller bag. She rummaged through the larger bag for a book she had picked up from the library the day before on the history of Pinedrop. She hesitated when she caught sight of something protruding from between the pages. It was a scroll, faded with age, frayed along the edges, and quite distressed from rolling around in the bag of books. Wedged into the ribbon that held the scroll closed was a folded piece of parchment, much newer than the scroll itself. Gemma freed the paper from the ribbon's clutches and unfolded it. It wasn't signed, but Gemma recognized Mr. Abernath's handwriting.

It was addressed to Richard the Elusive.

CHAPTER 6
ARNEM

Arnem was back on a train toward home, but this time it was a passenger train. He probably could have afforded a first-class ticket if he'd really wanted to spring for it, but it would've eaten into his profits, and he was already thinking about how much he'd have to save up for his daughters' weddings when they came of age in the next few years. So here he sat in a coach dining car that was not completely filled, but the seat facing him at his table was occupied.

Across from the modest merchant sat a boy in fresh new clothes. Denny was greedily scarfing down what had begun as a plate of over-easy eggs, two buttered, flaky biscuits, and two strips of bacon but now amounted to a puddle of yolk that the boy began lapping up like a dog. As Denny looked up from his plate, Arnem couldn't help but chuckle at the yolk residue that had soaked into the boy's already-greasy hair. Denny was too satisfied with his first real meal in months to even notice.

"Well, now, it seems you could probably polish off another

breakfast plate, but let's save some room for lunch, shall we? It's a long ride back." Arnem handed Denny a napkin. "Are you ready to explain what you meant last night about friends in trouble?"

It had been quite a night. After the ordeal outside the tavern, Arnem had brought the boy to the only medical clinic he could find open at that hour. While they sat, waiting for the nurse to stitch the wounds Denny had gotten from jumping into the rubbish bin full of glass bottles, Arnem had heard the whistle of the cargo train in the distance as it left Esteron. The clinic staff had allowed Arnem and Denny to stay in the waiting room for the rest of the night. In the early morning, while Denny continued to sleep, Arnem had ventured out to find a clothing shop, where he procured slacks, a button-down shirt, and a pair of lightly used boots that he thought would fit the boy. He couldn't help but notice that he would probably be buying similar-sized clothing for his oldest daughter, Lyria Marinah, had she been a boy. For a brief moment, he'd thought, *Maybe it's not too late to try again*, but then he reminded himself that he and Selah were pushing half a century and that yes, it was far too late for them.

When Arnem had arrived back at the clinic, Denny had turned to him with relief. It was clear from the look in Denny's eyes that he had thought he'd been abandoned, that Arnem wasn't the hero he'd thought he was, or that the previous day's ordeals were just an elaborate dream. But seeing Arnem again that morning had meant there was still hope for the boy. Arnem had been in a hurry to drop the clothing off with Denny and head back to the train station to catch the morning passenger line. As soon as Arnem had handed the clothing to Denny, however, a pang of guilt had washed over him.

Is it guilt, though? Arnem had thought to himself. *It feels much stronger, like something tugging at me—a sensation like when Maachel and I got pulled into the Journey and we just knew we had to go...*

And so Arnem had bought two tickets for the train back home, and they'd caught it just minutes before departure. *I don't know how I'm going to explain this to Selah. At least I'll have another hand to help out at the shop.*

Denny pulled the distressed book off of his lap and dropped it on the table next to the empty plate. He looked at Arnem and tapped the book with greasy fingers, not worried about dirtying it further.

"Is it all true?" Denny asked.

Arnem looked at the boy as he collected his thoughts.

"All of it? Well..." By now, he was looking past Denny, or maybe through him, as his mind raced over what was in the book, or at least in the volume he'd read more than a decade ago. He'd spent years evading conversations about the Journey and about Jestan and the others. "Well, it's complicated. Jestan is, um... well, a bit of an eccentric storyteller. Not a historian. A lot of what he describes—the big events, at least—happened in some form, but not quite in the way he spun the tales in there."

He paused, attempting to think how else he could describe it without breaking the kid's heart. But before he said anything else, Denny spoke up.

"No, I mean, I understand that Jestan is probably a bit of a liar," Denny said. "He clearly writes in a way that makes him out to be the hero of a fairy tale. But the rest of it—the magic, the darkness. Did you really see it?"

"Listen, Denny, let me be honest. We were in distress the whole time. We wandered through the mountains and forests for months on end with very little sleep. We ate food that turned out to be poisonous and hallucinogenic. We weren't cut out for that kind of living. We all thought we saw things that could be explained as magic and sorcery, but—" Arnem broke off. He realized he had said those words too loudly. Words were words, but the concepts themselves were forbidden in Aepistelle under King Davin. The last thing Arnem needed was to be thrown in jail because someone on the train reported him to the Royal Mystic Committee. He peered around, but nobody seemed to be looking their way.

"What I mean is," he continued, "things may not have gone the way we thought they did at the time. There is a lot to explain the things we saw. Those natural gasses that come out of the earth in the Forest of Despair are known to warp the minds of those passing through."

"But the fires that burned down the forest and everyone in it? Those weren't delusions of a warped mind," Denny fired back.

"Well," Arnem answered, "if the gasses were released in large quantities, and the soldiers lit fires at night where they camped... the gasses are also known to be highly flammable. There were thousands of soldiers, probably hundreds of fires burning at once throughout their camps."

The look Denny gave Arnem was one of disbelief. Heartbreak, even. "Please, Arnem. These are all the official explanations that King Davin's people have given, but there are so many holes in them! I just thought you could be honest with me."

Deep down, Arnem knew that he was rehashing those ridiculous explanations. There were so many more that he'd been made to memorize when King Davin and the Committee had summoned him years ago. The only reason Jestan had gotten away with writing about so much of it was that his style was so outlandish that many people treated his work as fiction, as an extension of Jestan's wild personality.

Arnem had spent so long memorizing and internalizing the officially mandated versions of events. He'd had to. For his own freedom. For Selah. For his girls. For Aepistelle's healing.

But inside, Arnem knew. He remembered.

As he sat in shame and silence, he observed Denny's frustrated demeanor. This wasn't just about being let down by an idol. It was clearly something deeper for Denny. Arnem wanted to let it go, but he had to press on.

"What is it, Denny?" he asked. "What's so important to you about the story being real?"

"It's just..." Now it was Denny's turn to dig deep into his memories, ones that were clearly painful to him. "My parents were taken from me when I was young. They knew it was illegal to study in the ancient texts. But they couldn't stop. They wanted to understand more about what they were. The Royal Mystic Committee couldn't make them forget."

"And what were they?" Arnem inquired.

"They had gifts. They were... prophets," Denny said in a hushed tone as he looked up bashfully.

Arnem didn't mean to, but he let out a small scoff at the word *prophets*. *Here we go*, he thought. *I'm being set up by the Committee, aren't I? After all these years...*

He didn't really believe it was a setup, but he knew it was dangerous to continue talking about the subject. Denny persisted.

"They had the gift," Denny said, and then his voice turned to a whisper. "And I do, too."

Arnem realized his throat had dried up. He took a sip of his tea, which had gone cold while they'd sat there talking. He didn't care. He started to fidget with the teaspoon as he looked around again to ensure they weren't being watched. Most of the passengers had moved back to the sitting cars by now, and only a few remained while they waited to pay their bills.

"I see things. In my sleep. I don't know how, but I do," Denny continued. "They're not usually clear, but they're more real than dreams—I know they are. I saw *him* a few nights ago, and he was in trouble. In pain. There was a castle of some sort, an abandoned village, something evil, some dark sorcery, something lurking, ready to pounce on him."

"Him? Who?" Arnem asked.

Instead of answering directly, Denny opened the book. It naturally opened to the illustration of Maachel and Arnem, but Denny flipped back one chapter to a picture of a tall, muscular figure with inquisitive, skeptical eyes and the furrow-browed expression of a man deep in thought.

"Richard the Elusive," Denny said. "Only he was older. Kind of leaning and tired-looking. And he wasn't alone. There's something dark out there, and they are about to fall into it, but we can save them. We have to."

Arnem sat in stunned silence, gripping the table, knuckles white.

He didn't want to admit it, but deep down inside, he believed.

CHAPTER 7
GEMMA

She should have rented a horse for the day.

Gemma's morning had started off with an illustrious breakfast of the innkeeper's finest soggy oats and nearly rotten blueberries. Clearly, she had been too busy yesterday to acquire fresh fruit and eggs from the farmers market in the town square. It was unfortunate that the woman didn't buy directly from Richard the Elusive. Gemma had chuckled to herself at the thought of Richard, a former war hero, going door-to-door in town to try and find businesses he could supply directly. Then she'd realized it wasn't so funny after all when she recognized that the man she'd witnessed leaving the market yesterday was still far more capable than her own father of taking care of himself.

The bridge she took to cross the River of Giants was in fine enough shape. The road beyond it passed a couple of fields where farmhands were hard at work reaping and sowing. But as she continued on her walk, it became apparent that the road past those farms was rarely used and not at all maintained. Weeds up to her knees jutted out from between rocks that were big enough to cause trouble for even the toughest horse-drawn carts. Gemma had to carefully avoid potholes, lest she break her ankle and get sent back home to Capital City. The potholes were full of muddy water from the midnight rains and morning dew. Mosquitoes flew out of the puddles all around her.

She knew Richard lived outside of town, but she hadn't realized it was this far out. Perhaps he really deserved the mock title of Richard the *Reclusive*. The knapsack she wore wasn't too heavy—she'd brought only a notebook, a pen, and a few other small supplies for the day—but it started to dig into her shoulders. Gemma took solace in the fact that the overgrown trees this far out provided shade and that the sun hadn't grown too hot yet, as blue as the cloudless sky was.

It had been half an hour since she'd passed the last farm when Gemma noticed the road and surrounding land had begun gradually sloping upward. She remembered hearing that Richard's farm was on a terraced hill that overlooked the edge of what was once the Forest of Despair. She started to think she must nearly be at her destination when she heard someone speak.

"Hello there," the gruff, husky voice called out from up ahead. Gemma saw Richard the Elusive standing in the shadow of a large tree on the side of the road.

"Oh, uh, hi," Gemma said. "I—"

"—was sent to spy on me," Richard responded. This shocked her. Richard continued as he walked toward her out of the shadow of the tree. "I could tell you were following me in town yesterday. You and that shifty-looking fellow at the market. Don't tell me King Davin's Committee is recruiting straight out of the university these days?"

"Committee? Oh, you mean the Royal Mystic Committee?" Gemma responded. "No, I think you misunder—"

"So you deny that you two are spying on me?" he interrupted.

"No, we—I mean, I—"

"We," Richard repeated.

"Huh?" Gemma wasn't expecting such hostility from him, but of course he would be defensive in this situation.

"You said 'we' just then."

"A mistake," Gemma replied, trying to recover from a bad start with the man she'd traveled all this way to talk to. "It's just me. I'm here to interview you. With your permission, of course. I'm with Capital University Press, and we're updating our history texts, but we're still missing facts about the Journey, and—"

"The Journey?" Richard interrupted again.

"Yes, the Great Journey taken by you and your friends," Gemma said, not understanding what the problem was. "It's been twenty-five years now, and still nobody knows all of the details about what happened."

"The Journey?" Richard repeated again, not quite directing his frustration at her but clearly letting out something that he had kept simmering inside for quite some time. "You know, they all make it sound like a fun little prance with pals through the wilderness. Sitting around campfires and singing songs to each other..."

"Oh, not at all," Gemma said. "A journey is for heroes. Like you."

"Is that what they call me now? A hero?"

"Yes, of course," she responded. "You're one of the four great heroes. We grew up telling tales and performing plays about you and Maachel and—"

"Stop, please," Richard said. "I don't need to hear their names."

Gemma noticed the wind for the first time at that moment. It didn't start softly and ramp up. Instead, it hit her like a force.

"What?" Gemma asked. "But they're your friends. Arnem, Jestan—"

"Jestan is a liar!" Richard said, his voice now raised, brow furrowed with what seemed to be more of a pained grimace than an angry one. "There is no truth to anything that comes off his tongue or out of his inkwell. Everything he says is full of deceit for his own gain."

Now something really seemed to be wrong with the weather around her. Gemma had to shield her eyes from the dust that was being thrown around by the wind. Her hair was blown off to the side with force. And the sky, so blue and clear a few minutes ago, was now dark and cloudy. Had a storm really come in so quickly?

"But—" Gemma began, but her voice was drowned out by the wind.

"They all make it sound like a frolic! Like a story people love to tell with smiles on their faces," Richard continued, just loud enough to be heard over the wind. "But they don't tell the truth. They don't tell you about the souls that were lost. The ones we didn't save. Or about the lives we took, no matter how evil they seemed in the moment. They didn't—"

Richard's voice was now fully inaudible to Gemma. She looked at the sky in horror.

"What's happening?" she asked as Richard stepped closer to steady her against the gusts of wind. She heard a loud snap as a large branch from the tree Richard had been standing under moments ago collapsed and crashed against the ground. "I've never seen clouds so black before. It's not possible!"

"What did you expect to find out here?" Richard responded, now holding her tightly to keep her from being bowled over. She wasn't afraid of Richard, as angry as he seemed. His large hands around her forearm and shoulder were gentle enough, even fatherly. "This isn't known as the edge of civilization for nothing. There's nothing but curses and death out here. You need to get back to town, now!"

"But it's not safe, is it?" Gemma asked, screaming into his ear just to be heard over the wind.

"You're right," Richard reluctantly replied. "Come with me."

———

THEY MADE IT UP THE HILL TO RICHARD'S HOUSE. HIS door flew open when he turned the knob. Gemma was afraid it would snap right off its rusty old hinges. It was a struggle to close it, and leaves poured in through the doorway before they were successful, but Gemma was relieved when they finally made it out of the freak storm.

She was shivering, panting, and in shock.

"What..." she started. "What... was... that?"

"It'll pass," Richard replied shortly.

"Okay, but—"

"Please, just sit. It will pass soon enough." Richard's voice softened, and his demeanor seemed to calm now that they were inside. Perhaps the wind had blown away whatever anger had been rising in him. He pointed to a couch in front of the fireplace. There was no fire burning, as the morning had been a nice one before the wind blew in. She sat down on the couch as Richard asked, "How do you take your coffee?"

"Black," she replied. "Like you do."

Richard had been walking toward what she assumed was the kitchen, but he stopped in his tracks when she said that.

"How do you know that?" he asked, looking back at her.

"Jestan," she said. "He mentions it in his books. It's not all lies, is it?"

Maybe it was a rhetorical question, but she hoped to get a reaction from Richard anyway. Instead, he continued into the other room to make the coffee with nary a grunt or eye roll.

I shouldn't have pushed him, Gemma thought. *What a way to make an introduction. So smooth...*

She could hear Richard shuffling around in the kitchen, lighting the stove, pumping water into a pot. From the couch, Gemma began to take in her surroundings. The room was lined with built-in bookcases. Not just one wall—every available space on every available wall was covered in books. Even though they appeared to be built of fine wood, some of the shelves were bowing under the weight of the leather-bound tomes. There were books stacked on the floor, on the end tables, everywhere. There were loose papers sticking out of some of the books on a writing desk at the other end of the room, filled with handwriting. Gemma saw quills and inkwells on several surfaces.

I don't know what I expected Richard had been doing here alone all these years, she thought, *but this is excessive. What could he be studying?*

She was just standing up from the couch, intending to peek at some loose papers, when she heard Richard's footsteps approaching from the kitchen.

"Please excuse the mess," he said gently as he carried in a tray with two mugs and a plate of pastries. "I wasn't prepared for a visitor today."

"No, I'm sorry to intrude," Gemma replied as Richard set

the tray down on the low table in front of the couch. It was the only surface that wasn't covered in volumes.

"You're wondering about the books," Richard said. Gemma thought she could hear a tinge of embarrassment in his voice.

"I—" she began. "Yes, but I don't want to pry."

"You do," he said with a wry smile. "You're here to pry. It's your job, isn't it?"

Gemma didn't immediately respond, so Richard continued amiably, "Well, we're stuck here for now, so I'll tell you."

"Thank you," she said.

Richard sat in an armchair next to the couch. He took a sip from his mug and nodded to Gemma to do the same. The first sip burned her lip a little, but she was more taken aback by just how strong the coffee was. She wondered if this was how they'd made coffee over the campfire during their adventures. She remembered that Jestan's books mentioned that Arnem fell into the role of campsite chef.

"Those clouds out there, black as death itself," Richard started. Gemma noticed that he looked a bit dazed, as if he were staring through the brick wall over the empty fireplace. "They're part of the curse that was put on the wastelands north of here, back in the midst of what you call the 'Journey.' Those lands were once lush and full of life. There was a seventh kingdom back then called Emyhrsen, as I'm sure you know. And a seventh king, before the rest of them gave up control to Davin. King Harold the Gracious. He really was a gracious and merciful king in his younger years, despite what came later."

Gemma noticed a sadness start to creep over Richard's face. She was reminded of her father, who also shifted quickly between emotions and moods. A byproduct of the war, most likely. She let him continue.

"Harold was good to his people, helped them in rough times, didn't overtax them even during the most plentiful seasons. But as he grew older, he became increasingly paranoid that his kingdom would dry up, that his people would face a famine that would destroy everything they'd worked so hard to build.

"He began to amass a library of books from the southern lands. Religious texts, ancient texts, full of alleged prophecies and magic spells and divine messages."

Everything the Royal Mystic Committee was created to stamp out of our world, Gemma thought.

"He brought in practitioners, so-called wizards and shamans, demon summoners and demon exorcisers, if you believe such things."

Gemma didn't, but she wasn't sure it was appropriate to indicate that. Richard hadn't snapped out of the trance he seemed to be in, anyway. She thought about reaching for her knapsack on the floor next to the couch to get her notebook and pen, but she didn't want to disturb Richard's flow of thoughts just yet.

"He brought in everyone he thought could stop what his paranoid delusions told him would happen to his lands one day," Richard continued.

"Did he find a solution?" Gemma asked.

Her voice shook Richard out of his daze. He looked at her as if he'd just remembered she was there, then took another sip of his coffee. He set the cup down on the tray and went on.

"What he found was prophecy after prophecy of famine, of plagues, of death," he answered. "All the religious texts, no matter their gods, all had stories of it. And he started to believe that all those stories validated his fears. So he decided he needed to look farther out for a solution. He commissioned ships, sent them down the Amassa River to the Western Sea, to the unknown lands beyond. Ours was never a seafaring people, though. When the shipbuilders decided they wanted no part in sending inexperienced sailors to their deaths, King Harold forced farmers to tear down their barns and use the wood to build makeshift boats. Then he sent them off to find help, as if farmers could do any better at sea than the others."

"He just sent them to their deaths?" Gemma knew a little about the ships, but the schoolbooks she'd studied had never spelled it out so clearly.

"By the dozens," Richard replied, with more than a hint of sadness in his tone. "And then one day, after months and months of nobody returning, a single boat was spotted coming upriver into Emyhrsen."

"One of the sailors?" Gemma asked, genuinely invested in the story. "Or one of the farmers?"

"Neither," Richard replied. He paused again, this time taking a bite of a pastry, but not looking at it. He didn't even appear to taste it. He looked completely dazed. "This boat was not one of theirs. It was a vessel made from a black lumber that has never grown in our lands. Dark as those clouds out there. The men on the boat were different as well."

"Different?" Gemma audibly gulped, as if swallowing back her fear. "Different in what way?"

Richard turned and looked into her eyes.

"You've seen the Vheisenia? What most of Aepistelle call the Ancient Ones?" Richard asked her.

"Well, no," Gemma answered. "They left after the Journey and the war, before I was born. They took Maachel with them back to their islands in the Western Sea. Was it them?"

"The Vheisenia—the Ancient Ones—aren't like us," Richard explained. "You just know when you see them. The texture of their skin. Their size. The way they move, how they walk over the most fragile of plants and don't seem to rustle a single leaf."

"I've heard stories," Gemma said. "But I didn't know they had anything to do with the evil that was brought here."

"Evil? No," Richard said. "I didn't mean that these mysterious sailors *were* the Ancient Ones. Maybe they were related in some way—I don't know. Their features were very similar. But the actual Ancient Ones we know, they came out of their forest and onto the shore, watching from the other side of the Amassa River as this boat made its way against the current like it was propelled by magic. It was clear that the Ancient Ones were frightened. They called these newcomers the *Tzakabya*, the Foreign Ones. King Harold and his men went out to the docks to greet these sailors, and they all disappeared into the castle. They held council for days in private with the king. Nobody saw or heard what happened in there."

At this point, Richard paused again and looked around the room. He was eying the hundreds of books that adorned his walls and tables.

"A few times, the king called in what remained of his advisors and secretaries, those who hadn't abandoned him. He tasked them with clearing out the books he had amassed about magic and religion. They were all to be burned."

Gemma, too, looked around at Richard's books.

"But they weren't, were they?" she asked. "Not all of them?"

"Many were," Richard said, his eyes now meeting Gemma's. This time, she detected a look of pride on his face. "But not all. My father had been a close trusted advisor to

King Harold in the better days, and until then, he'd even stuck with him in the difficult times. But the more King Harold relied on those texts, the less he needed his advisors. So my father had been assigned the role of archivist and librarian for those books. And when the Tzakabya leader demanded that the books be burned, my father smuggled out what he could. He sent most of them off to the south of the Amassa River, beyond the Forest of Despair that he knew King Harold wouldn't cross. He burned the rest in a show of submission."

"And here they are," Gemma said. "But it sounds like King Harold finally saw the books for what they were—superstition and lore. If the king went through all the ancient texts and could not save his kingdom, why did your father think he could do any different?"

"My father didn't believe in the power of these religions at first," Richard said. Gemma thought she saw a look of distrust on Richard's face, but it quickly faded. "He wasn't raised to believe in the gods or the power of magic or any of that. But the more he studied them under the direction of the king, the closer he came to seeing something, like a puzzle whose pieces were scattered among the books. He needed more time to figure it out."

"You're continuing his work, then," Gemma surmised. "What have you found in your studies?"

Richard was quiet for a moment, obviously thinking carefully about what to say next. If Gemma truly was a spy for King Davin and the Committee, he'd already said enough to be tried and executed for treason. Just owning these books was sufficient, let alone lending credence to their power. But as he studied Gemma, she didn't think he saw malicious intent, only the skepticism that all children were trained to have in this new world under the rule of King Davin. And beyond that, she thought he could see her genuine curiosity and wonder.

"I've found..." Richard hadn't said this out loud to anyone, despite his years of studying and verifying it across the texts. "I've found that time is running out. For all of us. While King Davin and his Royal Mystic Committee attempt to crush the religions out of existence, the clock is ticking. Ignorance will not halt what is prophesied to destroy us all."

CHAPTER 8
GEMMA

If there hadn't been fallen tree branches still gracing the pathway leading up to Richard's front door, leaves lining the porch, and gardening tools scattered all across the yard, Gemma would have sworn she'd been dreaming just an hour earlier.

The wind had reached its climax during their conversation about the prophecies in Richard's library, and then it had quieted almost as quickly as it had begun. When that happened, Richard didn't seem to be as open to incriminating himself with talk of an impending apocalypse. As drawn in as Gemma had been, the fresh air was like a splash of cold water, waking her from the trance Richard's story had put her in.

Reality sank in as she looked around at the calm blue sky and listened to the birds chirp. She had never witnessed any magic while growing up in postwar Capital City that couldn't be explained by sleight of hand or hypnotic trickery. She didn't feel that Richard was a danger to her in any physical way. Sure, he was large and imposing, but he didn't give her any creepy vibes, though she could see he had trouble maintaining a single emotional state for long. In that way, he really did remind her of her father, whose mind had rapidly deteriorated while Gemma was still just a child. But she knew how to handle her father, and she was quite certain she could handle Richard.

As she walked across his yard toward the road, observing the damage that the freak storm had caused, she heard Richard calling from the porch.

"Are you leaving?" he inquired.

"No, sorry," Gemma said as she turned back toward the house. "I'm just trying to understand what happened here. I've never heard of anything like it! By the way, I have something for you."

Gemma jogged into the house and reemerged seconds later with the scroll in her hand. She pulled the letter free of the ribbon and handed both to Richard. He looked at her with apprehension.

"I think it's from Mr. Abernath at the Royal Library of Aepistelle," Gemma said. She took a step back as Richard read the letter. A look of wonder filled his face as he folded up the letter and unrolled the scroll. Gemma stepped to Richard's side to get a look, but she couldn't decipher the strange, flowing figures on the page.

"I have something else to show you," Richard said a minute later as he rolled up the scroll. He pulled the door shut behind him, stepped off the porch, and motioned for Gemma to follow him as he headed around to the back of the house.

On the other side, the hill continued to rise for a few hundred feet. They walked past rows of crops on which Richard toiled away daily, with several flat, terraced sections that he must have cut into the hillside over the years. She wondered what this hike up the hill was all about.

And then she spotted it.

As they reached the peak, she could see what lay beyond to the north.

"Do you remember how I described the boat that those foreign beings sailed in on?" Richard asked.

"You said it was made of black wood that doesn't grow in Aepistelle," Gemma began, then paused as she squinted at what lay before them. "If that's true, what are we looking at?"

"As you can see, a forest black as night," Richard replied.

"But I thought there was no forest here anymore," Gemma said. "I mean, it's literally nicknamed the *Decimated Forest*, and that's why nobody will come this far north of the River of Giants."

"When I mentioned that the boat was made from wood that didn't grow on our continent, I should have been more specific," Richard said, taking steps down the other side of the hill toward the abomination below them. "It never grew here until just fifteen years ago. It—"

"Impossible," Gemma interrupted. "I mean, look at it— it's as thick and overgrown as any forest that's been growing for centuries!"

Down the north face of the hill that sloped toward the forest, Richard's terraced fields continued, with berries growing aplenty at the peak of their season. But Gemma noted that Richard had abandoned the lower tiers.

"During the height of what you call the Great Journey, when the six kingdoms south of the River of Giants finally organized an army to send north to fight alongside us, this entire forest was destroyed," Richard explained.

"The flash, some people call it," Gemma said. "One of the sides set fire to it, either by accident or as a tactic of war." She knew the forest fire explanation was the official one, even though it wasn't what her father sometimes whispered in the rare moments when he let down his guard.

"Set fire? Not quite," Richard said. "It was the work of some kind of dark, evil magic. Several battalions of soldiers—thousands of men, and even some of the Ancient Ones who were sent to meet them and serve as guides—were heading north from here toward Emyhrsen. They were supposed to join us while we were camped at the Ancient Ones' castle."

Richard trailed off with a faraway look in his eyes, gazing over the black forest in front of them. Then he seemed to snap out of his nostalgic trance and continued his story.

"We were going to make our way farther north, beyond King Harold's kingdom, when the soldiers got there; they were to protect us from the Foreign Ones who didn't want us to pass through those lands. But most of the soldiers never arrived." Tears formed at the edges of Richard's eyes, but he didn't seem ashamed enough to look away or hide them. "As they trekked through the forest that was here, thousands of square miles of it, the whole thing disappeared in a flash of brilliant light. There wasn't even a fire to put out. All that life, all those trees... it was all just gone, replaced by charred remains.

"We were cut off from any assistance from the kingdoms after that," Richard said as they neared the border between his farm and the regrown forest ahead. "A single company of soldiers had made it through the forest already, and they found their way to us at the Ancient Ones' castle."

"My father was part of that company," Gemma said.

Richard seemed not to hear her as he continued his story. "But there was nobody else to send. Nobody would dare walk through the wasteland that remained. The only other ways to get to us were by crossing through the mountains in the east or by boat, sailing against the current of the Amassa River."

"But this is all impossible," Gemma said. She knew from her father's stories—when they were coherent enough to follow—that his company had set out from Capital City, camped much farther west of Pinedrop, and then crossed north through the forest ahead of the rest of the army. They'd made it to a peak overlooking the castle of the Ancient Ones when, as her father described it, rays of sunshine blasted not from the sky but from the floor of the forest that surrounded the mountains on three sides. The mountains they were trekking through were safe, as was the valley that held the castle below them, as if there were a large hedge of protection surrounding all of it. But Gemma had never believed magic had caused it all to combust in the blink of an eye. Rather, she bought into the theory that the armies must have lit their campfires in unison throughout the forest, which then ignited the natural gasses that were known to seep from the forest floor. It was a well-documented period of drought, so the trees would have practically been dry kindling.

"Impossible," she repeated again.

"Impossible?" Richard asked, this time sounding personally offended. "Impossible in a world governed by the laws of nature, perhaps. In the world that King Davin and his Royal Mystic Committee would have you believe you are living in. But here we are."

He waved his hand toward the forest.

"These trees popped up and grew in a matter of months," Richard said. "You can see it for yourself. You can touch the bark."

"Touch it?" Gemma asked. "You mean you've gone in there?"

"Not too far, but yes," Richard said.

They stood in silence, looking out at the strange trees beyond Richard's farm. Gemma was surprised to feel herself shuddering in fear. She wasn't superstitious, didn't believe in magic to back up that fear. If these really were the same trees the mysterious travelers had used to build their boats, those travelers could also have brought seeds with them, intentionally or unintentionally. And maybe something in the soil or weather of northern Aepistelle had caused the trees to grow as rapidly as weeds. She'd heard of stranger things.

"This scroll," Richard said, tapping the roll of parchment Gemma had delivered to him, "is a very old piece of *The Illuminarion*—"

"The sacred text of the Order of Solendaron," Gemma interrupted.

"Yes. I know their book front to back, but this isn't a part of any translation I've gotten my hands on. One of the many prophesies that were left out over the centuries, I figure. It mentions a dark forest that rises up out of the ashes in the years before the fall of Aepistelle."

"And you believe this?" Gemma asked.

"It lines up with everything I've been studying, but I'm still missing pieces of the puzzle. I do intend to go deeper into the woods. The village of Ferathan still stood the last time I was near the Amassa River, twenty-five years ago. There was a cache of books my father wasn't able to smuggle out of the north, books he held on to longer than the rest, so he hid them away in Ferathan. I believe these were the final books my father studied, along with the last journals he wrote before he was forced to permanently suppress his thoughts.

"They may confirm my suspicions," Richard continued. "I believe that a new evil is rising up north in Emyhrsen, one that will come south to Aepistelle. The brute strength of man alone will not be enough to stop it, but the banished elements of ancient magic might be. If Abernath risked everything to get this scroll to me, he must understand the urgency. I believe that time is running out for Aepistelle."

Richard stopped and looked at Gemma. She thought he was searching for one last sign that she had no intention of betraying him to the Royal Mystic Committee. He must not have seen any hint of devious intent in her, because he turned back to face the forest and looked into the distance, to the great mysteries hidden beyond.

Gemma also shifted her gaze back to the land once known as the Forest of Despair. The impossibility of what had happened in that forest perplexed her more than ever before. She thought back to her childhood, when she had witnessed the progressive decay of her father's mind. The way the liveliness in his eyes had faded away. The complete absence of awareness, of love, of presence that had replaced the man who had brought her into this world.

Somewhere out there, Gemma thought, *the story of my father's downfall played out. But that story doesn't have to be over. If magic truly caused the destruction and the decay, perhaps there's also magic that could bring back the life that was taken from him.*

Gemma contemplated going back home. It wouldn't be hard to tell Hannon that Richard was already gone by the time she arrived at his home to interview him. She was certain that Walker wouldn't dispute her story, as long as he hadn't already sent a report back saying otherwise. What would she be going back to, though? Being trapped at home to take care of her father? Hiding away from friendships, from love, from life? That didn't seem like a life worth living.

"I'm coming with you," Gemma said. "You can use the time we spend walking telling me more of your story for my assignment. I think being there in the middle of where you went on your journey will help me to really understand it all."

And perhaps it will help me understand my father, if I can follow the steps he took before it all went wrong for him, she thought.

Richard started to argue, but then he stopped and thought about it. "I could use some company, I suppose. I tried for years to get my old friends to come with me. They didn't so much as write me back."

"We'll get you those books," Gemma said. An unexpected confidence washed over her. It was something she'd never felt before, but she liked it.

And so a new journey to save the people of Aepistelle was set into motion.

CHAPTER 9
DENNY

About a third of the way through the journey back to Plentimore Valley, the train conductor had called out that the next stop would be Pinedrop Station. Arnem could have opted to cut short the journey home and gotten off the train there with Denny. They could have hiked out to Richard's home to check on Arnem's old friend. But when Denny had looked at Arnem, he could tell that the man was pretending not to have heard the conductor. Instead, Arnem seemed to be trying his best to convince himself that there wasn't any truth to this business of dreams and troubles that Denny had warned of. He caught Arnem's disdainful looks at his book.

He's wondering how much of this is all just a child's imagination and how much was caused by Jestan's book, Denny thought. It's clear from its condition that I've been reading it a lot. He probably thinks it's gotten to my head. Maybe he doesn't believe in my visions at all.

And now, before there was time to have another meal in the dining car, they arrived at Plentimore Station.

"I hope Selah prepared a large breakfast this morning," Arnem said. "You ate about three times as much as I did on this trip. Where all that food fits in such a twig of a boy, I couldn't say. Though I was in quite good shape at the end of the Great Journey. You wouldn't know it by the look of me now."

Denny noticed Arnem looking down at his paunch with disappointment. They locked eyes and laughed. Denny felt more at ease again.

A relatively small crowd stood up to exit at Plentimore Valley as the train came to a halt. It wasn't the biggest vacation destination, but some travelers visited the local wineries in the valley, and others would head west to the coast, just a half day's ride by carriage. Most passengers on the train were likely traveling to Capital City or farther toward the Southern Reaches. Arnem and Denny had no bags—Arnem's one light travel bag was on the cargo train he was supposed to have taken home—so they were the first two people off of the train. Arnem's first point of business would be to stop by the cargo office in hopes that the conductor had dropped off his bag.

The platform was fairly empty compared to the bustling Esteron Station Denny called home. Denny looked around in surprise. He observed a young woman only a few years older than himself, carrying a baby in one arm and a sign that read WELCOME HOME, FRANCES in the other hand. There was an elderly couple embracing. A group of children ran too close to the train while their mother yelled at them to stand back, lest they get run over. What caught Denny's eye, though, was a tall, mustachioed fellow, dressed in a fine suit that Denny wouldn't have expected on a resident of a farm town like this. The man's head was shaved completely bald. He was holding a newspaper, the *Capital City Courier*, but Denny couldn't help feeling like he was looking over the paper in the direction of Denny and Arnem.

Denny shook the thought from his mind as Arnem led him past the main station building toward a warehouse that served as the cargo railway's distribution center. They walked inside the office, a dusty room with desks covered in shipping records, forms, and schedules. A bulky woman with spectacles greeted Arnem with an annoyed glance and a grunt. She shifted her eyes to Denny, and her expression somehow got even more annoyed.

"Did you drag home a stowaway this time, Arno?" she asked.

"This is my friend Denny," Arnem said. "Listen, do you have my bag from the line that returned late last night? I missed the departure and had to catch the passenger line."

The grouchy clerk rolled her eyes, let out another grunt, and said in her husky voice, "Let me check."

She got up and walked at a snail's pace through a doorway into a rear room. Denny turned to look around. Outside the window facing the platform, he saw the mustachioed man again, this time leaning against the wall of a ticketing stall, newspaper still in hand, eyes still glancing over the words and toward the cargo office in which they stood. Denny turned to look at Arnem, but he apparently didn't share the feeling that they were being watched. Denny thought Arnem was probably trying to formulate an excuse for why he was bringing a homeless teenager back to the family.

"You are a true angel, Berna," Arnem called as the clerk waddled back out. She was holding a leather bag that looked like it would hold one day's worth of clothing. "Thank you. I promise it won't happen again!"

After another grunt and what may have been the slightest hint of a smile from Berna, Denny followed Arnem back out the door. Arnem didn't seem to notice the man watching them as they walked in front of him, and Denny tried his best to avoid eye contact.

"—wasn't the first time I left my belongings on one of the trains. I mean, it's bound to happen when you travel as much as—"

Arnem rambled on, but Denny was distracted. He knew that they had passed right through Pinedrop, even though Arnem hadn't said a word about it. Why had Arnem bothered to bring him home if he didn't believe what Denny had said about the prophetic dream? Jestan's book described Arnem as a loyal friend with a heart of gold. That generous heart was surely the reason why he was helping Denny put a roof over his head, but what about the loyal friend part? And why were they being watched at the train station?

Tsechev... ni-fellen... The strange words ran through the boy's mind, but he still didn't know what they meant. *Szoren al-zar...*

~

"YOU CAN'T JUST BRING HOME STRAYS, ARNEM!"

Denny sat in the dining room of the Wynstone family home, chewing on his third sandwich of the afternoon. He was between Arnem's two daughters, Lyria and Rosaline, who watched him in silence. In the other room, he could hear Mrs. Wynstone's patient but perplexed voice as she spoke with her husband about him.

"If Richard really is in trouble, I have to know. I can't just ignore that without finding out," Arnem said.

"But he's talking about seeing visions in his dreams, Arn," Selah said. "You know the damage that could bring to our family if someone reports it to the Committee."

"It'll be okay," Arnem replied. "Besides, you know I've always wanted more help with the business. He'll fit right in. He's a good kid, Selah."

Selah seemed to resign from the argument for now, as Arnem walked back out and beckoned for Denny to follow. He led him to the front door. Denny turned back to see Selah watching from behind the table, where she flashed him a concerned and motherly smile. He felt a bit of comfort in that moment of the type he hadn't experienced since his parents had vanished all those years ago.

Arnem led Denny past two large barns that served as warehouses for the farming supplies he distributed, and then they arrived at a smaller building that was used as an office. Arnem motioned for Denny to sit in a chair. Arnem plopped down behind a desk, his usual place for doing business.

"I'm sorry to cause problems with your family, sir," Denny said.

Arnem looked shocked at first, then let out a fatherly laugh.

"No, no need for apologies, Denny," Arnem said. "Selah will warm up to you very quickly, I'm sure. Besides, those girls of mine can use someone new to pick on around here!"

"I don't plan to stay, though," Denny said. "What I told you before, it wasn't made up. I need to help Richard, and I'd prefer to have your help, but I can do it myself if I need to."

"Denny..." Arnem began, then paused while he tried to frame his thoughts. "Look, I get why you might feel a connection to my friends and to me. Jestan is a very gifted writer, and he made the Journey sound like such a fun adventure in spite of the great dangers we faced every step of the way. But what happened in the past is in the past. This is a new world. One without magic. Without danger. A world my daughters have a chance to grow up in without sorcery threatening their well-being. There are consequences for practicing or promoting magic and prophecy in this new world. If Richard has been toying around with all that, maybe he really is in danger, but he brought it upon himself. You don't owe him anything."

"But you can't believe that, can you? You have to listen to me. This is very real." Denny had tears in his eyes as he tried to explain this to the one man who had afforded him dignity in all the years he had been alone, living on the streets of Esteron. "I know there's danger in all this prophetic business. My parents are dead or rotting away in a cell because of it. But they never chose to have these gifts. I never chose it. And I can't ignore the call. Maybe you and Richard are my heroes because I'm just a stupid kid reading stupid fairy tales, but maybe we really are connected through some mystical powers!"

"I..." Arnem didn't seem to know where to go with this. Denny had full faith in his visions, but he needed Arnem to believe in them as well. He knew how much Arnem had witnessed on his journey—not just the destruction, but the creatures they'd fought, the things he couldn't explain, the devastating disappearance of those soldiers in the woods. Pure evil born at the beginning of time, and a corruptive evil holding power over those who had once been good. It was still out there, despite King Davin's best efforts to drive it back underground.

Denny saw a change come over the man's face as he sighed.

"I need to write a letter for Selah and the girls," Arnem said at last. "If I look my girls in the eyes or feel my wife's embrace, I may not be able to leave again. So I'll write a letter instead. Selah will find it here on my desk tonight when I don't return for supper."

Denny wanted to feel relief, but he couldn't help feeling something else instead. It was what he'd felt when they'd gotten off the train that morning, when he'd seen the man with the newspaper. The man who was so much taller than Arnem and the other locals. He shrugged it off as Arnem wrote a letter of apology to Selah and their daughters.

Denny's mind turned toward the girl he'd been seeing in his visions more recently. She was older than Arnem's daughters. He didn't think Richard had a daughter of his own. He wondered how she had come to be with Richard. He wondered why Richard trusted her. He wondered how Richard hadn't seen the trap that must have been set just for him.

He wondered if they would be too late to save Richard the Elusive.

CHAPTER 10
GEMMA

"Well, you must have had quite a night, young lady," said a woman's voice, followed by a disturbing cackle.

As Gemma walked into the inn's dark interior, her eyes filled with white-and-yellow orbs while her vision adjusted from the brightness outside. Once her pupils settled, she saw the innkeeper giving her a mocking smile from behind the front counter.

"Breakfast is over now, but come back down in an hour, when I'll be serving my famous split pea soup," the innkeeper said. Gemma's thoughts turned to the previous morning's excuse for breakfast, and her stomach turned sour.

"Thanks," she said as kindly as she could, "but I'm actually going to be checking out soon. I need to gather my belongings."

Gemma climbed the stairs to the third floor. She was exhausted, so the hike to the top felt like climbing up the tallest tower of King Davin's castle back in Capital City.

When she'd set out for Richard's house the day before, she had fully intended to return to the inn by the evening, eat whatever gruel was being served by the innkeeper, and begin taking notes on the day's happenings. But after the trek down to the forest's edge, Gemma and Richard had sat on the porch for several hours as Richard opened up about more aspects of his life during and since his journey. Gemma had shared her father's story. Richard had admitted that he hadn't interacted much with her father's company and that he couldn't remember Geoffrey Calvertson specifically, but he had praised the bravery of those surviving soldiers and had seemed to respect Gemma more because of that connection. The glaring distrust he'd had for her when he'd seen her approaching on the road to his farm had faded by that point. And now they were going to explore those dark woods together. Richard had allowed Gemma to take notes as he spoke about the Journey, but not about his studies in the house full of banished books. He had also given the condition that he would be able to read all of her notes before she took them back to the university.

Gemma walked to her room on the third floor of the inn. It was the last door on the left. She unlocked it, turned the handle, and let out a shriek.

"Walker? What are you doing here?"

"Quiet, Gemma!" Walker ran up to her, pulled her inside, and slammed the door shut behind her. "Calm down, please."

"How did you get in here?" Gemma asked.

"I told the innkeeper that I was your husband. She let me in easily enough. I waited all night for you. What happened? Did you talk to Richard?"

"Walker, I told you, I have no ulterior motives with this assignment. I won't help you spy on him or whatever it is you're here for. I'm here to talk with Richard, to get his perspective on what happened during the Great Journey and document it for the university. That's it."

"Oh, Gemma, you're so naive," Walker said. It took every ounce of Gemma's willpower not to strike at him. "I'm here under official orders, not just to protect you, but to see if Richard is violating the laws. Some of the locals suspect Richard of studying magic. That is expressly forbidden, and you know it."

"Of course I know it. But—"

"Listen to me," Walker interrupted. "The Royal Mystic Committee got word that Hannon was sending you on this assignment, and it was the perfect opportunity to act. They've had a strong grasp on Jestan and Arnem for years. Maachel is out of the picture completely. But Richard is the wild card. The Committee doesn't trust him. I don't trust him, either."

"Well, you're going to have to trust me, then," she replied. "I've already gotten him to open up a lot about the events leading up to the Great Journey and the start of the war. I need more time, though. Please stay away from us!"

Walker was about to respond but swallowed back the words. He opened the door, peeked down the hall to make sure it was clear, and walked out in silence.

Gemma sat down on the edge of her bed, shaking from the confrontation. It wasn't her first time fighting with Walker. They had a history together; they'd been students at Capital University at the same time. After graduation, Walker had gone on to work for the security arm of the Royal Mystic Committee. Gemma also knew about Hannon's involvement in the Committee. Garrod Hannon had served two terms as King Davin's Minister of Propaganda before joining the university to oversee its publishing arm. The decision to hire him had been controversial. There had been some student protests that Gemma did not participate in; she was only a freshman at the time and not yet politically educated. She now agreed that it was a conflict of interest to have one of the architects of the laws that quashed the mystic arts and religions in Aepistelle overseeing the leading academic publishing branch. But she was able to overlook the conflict as long as it didn't interfere with her assignments. She hadn't witnessed any obvious attempts by Hannon to tamper with the work that Gemma and her colleagues did.

But this time, it felt different. Walker seemed like he was after blood. Gemma couldn't help but feel like she, too, was actually here to spy on Richard, like he was an enemy of the state. As if Richard was somehow a person to be feared, some practitioner of dark magic bent on the destruction of the kingdom. A danger to public safety.

Had Hannon really been a part of this setup? *And here I am*, she thought, *about to head out on some kind of journey into the unknown with Richard...*

GEMMA DIDN'T DWELL FOR TOO LONG ON THE confrontation with Walker. She had a job to do, regardless of Walker's part in it. Richard trusted her, had opened up to her, had shared incriminating secrets with her about the books that filled his home. And now he was waiting for her not far from the inn.

Richard was gathering supplies for their journey. He had pulled the same cart into town that Gemma had seen him pulling home from the market two days prior. His plan was to fill it with fruits, bread, dried meats, blankets, lanterns, and other supplies for their trek through the woods. Gemma didn't know how many nights they would be away, so she thought it best to gather her belongings and check out of the inn. She was fairly certain there would be vacancies if she needed to check back in a couple of nights later. She descended the stairs, paid the sneering innkeeper for the two nights, and headed down the street to the general store.

As she approached the storefront, Richard stepped outside, arms full of newly acquired goods. She watched him place the purchases in the cart next to the food he had picked up from the neighboring grocer. In that moment, Richard reminded her of her father, back when she was a child and her father still looked at her with eyes that knew her. Before things really got bad for the family. Richard didn't look threatening. Sure, he was large and physically capable of overtaking her, despite his arthritic posture. But everything else about him assured her that he was not a threat.

"Are you all set?" she asked him. He looked at her with a half smile and nodded. Gemma thought she could see a bit of suspicion under that smile, causing her to wonder if Walker had passed by the shop after leaving the Frontiersman Inn.

"We have a good seven hours before sundown," Richard said. "By the time we arrive back at my house and prepare our travel packs, we'll have four or five hours to walk and make camp."

Richard grabbed the handles of the cart and started north toward the bridge at the edge of town, and Gemma followed.

THEY WERE JUST PAST THE SECOND FARM ON RICHARD'S side of the River of Giants, where the road started to softly incline toward his property, when a man stepped out from behind the trees. He looked to be around Gemma's age and was somewhat disheveled, as if he had passed out in the bushes, but not dirty enough to be homeless. A semifunctioning junkie, perhaps. Richard and Gemma stopped in the middle of the road.

The junkie held something that Gemma mistook at first for a knife, but then she realized it was actually a machete. Perhaps he had stolen it from one of the nearby farms, maybe even Richard's own.

"Stop right there and give me your cart!" the junkie yelled, waving the machete. "What do you got in there? It's mine!"

The junkie turned his gaze toward Gemma, then pointed the machete in her direction. Gemma gasped.

"And the girl! I'm taking her with me!"

Gemma looked toward Richard, careful not to make any sudden movements that might set off the junkie. She noticed that Richard didn't cower. In fact, his notable hunch was replaced by a straight spine and broad shoulders, and he wore a determined expression. In that moment, Gemma felt like she was looking at the cunning warrior depicted in the illustrations in Jestan's books.

"Put it down, friend. This is your only warning," Richard said to their opponent.

The wind began to pick up. Gemma glanced up at the sky. *Has it been this dark all morning, or did these clouds just come?* she wondered.

"Do you want this through your throat, or will you do what I say?" the junkie threatened as he started to wave the machete around wildly. Gemma jumped back a few steps. Richard didn't budge at first, but then he moved quicker than Gemma would have thought possible after seeing the painful way he'd moved the past two days.

Richard somehow lifted the entire fully loaded cart into the air, swung it in the direction of the junkie, and hurled it. The weight of the cart bowled the junkie over as an audible snap of bones rang through the air.

Gemma screamed in terror.

Richard leapt onto the overturned cart, crushing more of the junkie's bones. Gemma observed the young man's face as the life left it. Richard lifted the cart again, then slammed it back down on the man.

"Richard, stop! He's dead," Gemma yelled.

Richard froze for a moment, then pulled the cart off the man's body. He turned to Gemma. There was a raging fire in his eyes that faded as quickly as this situation had fallen upon them.

"Please help me pick all this up," Richard said to her in a calm voice, motioning to their supplies, which were scattered on the road around the junkie's body. Richard grabbed the filthy corpse by the arms and dragged it to the side of the road. Gemma shook with fear and adrenaline as she picked up the supplies and placed them back in the cart. Without another word, Richard began to pull the cart up the road toward his farm. The air was still, the sky clear and blue once again. The only sounds were birds chirping and a train whistling as it pulled into Pinedrop Station a few miles south.

Gemma stood there for a moment, glancing down at the body, then up at Richard. She thought of Walker, about his warnings that Richard wasn't to be trusted. She thought of her brother George and how he was worried that Richard may be a violent, damaged war veteran. She thought of the danger she may actually be in, about her blindness to the fact that Richard may really be as unstable as the rumors often said he was. Finally, she thought of her mission: to document the truth about what happened years ago so the mistakes of the past wouldn't be repeated, and perhaps also to help her own father recover from that past and have a future of his own.

And so she followed Richard the Elusive without another look at what was behind her.

CHAPTER 11
ARNEM | WALKER | DENNY

Arnem and Denny had arrived in Pinedrop.

It hadn't been a comfortable ride at all. Arnem had wanted to leave home right away, knowing that another look at his family would take away all of his willpower. But when he and Denny had arrived back at the train station in Plentimore Valley, they'd found there were no more eastbound passenger trains until noon the following day. However, Berna at the cargo distribution office had helped them secure passage on the cargo line that left around midnight. The catch was that they'd had to sit in the livestock car with a group of horses. The engine car was full already, and there was no other choice. For Denny, who'd slept under the stars and eaten out of rubbish bins for the past few years, it was no problem. But Arnem realized that his days of luxury were over for quite some time. He had survived out in the elements for several months with his friends all those years ago, so he knew he would survive this as well. He had to. Selah and the girls were counting on him to return home.

"Do you know where Richard lives?" Denny asked as they stepped off the train in Pinedrop the following day.

"You're the psychic, aren't you?" Arnem asked in jest. "I thought you could take me right to him."

They walked toward the town square. Arnem saw a diner that was open for breakfast. He motioned for Denny to follow him as he shuffled down the street toward it. The restaurant was nearly empty, so Arnem was comfortable enough to speak freely with Denny once they were seated.

"I can imagine how this is going to turn out," he said to Denny with a chuckle. "'Hey, Richard, old pal, it's been twenty-five years and all, but we're not out of danger yet! There's a monster after you, so let fat old me help you fight it!'"

Denny didn't seem to know how to respond. Perhaps the boy thought Arnem didn't have faith in his visions.

"I'm just playing, Denny. We've come all this way already. There's no sense in turning back now."

"He'll believe you," Denny said after the waiter brought their food. "He already knows that the evil has returned, and besides, he—"

Denny broke off, breathless. He was facing the front window of the restaurant and had a view of the sidewalk and street outside. Arnem turned to follow the boy's gaze out the window. All he could see was a tall, bald man with a curled mustache. The man didn't look their way, just continued walking down the street as if he had somewhere to be.

"Everything okay?" Arnem asked. "What is it?

"It's... it's nothing. Sorry," Denny stammered. He took a bite of bread and chewed it joylessly. The way he picked at his food was much different from how he'd eaten the day before. Denny pushed the plate away and spoke again. "I remember when my parents had these visions. For days afterward, they were on edge. Jumpy, paranoid, excitable. I think I'm becoming more like them every day. I don't know if I have the strength to see this through."

"We'll get through this together, Denny. We'll figure it out."

Arnem thought about how he'd been very much like the boy at Denny's age. He had relied on Maachel to motivate him to keep moving. He had looked to Richard and Jestan to protect him. Now he would have to be the stronger one. He would have to take up the mantle of a leader, no matter how uncomfortable it made him. He had to protect the boy.

—

THE LOCAL MILITARY UNIT HAD OFFICES AND BARRACKS stationed on the western edge of town. That's where Walker was supposed to be working on this assignment, and that's where he headed after confronting Gemma at the Frontiersman Inn.

He had hoped this trip would start off better. Gemma had been his girl during their years at the university. She'd broken it off with him in the end, but he was certain she still loved him. He'd been sure that traveling together would excite her, ignite a new spark between them. He had imagined she would come back to her hotel room the night before, as filthy as it was, and be pleasantly surprised to find him waiting there for her. And he knew that she wasn't seeing anyone else at the moment. He watched her closely enough back in Capital City to be certain.

Sure, she was lower class than his own family. Her mother washed the dishes that Walker's parents ate off of as regular guests of King Davin. Her father had fought in the war while his father had profited from it. But Walker believed that

Gemma was destined to overcome the failures of her parents. Her intelligence, her inquisitiveness, her ambition—they drove him wild in ways he didn't understand. Before Gemma, and even after her, his rotating lineup of girls had all been much more passive, no thoughts in their pretty little heads except about what to wear, who to impress, and how to please people. They were from wealthy families like his own. They weren't Gemma.

But now, Walker wasn't sure how this would turn out. Gemma was seemingly aiding and abetting Richard the Elusive in his crimes. Walker was going to bring the hammer down on Richard, and he feared Gemma would get caught up in it.

"Hello, sir," said the military clerk in the front office of the base as Walker arrived.

"Get me two men, please," Walker commanded, skipping over any pleasantries. "We have an arrest to make."

"Right away, sir," the clerk said. He ran off to consult with the commanding officer, who sent out two young privates.

"How old are you two?" Walker asked with disdain.

"Eighteen, sir," one of them replied. The other nodded in agreement. "This is our first posting. It's an honor to serve you."

"Yes, I'm sure it must be," Walker replied. "Well, let's get on with it. I do hope our man won't fight back, or this won't be pretty."

The soldiers looked at each other with confusion and more than a hint of fear on their faces. They followed Walker outside to the military stable, where all three men mounted horses and rode northeast through the streets of Pinedrop toward the bridge. They'd grown up on stories of Richard the Elusive, and now they were going to be his downfall.

AFTER THEIR MEAL, ARNEM GUIDED DENNY THROUGH town and over the bridge that led north. They had just walked past the second farm on that eerily quiet side of the river when Denny froze in his tracks.

"We're too late!" he yelled out.

Arnem turned to face Denny.

"What? What are you talking about?" He was genuinely confused about what the problem was.

"Horses are approaching," Denny said. He darted toward the trees at the edge of the road. "Hurry!"

Arnem couldn't yet hear any horses, but the boy was clearly frightened, so he followed suit and hid behind the trees and shrubs. A moment later, the sound of hooves on rough gravel hit Arnem's ears. Within half a minute, two young soldiers and what looked to be a civilian in his midtwenties sped by on their steeds, taking no notice of the old man and the boy lying low next to the road.

"Is that your monster?" Arnem asked.

"No, but we should stay off the road from here on out," Denny replied.

Arnem stood up. His knees audibly cracked as he straightened. He looked down to see his clothing covered in dirt and weeds from lying on the ground.

And of course I didn't bother changing out of my business clothes into something more suitable for a journey, he thought with embarrassment.

"HALT," WALKER YELLED AS HE PULLED BACK ON HIS horse's reins. The soldiers came to an abrupt stop behind him and followed his gaze up the road. Walker dismounted and walked toward whatever it was that he'd seen lying on the side of the road. The soldiers looked at each other with fear and confusion but kept their distance.

Walker stood over the mangled body of a junkie. Next to him was a sizable machete, but no blood dripped from it.

"There aren't many flies or maggots on him," he called out. "This man hasn't been dead for long."

Walker looked back at the soldiers as they slowly made their way toward him. He was quite sure they had never seen a dead body before. And if he was honest, neither had he, seven years their senior.

"I need one of you to ride back to base as quickly as possible," Walker directed. "Tell Commander Magellan to send word back to headquarters that the boar has broken loose. He'll know what that means. The other of you will continue on with me."

Walker left the body to rot on the side of the road and hopped back onto his horse. He paused, rode back to the body to grab the machete, and then continued forward. The soldiers divvied up their responsibilities wordlessly; one followed Walker, and the other raced back to base as commanded.

"What is your name, soldier?" Walker asked when the remaining young man caught up to him.

"Millness, sir," he said. He didn't need to call Walker *sir*, as Walker was not in the military and thus not part of the chain of command. The Royal Mystic Committee was its own part of the government under King Davin, and it was feared even by the most hardened of soldiers. Though in truth, there were barely any hardened soldiers anymore. Aepistelle had known years of relative peace outside of the work of the Committee, and even things with the Committee had calmed down before

Walker was old enough to serve on it. Now they were mostly involved in clandestine operations, rarely calling in the military to assist with arrests of practitioners unless they were especially dangerous.

Walker had seen Richard at the market two days prior. Sure, Richard was a good hundred pounds larger than Walker, but he was also a husk of the man who was portrayed in Jestan's book. The old man's body was frail, bent, and probably more fat than muscle. And as reclusive as Richard had become, Walker had been convinced when he'd set out that afternoon that the man would still have enough honor and sense to surrender without a fight. But now, after witnessing the dead body in the road, Walker wasn't as sure. He wouldn't express his fear in front of the soldier, but he worried all the same. If Richard had killed that man back there, there was no telling what he might have done to Gemma.

They rode on, up the incline toward Richard's reclusive estate at the edge of civilization.

ARNEM AND DENNY DROPPED TO THE GROUND AGAIN, THIS time below the road but without trees to hide them, as a single horse sped by in the opposite direction. Denny was certain the soldier had spotted them, but even if that was true, he didn't slow down or give them a second glance. They got back to their feet and continued on.

Denny didn't know what was ahead, but he suspected it wouldn't be pleasant. He could feel it even before Arnem pointed out the crows circling overhead. It was Arnem's childish cry at the sight of the body a few minutes later that confirmed the danger they were in.

CHAPTER 12

GEORGE CALVERTSON | JESTAN
THE JUST

George had tickets, and he intended to use them.

It wasn't often that George Calvertson had cash to spare, especially not enough to take Wellyn out for a nice night on the town. Fortunately, he'd been offered two tickets for that night's spoken word performance by the one and only Jestan the Just. Jestan was in the city all week for performances at the University Theater, as well as private engagements for the royal court. Jestan's business manager, Rodnego Deveron, had arrived at the shop that morning, needing repairs on one of the tour's carriages. The tongue of the carriage had loosened repeatedly, indicating that the metal harness needed some work. George had wanted to explain that he was in the business of forging and fitting shoes for horses, not repairing the carts they pulled, but money was tight and business was slow. He'd decided that beggars couldn't be choosers. To sweeten the deal, Deveron had offered tickets for Jestan's performance that night. In exchange, Deveron had asked him to begin the work right away, ahead of the other projects George had intended to work on that morning.

If only Gemma could have waited a couple of days, George thought as he set to work casting new steel pieces for the wagon's tongue. *She could have interviewed Jestan for her research assignment right here in town instead of abandoning us for that Richard fellow.*

It wasn't that George didn't support Gemma, but he was humiliated to have to ask his girlfriend to take care of his father. Wellyn seemed glad enough to help, but watching his father was not a stroll in the park. At least she'd be pleasantly surprised by the date he was going to take her on, George hoped.

He had a smile on his face and was humming a song when the sound of rushing hooves reached his ears. He turned to the open doors of his shop as two riders jumped off their horses in a hurry. The taller of the two, a soldier in uniform, stayed back with the horses while the shorter man walked into the stall. George recognized the man, who was wearing a light tweed suit. He was the stable master from the local military base.

"Welcome, Mr. Byers," George greeted him. He hoped there would be a large order to fulfill, as the military always paid promptly and in full. "How can I help you today?"

"I need you to drop everything, George," Byers responded. "We're gearing up the boys for a run up north, and we need them ready by tomorrow afternoon. We need full replacements for thirty-six horses from our unit."

"Thirty-six sets by tomorrow afternoon?" George asked in disbelief. "That's a lot for that turnaround time. Let me see what I have in stock."

George walked back into his storeroom. He had spent much of his downtime over the last few months stocking up on different sizes and styles of shoes. His speed and efficiency helped set him apart from other farriers in town. But this number of shoes by tomorrow? That seemed like a tall order. As he shuffled through his inventory, he remembered the tickets for Jestan's appearance at the theater. That date with Wellyn no longer seemed possible. At least he hadn't gotten a chance to tell her about it; she would have been crushed.

He walked back out to the front of the shop. "It looks like I have the inventory I need," George said. "I'll have to get started on fitting them this afternoon, work through most the evening, and start again first thing in the morning."

"Thank you, George," Byers responded. He mounted his horse, and his companion did the same. "Bring us the invoice when you're done. See you down at the stable."

George watched as Byers and the soldier rode away. He pulled the tickets out of his back pocket and looked at the showtime. "I might be able to pull off an eight o'clock show," he said out loud, then set to work.

It wasn't enough that the matinee performance had been held in the grand banquet hall of the castle that afternoon; King Davin and the Royal Cabinet of Aepistelle decided they also wanted to be in attendance for the evening show. Many of them were busy with deliberations and duties earlier in the day. Because of their high status, they were announced from the stage, and all eyes turned up to their balcony boxes as each name was called out.

Jestan peeked out from behind the curtains to get a glimpse of them. Secretary of Commerce Marilu Llywin. Secretary Ecclese Holmann of the Tax Board. John Coggsworth, Secretary of Foreign Affairs. Defense Secretary and Supreme General Hark Lionskin. Many visiting duchesses and dukes, ladies and lords. And of course, King Davin himself, along with Queen Elise.

Jestan exhaled in relief. The one person he dreaded seeing was not in attendance. He turned away from the curtains and listened as the announcements of the royal family and cabinet members ended and everyone was asked to be seated. The maestro conducted the band through the overture, and the crowd cheered. It was a symphonic version a song written by Willem Lark, a renowned composer, which had originally featured lyrics sung by a full ensemble back when Jestan's show was a larger dramatized production of the Great Journey. Those days had been grand—and highly profitable. Now the tour was a subtler affair. Just Jestan, his manager, and a few stagehands. The orchestras were local to the regions he traveled to. The auditoriums were sometimes half filled at best. Jestan was relieved that tonight was an exception; Capital City was unusually kinder to him, especially when townsfolk knew that royalty would be present.

Who am I kidding, he thought to himself. *It's me they want to see, not actors and actresses. Not fancy sets and props. Just wonderful, illustrious me.*

As the orchestra approached the final verse, Jestan walked to center stage, and the curtains opened. By the last clanging cymbal hits, he was fully revealed. The audience cheered. Jestan looked at them, smiling. The applause and fanfare never grew old. The adrenaline of appearing in front of an energetic crowd made him feel as alive as he had during the battles he'd fought alongside Maachel, Arnem, and Richard. It even kept him from drinking, at least until the curtains closed at the end of the evening.

He flashed his beautiful, pearly white teeth and waved at everyone who was there to soak up his charisma and handsomeness. He then turned his attention up toward the balcony sections, where King Davin and the court secretaries all sat. He gave them a bow to show his respect, or maybe to make some of those powerful women blush over him.

This will be a beautiful night indeed, he thought as he bent low.

As he returned to standing, still facing the balcony, he froze, his smile fading. Walking in and taking a seat next to King Davin, a full grimace on his face, was Sir Marin Allemon, Secretary of the Royal Mystic Committee.

IT WAS SUPPOSED TO BE A ROMANTIC NIGHT OUT. GEORGE had imagined that Wellyn would be ecstatic at the prospect of dressing in her finest gown, smiling through the evening's entertainment. The show would be followed by a delicious dinner, though he hadn't thought to make a reservation at any of the nice restaurants on that side of town.

However, George arrived home from fitting shoes on two dozen horses in the military stable only an hour before the show was to begin. It would be at least a twenty-minute ride to the theater. Oh, and George had not had time earlier in the day to actually *tell* Wellyn about his plans for the evening. She was at his house in what she regarded as her rags, filthy from a day of cleaning up after George's father and bringing some order to the Calvertson family home. Her hair was up in a makeshift bun, and she was barely hanging on to the last thread of her patience.

"Out of your frock and into your finest!" George said, with only the best intentions. "We're off to the theater, but we have to leave right away!"

"Right away?" Wellyn asked incredulously. "You expect me to be ready for the *theater* right away?"

"I'm sorry, I should have sent word to you sooner," George said. "It's been a crazy day. First Jestan the Just's manager came in for repairs on one of their tour wagons. He gave me tickets to tonight's show. Then the military stable master stopped in with a request for—"

"What were you thinking, George?" Wellyn asked. "There is no way this is happening tonight after everything I put up with from your father, plus cleaning up after your cats all over this house. I have my own parents' home to take care of now that you're here. Go to the show on your own, you big hopeless slob. Good night!"

Wellyn didn't even look back at George as she walked quickly past him and out the front door.

For a moment, George felt anger toward Gemma for leaving the family that week for her assignment. He was jealous that she was out having a good time on the university's dime, riding the train and seeing the country. He picked up one of his small black kittens and stroked its fur for a moment.

George didn't want to let both tickets go to waste. His mother wasn't home from work yet, and his father was already passed out in bed, so he decided he would just go alone. He quickly changed into some more presentable clothes—as in, clothes that didn't smell like horses or forges. He walked to the kitchen, where a plate of food was waiting for him. He took one look at the fat congealing on the meat, set the plate on the floor for the cats, and darted back out the door.

He was late by a good twenty minutes, out of breath, sweat soaking through his layers of clothing. The show had already begun.

"AND THERE WE WERE," JESTAN PROCLAIMED FROM THE stage. The audience was fully invested in the story, hanging on his every word, leaning in, perfectly silent. "Rain pouring, thunder crashing, the only light the occasional flash of lightening. Face-to-face with one of the creatures, no weapons in my hands, no weapons in its hands. Just man versus beast. My magnificent eyes meeting its hateful, evil, red-and-black eyes. No one around to intervene. I could feel its breath on me. Hot, sulfuric, sickening. I could see its rough, crusted fur standing on end, its massive fingers ending in razor-sharp claws. And then... then..."

Jestan's voice was so smooth, softening to a whisper, or as close as one could get to a whisper in a theater of hundreds, as silent as they were. They were on the edge of their seats. Not one person even seemed to breathe in that moment. He paused for maximum effect. Then...

"It POUNCED!" he yelled, accenting the words with a pounding stomp of his right boot. As if on cue, the entire audience jumped back. Several women gasped. Men were visibly startled, even angry at being so vulnerable in public. And then they all let out nervous but relieved laughs at their collective reactions.

Jestan still had it. He was a master of his craft.

He continued on, telling the carefully crafted version of what happened on the Great Journey, sidestepping any mentions of the sorcery used against them, the magic that may have been used by one of his companions, or about the Ancient Ones who had joined them on parts of their adventures. He described his opponents as either more animal or more human than they were in reality, casting the more fantastic elements as merely the deeds of twisted people or rabid wild animals. He was vague, leaving the truth open for interpretation just enough to avoid the consequences that had been threatened years ago by the Royal Mystic Committee.

He knew he was being watched at all his shows by spies for the Committee. They scrutinized his scripts and required first approval on all of his book manuscripts. They were watching at all times. But tonight, Sir Marin Allemon, Secretary of the Royal Mystic Committee, was there in person.

Even now, as hundreds of men and women enjoyed themselves in the audience, from servants and housewives to the king himself, Allemon was picking apart every word Jestan said. He was looking for any excuse to put an end to Jestan's act.

Jestan worried that tonight was as good a time as any.

———

As George sat and listened, he found that he couldn't enjoy the show as much as everyone around him. Every mention of Richard the Elusive or the Forest of Despair made him shudder. *Gemma could be in danger,* George thought. *She is too close to it all now. Why couldn't she have continued her research on the tribes of the Great Eld Desert? Or anything that doesn't involve dark magic and a cursed forest and an unstable survivor of such a terrifying war? I never should have let her go.*

George was so lost in his thoughts and worries that he didn't realize the show had come to an end until everyone around him rose for a standing ovation. He joined the crowd, though his clapping lacked the vigor of the rest of the theater patrons. People threw roses up onto the stage as Jestan took repeated bows. Jestan gestured to the orchestra, and the applause grew even louder as the musicians stood up for recognition. The musicians then sat back down and played a triumphant closing piece while Jestan walked offstage.

George decided he needed to speak directly with Jestan.

"Excuse me, sorry," George said as he quickly walked through the narrow row of seats toward the outer aisle. He stepped on a few toes, bumped a few knees, but he didn't let that slow him down. He hurried toward the exit into the lobby and looked around. There was a guard at a door that he presumed led to the backstage area. He decided to give it a try.

"Hello," George said to the guard, who had quite an annoyed scowl on his face. "I'm, uh, I'm the repairman of Jestan the Just's traveling coach, and I was hoping to speak to him about the repairs..."

He trailed off, embarrassed, knowing it was a lousy story even if it was true. The guard rolled his eyes.

"And I'm his gardener, but even I don't get an audience with Jestan," the guard joked. "Now kindly clear this area, sir."

Defeated, George turned and walked away. The audience was now pouring out of the auditorium and into the lobby, but George managed to squeeze through the exit and out into the cool evening air. He walked around to the alley next to the theater, where there were two carriages parked, the horses tied up under an overhang. The vehicles were the same gaudy colors as the one that had been dropped off in George's shop that morning. He made his way down the alley.

"Good evening, Mr. Deveron," George said. Jestan's business manager was leaning against one of the carriages, puffing on a cigar. When he looked up at George, he was initially perplexed, but soon recognition dawned on his face.

"Oh, um, our blessed repairman, Mr... uh..."

"Please, call me George. Is Jestan going to be out soon? I'd love to speak with him."

"Speak with him?" Rodnego Deveron laughed cruelly. "Look, I'm sorry, but there is an entire theater full of ladies and blokes who want to speak with him, including the bloody king of Aepistelle, but we can't have that happen, now can we?"

"Oh, I'm sorry," George responded. "It's just that I—"

"We will give you full payment tomorrow when we pick up our cart," Deveron responded. "Thank you for your service. I will drop in an hour after sunup at the latest." Deveron threw what was left of his cigar onto the street and walked in the back door of the theater without another word.

George stood in stunned silence for a few moments. Then he turned around to head back out of the alley when he spotted a well-dressed man, flanked by three soldiers on either side, coming in his direction. He moved aside to let them pass, trying to think who the man might be. He was clearly wealthy and powerful but did not necessarily appear to be a military general, despite the ensemble of soldiers. George crept into the shadows and watched the soldiers halt as the man pounded on the door that Deveron had just passed through. Deveron opened the door.

"No visitors, plea—" Deveron's voice came to a sudden stop; he clearly recognized the man.

"Hello, Rodnego," the man said in a mocking tone. "Please send out Jestan. Immediately."

"Look," Deveron started. George could hear fear in his voice as he continued, "We are in town at the invitation of King Davin himself. Jestan followed all the guidelines you set for his performance tonight. It was no different from any other night, Allemon."

"It's *Sir* Allemon to you, and I appreciate that he's following the rules of the Committee," the man said. "But I must speak with him all the same. Now, send him out before my men force their way in and cause a real scene he won't be able to steal."

Deveron nodded. George couldn't help but think that he looked like a dog that had been beaten into submission by its master. He watched as Deveron turned and went back inside the theater to fetch Jestan. George decided to continue lurking in the shadows to see what would happen. It wasn't that he was looking for gossip to spread; he genuinely felt that there must be some kind of trouble. *And if Jestan is in trouble*, he thought, *then Richard may also be in trouble. Which means that Gemma could be in danger, as I feared.*

Deveron returned to the doorway and beckoned for Sir Allemon to follow him, which he did, along with his cadre of soldiers. The last soldier to enter the theater pulled the door shut behind him. After several minutes of waiting, George gave up. He sighed and walked home, feeling defeated and hopeless.

CHAPTER 13
GEMMA | WALKER

She had come so far, and she knew it was too late to go back. She was a witness, maybe even an accessory, to murder. The more Gemma thought about it, though, the more she realized she would be okay. It wasn't as if anyone was likely to miss the vagrant who had attacked them on the road. She also didn't think anyone else would venture in this direction on purpose. The road led only to Richard's house and the forest. The forest was universally condemned, and Richard surely wasn't expecting anyone for a social visit. Still, perhaps someone would come look for Richard when he didn't show up for the market next weekend. Even more likely, someone might come look for Gemma when she didn't report to Walker, or when Hannon at the university didn't hear from her for several weeks, or when George realized something was wrong and sent the entire military to rescue her. She didn't doubt that Richard would admit that he alone had killed the man if necessary. After all, it was self defense. That creep had been waving a machete around and trying to abduct Gemma.

But none of that mattered now. Gemma tried to push it out of her mind. She needed the headspace for what they were about to do. They were nearly finished preparing their travel packs. Then they would head out into what remained of the early evening sunlight.

They would head into the Forest of Despair.

From the coast of the Western Sea in the west to the Esteron Mountains in the east, it was about five hundred miles, with two smaller mountain ranges in between. But they'd be traveling north. From the River of Giants near Richard's farm to the Amassa River in the north, it was about one hundred and fifty miles. They planned to stop first at what was left of the village of Ferathan, which was just over a hundred miles through the forest. Ferathan looked out over Amassa Lake, which fed into the Amassa River. Across that river was King Harold's Keep and the fallen kingdom, Emyhrsen.

These were all places of legend, forbidden lands and villages and castles that the people of Aepistelle dared not speak of except in whispers, lest they be arrested for treason by the Royal Mystic Committee. Even though these mysterious landmarks still appeared on the old maps she liked to dig up on the fifth floor of the library, Gemma and her generation could not even ask questions about them without fear of consequences. Newer maps that hung in classrooms throughout Aepistelle pictured the River of Giants as their northernmost feature. Gemma felt both fear and excitement at the prospect of breaking one of the taboos of the age. She was about to head into the Forest of Despair.

As Richard latched the packs closed and handed Gemma the lighter of the two, he suddenly paused and held up a hand to signify that she should hold still. She watched him as he cocked his head to listen while his right hand instinctively moved toward the hilt of the sword he had strapped on minutes ago.

"What is it?" Gemma whispered, breaking the silence, but then she heard it too. Two horses were racing up the road toward Richard's farm. Gemma raced to the front door.

"We can make it out to the woods if we run," she said. "Let's hurry!"

"No, we'll never make it over the hill in time," Richard said. Most of the windows in his front rooms were covered by bookshelves, but there was one filthy pane accessible. Both Richard and Gemma moved toward the window, keeping low. Gemma already knew who one of the riders would be.

"Your friend," Richard said angrily.

"Walker. He was sent to spy on us—or on you, I guess. But Richard, please, I had nothing to do with it, I promise." She looked at him with regret, half expecting Richard to throw her through the window or crush her under a shelf of books, but to her relief, she could tell by his reassuring glance that he believed her.

"There's one soldier with him, but soldiers never travel alone," Richard said. "There's bound to be more on the way. Come on."

Richard left the window and walked to the kitchen. Gemma took one more look outside to get a glimpse of Walker. She wanted to hate him, but she recognized a look of concern on his face.

He's seen the body, she thought. *He's worried I'm in trouble. If I walk out there, this is all over, and my assignment is a failure.*

"Gemma, quick," Richard called from the kitchen.

She ran across the front room and through the kitchen doorway. Richard had opened his pantry. Behind shelves filled with glass jars and clay pots, there was a cellar door, also open and waiting to swallow them into the darkness below. Gemma felt damp, frigid air blowing up from the depths. Richard lit one of the small lanterns that had been hanging from his pack and handed it to Gemma.

"Watch your first step. There's a rail to hold on to the rest of the way down."

It was a large drop to that first step, which she couldn't even see when she put her right leg into the black maw. Once she felt it with her foot, she pulled her left in behind it. Then she grasped around with her left hand until she found a rope, knotted through a metal loop at the height of her waist. It took a couple more steps down into the dark cellar before her eyes adjusted. The lantern in her right hand was hardly enough to illuminate more than one step ahead of her at a time, but she was relieved to reach the floor of the cellar after a few more steps. The ground seemed to be dirt and rock. It smelled like the caverns she had explored as a teenager off of the rocky beaches southwest of Capital City, though those were far less creepy and dark than this one.

She turned and looked up to the top of the cellar stairs. Richard closed the door from the kitchen to the pantry, then the door from the pantry to the cellar. He bolted the door from the inside. *Why would there be a lock on the inside of the cellar rather than on the outside?* Gemma wondered. Richard descended the stairs, and Gemma stepped aside to let him lead.

As they walked across the floor of the cellar, they passed shelves full of jars, junk, and deteriorated books that Richard had apparently decided he didn't need anymore, and finally, they reached a rough stone wall. Gemma watched as Richard felt around on the wall, stuck his fingers into a crevice, and pulled. To her amazement, part of the wall opened on unseen hinges. The groans and creaks of the hidden hinges were evidence that the secret door had not been opened in decades. The cold, damp atmosphere she'd noted at the top of the stairs was now a hundred times stronger, and somehow, the darkness was, too.

—

RICHARD THE ELUSIVE IS A DEAD MAN.

That was all Walker could think about. Well, not *all*, exactly. He also thought about the forms of torture he would make sure the Committee allowed him to do on the man who had put his Gemma in danger. Richard must have used some kind of magic on Gemma to get her to follow him. That slain man in the road must have been trying to defend her, but the crazy brute Richard had murdered the would-be hero and dragged Gemma the rest of the way back to his house. Walker was sure of it.

"Shall we go up and knock, sir?"

Walker turned to his companion, the soldier Millness.

"Knock?" Walker said in disbelief. "Just walk right up and knock on the damn door and ask politely for Richard the Elusive to let the girl go?"

Millness stared at Walker, wanting to nod but thinking better of it. He sat in silence instead. They both did, just looking at the house about fifty feet away, waiting for signs of life. It was at least two minutes before Walker broke the silence.

"And where are those damned compatriots of yours, anyway? They knew the code words. They were to send a message back to Capital City and then rush out here to assist us with every man they had."

"They must be preparing the horses for a chase, sir," Millness replied.

"A chase? Through the forest? Horses won't get us

anywhere in that forest, you fool. If we have to go in there, we go on foot."

Walker could see the terror on Millness's face at the prospect of entering the forest. He figured Millness was a local boy, meaning he'd grown up on ghost stories about the so-called *Decimated Forest*. The superstitious folk of Pinedrop avoided the country north of the river almost entirely, all except a few farmhands who tended the fields and of course the mysterious Richard. *Any man living this far from civilization is hiding something, some terrible secret. Well, we're about to uncover it, Richard. We're about to ruin you.*

There wasn't a sound or even the spark of a lantern coming from the house. Half an hour went by while Walker and Millness took turns steering their horses in circles around the house. Walker even sent Millness up the terraced hill to make sure they weren't hiding on the other side, but there was no sign of Richard or Gemma. Walker hadn't expected they'd be on that side of the hill; mostly, he just wanted to strike fear into Millness by sending him closer to the forest.

Walker decided he had done enough waiting. He ran right up to the porch and kicked in the door. It flew open easily enough.

He stepped inside, grasping the machete he had stripped from the dead body on the road to this pitiful farmhouse. Dusk was falling outside, and there wasn't enough light in Richard's dank, filthy dwelling. There was a candle on the table next to the door. Walker pulled out a match, struck it, and lit the candle. He carried it into the sitting room. Noticing stacks of paper on a desk, he picked up a few, lit them, and threw them into the fireplace. Millness entered the house and followed suit, lighting additional candles. When their eyes adjusted, they could finally see the objects of Richard's obsession.

"What in the name of the king is all this?" Walker muttered.

"Books, sir," said Millness without a hint of malice in his voice.

Walker turned to him, picked up a book, and lobbed it at him. He then chose another book off the shelf at random and observed the title scrawled into the leather.

"*Incantations for Infinite Health*," he read aloud, then dropped the book to the floor. He picked up another one. "*Kzeneron Solstice Rituals*," he read from its spine.

"I know that name, sir," Millness said. "The Royal Mystic Committee has banned the Kzeneron practices in Aepistelle."

"Yes," Walker said as he paced in front of the dusty bookshelves. "Yet, Richard the Elusive has volumes upon volumes of these. Spells. Journals. Holy books from every religion and tribe you can imagine. Even without the corpse in the road, there's enough here to torture, imprison, and execute that despicable brute. His days are finished."

CHAPTER 14
GEORGE

George got to the shop a good half hour before sunrise to start what promised to be his busiest day in the three years he'd been in business for himself. He hadn't even waited for Wellyn to arrive at the house to take care of his father. In fact, he didn't know if she would come at all after the ordeal of the previous night, and he wouldn't have blamed her if she didn't.

Jestan the Just's smaller touring wagon awaited George, as did the remainder of the fittings at the military stables. George prayed that Deveron would arrive as early as he had promised, or else there would be hell to pay with the military stable master. George set to work on finishing the repair.

True to his word, Deveron rode up to the shop an hour after sunrise on the same horse he'd used the previous morning to pull the cart in. George was just finishing up the final touches and crawling out from underneath the cart when he heard the hooves outside.

"Good morning, Mr. Deveron," George said. "I trust you had a pleasant evening."

"You misplaced your trust, then," Deveron replied. His stare was cold, and George knew then that things hadn't gone so well for Jestan with the Committee. "How goes the repair? We're heading out of town sooner than expected."

"How soon?" George asked.

"Soon," Deveron said, "as in right now. Let's get this draft horse hitched so I can leave while I'm still able to."

"Not a problem," George said. He set to work hitching the horse as requested, biting his tongue until he'd finished. He worked in silence until he could no longer stand it, and then he decided to take a chance. "Listen, I don't mean to pry, but I couldn't help noticing that the gentleman from the Royal Mystic Committee was a bit on edge about something last night. Might I inquire what that was about?"

Deveron gave George a hard stare but didn't immediately respond. He reached into a satchel that hung over his shoulder and pulled out a cigar, which he lit with one of the candles that brightened up George's shop in the early mornings.

"Look, we get that treatment all the time from the Committee. We ride into town at the invitation of King Davin, and then we get driven out by Davin's own man. Jestan the Just is a hero from a time in history that the Committee was organized to rewrite. They certainly rewrite Jestan's books. And still they blame him for corrupting the public with thoughts of magic and mysticism anytime something happens halfway across this forsaken country. Something has them more worked up than usual this time, though. That's all I can say, and you'd best keep it quiet."

George was surprised that he got even that much information from Deveron, a man who seemed rough from his life of late nights on the road. But George wouldn't be intimidated this morning. He decided to take advantage of the opportunity.

"I need to speak with Jestan, if I may," George said. "I know he's a busy man, but I'm not asking as a fan. I fear my sister may be in danger, and Jestan is uniquely qualified to help."

Deveron looked at George incredulously. He let out a puff of smoke and then belted out something between a cough and a laugh.

"You just don't give up, do you?" Deveron asked.

"It's about Richard," George said. "Richard the Elusive."

George took notice of the way Deveron furrowed his brow, perhaps confused about how this soft-spoken little farrier in a back street shop in Capital City could have anything to do with the legendary Richard the Elusive.

"Listen," Deveron started. "I'm tired of Jestan and our crew being set up by the Committee. We run into their spies in every city. They harass us at every opportunity. I know one when I see one, and you're nothing but trouble for us. We know nothing of Richard the Elusive. Jestan can't help you, and I can't help you either. We're heading out of town to give Sir Allemon what he wants. Here's the money for your services. Goodbye."

Deveron pulled a stack of cash from his satchel and slammed it onto one of George's workbenches. He climbed up onto the cart, took the reins, and directed the horse out of the shop and down the street.

Well, now you've done it, George thought to himself. He snapped out of his self-pity as he remembered he had a job to finish at the military stables. He grabbed his supplies, locked up the shop, mounted his own gelding, Melvin, and dashed across town.

THE SUN WAS CENTERED IN THE SKY HIGH ABOVE GEORGE as he fitted the final set of shoes. His fingers were blistered from the morning's work, his stomach was calling out like a feral cat from hunger, but he was going to meet his deadline. The stable master, Mr. Byers, had yelled at him in jest a few times already, but George was working as fast as humanly possible, and Byers knew it.

George was shoeing the final hoof of his marathon assignment when he noticed a group of soldiers running out to the stable where he toiled. A lieutenant around Gemma's age called out to Byers, who walked over to meet them with an honest smile on his face.

"Sir, we need to saddle up right away," the lieutenant told Byers.

"I was told we have until late afternoon, so what's the rush?" Byers seemed to lose any goodwill he had possessed. "Would they make up their damn minds?"

"Sir, a courier just arrived on an overnight train out of Pinedrop," the lieutenant said, a hint of fear in his voice. "There's been a situation that threatens the kingdom's security. That's all I know. We need to leave immediately, so we'll be loading the horses into the livestock car down at the station."

George knew he shouldn't be listening, but listening he was. He was sure his instincts were right, that Richard the Elusive was causing some sort of trouble up in Pinedrop and that Gemma would be caught up in it. He rushed to secure the final shoe while Byers completed his own work of saddling up the horses. Soldiers approached the stables and mounted their designated horses as George gathered his supplies, mounted his own horse, and sped off without his payment. He knew Byers would be good for it later.

George and his gelding didn't head southwest toward the shop, nor south toward George's house. Instead, they sped north, up the main road that led out of Capital City and toward the coastal town of Seahaven. He knew Jestan the Just was headed in that direction with a few hours' head start, fleeing from the Royal Mystic Committee with his wagon train.

He really hoped someone would remember to feed his cats.

IT WAS A HARD AFTERNOON OF RIDING—HE WAS SORE beyond belief, and his horse had long since started to slow—but George was relieved to catch a glimpse of three elaborately painted wagons up ahead. He tried to yell out to them, but his throat was parched. He could only imagine what his horse's throat felt like in that moment, as all George had to do was sit in the saddle and hold on. He gave up on trying to yell and instead tried to get Melvin to engage in one last sprint.

"Come on, old boy," he coaxed the gelding. "I promise I'll let you rest after this."

As he got closer to the caravan, he recognized Rodnego Deveron at the reins of the rear wagon, the one George had worked on that morning. Deveron turned his head at the sound of the approaching horse. When he recognized the rider, he put two fingers to his lips and whistled loudly.

"Hold it!" Deveron yelled out to the other wagons. He pulled back on the reins to halt his draft horse. George was finally able to catch up and allow his horse to rest at the side of the road. He dismounted and jogged over to Deveron.

"Mr. Deveron, thank you for stopping!" George shouted up to him.

"Mr. Calvertson, I can't help but feel that you're following me even though I clearly remembered paying you this morning," Deveron said.

"Yes, you certainly did, and thank you for that," George said as he caught his breath. "Look, I told you this morning that I needed to speak with Mr. Jestan, and it's even more urgent now. Please, I—"

"You certainly have come a long way for an autograph, Calvertson. Jestan owes you nothing, and I refuse to disturb him while he rests during his journey home. It's been a long tour, and we're all exhausted. Now, if you'll kindly—"

Before Deveron could finish, the door to the most elaborate of the three wagons flew open, and out poked a head of long, raven-black hair peppered with streaks of amber and ash gray.

"Rod, is everything okay out there?" the long-haired gentleman called out. "Who's that, a fan?"

Deveron rolled his eyes, pushed his palm to his face in annoyance, and then yelled back. "It's nothing, Jes! Go back to relaxing in there, please."

Instead of listening to his manager, the man pulled himself up to standing position, already half out of the open doorway of the wagon, and jumped down to the ground. He was wearing boots and dark brown slacks but no shirt. George blushed at the sight of his bare, russet-brown chest and muscular build. As he approached, George noted how badly the man seemed to be stumbling. When he was still a good ten feet from them, George smelled the wine that seemed to be aerating through the man's pores.

"Well, hello, my good man," the topless wino said to George. He reached out his bulky right arm with his hand open. "Jestan the Just; you may have heard of me."

Even with the stress of the day and his own fears for his sister, George couldn't help but chuckle at the situation. He was meeting not just any author or a stage performer that he'd known about all his life; he was meeting one of the legendary members of the Great Journey. George met Jestan's open hand with his own, and they shook.

"Pleased to meet you, sir," George said. And just as quickly as his urgency had faded, it came right back. "My name is George Calvertson. I'm so sorry to disturb you, but I believe Richard the Elusive is in a bit of trouble."

"Ah, Richard; old stubborn Richie boy," Jestan slurred. "I... excuse me for a moment."

Jestan took a few steps away from George and vomited in the middle of the road. Feeling awkward, George turned away and met Deveron's eyes. Deveron didn't look at all surprised, only annoyed. After a few wretched-sounding dry heaves, Jestan walked back over to them, wiping his mouth with a bare forearm. He had somehow managed to keep his luxurious hair clean while he lost the contents of his stomach, George noticed.

"Sorry about that, friend," Jestan said, sounding as if he'd already fully recovered from what just happened. "Now, listen, I haven't even seen Richard in more than twenty years. We pop into Pinedrop on tour every few seasons, but he never comes out to see me. I'm afraid I don't have any more to say to you than I did to Sir Allemon last night."

"Oh, I'm not with the Committee," George said. "It's just that my sister, Gemma, is with Richard, and I overheard this morning that the military is being sent to arrest him. Apparently, he's in it deep for something. I'm terrified for my sister.

She only went there for research, but I'm afraid she's gotten caught up in whatever it is they're after him for. There has to be something you can do to help her."

"Richard hasn't even returned any of my letters, and I did write him all the time to try and get him to join me on the road," Jestan said. "Imagine the extra seats we could fill in theaters with two members of the Journey on stage."

"Ahem," Deveron started. "That's not entirely true, sir."

"What do you mean, Rod?" asked Jestan. "Speak up, now."

"Well, how do I put this? I..." Deveron seemed afraid to speak, lest he anger the immensely strong Jestan the Just. George wondered if Jestan had a temper when he drank, though he didn't think Jestan seemed at all threatening at the moment. "Richard *has* been writing you, Jes. Quite regularly, in fact. But his letters are treasonous. I couldn't let them reach you so you wouldn't become an accessory to his crimes."

"What do you mean? What crimes? What treason?" Jestan seemed genuinely perplexed.

George could see sweat forming on Deveron's forehead. He heard the man swallow nervously.

"He rambles on about prophecies," Deveron continued. "About darkness and suffering. About the end of the Age of Peace. Everything the Committee is hoping you'll slip up and talk about in your shows and books so they can finally lock you away. I couldn't let him incriminate you like that, Jes."

"And these letters—where are they?" Jestan asked.

"I have them back home, tucked away safely in my office," Deveron said. "I didn't want to burn them in case we needed them as evidence if they tried to tie anything to you. We're an hour from home, Jes. You can read them by nightfall."

Jestan gave Deveron a long, disappointed stare. Then he turned to George with a more sympathetic look and put his hand on George's shoulder.

"I'm sorry to hear about your sister, friend," Jestan said sincerely. "Please, follow us the rest of the way home, and I'll see what I can do to help. Maybe there is something in those letters that will tell us more."

George noticed that Deveron had shrunk down in shame. Jestan returned to his carriage. George mounted his own horse, who was now a little rested, and tagged along with Jestan the Just's caravan for the remainder of their trip home.

PART II
TREES

CHAPTER 15
GEMMA

In pure darkness, they fled.

The smells of dirt and decay filled the air around them. They slammed their heads frequently, as the ceiling of the tunnel sloped dramatically without warning. They tripped and fell with regularity, as roots and rocks jutted out of the ground they couldn't see.

The sounds that followed them kept them moving. Wet, snarling, animalistic growls clashing with humanlike whispers of words they couldn't quite make out.

The sensation of being touched by something wet and cold haunted them. They swatted back to find nothing but spiderwebs or the narrowing walls that surrounded them like a tomb.

Neither lanterns nor torches would remain lit, but even when they struck matches, they couldn't see anyone or anything behind them before the flames inexplicably extinguished.

Hours upon hours passed, but they didn't stop to rest. They refused to slow their pace.

And finally, there was hope up ahead. Blessed, illuminating light.

"We've made it at last," Richard said as they approached the narrow rod of sunlight that pierced the darkness from some crack in the earth above.

Gemma waited in silence as Richard reached up toward the hole to the outside world. He grunted with exertion and frustration as he pushed with all his remaining strength on the large boulders that covered the tiny opening above their heads.

"Richard, what's wrong?" Gemma asked.

"I thought this was the exit, but these boulders won't budge," Richard said. He unsheathed his large sword and attempted to pry the rocks out of the way, but it appeared to do no good. He put the sword away and continued to try his own brute strength. As he toiled, his breathing became louder and more rapid.

"No, no, no," Richard grunted. "This has to work! This is the exit chamber!"

Gemma couldn't see his face from where she stood in the dim cavern, but she could guess that he was visibly cycling through shock, anger, and frustration, just as he had on the road to his farm or when he had recounted the downfall of King Harold. She gave him space while he worked through it.

As Richard continued to toil away at their escape route, Gemma noticed that her eyes were adjusting to the light the small hole provided. This section of the tunnel was wider, as if they were in a chamber. She walked to a wall and leaned against it to catch her breath, then jumped and let out a cry as she felt something dangling down, brushing against her shoulder. At first glance, she thought it was a large snake, ready to consume its first warm meal in years. But her eyes focused on it when she took a step away, and it wasn't a snake at all.

"Richard, this might be it," she said.

Richard pulled away from the crack between the rocks in the ceiling and looked toward Gemma.

"What did you find?" he asked. She noted a strong sense of desperation in his voice. She wondered if he was suffering from claustrophobia in these dark, narrow tunnels.

"This rope passes through some sort of pulley," Gemma explained.

Richard walked over to get a better look. Together, they examined the contraption above their heads. The rope fed through the pulley Gemma had mentioned, then hung back down, where it was secured around a rectangular boulder about three feet high.

Both Richard and Gemma took hold of the dangling rope, set their feet, and pulled in unison. At first, it seemed hopeless; the boulder didn't seem to budge. Gemma grunted as she exerted every last bit of her strength, and Richard did the same. She felt her skin burning as her hands chafed against the rough and weathered rope. Then another blessed crack of light streamed in from under the boulder. This gave a glimmer of hope to both of them, and they somehow found the strength to pull even harder. As if by some miracle, the boulder began to lift with more ease than Gemma thought should be possible.

"It's on a track," Gemma said. As more light streamed in, Gemma could see a series of gears in the wall, and she realized the edges of the rock had cogs in them that allowed it to catch on the track and rise more easily.

"It's holding," Richard said. "I don't know how long it will stay up, but I'll keep hold of the rope while you go under."

Gemma didn't hesitate. She ran over to the first stream of

light, grabbed the pack Richard had dropped, rushed to the opening, and threw it and her own bag out. She crouched down and started to crawl under the hundreds of pounds that loomed just above her.

She heard a loud *snap* as the rope tore in half from the weight of the boulder it held. She rolled out of the way and into the brightness beyond just in time. She felt the rush of air as the great weight dropped beside her. There was a muffled *boom* as it hit the ground, followed by a loud *clank* as the track of gears broke to pieces and the boulder fell inward.

Gemma gasped, afraid Richard had been crushed. But then she heard something she didn't expect.

Richard was chuckling.

"Are you all right?" she called into the dark cave. She sighed with relief when she saw Richard squeezing through the opening.

"It sure feels good to breathe fresh air again," Richard said with a smile on his face.

They looked around. They were standing partway up a mound piled with large boulders and rocks, but all around them for as far as they could see were the same eerily black trees that had sprouted up behind Richard's farm. They were in the middle of the Forest of Despair.

"I believe we traveled about ten miles into the forest as the crow flies, but we probably ran closer to fifteen with all the twists and turns in that dark maze we just escaped from," Richard said.

Gemma recalled that it had been nearly dark the previous night when they'd descended the stairs into the cellar and started working their way through the tunnels. It was probably an hour or two after sunrise now. After the initial shock of brightness wore off, Gemma realized how dim and gloomy it was. The trees all around them seemed to absorb the sunlight, even dampen it somehow, and they weren't even under the canopy of the forest yet.

Ten miles down, a hundred to go, Gemma thought.

Richard picked up the smaller of the two packs and handed it to her. He picked up his own, put it over his shoulders, and climbed down the rocky mound.

"Where are you going?" Gemma asked. All she wanted was to rest now that they were out of that dark hell.

"North," Richard said without a hint of sympathy or weariness.

And so she followed.

———

It didn't take long before Gemma started coughing. There seemed to be fine particles floating through the air. She had thought coming aboveground after a night of running through caves would be a relief, but the air did not seem any fresher up here. When the occasional beams of sunlight shined through breaks in the forest canopy, before it hit the dark trees and was absorbed, Gemma could see what appeared to be black and gray dust floating all around.

"Please don't tell me we're breathing in the burned remains of the soldiers who were killed in the flash all those years ago," Gemma said.

"The trees are shedding their skins," Richard said. He balled his right hand into a fist and pounded it against a tree he was walking past. The impact caused a large section of the bark to crumble. As she approached the tree, Gemma looked at the newly exposed area. She gasped loudly when she saw what the new layer looked like.

"How can that be?" she asked. "It looks like a snake! Is it safe to touch?"

"It won't hurt you."

Gemma reached her left hand out and rubbed her fingers across the exposed portion of the tree. It was cold and unexpectedly wet. Its skin looked like the scales of a serpent.

"The trees must be unhealthy if they're falling apart like this," Gemma said. "Maybe they can't grow in this climate."

"On the contrary, they're spreading like weeds," Richard said. "They are growing too well here. I believe the fragments of molting bark serve as seeds, and the breeze carries them away, only to deposit them farther on and cause more of them to grow. It would have taken decades for the native trees to repopulate and grow like this."

They kept walking. After another hour of swatting away the black tree bark dust in front of her face, Gemma realized something.

"Richard, there aren't any bugs flying around," she said. "We should have been attacked by dozens of mosquitoes by now."

"No animals, either," he replied. "I've been looking for tracks to see if we can find some fresh dinner, but there's nothing alive out here at all. We'll be dining on our dried provisions tonight."

There was an eerie feeling Gemma couldn't quite wrap her mind around. Part of it was the lack of animal and insect life in a forest that should have been teeming with it. But there was also some other sensation nagging at her. It was as if she were being watched, but not by a predator or person. She rubbed her fingers together, remembering the wet, reptilian feel of the tree's inner layer.

Richard stopped up ahead. Gemma caught up to him in a small clearing as Richard pointed to two large rocks that looked just flat enough to serve as seats. They sat and split up their food. The dried fruits, nuts, bread, and jerky didn't quite make up for the last couple of meals they'd skipped, but Gemma was satisfied all the same.

"I need to relieve myself," Gemma said as she finished eating. She walked away from the clearing, heading off to the east, where the trees were a bit closer together. Gemma lowered her slacks and undergarment and hunkered down. Just as she was pulling herself back up, she looked at the tree against which she'd been balancing.

"A symbol," she said. She ran her fingers over what appeared to be a carving in the tree. It was in a language she didn't recognize, possibly something from one of the northern tribes.

"Richard!" she called out after pulling her slacks back up. Richard came running up a moment later.

"Why are you yelling?" he asked. "We're being pursued, let's keep it down!"

"Richard, look," she said.

Gemma pointed to the carving on the tree. She watched Richard's reaction; his brow furrowed before it shot up in seeming recognition. He walked past her to another tree and felt its surface but didn't find another carving there. He moved on to the next tree, and the one after that.

"It can't be an old carving," Richard said. "You saw how tender the bark is, and these trees replace their outer skins in a matter of days."

"So someone else may be near us?" Gemma asked with a sudden shudder. She began to follow Richard more closely.

"I knew something, or someone, was alive out here," Richard said.

They walked on, continuing north. It was another several minutes before Richard slowed, tapped on a tree, and turned to Gemma.

"What is that symbol?" she asked. "Part of a northern tribal language?"

"A marking from the Nazseke. It represents Peltreze Ah Kutsar, which means 'God of Clouds.' It's their deity of protection. The Nazseke carved this symbol on the outsides of their homes during times of war or strife, when their lives were threatened."

"But the Nazseke lived up in the mountains."

"More than a hundred miles northeast of here, yes," Richard said. "Something drove them out of their homes."

"They must have been trying to reach Aepistelle, looking for safety," Gemma reasoned. "In theory, traveling south through the Esteron range would have been much more difficult than trying to cut through this forest."

"And clearly they made the wrong choice," Richard said, his voice full of sadness. He pointed to another tree a few feet away. "There's another one. Same symbol."

They walked a bit farther until they reached another clearing. Gemma gasped at the sight of a camp torn to pieces. Something appeared to have ripped open the canvas tents, rifled through them, and crushed them down into heaps. Sacks of supplies were scattered around the clearing in shreds.

"They must have been trying to avoid attention by not building a campfire," Richard observed.

Gemma thought about it, then gathered some of the fallen branches from around the clearing. She laid them out and prepared the area as she had been trained to do by her father when he was still lucid enough to teach her things like how to start a campfire. She tried to get a spark to hold, but after several matches burned out on the black wood, she gave up.

"I've never seen dry wood that wouldn't burn," she remarked.

"And I've never seen an attack on an entire camp with no sign of blood or bodies," Richard said. While Gemma was attempting to work on the campfire, Richard had been poking through the collapsed tents, grunting in dismay. "We should move on immediately."

Gemma didn't look back as they walked out of the camp and continued north. It was nearly too dark to see again, but they didn't want to stay in that accursed death trap. It was another hour before they hunkered down in a flat clearing, laid out their blankets, and slept the night away.

CHAPTER 16
LETTERS | JESTAN

*E*xcerpts *from assorted letters written to Jestan the Just from Richard the Elusive, sent over the last twenty years:*

JESTAN,

I apologize for the way we all parted after everything we went through together. I've also drafted an apology to Arnem, which I will send out at the same time as this letter. Of course, it is too late to reach Maachel. After the burdens we placed on him, I could not expect him to do anything but take the white ships to that place beyond the seas with the Vheisenia.

I have taken it upon myself to find a quiet cabin where I can't be reached easily, yet not so far away that I'll be able to forget what we have faced, what we have seen, what we have done. My nightmares wouldn't let me forget it even if I wanted to, but I do not want to. I would not want to spit on the piles of ashes that remained of the soldiers who tried to come to our aid. Nor would I want to forget those who were left behind up beyond the Amassa River. We failed so many. I wonder if all we saved was worth it when so much was also lost.

I have obtained a copy of your book. What an accomplishment it is. I do hope you find not only success but an outlet to process any grief or fears you may have—much the opposite of me, as I don't find myself able to leave it behind.

Your friend,

Richard

JESTAN,

I was recently visited by men sent by King Davin. They are calling themselves the Royal Mystic Committee. They want us to keep quiet about many aspects of what we faced up north. I fear for the people of faith in the community around Pinedrop and all through Aepistelle. The men also said they are confiscating copies of your book and that you are retracting much of what you wrote and spoke of. I pray that you are safe.

Yours,

Richard

JESTAN,

What a turn things have taken in Aepistelle. All we fought for is lost under the iron thumb of King Davin. How many hundreds or thousands of ministers, clergy, and practitioners have Davin's Committee slaughtered for keeping alive their traditions that have graced these lands since the earliest days of civilization? And your newest publication was received by the local bookshops in the midst of the national purge. Curious that you have changed so much of what happened, left out so many important details that our society could have learned from. I know not how you could lie like that. What would Maachel say? What does Arnem think?

Signed,
Richard

JESTAN,

I know how dangerous these letters are. I don't know if you don't reply because you hate me or because you fear committing treason, but I must speak to you. You are in a unique position. You have an audience in the citizens of Aepistelle. I urge you to use your platform to tell the truth. I am reading some volumes that my father stashed away, smuggled from King Harold's Keep long ago. What Davin and the Committee see as contraband is in reality the only thing that can prevent the total annihilation of every man, woman, and child in the land. Here is a sample of the Nazseke prophecies I've translated, but I've found almost identical warnings in the *Rylliad* of the southern mystics, the *Kruulen ti Avar* of the early Centeron tribes, even in the writings of the Vheisenia themselves. What does this passage remind you of?

THE REAPING COMES AS A RECKONING,
FROM THE RUINS IT DOTH SOW.
DARKEST DEATH IS BECKONING,
FROM ASHES IT WILL GROW.

.   .   .

I SET UP MY HOME AT THE BORDER OF WHAT WAS ONCE THE Forest of Despair because it unsettled me so. Now that I've uncovered instance after instance of this warning in the sacred texts, I keep watch for what may come across the wasteland. That cursed stretch is all that separates the things that haunt the north from the peace and well-being of the rest of Aepistelle. Perhaps you will find a way to warn our countrymen. The way people look at me in town, it's clear they think me a madman. I suppose I don't blame them, but the latest volume you published isn't helping, either. It's okay. I know Davin's men are pressing your hand, so I will not fault you.

Faithfully,
Richard

OLD FRIEND,

I don't know how far from here the Vheisenia reside. Their island doesn't grace any map we know of in Aepistelle. I pray they are not too far to signal when things go bad here again. We never would have been victorious without them. I'm certain we would not have made it home alive had it not been for the Vheisenia and their wisdom and strength. Please, should you not hear from me when evil rises again, signal for them. Only you and Arnem know how, and we can both admit that Arnem alone couldn't do it.

Your friend,
Richard

JESTAN,

Do you not understand what I've been telling you in all my letters these last few years? Darkness is on the horizon. I've seen the signs. The black forest that grows behind my farm is exactly what was prophesied. Our entire civilization is now severed from reality, thanks to the Royal Mystic Committee, thanks to King Davin, thanks to *your* spin on the truth of what happened. It may be too late to stop it now. The people of Aepistelle think of you as a hero. You've convinced them it is so. But I know the truth. You are a coward. I understand the kind of man you are now. This will be my last letter.

Regretfully,
Richard

IT WAS THE LAST LETTER THAT STUNG JESTAN DIRECTLY IN the heart. There were some fifteen letters spanning a period of about twenty years—two decades during which Jestan had thought Richard had completely faded away, maybe somehow forgotten about Jestan, or hated Jestan's guts for something. Okay, so it *did* seem that Richard hated his guts in the end, but if Jestan could have responded to those earlier letters, maybe it wouldn't have gone down that way.

"When was this last letter received, Rod?" Jestan asked. Rodnego Deveron was sitting across the table from him. He'd watched with trepidation as Jestan read letter after letter from the stack he'd hidden away in a safe in the business office of Jestan's estate.

"That last one came just before we left on this tour, so just two months ago, I guess," Deveron responded. "You haven't touched your cup, Jes. Is the wine bad?"

Jestan looked up from the letter and stared at Deveron in disbelief.

"You think I can enjoy a drink after all this?"

"You usually enjoy a drink after anything," Deveron pushed. "*Before* anything, even."

That was enough. Jestan knocked his chair back as he rose in haste. He pointed toward the door.

"Rod, you've guided me in my work for two decades now, and you've been my friend since childhood. You've lifted me up at my best, and you've shared my vices at my lowest. I know you hid these letters in what you thought was my best interest. But I'm going to need you to walk out that door before I say something we'll both regret."

"But Jestan, I—"

"Go," Jestan reiterated, using every ounce of his willpower not to direct a string of obscenities at his friend. Wisely, Deveron made his way out of the office and headed across the courtyard to his own apartment on the estate.

Jestan sat back down and spread out the pile of letters. It hurt him to see the change in Richard's tone over the years. About halfway through the stack, Richard really went into detail about ancient books and prophecies and spells. Jestan knew he owed a lot to Deveron for his discretion with these letters, even if he'd have preferred that Deveron hadn't completely hidden them from him. This was exactly the kind of rhetoric Sir Allemon was looking for in Jestan's books and performances, hoping to lock him away in a cold, dark cell for the rest of his life.

He couldn't help but feel sorrow and pity for Richard. In that day and age, the things Richard had written weren't just illegal—they also sounded like the rantings of a madman.

And perhaps I'm to blame, Jestan thought.

Jestan had always told himself that what he wrote and

preached was a coping mechanism, a way to forget the difficult times the country had faced during the war. Most of the world was moving on, and those who weren't willing to do so on their own were forced to by the hard rule of King Davin and the Royal Mystic Committee. The people were safer without the dangers of wizards and witches, without fears about monstrous creatures and vengeful gods. So Jestan had gone along with it. He'd retracted his first volume and replaced the more supernatural elements with things that were more easily explained. That Ogressi he had battled in the Swamp of Steinhold became an ape that had wandered down from the Esteron Mountains. The flash that had annihilated thousands of soldiers in the forest was now a forest fire caused by an overabundance of the natural gasses that had always plagued the forest. These were now the official stories, carefully crafted by Davin, Sir Allemon, King Davin's chief propagandist, Garrod Hannon, and of course Jestan himself.

He had done it all to save his own skin, but perhaps what he'd really done was put his friend in danger. Worse, he had put his entire country in danger.

It may be too late to save Richard now, Jestan thought, *but it's not too late to save Aepistelle.*

Jestan's bags were still packed from his travels. The clothes may have stunk from being worn on the road and in the theaters over the past several weeks, but there wasn't time to get them cleaned now. He wrote a note to Rodnego Deveron, left it on the table, and then rushed across the property to the guesthouse where George Calvertson awaited him.

George and Jestan mounted horses and headed for the docks to charter a ship.

CHAPTER 17
GEMMA

Two long days passed without event for Gemma and Richard after they left the abandoned camp. The more tired Gemma felt during their long and silent hike through the forest, the more she tried to focus on the fact that the adventure brought a new spark of life to her companion. When she'd first seen Richard just a few days earlier, he'd been an exhausted, hunched old man, much like her father had been for as long as Gemma could remember. But now, Richard was standing tall, walking without that crooked gait. His eyes looked more alert, more full of life. He didn't seem to fear their situation as she did. He looked very much like the hero she'd grown up reading about in Jestan the Just's *Journey of Perils* book.

Gemma, on the other hand, was terrified by the very trees that surrounded them. She still couldn't shake the feeling of being watched, even though they hadn't heard a single footstep, animal call, or even the buzz of a fly. Other than the trees that were dark as death, there was no other living creature to be found anywhere. They had not found any tracks that led toward or away from the ransacked camp they had stumbled upon. The sun was rising on their fourth day since escaping the tunnels, and Gemma had questions.

"Richard, those tunnels we used to escape your house—where did those come from?"

Richard looked up from the sack of dried fruits and nuts that he was picking through for breakfast.

"As far as I know, the tunnel system is part of a series of mines from hundreds of years back," Richard said. "There was an ancient tribe, the Hathdrak, that resided in the river lands where my farm is."

"I learned about the Hathdrak in school," Gemma said proudly. "I studied Aepistelle history at Capital University. The older history books say they mostly wiped themselves out when a group ritual went wrong, but most of those books have been destroyed by the Committee."

"That's partially right, I suppose. They mined a mineral from the rock at the edges of the forest for centuries, then ground it into a fine powder and inhaled it. It seemed to put them into some kind of trance where they could talk to the spirits. I don't know if it was their gods, or maybe their own dead ancestors, but they claimed it helped them gain wisdom and insight into the future. After centuries, they used it all up. They continued to dig tunnels, hoping to find more of that special rock, and they were soon several miles deep into the Forest of Despair. After so long under the ground, they started hallucinating.

"The hallucinations came from the natural gasses this wretched place emits. Their minds warped. They turned against one another, using their digging tools or their bare hands to slaughter each other. Some fled back to their villages, but the harder they ran, the more of the gasses they breathed, and they slaughtered the women and children when they returned."

"That's when the early Pinedrop settlers stepped in, right?" Gemma asked.

"That's right. Pinedrop was settled by a group of soldiers who fled after a failed uprising against the king of Esteron. They heard the screams from across the river, so they gathered their weapons, crossed over in their rafts, and put an end to the rest of the Hathdrak. The story goes that when the soldiers found them, the remaining men were covering themselves in the blood of their own wives in some kind of sick ritual to appease a spirit of the forest that made them do it."

"So, that explains why I was hallucinating that I heard whispers when we were running through those tunnels," Gemma said. "It seemed so real, too."

"If you couldn't tell, it filled me with terror as well," Richard admitted. "I know those tunnels were used by smugglers and others over the years, even after what happened to the Hathdrak down there, but I didn't expect there to still be gasses that powerful. Somehow, I thought the destruction of the forest twenty-five years ago may have cleansed it."

"Or it was the gasses that caused the explosion," Gemma proposed.

Richard shot a betrayed look at her. "Do you mean you believe Davin's retelling of events?" he asked.

"Well," Gemma began, "I know there are some horrendous things that King Davin and the Committee have done to cover up so much of the past. As a student of history, it's been a nightmare trying to get access to old books when so many have been confiscated from the libraries. But so much of what I've studied about the old tribes, about the religions around Aepistelle, even about the years leading up to the war... a lot of it can be explained logically. Like how those hallucinatory gasses explain why I thought I heard ghosts whispering to me down in the caves."

Richard sat in silence. After looking at her, stunned, for a few more seconds, he turned away and gazed off into the trees. Finally, he turned back toward her and broke the awkwardness.

"When were you born?"

"About a year after the war ended," Gemma responded. "Why?"

"By the time you were old enough to be aware of the world around you, Davin had formed the Royal Mystic Committee. He had his men writing their propaganda. His soldiers were killing helpless ministers and practitioners in the streets, smashing houses of worship to pieces. All for the sake of creating a new generation that would fall easily in line under his rule."

"I can't help when I was born," Gemma said. "But that doesn't mean I'm some mindless wench who can't think for myself."

"You're right," Richard said. "I'm sorry I said it that way. But if you don't believe in what I've experienced, why are you out here with me?"

"I'm here because it's my assignment, because I want to contribute to documenting our past. Outside of Jestan's books, there's not much on record about what happened during those dark years. You are one of the most important sources of knowledge. And yes, I admit that the official stories from King Davin don't completely add up, nor do Jestan's versions, which were obviously tampered with by the Committee. So I truly want to learn more, even to be proven wrong. And I want to return home with your story, whether or not it lines up with everything else."

"They'll kill me," Richard said bluntly. "Once you're done,

if I go back to Pinedrop, they'll have what they need to kill me. Hell, those soldiers were already there for me when we fled. I'll give you my story. But they'll force you to change it, and then you'll be in danger, too."

"I won't let anything happen to you, Richard. That man who was with the soldier will stand up for me, and I'll make sure he stands up for you. Walker works for the Committee, but he's not a terrible person, I promise."

"Power makes good people do terrible things," Richard muttered. He gathered his belongings, secured his pack, and stood up. "But thank you. We better move while the day is still young."

As much as Richard had appeared to be in his element over the past two days, he was now back to being a slow-moving, aching old man. Gemma felt like she'd deflated what confidence and ego Richard had built back up over the course of their trek. She didn't think they were covering nearly as much distance that day as they had during the past two, and she thought she was to blame for it. It also didn't help that her feet were aching, her thighs were chafing, and her stomach felt unfulfilled by the dry snacks they had to call meals. The waterskins were less than half full, but she didn't think they'd covered half the distance to their destination yet.

Still, she kept on walking. It was easier to keep pace with Richard now, and she even found herself passing him up on occasion. She slowed down anytime she thought she was veering off their northerly course, and he would wordlessly take the lead again.

As evening closed in, a cold wind blew through the forest. The sun was far off to the west and falling lower behind the trees. They reached a clearing on an incline. They climbed the dirt hill, which seemed naked without the black trees. Gemma felt exposed without the close cover of the trunks and branches. She stopped and turned her head quickly to glance behind her. There was movement in the trees, she was sure of it.

"Richard," she whispered. He stopped in his tracks and turned.

"What is it?" he asked, but he didn't seem alarmed. The wind blew even harder up on the crest of the hill.

"I thought... never mind. Just the wind, I guess." She turned forward, shivering from the cold wind, and they continued walking. They descended the hill, and she actually felt some relief to be back under the cover of the forest.

After another hour of walking in silence, they stumbled upon a camp. Unlike the previous camp, which had been in tatters, this one contained three canvas tents that looked like they could have been set up that morning. Richard held out a hand, gesturing for Gemma to stop and remain silent. Then he pointed to a carving in a tree to their right. It was the same symbol that had been engraved in the trees surrounding the previous camp. They stood still for a few more seconds but did not hear any noises. Richard crept toward the center of the camp, wordlessly observing the surroundings. Gemma quietly treaded a few feet away from one of the tents.

"Gnnugh," a woman groaned as she emerged from a tent about fifteen feet away from Gemma. Richard was in between her and the woman, but Gemma could still see her. Her hair was orange and wild. Her clothes seemed to be made of brown animal skin. She was filthy from head to toe. She was close to Gemma's height, but she must have weighed thirty pounds less, and Gemma was not heavy by any means. The woman stumbled toward Richard, continuing her groaning sound. She didn't look vengeful. She looked terrified, as if she were running to Richard for help. Gemma got a better look at her open mouth.

Her tongue had been cut out.

The woman extended her hands to Richard, who must have also felt that the woman was not going to attack him, as he did not bother reaching for his sword. She came within three feet of Richard when a *thwang* sound rang out.

The woman fell to the ground, an arrow lodged through her head.

She was dead.

Gemma didn't hesitate to move. She turned back toward the tent nearest her and dove inside. She pulled the canvas flap closed, lay belly-down on the ground, and covered the back of her head with her hands in case any arrows came flying in.

Was it a trap? Gemma wondered. *She didn't want to hurt us. Maybe she was trying to warn us.*

She heard the sound of Richard unsheathing his sword. She heard another bowstring snap and an arrow hitting a tree. She heard several pairs of footsteps running toward the group of tents and Richard's heavy steps running to meet them. The unsheathing of more swords. The clash of steel. Screams of pain. More clashing steel. More screams. Painful grunts. Bodies falling to the dirt.

And then silence.

Not for long, though. She heard a whimper, a person begging for their life to be spared. It was a voice she knew.

"Walker!" Gemma jumped out of the tent as she yelled the name. "Walker, what—"

Gemma broke off in shock. Above them, the sky seemed to have gone nearly dark, filled with black clouds that Gemma didn't remember seeing just minutes before. Her shock grew when she saw Richard. He was standing, his face, arms, and torso covered in blood, though it appeared he had no wounds of his own. He held his imposing sword in his right hand, aiming it down toward Walker, who was lying on his back and whimpering like a battered dog, his own sword a few feet away in the dirt.

Sprawled out on the ground around them were soldiers.

Dead soldiers.

Nine of them.

Richard the Elusive had killed them all.

CHAPTER 18
MARZELE

On the northeastern edge of the town of Pinedrop, wedged between the River of Giants and a long stretch of farms that continued to the foothills of the Esteron Mountains, there lay a large building, dark and gloomy, as if it were there to scare off any intruders that may be approaching the town from the east.

In the light of the sunrise, it cast shadows westward over the outskirts of town, and in the evenings, the shadows dropped over the nearest farm. But throughout the day, the inner rooms of the building were in constant shadow. The windows were boarded up with pieces of old fencing and wooden signs from shops that had long gone out of business. Compared to the rest of Pinedrop, this was a dreadful place to be. Some townsfolk said blood still stained the floor. Others swore they could hear screams of the dead coming from the building at night. Children dared their schoolmates to run up to the door and knock, but none ever mustered up the courage to do so, despite the goading of their peers.

The entire town agreed, though: the former Temple of Solendaron the High was a cursed place.

Even before the Royal Mystic Committee's bloody purge of the Order of Priests of Solendaron two decades prior, many in Pinedrop did not go near the place. Since the founding of the town many centuries earlier, Pinedrop's people had largely stayed away from the various religions of the land. The earliest settlers had fled Old Esteron because they disagreed with the religious customs the king forced on his citizens. Those settlers had also seen the dangers some traditions could bring when they'd witnessed the self-imposed genocide of their nearest neighbors, the Hathdrak. Yet when the Solendaron priests arrived, the townsfolk had allowed them to build their great temple out by the farm the Order had purchased, as it was the landowners' right to do so. People were sometimes suspicious of what went on in the temple, but never enough to approach it with pitchforks and torches and destroy the place.

A whole host of followers of Solendaron had made pilgrimages to the temple in the better days. They were nice, seemingly ordinary people from other parts of Aepistelle, and they visited local restaurants and shops, spent good money, and contributed to the local economy. So the people had grown more comfortable with the Solendaron, and all was well for several generations. That is, until King Davin's Committee came to town. The people didn't think the Solendaron had done anything to deserve what happened, but the law was the law, and the priests had refused to obey it.

The temple had stood empty ever since.

Until this evening.

Marzele of Southplains pushed past the gate that the children of Pinedrop dared not open. His long legs had no problem navigating the weeds that hid the pathway, even though they grew past his waist. The strong evening breeze chilled his hairless scalp, but his face stayed warm under his considerable and well-groomed mustache. Marzele ascended the steps that led to the large iron doors of the massive temple. At the top, he reached down and rubbed off the burrs that had attached themselves to his nice suit.

Marzele reached for the handles of the doors, but his hands stopped a few inches away. In the dim light emanating from the moon on that clear but cold evening, he could make out many of the dents in the door from when the Royal Mystic Committee had forced its way in. Chains and locks had been placed on the handles to keep intruders out. He gave a tug, but it did no good.

Marzele smiled. He wrapped both hands through the chains, bowed his head, and whispered words of a language not heard out loud in Aepistelle for quite some time. The wind died down almost instantly. The moon's radiance began to increase, as if there were a full moon instead of the crescent that presently flew high in the clear night sky.

A bright light sparked within Marzele's hands. As he continued to grasp the chains on the door, smoke drifted out from between his fingers. The chains glowed a bright, burning red. They pulsed brighter, then shattered into hundreds of shards.

The moon faded to its normal brilliance. The battered, hulking doors opened inward. Marzele spoke again.

"Please accept the gratitude of your humble servant, oh generous Solendaron," he said quietly, this time in the common tongue of Aepistelle.

His hands were still glowing, lighting his path as he entered the desecrated house of worship. The smell of rot and decay was strong. He knew the Committee had taken the bodies out and burned them after their show of force twenty years ago. But rats had called this place home ever since, and who knew what else. He reached his hands out toward a wall and saw that it was covered in black mold. Weeds were growing out of holes in the floor, and he carefully stepped around those areas to avoid falling and breaking his ankle.

Marzele walked into the cavernous sanctuary. The wooden pews had been tossed all around by the Committee when they'd conducted their raid, and nobody had been back in to clean it up. He carefully made his way toward the altar, climbing over pews and stepping around holy books that were strewn all over the floor. Up on the dais, Marzele found the charred remains of what he could only guess was the Ever-Giving Sun, which had once adorned the wall the worshippers faced. It represented the Great Lord Solendaron, and the Committee had ripped it off the wall and set it ablaze.

Mournfully, Marzele turned to the side of the dais, where a rotted curtain hung. His right hand dimmed and cooled as he reached for the fabric so as to not set it on fire. He pulled the curtain aside and walked down the hall that led to the residential quarters for the priests that had once served in the temple. His hand returned to its former brilliance to illuminate his way past doorway after doorway. At the end of the hall, he found himself at the foot of a staircase. He climbed.

As he ascended the stairs, he couldn't help but sweat from the heat trapped in the upper floors. The heat his own hands generated didn't affect him for reasons that could only be explained by the Order's sacred text, *The Illuminarion*, but natural heat bothered him in his fine suit. Fortunately, the heat began to fade as he reached the highest point of the staircase and was met by a cool breeze. These windows weren't barricaded with wood scraps. The panes had been shattered by inclement weather over the years, or by stones thrown by the locals. But even if the windows had been fully intact and the temple had been in regular use by those of the Solendaron faith, they would have been left open up here anyway.

They would have been open for the sake of the birds.

Marzele clicked his tongue when he reached the top step.

"Hello, little friends," he said. The glow from his hands pulsated momentarily as Marzele listened to the sounds of the birds. He looked around the upper chamber of the Temple of Solendaron and smiled with joy at the hundreds of pigeons, all looking his way and cooing wildly.

Marzele shushed them, then began reciting an old incantation in that ancient tongue. The birds sat in silence, tilting their heads toward the tall, mustachioed man. It was as if they understood every word he was saying, even though nearly no man or woman in Aepistelle would've been able to decipher them. Then he switched back to the common tongue as the birds remained in their silent trance.

"The great and merciful Lord Solendaron has granted me success on this part of my quest. It is my honor to report that events are in motion. The Dreamer and the Loyal One have reached the Forest of Despair. The Protector and the Inquisitive One are already closing in on Ferathan, where they will meet an agent of darkness. The Committee and the military will pursue them, and Capital City will be vulnerable. Let it begin."

For a moment, it was silent. Then the birds seemed to snap out of their trance. They cooed all at once, then rushed toward the open windows. Out they flew into the night, some headed east, some west, some south.

"Let it begin," Marzele repeated with an accomplished, confident tone as he watched the birds fade into the distance.

CHAPTER 19

GEMMA

When Richard had packed for this journey a few days earlier, he hadn't thought to include a shovel. He hadn't assumed he'd have to bury nine soldiers, nor one Nazseke refugee with an arrow through her head. Yet here they were with ten bodies sprawled around the camp. Fortunately, there were mounds of fairly large rocks in the nearest clearing, and after tying Walker to a tree, Richard dragged the bodies one at a time to the rocky area.

He would have done well to have brought that silly old cart with him for this job, Gemma thought with a good-natured half grin on her face. She caught Walker staring up at her in that moment, and guilt flushed over her.

"Something on your mind, Gem?" Walker asked her.

She turned to him. He was sitting on the ground with his legs sprawled out in front of him. Richard had wrapped rope around his torso and arms and tied him to the solid trunk of a tree away from the blood that had spilled all around the camp.

"I'd like to know what was on *your* mind when you led those men out here after us," Gemma said. "And why you killed that poor woman."

"I thought she was going to attack you," he claimed. "We were watching you and Richard from the cover of the trees, and that lady just jumped out of nowhere and ran at you. She looked insane."

"She looked scared! Desperate! That is so different from threatening or insane, Walker. She clearly needed help."

"Well, you *are* one to sympathize with the crazy types," Walker said as he eyed Richard approaching for another body.

"What's that supposed to mean?" Gemma demanded. "Because of my father's condition from the war?"

"I only meant your friend over there," Walker said with a sigh. "You know I respect your father."

"Dad always said you were no good for me. Even with his condition, he can still read people. He could read you just fine, Walker."

Gemma got up and walked over to where Richard was stooped. She grabbed one leg of the body he was gathering. Richard looked up at her, surprised yet grateful for her help. She looked back at him and noted the sweat pouring down his forehead. Richard grabbed the other leg, and they dragged the soldier through the trees to the rocky clearing. It was harder than it looked, and Gemma sat down on one of the boulders once they had brought the body far enough.

"Richard, what are we going to do with Walker?" Gemma asked. A look of rage came over his face at the mention of Walker's name. She didn't know why, but she decided then that she needed to advocate for Walker. "He's a despicable man, but he cares about the safety of our people above all. He follows orders. That's all this is. We can't just let him die here."

"He was sent out here to kill me and arrest you," Richard growled. "He *led* those soldiers here. He didn't follow their orders—he ordered them around. They murdered this woman. So why, then, should we spare him?"

"Why did you spare him earlier?" Gemma genuinely wanted to know. "You killed all the soldiers, but not him. Why?"

"It's..." Richard's hard glare softened, as did his voice. "I know you two traveled to Pinedrop together. You seem to know each other well. I just... I didn't want to turn you against me."

"We did know each other well. We were friends," Gemma said. "No, more than just friends. There was a time when I thought I was going to marry him. But we found out that we were just too different, especially our positions on King Davin and the Royal Mystic Committee. And then Walker went to work for the Committee, so that was the end of it. That doesn't mean he deserves death, though. Nor does it excuse what he did."

"If we let him go," Richard said, "Walker will just run back and gather more soldiers. They'll come back with a full army."

"It looks likely they'll come after us with a full army anyway, right?" Gemma asked.

"I suppose so. Perhaps we better take him with us after all."

Richard walked back to grab the last of the bodies. Once he'd dragged it to the clearing, Gemma helped him pile rocks on all ten of them. It was the middle of the night by that point, and despite their long day of hiking through the forest, the events of the evening had filled Gemma with too much adrenaline for her to even think about sleep. But once the bodies were covered, the exhaustion really hit her. She found Walker's pack, removed the blanket he had brought with him, and covered him with it. He looked away from her in shame and didn't speak.

Gemma decided to sleep in the tent where she had hidden during the attack. Richard stayed outside to keep an eye on Walker, but Gemma knew he wouldn't try to escape that night. She quickly drifted off to sleep.

"Off we go," Richard said, his head poking into Gemma's tent.

Gemma slowly opened her eyes and wiped away the sleep. The sun shined brightly through the flap as Richard backed away from the tent. For the past few days, they'd been waking up at sunrise to continue their journey, but Gemma realized that Richard had let her sleep in this morning. She was grateful for that.

She folded her blanket and then crawled out of the tent, dragging her pack out with her. She stuffed the blanket in, pulled out her sack of snacks, and got ready to eat yet another unfulfilling, dry breakfast.

"We have military rations, Gemma," Richard called from across the camp. She glanced over and saw him digging through the supply packs of the soldiers, taking what he needed, including all of the food. He also combined the contents of the waterskins. "When we packed for the trip, I thought we'd be able to hunt and forage. I didn't even consider that only these fruitless black trees grow out here, and no animals roam about."

Richard pulled an apple out one of the packs and looked at Gemma questioningly. She couldn't help smiling. Richard smiled back and tossed the apple to her. It was quite bruised from getting pushed around in the bag during the soldiers' pursuit of them, but she didn't mind at all. She took a bite. The sweetness, the juiciness, the freshness was beyond satisfying after several consecutive days of dried meats, dried fruits, and nuts.

"Care to share a little with dear old me?" Gemma heard from behind her. She turned and remembered for the first time that morning that Walker was there, though he was now tied to a different tree. She glanced at the tree he'd been tied to the previous night, then back at him, looking alarmed.

"How did—"

"My kind host, Mr. Elusive over there, graciously allowed me to defecate out in the trees," Walker said as he rolled his eyes. "Not that I could really get it all out with him standing there, staring. I wasn't going to run, and even if I'd tried, I wouldn't have gotten far with my pants around my ankles. I sure hope he gives *you* more privacy than that."

"Did you eat yet?" Gemma asked.

"Oh yes, he fed me, too. I felt like a helpless little baby."

Richard walked over, his pack stuffed full of extra supplies. He began to untie Walker.

"What will you do with me now?" Walker asked him.

"For Gemma's sake, I'll allow you to live," Richard said. "You may continue with us if you behave yourself. Otherwise, it's at least three days back on your own, if you can find your way, and you won't have any weapons on you."

"Well, I sure as hell don't want to walk back alone," Walker responded, and Gemma could tell he was actually being honest under his sarcastic tone; she could sense his fear, having known him for so long. "I do hope you'll at least keep my legs untied. I won't be running anywhere."

"There's one more choice," Richard said, turning to

Gemma. "It's yours to make, Gemma. You can go back with him. The two of you will be safe together as long as you head straight to the south."

Gemma stood silently, looking at Richard. Going back to the safety and comfort of home sounded so nice to her in that moment. She almost considered it. But then she looked back at Walker, and her heart sank as she thought of going back home a failure.

"No," she said with confidence. "We continue on."

Gemma turned away from both of them and started walking. Richard and Walker looked at each other. Walker's face was filled with dismay, but Richard looked quite relieved.

"Great," Richard called out to her. "Though you're heading east."

Gemma turned and laughed. Even Walker had a good-natured smirk on his face. Gemma figured he was mostly just happy to have the ropes off for now after a good twelve hours tied up.

They walked for several hours with Richard in the lead, Walker in the middle, and Gemma behind to keep an eye on him. They were mostly silent, and Gemma noted that Richard kept his hand closer to his sword hilt than usual. He clearly didn't trust Walker. Gemma couldn't blame him. She also thought she caught Walker stealing glances at the bow and quiver of arrows Richard had slung over his left shoulder and the machete that now hung from a clip on Gemma's belt, but he was wise enough to not make any move to get his weapons back.

She remembered how proud Walker had been of his bow skills back when they were dating. They had often ridden out east of Capital City and into the open fields on weekends, where Walker practiced firing off arrows while Gemma sat in the shade of a tree, reading history texts for school. Walker had even given Gemma his old bow when he'd upgraded to a military-grade one. She was a great shot, too, and she had laughed at how jealous Walker got when she showed him up in target practice. Even now, she let out a laugh as she thought of it. Walker turned around and looked at her, confused.

About midway through the day, they came upon a large open area where the black trees didn't grow for several hundred feet. Without those blackened monsters towering over them, it was quite sunny and even warm in the empty field. They were able to see far into the distance, where Gemma spotted foothills leading northeast to larger mountains on the horizon.

"The Fingers," Richard said. "They jut off the Esteron range. The runoff from the mountains feeds into the Amassa Lake in the west. By late tomorrow morning, we'll hit the hills and turn west. We'll get to Ferathan by nightfall tomorrow, if all goes well."

Gemma shivered. It certainly wasn't from being cold, as the sun was burning hot. She dreaded what they'd find in Ferathan. According to Richard, the town was still standing after the decimation of the forest. It sat on the northern edge of what had been the Forest of Despair and was apparently immune to whatever had caused the fires that had killed so many of Aepistelle's soldiers.

"My grandfather used to tell me stories about the Fingers," Gemma said when they approached the cover of the trees again. "About trolls that climbed down from the peaks above to feast on the villagers of Ferathan."

"My mother told me similar tales," Walker said. He sounded surprisingly calm for a man who had failed in his mission, seen his traveling companions get slaughtered, and been taken prisoner. "Only the trolls were never successful because of the old witch who defended the village. But it wasn't without a price. They had an agreement with the witch. She would protect the people of the village from harm —not just from the trolls, but from the bears that came down from the hills, and any other person or creature that posed a threat..."

"They got to a point where they couldn't pay her," Richard interrupted, taking over the story. "They had previously prospered from trade with other villages in the northern kingdom, but once they started working with the witch, their trade partners no longer wanted anything to do with them. They cut off all commerce with Ferathan. Once their money dried up, the witch extracted payment in other ways. She demanded that they give up their own children to her. They gave her the large estate at the edge of the village, practically a castle that rivaled King Harold's own. She lived in it with all the children, who weren't allowed to leave. Nobody knew what went on in there, but they didn't dare anger the witch by asking."

Richard trailed off. Walker turned his head and looked at Gemma, rolling his eyes. Gemma was surprised that Richard sounded like he believed what he was saying, as if those old bedtime stories were the truth. He didn't seem to want to finish the story, so they walked in silence again for quite some time.

The dark forest thinned out by evening. Gemma knew she should be happy about it, but a murky feeling plagued her. She stopped and looked around, but there was no sign of life. Were there more soldiers following closely behind Walker and his unit? Surely they'd slaughter Gemma and Richard to avenge their comrades, if so.

She turned back in the direction she had been walking. Richard was in the lead; he seemed lost in thought and hadn't noticed that Gemma was falling behind. Walker was halfway between them, turning back repeatedly to check on Gemma but maintaining his pace so as to not provoke Richard's anger.

Gemma heard a noise.

It was a wet, sticky sort of sound. She turned around again, this time seeing what appeared to be a black snake coming toward her, hanging from one of the dreadful trees. It was faceless, though. There was no protruding tongue, no razor-sharp teeth, no hissing, but it glistened damply in the evening's setting sun.

Gemma gasped instinctively but immediately felt silly. *There are no living animals out here—we've already discovered that*, she thought. As she looked at the other end of the object, she noticed that its rear side was definitely just a tree branch. *Perhaps the wind blew it.*

Then the serpentine branch coiled back on itself.

"Guys?" Gemma called to her companions. "Something weird is going on with this—"

The branch shot forward, stretching impossibly far from its trunk. Gemma jumped back, but she tripped over a stump. As her right elbow struck the ground, something grabbed her left ankle. She looked down to see the branch wrapping itself around her. It began to pull her toward the tree it stemmed from, and as it did, it coiled its way up her calf, then her knee. It started to tighten its grip. Gemma screamed.

"Gemma!" Walker yelled with genuine concern. She looked in his direction frantically as Richard turned and ran toward her.

"Use the machete, Gemma!" Richard yelled.

The pressure on Gemma's leg was immense. She was sure her bones would be crushed if the serpent continued to tighten its grip. Then a second branch shot out and wrapped itself around her left arm. The branches seemed to work together to yank Gemma up into the air. She reached for her machete, fumbled with the clip on her belt, and finally unlatched it. She pulled it free, her right hand shaking in fear.

Richard arrived at the base of the tree, but a third branch slammed against him and sent him flying back fifteen feet into another tree trunk.

"Gemma, slice it up!" Walker yelled as he made his way over.

Gemma couldn't calm her trembling right hand. The machete fell. Walker dove, caught it by the handle, and stood back up. The branch that had knocked Richard back now made its way toward Walker, but he swung the machete and sliced a full foot off of the tip. Then he plunged the blade through the branch that was wrapped around Gemma's leg, careful to not get her foot. In apparent pain, the tree recoiled, loosening its grip on Gemma's arm. She fell atop Walker, and they both tumbled to the ground.

Gemma pushed herself up on her elbows. Her face was inches from his. They both froze and looked at each other. Memories from their time together swept over both of them, until Richard ran over and slammed his boot down on Walker's right forearm, forcing the captive to drop the machete.

"No weapons for you, prisoner," Richard said. He picked up the machete, then used his other hand to pull Gemma up. He looked her over. "Are you okay?"

"It's..." Gemma was still shaking. "I don't know what that was. Can we get out of here? Like, right now?"

"Yes, and we'll walk through the night. We shouldn't be in this forest any longer than we have to. Not anymore. I fear it's all beginning."

"What's beginning?" Walker pulled himself to his feet. He rubbed his arm and wiggled his fingers to make sure Richard hadn't damaged anything. "And why did you need to do that to me, old man? I saved the girl, and that's more than you could do."

"You're right," Richard said. He turned to Gemma. "You cannot hesitate when danger strikes, Gemma. We're lucky you weren't torn in two just then. When the opportunity presents itself, you strike. No thinking, no worrying, no crying out in pain. Just strike at your enemy as mercilessly as it would do to you."

Richard turned and walked north without another word. Gemma looked at Walker, who winked at her, and they both continued on.

They reached the foothills by midnight, earlier than Richard had predicted. By that point, the black trees were a mile behind them, and now plants—regular, normal shrubs and trees and flowers—grew all around them under the clear night sky. Gemma was relieved to spot a cluster of blackberry bushes, and they all ran over and ate the fresh berries with smiles on their faces. Much of the tension they had all felt in that dark forest had faded away.

After they were full from the berries, Richard reached into his pack to pull out the rope.

"No, please," Walker said. "I'm not going to try anything!"

"I have a sword and your bow, and she's got your machete," Richard said. "I'd like to sleep a few hours tonight, and I can't do that knowing your hands are untied and ready to grab the weapons. Don't make this harder than it needs to be."

"Point taken," Walker said. "Though Gemma deserves that bow. She's quite a shot. I might even venture to say that she's more skilled than me. Maybe."

Richard looked at him and grunted but did not take his suggestion.

After Walker resigned himself to being tied up, Gemma

walked toward a patch of trees—normal trees—and collected kindling. When she returned with her arms full, she was delighted to find Richard skinning a rabbit. All three of them ate well that night and fell asleep soon after.

They didn't know it, but it was to be their last comfortable night for quite some time.

CHAPTER 20
GEMMA

It was a luxurious morning.

At least, compared to the previous few mornings. It was pleasant waking up next to a campfire, feasting on a crisped bird of some sort that Richard had managed to catch at daybreak, and knowing how close they were to their destination. Gemma felt relaxed despite the soreness in her leg from the previous evening's attack. Richard had untied Walker, who seemed fairly content, all things considered. While they ate, Gemma took notes as Richard explained elements of the Great Journey that he felt Jestan had failed to accurately capture in his published works. After they all felt full, Walker put the fire out while Gemma and Richard packed up their things.

"Since we got this far last night, we should make it to Ferathan late this afternoon," Richard said. He was standing tall and confident, ready to lead Gemma and Walker, apparently familiar with his surroundings now that they were away from the Forest of Despair. "Let's keep a good pace. I don't know what we'll find there after all these years. Arriving after dark may not be such a good idea."

Richard's pace was much faster than they'd gone since escaping the tunnels that connected his house to the heart of the forest. She and Walker rapidly fell behind. Walker decided to take advantage of the distance and talk, albeit low enough that the warm breeze wouldn't carry his voice up to Richard.

"Maybe Richard will let you have my bow and send you out to hunt for lunch," Walker said.

Gemma turned and looked at him, at first not knowing if he was being sarcastic, but she realized he was honestly just trying to make conversation. "Hitting targets on trees is one thing," she said, a smile forming. "But hunting a moving animal? There's no way I would hit one."

"Give yourself some credit, Gem. You sure outshot me back then."

"Okay, you have that right!" Gemma laughed.

"Really, though, you could do it. You're one of the most capable people I've ever met at just about *anything* you try to do." Walker turned and looked at her. Gemma met his eyes and gave him a half smile. Walker went on, "We had some good times, didn't we?"

"We don't need to do this, Walker."

"Do what?"

"Talk about our past."

"It's just... I'm sorry, Gemma. I'm sorry for disappointing you back then, for the way things ended between us. And I'm sorry for getting you into this mess."

"I would have come out here with Richard whether you'd chased us out of his house or not," Gemma said.

"Not just that," Walker said. He winced as he continued. "I set up your whole assignment. It was my plan to get you close to Richard. We were in a meeting for the Committee, and Sir Allemon made it clear that he meant to ensnare Richard but needed a way to assess his threat level. With what you've been studying, and since Hannon is both your boss and an extension of the Committee, it was easy to work it out. He seemed all too willing to let you do this."

Gemma stopped walking, and Walker followed suit. She glared at him, and he took a step back.

"I earned this assignment," Gemma said. "Even if you hadn't suggested it to Hannon, I would have made it to Pine-drop on my own. And it would have gone much more smoothly than it did, no thanks to you."

Gemma turned and started walking again, picking up her speed to get closer to Richard. After a few moments, Walker jogged to catch up to her.

"Gemma, wait. I really am sorry. It was because I had faith in your abilities, even if I wasn't honest about everything. I'm sorry I used you, though. Hey, do you remember that time we went to the cabin on the coast with my parents?"

"Of course. I remember almost smashing against those rocks when you convinced me to jump off the cliff and into the ocean."

"Well, I knew you wouldn't hit the rocks," Walker said. "I went there with my family every year and was always safe when I jumped. But if I had told you how close the rocks were, you might not have jumped. We wouldn't have been able to swim behind them into that little cave. You know, where my parents couldn't see us."

"What's your point, Walker?"

"My point is, if I had told you to spy on Richard, you wouldn't have done it. But because you did do it, you also have the chance of a lifetime with this assignment. You can make a name for yourself and help protect Aepistelle at the same time."

"You did this for your own benefit," Gemma said. "Besides, this isn't about making a name for myself. I feel like the more I can learn about what happened during the Great Journey and the war, the better I might be able to understand my father, maybe even enough to help him snap out of whatever it is that has taken him over."

"It's not something he can just snap out of, Gem. I just don't want to see you get crushed over that."

"I guess I know that," Gemma sighed. "But I still feel like I can learn some things that I can talk to him about to help him remember. I'm losing him. Every passing day, it becomes more clear that his mind is being eaten up by some hidden evil in his head. By his past."

Gemma shifted her eyes toward Richard up ahead, and Walker seemed to notice.

"And Richard?" he asked. "Does he seem to be afflicted with the same thing?"

"Not the same," Gemma said. "I've been having trouble reading him, but he's different from my father. And I don't feel threatened by him, even though I've witnessed his violent side."

"That man in the road near Richard's farm, for starters," Walker said.

"Yes. Richard rescued me. That creep was threatening to kill him and abduct me to do who knows what, but Richard didn't hesitate to stop him."

"Nor did he hesitate to take out the soldiers I was traveling with," Walker said. He seemed to be annoyed by any praise of Richard—jealous, even. "Poor little Millness. He accompanied me to the farm before the other soldiers met up with us. They gave him the option of going back to the base, but he wanted to see this through. He was a good kid on his first tour of duty."

"I can't justify what Richard did any more than you can justify killing that woman with an arrow to the head," Gemma retorted.

"Look, it was a mistake! Maybe I was out of my element, coming here with the soldiers. I should have left it to the more experienced agents in the Committee. But I need this to go right. I can work my way up. Sir Allemon sees promise in me. Who knows, maybe I'll be knighted someday."

"You always did aim high," Gemma said. She found herself forgiving him, in a way. Not completely—she knew she could never fully trust him again—but she didn't hate him, either. They walked on, closing the distance between them and Richard.

THEY STOPPED FOR A SMALL LUNCH. RATHER THAN WASTING time on hunting, skinning, and cooking game, they feasted on rations Richard had salvaged from the soldiers' packs the previous day. Gemma couldn't help feeling a little let down by the dry meal after having fresh meat for breakfast that morning and dinner the night before, but she was as anxious to get to Ferathan as Richard was. A stream ran through the meadow they were stopped in, and Richard filled up the waterskins.

"The Nazseke people up in the mountains believed that their water was the purest in all of Aepistelle," Richard said between gulps from his waterskin. "I didn't believe it until we were there during what you call the Journey. I'll never forget the first sips of water I drank up there."

"I suppose some of that magical goodness must have

gotten filtered out on its way down the mountain," Walker said with a devious smile. "This tastes like plain old river filth to me."

Gemma gave a little laugh, but quickly stopped herself and felt guilty. Walker had always gotten her into trouble in their younger days. She didn't want to fall back into her old ways. She decided to change the subject instead.

"I expected it to be colder here near the Fingers," she said. The Esteron Mountains off to the east were snowcapped despite the heat down below the foothills.

"Blame the Witch of Ferathan," Richard said. "As part of her protection agreement with the people of Ferathan, she keeps the weather around their village and farms ideal for growing crops all year long."

"Or perhaps the low altitude, combined with the mountain ranges blocking heavy, cold winds and the Amassa Lake just north of the town, make it a pleasant and fertile land," Walker said. "No magic needed for that. Nature at its best."

Gemma didn't want to upset Richard, but she found herself nodding in agreement with Walker.

"That's okay," Richard said. "You'll see for yourselves when we arrive. We should be off."

They put away their remaining rations, capped the waterskins, picked up their packs and weapons, and continued on their way. After another three hours at a reasonably brisk pace, they found themselves crossing an apparently well-maintained vineyard, and they knew they were on the outskirts of Ferathan.

A SEEMINGLY IMMACULATE LITTLE FARMHOUSE STOOD BESIDE the dirt road, though there were no immediate signs of life.

The road headed northwest, the same direction Richard was leading them toward Ferathan. For the first time since leaving the outskirts of Pinedrop and Richard's home, they had a clear path to their next destination.

Farther up the road, they passed an apple orchard. Again, there was no one about, no farmhands out harvesting crops, so Walker strolled off the road and started picking apples.

"Heads up, big man," Walker called as he tossed a plump red apple toward Richard. He reached up and caught it just before it crashed into his face. Walker and Gemma both laughed playfully, but Richard didn't react other than slipping the apple into his pack. Walker offered another apple to Gemma. She declined.

"Suit yourselves," Walker said as he tucked the extra apple into his pack. He bit into his own apple, chewed, and swallowed. Gemma glanced over at him as he took another bite and was surprised to see Walker's face turn sour.

"What's the matter?" Gemma asked. She watched as he chewed a few more times, then spit the contents into his cupped left hand. He grimaced as he stared into the mush of apple and saliva. Then he dropped the apple, reached into his left hand, and pull out what appeared to be a long black worm.

"Excuse me for a second," Walker uttered. He turned away from Gemma, spit the rest of the apple fragments from his mouth onto the side of the road, shook off his hands, and wiped them on his trousers. He reached into his pack and grabbed the other apple.

"Is that one any better?" Gemma asked.

Walker looked at it, turned it around a few times, and shrugged. Richard turned back to watch him as well. Walker took a bite, chewed, and again spit out the contents. This time, however, it wasn't a worm. Instead, the chewed-up apple appeared to be made of dirt. Walker looked at the spot he'd just bitten from and immediately dropped the apple.

"That's impossible," he said.

Gemma leaned down to examine the apple. "Why would you even bite into that? It's completely rotten!"

"It wasn't rotten when I picked it. Or even when I took the bite! How can that be?" Walker looked over at Richard, who shrugged. He reached into his own pack, pulled out the apple Walker had given him, and tossed it on the side of the road without even looking at it. He turned and continued walking. Gemma and Walker looked at each other with confusion and followed.

After climbing a slight rise in the road, Richard halted at the peak. Gemma and Walker caught up a few moments later and stopped next to him, following his gaze. They all stood in surprise as they saw the town of Ferathan for the first time.

"It's flawless," Gemma uttered.

"How can that be?" Walker asked.

Richard looked over at them with disbelief, nodded, and let out an irritated chuckle.

"I told you already. This is the domain of the Witch of Ferathan. She protects those farms, and she protects that village. You can't trust your eyes in Ferathan, unless you wish to end up disappointed, like Walker here with his apples."

CHAPTER 21

GEMMA

On the main avenue of Ferathan, they walked past businesses and restaurants. Gemma peered into windows of well-organized tailor shops full of suits and dresses, a pottery shop with elaborate vases and plates, an art gallery with beautiful paintings and sculptures on display, and a bakery with all kinds of cakes and breads in glass cases.

And yet there was not a person to be seen. Every door was closed.

"Is this a day of rest?" Gemma asked. Richard gave her a look that she didn't know how to interpret, but he said nothing.

For as well maintained as everything in the town seemed to be, Gemma expected to see people cleaning the windows and dusting the gas lamps that lined the sidewalks, or even just enjoying the warm sun shining on the grass in the park across the street. Instead, it may as well have been a ghost town. Walker stopped suddenly and held up a hand.

"Does anyone else hear that?" he asked, his head cocked at an angle.

Gemma nodded. Richard stopped, turned, and listened as well. Gemma watched his eyes narrow in thought. She wasn't sure if the look on his face was nervousness, but she was certain he also heard the sound.

It was music.

At the end of the block, they turned the corner just in time to see a door closing up ahead. There was nobody standing outside, but the music was much louder there. They walked past a few more storefronts toward the door. They could not see through the opaque windows, but a beautifully painted sign hung above the door, reading MEAD, MEET, AND EAT.

Richard reached down, touching the hilt of his sword, and looked at Gemma. This time, she was sure there was a nervous expression on his face. She found herself reaching for the machete she now carried. Walker had no weapons, so instead, he reached for the doorknob.

"I surely can't be the only one ready for a real drink," he exclaimed with a laugh. Before Richard or Gemma could say a word, Walker pulled the door open.

The sound coming out was unexpected. A live band was playing a lively tune. Dozens of men and women chattered excitedly, attempting to be heard over the music. This was not what Gemma had expected to find in a small town under the oppressive rule of an alleged witch, far across a deadly forest, less than a hundred miles from a kingdom of pure evil.

Walker stepped inside. Gemma and Richard followed. All around them were happy, healthy adults, socializing in their finest clothes. Tables were covered in mugs of ale and mead. Servers delivered platters of meats to the patrons. The band was set up on a low stage in one corner. Nobody turned toward the three travelers.

They headed toward the bar, where three empty stools

stood side by side. Walker sat down confidently. Richard and Gemma hesitated at first, then took the seats on either side of him.

"One double shot of your strongest, please," Walker said, arm raised to flag down the bartender. He turned to his traveling companions. "And for you two?"

"That's not a good idea," Richard said gravely. "You remember the apples."

"Yes, they were apples. And they were disgusting. And I need to get the taste out of my mouth with some very good, very strong liquor. Thanks for the reminder."

"There was rot and filth for a reason, Walker," Richard warned.

The bartender set a glass down in front of Walker and walked away. It was filled to the brim with a dark brown liquor of some sort. Gemma enjoyed a good social drink every once in a while, but she didn't remember ever seeing a liquor so dark back in the Capital City taverns. Walker didn't seem concerned. He picked it up, put it to his lips, and downed the contents without giving it a second look. Gemma and Richard watched him.

He swallowed, set the glass down on the bar, and sat silently for a moment. Then he exhaled loudly and grinned.

"Wow, now, that was spicy!" Walker proclaimed. "Whatever they make their liquor with up here in the north, I want more of it!"

Walker flagged down the bartender again. The man walked over. He was an older gentleman, perhaps a decade older than Richard. He was somewhat thin and balding with a friendly smile and kind eyes.

"Another for you, sir?" he asked, taking Walker's enthusiastic nod as confirmation. "And for you two?"

"Nothing for me, thank you," Gemma said. Richard gave a

declining wave but didn't speak. The bartender turned his back, pulled a bottle of the house-made liquor off the shelf, and filled Walker's glass again. He set the glass in front of Walker and stepped away to help other customers.

Walker looked down at the alcohol contentedly. He reached for it, then hesitated as he broke into quite an intense coughing fit.

"Pardon me," Walker said. "I don't know where that came from."

Once his lungs were clear again, he threw back the second glass of that brown stuff as quickly as the first, then let out a satisfied, burning breath. Richard turned to look around the room, then pointed to an empty booth along one wall.

"Let's go have a seat over there," he said.

The three companions got up from the bar stools, picked up their packs, and walked to the booth. Richard sat on one side. Gemma scooted in toward the wall on the other side, and Walker sat next to her.

"I feel like nobody even notices we're here," Gemma said. "The bartender didn't look at us twice. It's not like they've had any visitors in decades, right?"

"I'm trying to figure it out as well," Richard said.

"Oh, lighten up, you two," Walker scoffed. He raised a finger toward the bartender, indicating that he'd like yet another drink. "Have a couple of drinks and loosen up. It's clear from the farms and shops we passed that these are hard-working folks. We caught them relaxing during their time off. More power to them, I say."

"Everyone here appears to be in their fifties or older, too," Gemma noted. "Where are the younger people?"

"It's like the taverns back in Capital City, Gem. You have the old folks' watering holes, and you have the clubs for the university crowd. We unfortunately walked into the former."

"That's not it," Richard said. "You don't see any younger folk because they don't get to walk free like these people do. They're under strict control of the witch. They are all locked up in her estate on the northeast edge of town. That's where we're heading after this."

"Right, your little scary tales again," Walker said. "Don't forget that you're speaking about these things in front of a deputy of the Royal Mystic Committee. I won't turn a blind eye."

"Cut it out, Walker," Gemma said. "You're not here as a Committee deputy or a spy. You're here because Richard let you live despite what you did. Besides, even I can see that something isn't quite right here. I don't know about any witch, but this whole place is just unsettling."

The bartender walked up to their table, set another glass down in front of Walker, and trotted away, again without any apparent notice of the presence of strangers in the secluded town.

It's not like these people are unfriendly, Gemma thought. *It's more like they see through us, like we're transparent ghosts, present enough to be served, yet not enough to actually be seen for who we are.*

Gemma watched as Walker reached down to pick up his glass. His hands were trembling wildly, and he hesitated.

"Are you okay?" Gemma asked him.

"I'm fine," Walker said, his voice just as shaky. He grabbed the glass and started to lift it toward his lips, but the liquid splashed out from the jittery motions of his hand. "I just—"

He dropped the glass. The rim chipped as the contents spilled onto the table. Walker broke into another horrible coughing fit. He curled forward, not caring that the liquid was soaking into his shirt.

"Oh my..." Gemma started as she looked at the table.

In the center of the brown puddle, she saw another black worm, flailing about. Then drops of red mixed into the mess.

"What's happening to him?" Gemma cried out to Richard.

Richard didn't reply, just sat and watched in stunned silence. Walker's coughs grew wetter as blood spewed out with each puff of air. Gemma reached over to pat his back, not knowing what else to do, but Walker fell right off his seat and onto the floor in front of their booth. He was bent into a fetal position, shirt soaked with brown liquid and crimson blood.

Richard got out of his own seat and helped lift Walker to his feet, guiding him slowly toward the exit.

"Grab the packs," Richard called back to Gemma, who was frozen in stunned disbelief. She snapped out of it, gathered their belongings, and started to follow her friends. She stopped and looked around before she walked out into the warm, fresh air. The patrons of Mead, Meet, and Eat were still engaging in lively conversation. The band had taken a break between sets but was getting ready to start another number. The bartender was serving more drinks to some clearly intoxicated women at the bar. Nobody even turned to see what the commotion was all about. Not one person appeared to notice the liquor and blood on the table and floor. Gemma shuddered as she turned and followed Walker and Richard outside.

Richard had guided Walker up the street past another couple of businesses and set him down on a bench. Gemma hauled the packs over to them, set them down on the ground, and then patted Walker's back again.

"I don't—" Walker was interrupted by his hacking coughs. "I can't—"

"Hush, it's okay," Gemma said.

"I feel... something... inside...moving ..." Walker's face was turning purple. Gemma had read phrases in books about people turning colors while choking or in pain, but she'd never actually seen it happen.

"Oh no, he can't breathe!" Gemma shrieked as she started patting Walker's back harder. She looked up at Richard with tears in her eyes, but Richard didn't give her any solace. He looked as terrified as Gemma.

Walker vomited what appeared to be gallons of blood. It narrowly missed Richard and Gemma, who stood on either side of him. Then he rolled off the bench and fell to the ground.

Gemma gasped in shock as she saw Richard reach for his sword.

"What are you doing?" Gemma cried. "You don't need that! Help him!"

Richard looked at her, now with a fearful sorrow in his eyes. Then he looked back down at Walker. Gemma followed his gaze. Walker's entire body appeared to be puffing up like a waterskin being filled in the river. Sweat poured out of him, soaking through his clothes, drenching his forehead and his hair. He started shaking so violently that Gemma couldn't help but stumble back a few steps. Richard took three steps back in the opposite direction and drew his sword.

"No!" Gemma yelled to Richard. "You don't need that! Put it away!"

The sound of tearing cloth hit Gemma's ears. She looked back at Walker and couldn't believe what was happening. His body was rapidly bloating, so much that it was stretching the stitches of his clothing past their breaking point. The skin of his chest was now visible. Gemma knew that chest well. She had rested her head against it many times in the past—in that cave on the coast after their leaps off the cliff, in the secluded fields where they had practiced archery under the warm sun. It had never been purple before.

Walker's body continued to bloat. He shook violently. Blood and saliva continued to shoot out of his mouth as the coughing went on.

"Gemma!" Richard yelled to her. "Draw your weapon!"

She looked up at him in shock and anger.

"What?" she screamed. "How could you?"

"I told you this place is cursed," Richard called out. "I warned you both that this is the witch's domain, that it can't be trusted. I'm sorry that I led you here."

Gemma was shocked by the mix of anger and fear that had overtaken Richard's face. She realized through her tears that the sky was getting rapidly darker. She looked up to see clouds of pure blackness, like the trees in the Forest of Despair, rolling overhead, accompanied by a fierce wind that suddenly ripped through the streets of Ferathan.

"No, not again," Gemma said. "Why is this happening again?"

She looked back down at Walker and screamed.

Walker had impossibly doubled in size in a matter of seconds. His clothes had almost completely torn off, with bits still wrapped around his arms and waist, but clearly so tightly that the circulation of blood was impeded. His eyes were open wider than Gemma thought possible, and instead of Walker's charming green eyes, she found herself looking into bloodred spheres. Then, before her eyes, Walker's mouth stretched fully open. His throat pulsed. A long, slimy, bloody antenna wriggled out of his mouth, then a second one. A head of something as wide as Richard's forearm began to slither out in the direction of Walker's feet. *A snake?* Gemma thought, but it didn't have the eyes or mouth of a snake.

It kept coming, at least six feet long now. Richard and

Gemma walked rapidly backward in opposite directions, away from what had once been their mischievous traveling companion. After about seven feet of the dark, slimy serpent had slithered out, Walker's ballooned upper half seemed to sit up, pulled forward by the girth of the creature coming out of his mouth. It turned toward Richard and started to move. Walker's body rose to its feet and involuntarily stumbled along behind the serpent.

Gemma froze. Her feet wouldn't work anymore. She was in complete shock. As she stood, bracing herself against the unnatural wind that accompanied the blackness of the sky, she thought she heard a sound coming from Walker's mouth. She didn't know how that was possible, or even whether he was alive, what with that thing filling his mouth and stretching his jaws beyond the limits of reality.

It sounded like, "Waaan, Ehrraaaah—" *Run, Gemma*, she thought he meant. But she couldn't run.

The thing was pulling Walker's body toward Richard. As if it wasn't already desecrated enough, the sound of crunching bones filled the air, and Walker's body seemed to go completely limp as the human life left it forever. It was now merely an extension of the serpent, which continued to grow not only in length but also in girth. It now looked to be about fifteen feet tall with the circumference of a wide tree trunk.

Richard swung his sword through the air to try and scare it off, but the creature that was Walker kept coming for him. Closer and closer it got. Richard swung again in a wide arc, this time connecting with the thing. Blood sprayed out of it and onto Richard, who kept trying to hack at it.

Gemma looked past the pile of vomit and blood in front of the bench where Walker had fallen moments ago, when he still had a human body. There, next to the bench, she spotted their packs. Hanging off of Richard's pack were the bow and quiver of arrows he'd confiscated from Walker back in the camp. She looked up the street at Richard, still fending off the monster that was attempting to pulverize him. She tried to move, but couldn't at first.

Run, Gemma, she repeated to herself. *Run!*

She ran to the bench, careful to step around the puddle of Walker's innards. She unhooked the bow and the quiver from Richard's pack, then slung the quiver over her head and onto one shoulder. She pulled out an arrow and nocked it. She started to pull back, but the fear made her arms feel as weak as a twig blowing in the wind.

Come on, she thought. *Come on.*

"Come on!" she yelled out loud.

And then, as if the wind had suddenly dropped dead in that instant, as if the world had gone completely silent and still, she felt totally focused. She felt strong. She felt fully in command. She pulled back the bowstring, took aim, and released.

The arrow flew through the air and right past the creature, missing it by several feet. It bounced off the window of a grocery shop down the street, the arrow clanking to the ground. Gemma realized that the wind had not died down at all.

Nor had the creature stopped its attack. Gemma watched as Richard took another swing at it, but this time he lost his grip on the sword. It bounced off the slimy mass and fell to the ground. The monstrous thing lunged at Richard, crushing him against the rough gravel of the street. Richard screamed in pain under the weight of it.

It seemed to dig its way under Richard, lifting his body, then wrapping around him. It was going to squeeze the life out of him.

Gemma reached back for another arrow. She set up her

shot, taking the wild wind into consideration. She took a deep breath, then let the arrow fly. This time, it hit its mark. She was careful not to aim for the parts of the creature that were wrapping around Richard for fear of hitting her only remaining companion. Instead, she shot at the lower part of the creature with success. Another arrow, another hit. And a third. The creature let out a piercing shriek. Richard screamed in pain as it tightened its hold around him. The arrows were hurting it, but it was clear to Gemma that they wouldn't kill it. She looked back at the pile of their belongings on the ground and picked up the machete.

As she jogged toward Richard and the beast that was wrapping around him, Gemma noticed Richard was starting to turn as purple as Walker had back in the booth. She picked up her pace when she was certain she heard the cracking of his bones.

A mouth at the tip of the creature opened up for the first time. It stretched its upper half high above Richard and arched back down, ready to bring its open mouth over his head. In that moment, Gemma swung the machete.

The creature's head fell to the ground. Its body clenched one more time, and Richard let out a pained groan. Then the creature's grip around him loosened, and he collapsed on top of it. The wind seemed to die away again. The black clouds, however, remained in the sky.

"No!" Gemma cried. "Richard, no!"

She tried to pull at the creature's carcass, which was wrapped around Richard like a giant, slimy vine, but it was too heavy for her to move. She took a step back and started hacking away at it with the machete.

"Wait, let us give you a hand," someone called out from behind her.

She turned, and through the tears in her eyes, she saw a

plump man around Richard's age and a boy who must have been ten years younger than her. They looked nothing like the patrons of the tavern.

"What? But who are you?" Gemma asked in shock.

"A friend of his," the man said in a gentle voice.

Gemma didn't know what to say, so she, the man, and the boy worked together in silence to pry the remains of the creature off of Richard. The creature that had *come out of Walker's body*, killing him. The creature that may have murdered her only remaining companion on this journey. It was too much for her.

Gemma stepped back, legs shaking, as the other two began pulling Richard from the grip of the dead creature. She sat down at the edge of the sidewalk and caught her breath. She looked over at Richard, his head in the lap of the man who was shaking him by the shoulders and calling his name. He wasn't responsive.

But he was breathing.

Richard the Elusive was alive.

CHAPTER 22
GEMMA

Gemma continued to sit on the sidewalk in shock. She was in shock over witnessing the disturbing and sudden transformation of Walker's body. She was in shock over the death of the boy she'd grown up with, dated during college, broken up with, resented, and reunited with in the strangest of places. She was in shock over her friend Richard nearly getting crushed to death by the impossible creature that seemed to have formed from Walker's innards. And she was in shock that one of Richard's companions from the Great Journey was here, kneeling over Richard, holding Richard's head in his lap.

She recognized Arnem from all the illustrations in Jestan's books. She didn't, however, recognize the boy who accompanied him.

Arnem's young companion had run off down an alley a few minutes prior in search of something. With everything going through her head, Gemma didn't catch what it was he was looking for. So she sat, tears streaming down her face, right hand still gripping the machete so tightly that her knuckles turned white. When she realized she was doing it, she set the machete down on the sidewalk next to her. She turned toward the tavern and realized that despite all the commotion out here, nobody had come out the door to help or even just to watch. Nobody had strolled by on the sidewalk. No riders on horses had come down the street.

Gemma jumped when she heard a sound at the mouth of the alley. She turned to see the boy approaching, pushing a cart that looked strikingly similar to the one Richard had used back in Pinedrop. Somehow, that small connection helped her snap out of her state of shock. She stood up and walked toward Arnem, Richard, and the boy with the cart.

"I don't know if I can lift him by myself," Arnem said to them.

Gemma and the boy both nodded. Gemma took Richard's right leg, the boy took the left leg, and Arnem gripped Richard's upper body, using the crook of an elbow to carefully cradle Richard's head.

"One, two, three," Arnem counted, and they lifted in unison. Arnem grunted loudly under the weight. They gently laid Richard down in the cart, though he was comically too large for it. His legs hung over the edge. Gemma lifted his dangling arms and crossed them over his torso. She ran back to the packs, grabbed two blankets, and placed one under Richard's head for support and spread the other over his body for warmth. He looked swollen all over, which she hadn't noticed right away. There was blood coming out of one of his ears. She was certain he had at least broken some ribs when the creature had squeezed him tight.

"What are we going to do with him?" Gemma asked.

"There's only one person around here who may be able to heal him," Arnem said. "The Witch of Ferathan."

Gemma shook with fear. She knew that Richard's plan all

along had been to go to the witch, but even an hour earlier, Gemma hadn't believed the woman could actually be a real sorceress. Nor had she believed this town was under any kind of magical spell. But after the events that had occurred since they'd entered this pristine yet silent town, she was willing to let go of some of her skepticism. No parasite, insect, or reptile in Aepistelle could have been responsible for what happened to Walker. It had to be some sick, dark magic.

"My name is Arnem, by the way."

"Oh, yes, I assumed so. You look just like the pictures in the books. Just older, I guess," Gemma said. The boy let out a good-natured laugh. She turned to him. "My name is Gemma."

"I said the same thing to Arnem when I met him," said the boy. "About the pictures in the book, I mean. I'm Denny."

Now that she was a little calmer than before, Gemma observed Denny for the first time. He was unnaturally thin, something Gemma could tell came from years of hunger and not from the few days they must have been traveling to Ferathan. His eyes were a dark blue, and Gemma couldn't help but notice there was something very deep and knowing in them. It was like he didn't see her as a stranger, but as someone he'd known for quite some time.

"Have we met before?" Gemma asked, unable to understand the look in Denny's eyes.

"Well, I've seen you before, if that's what you mean," Denny replied.

"Where?" Gemma asked.

The boy looked at Arnem, as if to ask for permission. Arnem gently nodded to him.

"I have these visions," Denny said with some hesitation. "In my sleep. My parents had them, too, and they were taken away for it. I can see some things about the future. Just quick glimpses. I have no control over it."

"You saw me in these visions, then?" This was the second time in a few minutes that Gemma realized she hadn't outright disbelieved some claim of the supernatural. "You knew I'd be here?"

"Well, it started off with Richard the Elusive. I knew *he* would be here. And things looked different. He was being attacked by that monster, but it was in a cave in my dreams. Not everything was the same."

"Was I with him in the dreams?" Gemma asked.

"Not at first," Denny replied. "He was alone on some kind of mission, which he failed to accomplish once the monster killed him. It was the same thing for several nights, but then one night, just a couple weeks ago, a girl came into the picture. I couldn't see her clearly at first, but as the nights went on, I got a better look. It was you."

"If you guys knew this would happen, why didn't you get here sooner?" Gemma asked.

Denny and Arnem looked at each other with a mix of guilt and sorrow. This time, it was Arnem who spoke.

"We tried to," Arnem said. "We wanted to get here in time to stop this from happening, but it just didn't work out. Any time we thought we were gaining ground on the journey, we would get turned around again. I've never been a very good leader, especially in the woods. I always relied on my companions to guide us."

"We finally made it here just as that creature burst out of your other friend," Denny went on. "But what the dreams have been showing me the last couple nights was that this would be *your* moment—"

"Your moment to step up and be a hero," Arnem said,

finishing Denny's sentence. "I know that sounds terribly hollow now that Richard is injured, but we felt like the dreams were telling us to help you in the aftermath, not to interrupt the attack from happening."

"A hero?" Gemma couldn't believe they had said that. "Like this is some kind of storybook? We're real people, not characters in some tale."

"Everyone has a role to play when the stakes are high," Arnem said. "I ran from my destiny, shied away from it until my best friend made me be a part of the solution when things turned dark for Aepistelle. Maachel pulled me in with him, and we set things right, along with Richard and Jestan. Something evil is at work here in the north. If Denny's visions aren't preparing each of us for something big, I don't understand the point of it all."

An agonized groan from Richard ended their conversation.

"We must get him to the witch quickly," Denny said. "My visions haven't shown me anything beyond this point. I can't guarantee that he'll survive."

Gemma grabbed her pack and Richard's, leaving Walker's behind for good. She gathered the bow and the remaining arrows, as well as the machete, and walked back over to the cart, sliding some of the items in beside Richard. Denny picked up Richard's sword and set it in the cart as well. Arnem started pushing the cart up the street, and Denny and Gemma followed.

They hurried through the town, heading northeast up the middle of the streets. Gemma was no longer surprised that they didn't pass a single person on the way out. There were two other taverns that appeared to have life in them, based on the sounds of joyous laughter and chatter that leaked out, but no people were visible from the outside.

Gemma and her new companions didn't speak during the rest of their journey through the eerie town, but Gemma thought she heard the boy muttering some strange words. She couldn't understand what he was saying, and she didn't feel that she knew him well enough to ask. But she felt no threat from Denny, nor from the man who claimed to be Richard's close friend.

They arrived at a road that led them up a slight incline to a large manor that overlooked the town of Ferathan to the southwest, the Amassa Lake to the northwest, and the foothills of the Fingers to the east. Even from a distance, Gemma could tell it was nearly the size of King Davin's castle back in Capital City. This was not quite a castle, but for all intents and purposes, it was the same thing. Instead of housing royalty, this palace held the feared witch, protector of the town, and whatever remained of all the children of Ferathan who'd been given to her as a sacrifice decades earlier.

***

THE GROUNDS OF THE ESTATE WERE AS WELL KEPT AS THE rest of the town and its surrounding farms, but Gemma saw no gardeners toiling away at the landscaping. The darkness of the clouds had not abated in the hour since they had left downtown Ferathan. The path to the manor was lined with dozens of statues of grotesque and monstrous characters. Some were leonine creatures with snarling mouths showing sharp teeth. Others were large birds of prey in flight, with razor-sharp talons ready to pierce some imaginary victim. Some of the more disturbing ones were humanlike, but with odd features, such as the heads of horses, fingernails that looked like claws, or the legs of beasts.

A set of stairs rose to a great arched porch. Two massive iron doors stood at the end. The tunnel-like arches were lined with burning torches, but the light didn't stretch far. It felt like a dark cave leading up to the entrance. Because of the stairs, they opted to leave the cart and the unconscious Richard down below. They would retrieve him once they had requested the help they needed and knew they were welcome.

Arnem was the first to reach the top of the steps. He continued walking toward the door. Gemma was just behind him, and Denny brought up the rear. After walking a few feet across the tunneled porch, Gemma stopped and turned.

"What is it, Denny?" she asked. Behind her, at the top of the stairs, Denny stood in fear.

"The cave," he replied. "In my dreams, the cave I saw—it was like this porch, only deeper and darker. It ended in the lair of the monster that would kill Richard."

Arnem turned and walked over to them. "But Denny," he said, "Richard already faced off against the creature from your dreams. You said so yourself."

"Things from my dreams do change, that's true. Even so, I'm frightened of this place, Arnem."

"So am I," Arnem replied. "So am I. But we have to move on regardless. For Richard. Come, my little friend. We have a protector here with us, and we've seen her in action once already."

Gemma thought she caught a wink from Arnem as he glanced over to her. He needed her to be the brave one, it seemed. She smiled and stood tall, then walked over to Denny and took him by the hand.

"Arnem is right," she said, trying her best to sound courageous and heroic. "If we could take on that creature back in town, not to mention surviving the Decimated Forest, we can do anything."

Gemma led the way with Denny at her side. Arnem stayed close behind them. At the end of the porch, they looked up at the large doors. Arnem closed a fist and knocked, which made very little sound due to the thickness of the metal. Denny noticed that there was a rope hanging down from a large bell. He looked to Arnem and Gemma, and they nodded to him. Denny pulled, and the bell clanged loudly. He hurried back over between his companions.

After more than a minute had passed, they heard a noise on the other side of the doors. Then the doors slowly open from the inside. The creaking sounds the hinges made caused Gemma to think that they must not have been opened in quite some time.

The light that shone from inside was almost blinding after the dimness of the porch. Warmth flowed out, greeting the travelers, along with the welcoming smell of fresh-baked breads and cakes. And there, standing before them, were more than twenty children, well dressed and smiling. The oldest appeared to be close in age to Denny. Several were as young as four or five years old.

"Welcome to Ferathan Manor," one of the older boys said. "The lady of the house has asked that you join us inside."

Gemma, Arnem, and Denny stood in stunned silence. A little girl who looked about five walked up to Gemma and took her by the hand.

"Come on," the girl said in a sweet voice as she smiled up at Gemma.

"Um..." Gemma struggled to speak. "We have a friend who is injured. He's down below the porch."

Four of the older children stepped outside. One of them turned to Gemma.

"We will take great caution in bringing him in to the lady

of the house," he said. "She will take good care of him, as she does all of us. And all of Ferathan."

And so Gemma, Arnem, and Denny were led inside the oddly inviting mansion to meet the fabled Witch of Ferathan.

CHAPTER 23
GEORGE

George's first two days at sea were long, bouncy, and sickening. He had never been on a ship before, and certainly not on a sea with waves that swelled and crashed. It also didn't help that the crew of the *Ales and Sails* was constantly... well, drinking ales while manning the sails.

Maybe *manning* wasn't the proper term. The captain and the entire crew of the brazenly named vessel were women. So *operating* was probably a more appropriate term. And operating the ship they were. It wasn't the fault of their ales or their sails that the tide was particularly strong that second morning, nor that the wind and waves were knocking the ship all around. It only got worse the farther north they sailed.

Two nights earlier, after they'd left Jestan's estate, George had followed Jestan to the nearest port town, aptly called Portsville, and into the dockside bar, aptly called Drink Lest Ye Sink.

"Can't we just ride northeast and cut through Pinedrop?" George had pleaded. "We're heading the completely wrong way. We're heading toward the Western Sea!"

"That's the point, my good man," Jestan had said. When he'd arrived at the guesthouse earlier that night, George could tell immediately that there was something wrong. Jestan was clearly hiding some kind of emotion beneath his big, boisterous exterior. "We're getting ourselves a boat. We have some lost time to make up for. There's something we have to do to help your sister and Richard."

"What did you learn about the situation?" George had asked as they'd ridden side by side on their galloping horses. He'd looked over at Jestan, who was lost in thought.

"Well, I learned that Rodnego was keeping some things from me. And I learned that Richard has been writing to me for help for years. I feel partially responsible for whatever situation your sister walked into. I'm not sure what it is, only that it isn't good."

And so they'd ridden on. They'd passed through the streets of nearby Portsville, which seemed to be a collection of taverns, cargo warehouses, seafood restaurants, and more taverns. Jestan had dismounted in front of the Drink Lest Ye Sink, which hung halfway over a wharf; part of the building was on stilts that plunged down into the water below. George followed Jestan's lead, dismounting and tying up his horse outside the tavern.

"This is the best place to find a crew," Jestan said as he placed a hand on George's shoulder. "Just let me do the talking, and don't say a word about Richard or our mission."

Jestan turned and headed into the tavern, and George followed. Before he went inside, he saw the painted sign next to the door, which featured an illustration of a woman standing on an anchor and holding a large glass of ale as waves crashed below her.

The inside was loud, the crowd full of rowdy drunks. *They've certainly lived up to the first half of the place's name,*

George thought, *but let's hope whoever we hire won't sink our mission, too.*

"Well, if it isn't Jestan the Jester," a woman's voice called out. George watched as Jestan turned to his right and put on a playful smile.

"Le'Nelle!" he called out with a forced laugh. "You old pirate, you! You don't write or visit me these days!"

"That's because I don't fraternize with cheats and liars," she replied coldly. She turned toward George and frowned before looking back at Jestan. "I see you finally ditched Rodnego. Congratulations."

"Hey, Roddy's not such a bad guy. We just got off the road and needed some time apart. Listen, Le'Nelle, I—"

"That's *Captain* Le'Nelle to you," she interrupted.

"Sorry, Captain Le'Nelle. I need a ship, and I need it now," Jestan said. "There's nobody better than you for a job like this."

"Job like what, Jestan?" Le'Nelle crossed her arms. "What kind of garbage are you trying to throw at me this time?"

"Let's have a seat," Jestan said. He led Le'Nelle to a recently vacated booth and motioned for George to follow. Once they were sitting, he said, "This is my friend George Calvertson. George, this is Captain Le'Nelle Nightstar."

George and Le'Nelle nodded to each other.

"We have an emergency involving a very old friend of mine," Jestan said in hushed tones. "An emergency that requires us to head north."

"How far north are we talking?" Le'Nelle asked. Her glare extended to George this time as well.

"Just north of the Amassa River," Jestan responded.

"So you've come to me because you think I won't turn you in for requesting a job like this?"

"I've come to you because I know I can trust you," Jestan

said. "And I know that if anyone is talented enough to get us past the Royal Navy patrol ships unseen, it's you, 'Nelle."

There was a long moment of tense silence born out of whatever awkward past misdeeds had occurred between Jestan and the captain. Le'Nelle rolled up her sleeves as she considered the proposition, but George couldn't help breaking the silence.

"Are those kitties?" he asked with genuine excitement.

"What?" Jestan asked, turning to George. He flashed the younger man a bewildered look.

"They are indeed," Le'Nelle said. Her tough demeanor instantly mutated into a warmth that George soaked in. The captain rolled her sleeve up farther to reveal a mural of cats tattooed elaborately across her left arm and shoulder. "We have a couple dozen little ones onboard!"

"I have six at home. Oh, and look at this!" George rolled up his own sleeves, and everyone watching them was shocked to see that the shy young man's surprisingly muscular arms were adorned with illustrations of his own feline friends. Le'nelle's crew gathered round, patting George on the back and offering to share their drinks with him. George looked over at Jestan and laughed joyously.

"I like this one, Jestan," Le'Nelle said. "Okay, I'll do the job, but it'll cost extra. Three times my normal fee, and all of it upfront. Plus extra for the casks you drain on my ship and whatever the tab is for my crew here tonight."

"Well, *I* won't be drinking on the ship, at least," Jestan said, and Le'Nelle broke into laughter.

"The day Jestan the Drunk goes an entire trip sober is the day this world nears its end. I'll believe it when I see it."

Jestan didn't respond. Instead, he looked at her with a dire expression. Her smile quickly faded.

"Wow, it really is something serious, then," Le'Nelle said

soberly. "Three times the fee it is. I'll pay my crew's tab tonight; I was only kidding about that part."

"Thanks, 'Nelle," Jestan said. "It'll just be me and the cat boy here, no cargo. We need speed and secrecy, though, please."

"You got it. We can be out of here in an hour. The sooner the better, if you want to keep this under wraps. We're docked at pier eleven. Head over there while I gather the rest of the ladies."

AND SO TWO ROUGH DAYS PASSED AT SEA. EVEN THOUGH IT looked like a straight northerly journey on the map, they had to head west, not only to attempt to find smoother waters—which they clearly did not find—but also to avoid the patrol ships that guarded the coast. The Royal Navy had several imposing vessels stationed in the northern waters of Aepistelle, particularly to ensure that no sailors made their way north of the mouth of the River of Giants.

George missed his cats fiercely, but he was comforted by a deck full of new furry companions. It was all that got him through the voyage. True to his word, Jestan didn't drink at all, and as far as George could tell from the expressions on the crew members' faces, that seemed to be quite a big deal for him. However, true to their ship's name, the crew engaged in quite a bit of drinking. It was nearly as rowdy onboard the ship as it had been in the Drink Lest Ye Sink tavern back in Portsville. And for all the dizziness and vomiting George had experienced over those two days, he may as well have been drinking with them the whole time. At least there would have been something joyous about the trip.

"How can there possibly be anything left inside of you?"

Jestan asked. He laughed as he patted George's back hard yet playfully, like he was burping a baby. George raised his head from over the port-side railing.

"How can you possibly be so cheerful?" he responded. "I think I left my stomach back on the docks in Portsville."

"I love being on the open sea. Rodnego hired Captain Le'Nelle and her crew years ago for our coastal tour. That was a wild time, let me tell you. Sure didn't stay sober on that one, but I couldn't outdrink these ladies. Back then Le'Nelle was first mate, and the captain was—"

"Destination ahead," a voice called out from across the ship, interrupting Jestan. The crew members moved to their positions, preparing to bring the boat in closer to shore. Jestan pulled George away from the railing and led him to the starboard side.

In the distance was a beautiful sandy beach. Beyond that strip of beach, a forest grew, the trees climbing up the foothills. Beyond that, mountains stretched up, and on the southwestern edge of the range stood a lone tall tower.

"That's it," Jestan said. "The Western Watch of the Vheisenia—the Ancient Ones."

"I don't know what you're up to, Jestan," said a voice behind them. George turned to see Captain Le'Nelle eying them suspiciously. "Just don't let it be known that my ship brought you here. I could lose my maritime license for this one."

"And George and I would end up in prison," Jestan responded with a wink. "I wouldn't do that to Georgie boy here any more than I'd do it to you, 'Nelle."

"This is about as close as we get, boys. Now would be a good time to gather your bags and load them into the boat. That extra fee I charged you will just about cover a replacement boat and oars."

"Wait," George said to the captain, "you won't wait out here for us to return? How will we get back?"

"That was never the plan, Georgie," Jestan said. "We don't know how this is going to go, but we'll play it by ear."

Jestan led George down into the cabin they shared with the crew. They grabbed their belongings, returned to the deck, and tossed the bags into the smaller boat. Once they'd climbed in, the crew lowered the boat down to the water.

"So long, boys," Captain Le'Nelle called down to them with a rowdy laugh.

"Until next time," Jestan said.

"There won't be a next time," she called back, "unless your money turns out to be fake. Then I'll hunt you down."

Jestan seemed to find this hilarious, based on the hearty laugh he let out. George sat in stunned silence.

"Time to put yourself to work," Jestan said to George. "Let's get rowing before we're dragged back out to sea."

They eventually rowed to shore, but the current took them much farther north than where they had started out. Jestan pulled the boat up the beach, away from the reach of the waves and under the first trees that lined the sand. George only hoped they'd be able to find the boat again if they needed it. He looked out to sea and watched the *Ales and Sails* fade into the horizon. He tried to swallow away his fear; he couldn't help but feel that he'd never see civilization again. He turned away from the ocean and panicked.

"Jestan?" George called out. "Where are you?"

Instead of answering, Jestan sent a fruit flying right at George's head. It hit him just below the hairline and fell to the ground. He bent down and picked it up to examine it.

"It's a rayfruit," Jestan said as he emerged from the trees with an armful of the fuzzy yellow fruits. "They grow along the beaches up here in the north. It's been a quarter of a century since I've had one. Since anyone in Aepistelle has had one."

George furrowed his brow and then took a bite. The juice dripped down his chin. His expression remained blank for a few moments as he chewed. Then his eyes widened.

"This is amazing," he exclaimed. "Sour, but not too much. Sweet, but not overwhelming. And that juice!"

He didn't let the next one hit him in the head. He caught it this time and devoured it. Jestan looked on and laughed.

"Let's fill up our packs with more of these and then get on our way," Jestan said. They walked in among the trees, picked a few more rayfruits each, and then began their trek toward the tower in the mountains.

<hr>

EVEN IN THE PALE MOONLIGHT, GEORGE COULD TELL THAT the tower that loomed above them dwarfed even the highest point of King Davin's castle back home in Capital City. Even more impressive, it was built on the steep edge of the mountain. As they approached, George nearly hyperventilated—the tower appeared to be ready to tumble down on top of them.

"It's stood for a thousand years like that," Jestan reassured him as they stopped for the night. "I think it'll stand for at least one more night."

They had originally intended to reach the tower by nightfall, but Jestan had underestimated the distance and the steepness of the hills they had to climb. Instead, they found a nice clearing, started a campfire, and roasted some sort of feline creature that Jestan managed to catch.

"Why did you want to rush here instead of to wherever

Richard and Gemma are?" George asked. "You've been quite evasive about that this whole time."

"We couldn't talk about it on that ship. I trust Le'Nelle enough to sail us here and keep quiet about it, but tell her any specifics, and she or her crew may give us up to the Committee. The reward for information on violators of their laws is quite high."

"She would have been locked up, too, though," George said. "She sailed past the border of the River of Giants."

"The Committee would have looked past that if they had any excuse to lock me up. They've been trying for the last two decades. Doing what we're here to do would be more than enough for that."

"And what are we here to do, Jestan?"

"To signal for help," Jestan said. "From the Lands Beyond. From the Ancient Ones."

THEY SET OUT EARLY THE NEXT MORNING. GEORGE'S BACK ached. He'd never slept outdoors before—and he wasn't sure if he could even count the night that had just passed, as he'd hardly slept a wink. He was shocked by how rested and full of energy Jestan seemed. Lying out under the stars must have brought back memories of his youth and the more pleasant aspects of the Great Journey.

The climb up the rest of the mountain was tricky and seemingly perilous in some spots.

"Great call on not doing this at night," George yelled ahead at Jestan, who looked back and winked.

After another couple of hours, George pulled himself up and over the crest of the steepest peak yet. He lay on his belly, facedown in the dirt. Jestan began laughing joyously, standing over George.

"We did it, Georgie boy!"

George raised his head, still panting. He looked up to see the ancient Western Watch towering above them, only a few hundred feet away. Jestan turned and headed toward it, arms held out as if proclaiming victory.

"Woo!" Jestan hollered, and it echoed all around them. His excitement was infectious, and George broke out in laughter.

They arrived at a door to the tower.

"You do have the key, don't you?" George asked, half worried and half joking.

Jestan smiled at him, then reached for the handle of the great steel door. The handle gave way, but the door didn't. Jestan's smile faded.

"Well," he said, turning to George with a defeated look on his face, "it appears we'll have to go back home. It's locked."

"What? But we can't go back home after—"

The smile returned as Jestan pushed his full weight against the door. It creaked open loudly, though it was barely audible under Jestan's roaring laughter.

"Very funny," George said.

A cloud of dust puffed out of the doorway. Wings fluttered somewhere inside the dim tower. Jestan let out another ecstatic "Woo!" It echoed even more inside the tower. George followed him inside.

George didn't quite know what he expected to find. Maybe the interior would be as elaborate as the castle he'd visited with his mother during King Davin's annual banquet for the servants and groundskeepers and their families. Plush red carpets that made him wish he could run about barefoot. An ever-present inviting warmth. Sofas that seemed so elaborate and stiff that he didn't think anyone had ever dared to sit on them.

Instead, the tower's lower level was a massive, empty cavern of a room with crumbling pieces of stone scattered over a filthy floor. The skeletal remains of several rodents were strewn about. Narrow window slits high up on the walls let in a little light, but not so much as to make the place vulnerable to attackers. A warm and welcoming palace this was not.

A large staircase spiraled upward along the rounded walls of the building.

"Onward and upward, my little friend," Jestan said joyfully.

"I can hardly feel my legs after all that climbing," George replied.

Jestan dropped his pack and began to ascend the tower stairs. George sighed, set his own pack down, and reluctantly followed. They climbed floor after floor, and George regretted not bringing his waterskin. The higher levels were broken up into rooms with larger windows that provided more light. Jestan didn't stop climbing to explore the rooms— he said there would be time for that later. Still, George was surprised to see glimpses of elaborately carved chairs and tables, inviting sitting rooms, what appeared to be an armory, and much more. Of course, it was all completely caked in an unhealthy mix of dust and bird droppings, then further draped in decades of spiderwebs and crusted with rodent urine.

George lost count of the levels they ascended before they finally made it to the very top floor. Rather than a penthouse or even a watchman's perch, the top floor reminded George of a giant furnace. The openings in the wall were massive, and the wind terrified George. There would be no saving him if a gust knocked him right out and down the full height of the tower, or if he was on the south side of the room, down the side of the mountain.

"This is the Great Hearth of the Western Watch," Jestan said. "When the flames are stoked, it can be seen for hundreds, even thousands of miles. We'll be able to send a signal from here."

And so they did. George was shocked by how easily Jestan got the flames going. Of course, the smoke was quite black at first, what with all the dust that had accumulated over the decades.

They descended the stairs, coughing from the fumes. When they reached the ground floor, George looked to Jestan as if to ask what was next. Jestan grinned at him.

"Now we wait for help to arrive."

CHAPTER 24
GEMMA

The halls of Ferathan Manor were warm and well lit. The floors appeared to be swept and mopped regularly. The upper corners of the walls had no visible cobwebs. The few doors that were open looked into rooms that were organized, decorated with decadent furniture and fine art. It was all inviting. Comforting. And not at all what the travelers were expecting.

Several times on their walk through the seemingly endless halls, Gemma found herself exchanging surprised glances with Arnem. She also noted that Denny still looked afraid, as if this was all part of the terrifying dreams he'd had in recent weeks. He whispered under his breath those same words Gemma thought she'd heard him say on the walk through Ferathan. *Tsechev ni-fellen szoren al-zar*, it sounded like. What did that even mean?

They approached the end of another hall, but this time there was no corner to turn. Instead, there were two large red doors, both shut. They had been led there by a boy slightly younger than Denny and the same little girl who had grabbed

Gemma by the hand in the entryway. She still maintained the trusting grip.

The boy knocked twice. Without allowing any time for an answer, he turned the handles on both doors at once, pushing them wide open.

The room beyond was a spacious, open sitting room. Plush carpet spread across the floor. In the center of the room were three armchairs and what Gemma could only describe as a comfortable throne. The seats were arranged in a square, with the throne facing the doors so that its occupant could see people's comings and goings. The throne was the only piece of furniture that was occupied.

Sitting on it was a woman that appeared to be close in age to Gemma's mother. She was beautiful. She stood gracefully, and her full height was revealed. Gemma's eyes widened as she realized that this woman was probably two or three inches taller than Richard the Elusive. A smile spread across the woman's face, and Gemma didn't think there was any malice in it. She beckoned for them to come in and sit on the chairs around her throne.

"Thank you, Alex and Rabia. Please close the doors so that I may speak to our new friends."

The woman's voice was as warm and welcoming as her demeanor. Gemma and Arnem walked toward the sitting area, but Denny hung back by the now-closed doors.

"My child, please—there's no need for fear in this house," the woman said. She flashed a smile at Denny, who finally followed Gemma and Arnem. They each took a seat on one of the chairs and faced the woman. They stared at her in wonder for a few moments until Denny broke the silence.

"Are you the Witch of Ferathan?" Denny asked.

The woman let out a warm laugh. "Oh, out of the mouths of babes," she said. "No, I am not a witch. A priestess, yes. A practitioner of the arts of Azhelda. A protector of the people of Ferathan, even. But not a witch. My name is Naliah Lunarra."

"Madam Lunarra," Gemma said, "I am Gemma Calvertson. Our friend is outside. He's badly injured."

"The children are bringing him in now, dear. Please do not worry. Nobody will die in my house tonight, I can assure you."

"My lady, thank you for inviting us into your home," Arnem said. "My name is Arnem Wynstone. We've traveled a long way, and we were surprised to find Ferathan in such a condition. Have the Foreign Ones not interfered with the people here?"

"The Foreign Ones?" Naliah stared deep into Arnem's eyes, and he looked down as if ashamed. Naliah continued in a polite but commanding voice, "The only foreign ones here are you three. Here in Ferathan, we take care of our own people. We are insulated from the corruption of the outside world. Of course, that doesn't mean we don't take in travelers once in a while. Those who are in need, such as yourselves."

"You know what he means," Denny said. "The Tzakabya. Those who came from afar, from up the Amassa River, to brainwash King Harold. The same way you brainwashed the people of Ferathan."

"Denny—" Gemma began, but Naliah held up a hand to silence her.

"Child—Denny, I mean—I can see you are no ignorant babe at all. You are correct that I knew what he meant, but I do not like to speak of that evil. The children may be listening."

At that moment, the doors opened. The older children who had gone out to fetch Richard entered the room, pushing the cart that still held Gemma's companion. Richard looked worse than ever. Sweat drenched his face, hair, and clothes. His labored breathing was accompanied by a significant wheeze. His open wounds still oozed blood and puss. Gemma stood up and wept at the sight of her friend.

Naliah also stood. She motioned for the children to bring Richard to her throne. They parked the cart where she requested and promptly left the room. Naliah put her left hand on Richard's drenched forehead and her right hand over his chest.

"It appears that the son has come to finish the father's work," Naliah said.

Arnem cocked his head at this. "What do you mean?"

"Richard came here to collect the books that belonged to his father," Gemma said. "The ones that were left here for you to protect."

The witch nodded. Her smile shifted to something more devious, and Gemma didn't like it.

"It's not quite as simple as that," Naliah said. "It wasn't just a benevolent act on my part. I made a deal with his father, and he did not fulfill his end of it."

"A deal?" Gemma didn't remember Richard saying anything of the sort. "What kind of deal?"

The tall woman turned and walked across the room to a buffet table that held a pitcher of water, a few glasses, a platter of fruits, and a stack of neatly folded cloth napkins. She filled one of the glasses with water, picked up a napkin, and brought both back to the center of the room. She dipped the napkin into the water and used it to wipe away blood and sweat from Richard's skin. His eyes remained closed, but he stirred.

"Richard's father came to me many decades ago. He was cutting through my town on his way south. He and his underlings, with their bags full of books and scrolls. They were smuggling those texts away from King Harold and what you called the Tzakabya, or the Foreign Ones, bringing them down south to his parents' farm a few at a time. But they could only take so many trips before King Harold realized he was disappearing for days at a time. So on his last journey, he came to me, knowing Ferathan was out of King Harold's grasp.

"He begged me to hold the wretched things for him. I laughed at his desperation. I explained why it was not safe for someone with the power of the Azhelda to also have in her possession the books of tricks and spells."

"So you refused?" Gemma asked.

"No, he was very convincing. He was a charming man. A looker, like his son turned out to be, and a very smooth talker, even in troubled times. I let him convince me, or let him *think* he'd convinced me, to store those damned things for him here. But only if he promised to return the favor."

The witch interrupted her own story to call in one of the children. Rabia, the girl who had led Gemma by the hand, came back through the double doors. Naliah instructed her to fetch her healing kit. Rabia nodded obediently and ran off. Naliah then walked over to the buffet table to refill the glass of water.

While they waited in awkward silence, Gemma looked over at Denny. His face still expressed a strong distrust of the witch, a feeling Gemma was beginning to share. Arnem sat in silence in the next chair over, staring at Richard with sadness and wringing his hands. It seemed that they were all growing uncomfortable in that room.

Rabia returned a minute later, leading their other guide, Alex, who was carrying a wooden chest about a foot long by six inches deep with a rounded lid that opened on hinges. It was not unlike the jewelry box that Gemma's mother had inherited from her grandmother, though she had never owned any expensive bracelets or exotic trinkets to fill it with. Alex handed the box to Naliah, then exited the room with Rabia, pulling the doors closed behind them.

Naliah set the box down on the floor next to Richard and lifted the lid. She rummaged through the tiny crystal bottles that were inside and selected what she was looking for.

"Richard's father, Edward, promised to return the favor by helping to free me of this place and the covenant that holds me here. The covenant I made with the people of Ferathan long ago was to protect them from harm in exchange for this manor and power over their children. But I'm a terrible negotiator. I never thought to specify an end date to my agreement with Ferathan, so I am still bound by it. I suppose it was by my own design; I'd been cast out of my hometown, poor and alone, and I was excited to come here and have power over these people. But eventually, I started to long for other things. Other people. And here I am, protector of this town, caretaker of these children, yet all alone."

Naliah mixed a few drops from the bottle into the glass of water. She put the cap back on and exchanged it for a second bottle, which she also dripped into the glass. She gave the water a stir with her right pointer finger, and then pulled Richard's mouth open. She carefully tilted the glass and poured a small amount of the mixture into his mouth. She pushed his mouth closed and gently lifted his head up to get him to swallow.

"Since outsiders were rare, I admit that Edward was pleasing to me. I hoped to win him over with a spell, if not with my beauty, which at the time, I assure you, was probably enough, even for a married man like him. But I needed to be free of my commitments first. The biggest threat at the time —and still to this day—is not these Tzakabya you speak of.

The real threat to Ferathan has always been the Ogressi that live up in the Fingers."

At this, Arnem lifted his head and laughed.

"I know about the Ogressi," Arnem said. "We came across them during the Journey. We were hiking the north face of the Fingers to head up to the Esteron Mountains when they attacked us. Big old things, they were. Like giant humanlike creatures with weird gray-blue skin. They use tree trunks as weapons, that's how massive they are."

"And they love to feast on the flesh of men," Naliah said. "Especially men from Ferathan. At least they did, before my protection spells kept them away. They haven't been back since, but I hear them out there sometimes, howling and hollering up in the hills like beasts."

"So you expected Richard's father to slay the Ogressi?" Gemma asked.

"It may sound like an impossible task, but it may not be that difficult. They are stupid creatures. Edward was clearly a bright man, so I figured he could outsmart them."

"And if we go out there and rid the Fingers of the Ogressi, that would free you of the covenant with Ferathan? And you'll let us have the books that belonged to Richard's father?"

"Yes, I would be free, and I would let you have the texts," Naliah said. "I might even be in your debt at that point, for I long to escape this prison I've trapped myself in."

Gemma looked over at Denny, who was slowly nodding as if desperate for any plan that involved them leaving Ferathan Manor.

"I only recall there being two Ogressi when we ran into them back then," Arnem said.

"That's because there are only two left in this world," Naliah said. "Bring me proof that they are dead, and I will terminate the covenant and follow through with the promise I made to Edward all those years ago."

"What about Richard?" Denny asked.

"I will heal him while you're gone. I must do it in private. There are things I cannot reveal to those not of the Azhelda. I had great admiration for his father, and I will take good care of him. Even the Azhelda are decent to travelers in need."

"Decent to travelers?" Gemma shot up to her feet. Her hands clenched into fists. "And what of Walker? He was killed by the spells that you put on this town! How is that decent?"

"I am sorry about your friend, my dear." Naliah stepped around Richard's body and approached Gemma. She reached up and wiped a tear from Gemma's cheek as the girl flinched from her touch. "His intentions were not pure, and he would have attempted to do harm to this town, either directly or with his southern army."

"But he—"

"Search your heart. You know it to be true. He was a man who put duty before honor, even though he served a reprehensible regime." Naliah's eyes met Gemma's, and Gemma found herself sinking into a strange calm. Once her breathing relaxed, Naliah stepped back to Richard's side and addressed the visitors. "Now, the children will have set up rooms for you to rest for the night, but you must leave early in the morning. I will be up all night working on your friend."

Denny, Arnem, and Gemma walked out to the hallway. They were led to their rooms, where they attempted to rest in anticipation of their journey to slay the giant beasts.

CHAPTER 25
GEMMA

They were armed and armored. Ferathan Manor had coats of mail and a cache of swords from the time when it was a stronghold for the region. Denny was given a slightly smaller sword than Arnem, and Gemma opted to stick with the machete and the bow and arrows. The stockroom had enough arrows to replenish her supply, and Gemma was glad for it, as she had already spent some of Walker's arrows when she had attempted to take down the creature that had killed him.

Gemma had told her new companions about what had happened to Walker after eating the fruits and drinking the liquor in Ferathan. They had all decided that they would not accept any of the witch's culinary offerings, as delicious as they all smelled. Instead, they each brought the rations they had left and hoped it would be enough, at least until they found wild crops and game in the foothills to supplement it.

About an hour past sunrise, after Naliah gave them what they needed from the armory, they set out, heading east toward the Fingers. They didn't have any specific information about the whereabouts of the Ogressi, only that there were two of them who lived somewhere among the rolling foothills that stretched east to the Esteron Mountains. There was an overgrown trail just outside of the expansive yards of Ferathan Manor that they located and followed.

By noon, they had already made it to the top of the first peak, which gave them a view of the hills beyond. They stopped and looked for any signs in the distance that the Ogressi were near, but they found nothing. After a quick bite to eat, they continued, hiking through the evening. It was much cooler up in the hills than it was in Ferathan, and Gemma regretted not asking Naliah for a heavier coat before they'd set out that morning. She hadn't anticipated the biting wind. As the sun made its way downward in the western sky behind them, they arrived at a grove of trees.

"This looks like a good place to stop for the night," Arnem said. "We should be able to gather enough wood for a fire."

"What about the Ogressi?" Denny asked. His terror hadn't lessened since they'd left Ferathan Manor that morning. "Won't they see the fire and attack us?"

"I don't know too much about the Ogressi," Arnem said, "but I do know that they are terrified of the flames. It may give up our location, but they'll stay away at least until the fire dies down."

"I suppose it would speed things up if they came to us," Gemma said. "Let's just draw them in and get this over with."

She shocked herself in that moment. *Is this bravery*, she wondered, *or is it recklessness?* With everything that had happened the previous day—the death of the man who'd been her only serious romantic partner, the monster she'd slain, the creepy town, and the creepier mansion full of ageless children and what seemed to be an actual witch—Gemma didn't know how to feel anymore.

She set down her pack and began gathering usable firewood. Denny joined her, while Arnem gathered rocks and arranged them into a circular firepit. They got the flames going a few minutes later and settled down to rest for the night. Nobody was particularly hungry for their dried snacks, and no words bothered to leave their tongues for quite some time.

A cracking sound from the woods pierced through the silence, and Denny gasped. Arnem reached over and patted the boy's back to calm him. Gemma smiled warmly.

"Denny," she said, "tell me more about your visions. How do they work?"

Denny glanced at her nervously, then at Arnem. Arnem nodded to him as if to tell the boy that it was safe to trust Gemma.

"Well, some things I see, and some things I just know. Like with Richard the Elusive, I could see he was in trouble, but it wasn't like there was a sign that said where he was. That part I just knew, even though I've never been to Ferathan before. I'd never even left Esteron until I met Arnem last week."

"But things have changed in your visions since the first time you saw them?" Gemma asked.

"Yeah. It's like, the future isn't set in stone. Not all of the details, anyways—maybe just some of the outcomes. I didn't see you with Richard at first. He was all alone. Then, a few nights before I met Arnem, the visions began to change, and suddenly, there you were."

"Richard told me he was already planning to make the journey before I met him," Gemma said. "I just happened to meet him at the right time, I suppose." *Or rather, Walker and the Committee got word from their spies that Richard appeared ready to make a move, and they set up my assignment before he could leave on his own*, Gemma thought.

"Denny, do you think the visions come to you so that you can change what will happen?" Arnem asked. "We didn't arrive in time to stop the attack on Richard. For that, I feel like I've failed my old friend."

"I don't know that we failed," Denny said. "I think it would have happened sooner if we had gotten to town in time. Maybe we couldn't change it once things got moving, unless we had gone straight to Pinedrop before Richard and Gemma left for their journey."

"That's what I keep thinking about. A part of me believed you when you told me he was in danger, but then I doubted it. I could have gotten us off the train when it passed through Pinedrop on the way home from Esteron, but I acted selfish."

"You were thinking of your family, Arnem. There is no shame in that."

Gemma was impressed by the boy's maturity. *If there are gods who grant powers like the one he seems to have, they chose a wise young soul to wield them*, she thought.

"Have you had any visions about this quest we're on now?" Gemma asked. "About how things will go for us with the Ogressi?"

The boy looked down, ashamed. The fire crackled, and he jumped again.

"Nothing. When I finally slept last night, there were no dreams. It may sound selfish, but I was glad of it."

"You deserved the rest, Denny," Arnem reassured him. "We all deserve some more tonight. Let's sleep, shall we?"

They threw some more wood on the fire to keep it going, then settled down as close to it as was safe. They tried their best to sleep the night away.

IF ONLY THINGS WERE THAT SIMPLE.

Denny was the first to fall asleep, and Arnem was soon snoring loudly alongside him. But every time Gemma thought she was about to drift off, the boy started talking in his sleep. It was like the strange gibberish she'd heard him say before, but the words were different this time. *Pylen far-wellen zal ul-goetz nohar*, it sounded like. Eventually, though, Gemma joined her companions in slumber.

After only three hours of sleep, the cracking sound from the grove of trees next to their camp returned. And again. Then soft footsteps made their way toward the sleeping travelers. Gemma awoke to a soft nudge between her shoulder blades. Her eyes opened slowly as she sat up and looked around.

Surrounding Arnem, Denny, and Gemma were twelve women dressed in animal skins that were torn, ragged, and filthy. In the flickering light of the dwindling campfire, Gemma saw that they shared many features with the woman Walker had shot and killed in the forest. They were the Nazseke, only these women appeared to still have their tongues.

The women held carefully crafted spears, each engraved with elaborate symbols not unlike the ones Gemma had found engraved in the black trees. The tips were sharpened to fine points, strong enough to pierce man or beast.

Denny opened his eyes and screamed at the sight of them. In turn, Arnem sprang awake and involuntarily made a shocked, wordless sound.

"Don't fear them," Gemma said calmly to her companions. She had no real reason to trust these women, yet she was sure they were in desperate need of help the same way the Nazseke woman in the dark forest had been.

"We mean you no harm," Gemma said to the women surrounding them. "We are out here to slay the Ogressi so that we may free the captives of the Witch of Ferathan."

The woman standing closest to Gemma looked around at the faces of the other Nazseke. Denny was shaking, and Arnem set his hand on the boy's shoulder to try and calm him.

Then the nearby woman burst into laughter. The other women followed suit.

"You wish to slay the Ogressi?" their apparent leader asked. "With those weapons? And that boy and fat man to help you?"

She spoke with the thick accent of the mountain tribes, which Gemma had read about but never actually heard with her own ears. She was relieved that the woman spoke the standard language of Aepistelle. At her questions, the women roared with laughter even louder than before. Gemma looked over at her machete and bow with embarrassment.

It was Arnem who spoke next.

"Teyla-te-Anya?" Arnem asked.

The woman took a step closer to the fire, and Gemma got a better look at her. Her face was strong and determined, and it was full of both beauty and loss. She appeared to be several inches taller than Gemma. She looked like a true warrior who served with a purpose. The woman squinted as she looked at Arnem in silence. Then came the look of recognition.

"The Weeping One," Teyla said in an awed voice. "How can it be?"

"Wait, you know each other?" Gemma asked.

Arnem rose to his feet with some effort. "I'm sorry you

remember me that way," he said. "It was a desperate time. I knew you understood, though, Teyla."

"Yes, and it was a shameful time for the Nazseke as well. We are still suffering from the elders' decision to this day." Teyla lowered her spear. The others did the same. "And if you are here, that means it is another desperate time."

"Yes. We have come to save the people of Emyhrsen from the grip of the Tzakabya. We believe the Tzakabya mean to extend their control to Aepistelle. My old friend Richard is badly wounded, and the Witch of Ferathan has agreed to heal him if we kill the Ogressi and free her from her deal with the people of Ferathan."

Teyla shifted her gaze away from Arnem, her face full of sadness and regret.

"Perhaps you may lead us out of these mountains as well," Teyla said. She wasn't looking at Arnem, though. Her eyes were fixed on Gemma.

"Why are you here?" Arnem asked, getting Teyla's attention back. "Your people live a hundred miles north of here."

"They may still, or what is left of them. A few years after we met, Arnem, some men from King Harold's dominion, agents of the Tzakabya, arrived in Nazseke to extinguish our flames. They were on some kind of mission to end all magical practices in those lands. They cut out the tongues of everyone in the village that day."

"Why their tongues?" Gemma asked. "Why leave them alive?"

Teyla turned back to Gemma and stared hard into her eyes. She didn't speak immediately. Gemma felt like the woman was reading her, assessing whether or not she could be trusted.

"Magic is like the blade of a sword. It is sharp and danger- ous, but it cannot be wielded without the hilt. The tongue and the voice are the hilt, required to unsheathe the sword. I don't know why they spared the lives of the Nazseke, but they made sure that my people couldn't rebel in supernatural ways. They left a village of broken souls behind."

"Why were you and your companions spared?" Gemma asked.

"We had already separated from our people by that point, after their refusal to aid Arnem and Maachel on their journey when they came to us for help. But we aren't the only ones who escaped. Several weeks later, one of the Nazseke ministers, Lyon-te-Sall, stumbled upon our camp here in the foothills. He had been away on a meditation retreat by himself when everything happened, and he fled once he returned home and saw what had been done to our people. When he found us here, he blamed us for not helping to protect the Nazseke, and he cursed us to wander these hills, unable to make our way out until we found a new female leader to obey and follow. He called it our punishment for not being there to protect the foolish men who led the Nazseke when they were attacked. And maybe he was right to do so. We were supposed to be the warrior protectors of our people, after all."

Denny stood up, and Gemma was shocked to see that his fear seemed to have been replaced by wide-eyed wonder. He spoke with confidence for the first time since she'd met him.

"Before you surrounded us, I saw a vision in my dreams that I did not understand," he said. "There were twelve silhouettes standing in a circle with swords raised."

"We have no swords, young one, only spears," Teyla said. Her eleven companions let out low but good-natured laughs. To Gemma's surprise, Denny laughed with them.

"I was just telling my friends here that my visions aren't

usually perfect, but they aren't wrong in their meaning. I just don't always know how to interpret them."

"So what are you saying, child?"

"I believe you and your warriors were destined to be here in this moment," Denny said, "to help us on our mission. To earn your freedom."

"Freedom?" one of Teyla's warriors asked. "As she said, we need a leader to follow in order for the curse to be broken."

Denny looked up. His eyes skipped past Arnem and landed on Gemma. "There is a leader among us," he said. "In my vision, the twelve silhouettes surrounded the one person whose face I could see clearly. She will be the one to guide us all to freedom."

Arnem, Teyla, and the eleven other warriors followed his gaze across the fire and looked directly at Gemma.

She looked back in surprise. Most of the women had incredulous stares, sizing her up, judging her, snickering to each other. She didn't blame them. She would have done the same, had she a mirror in front of her face. Teyla, however, gazed at her with a different expression, and when the others realized, they too regarded Gemma with wonder on their faces.

"Freedom it is," Teyla proclaimed. "Freedom it is. Now, let us make a warrior out of this girl. Those Ogressi won't defeat themselves."

CHAPTER 26

GEMMA

The two days that followed were full of training. Teyla and her companions were unrivaled with their spears, and they taught Gemma to expertly wield the machete she had taken to over the past few days. They also gave lessons to Denny and Arnem, who was accomplished but decades out of practice with a blade, but most of their efforts were spent on Gemma. They did all they could to try and find something special in her. They didn't want to see merely a young historian, a city girl, or a hero's companion. There had to be true potential buried somewhere within her, a slab of clay waiting to be shaped into something brilliant. The Nazseke needed to uncover the leader inside Gemma Calvertson. If her natural abilities with the bow were any indication, it could be done.

Throughout their time training, there was no sign of the two Ogressi. The warriors used their spears to hunt for food and even got Gemma involved by encouraging her to practice with her bow. The first time one of her arrows took down a rabbit, she nearly wept at the sight, but it helped her confidence grow.

"What are the Ogressi like?" Gemma asked on the second night as the group sat around a large fire.

Teyla took a bite of freshly crisped rabbit leg, chewed, pulled out a piece of ligament, and threw it into the flames. "Some say they are dumb beasts," she answered after swallowing her food. "They don't speak like we do, but they are intelligent. As large as five fat men combined, but not quite giants in the historical sense. Their skin is almost slate gray and scattered with white, wiry hair."

"They're man-eaters, too," Arnem said from across the fire.

"Well, then, it's a good thing the women will be hunting them and the men will be the bait," Teyla said, and her companions had a good laugh.

Denny shot a terrified glance at Arnem, who patted his shoulder and winked.

"You think I'm kidding, Arnem, but I'm not," Teyla said. "You and the boy will draw them out, and we'll lead Gemma in for the kill."

"I don't feel ready for that," Gemma said. "I appreciate all the training you've given me, but I'm no warrior."

Teyla looked deep into Gemma's eyes.

"If you said you *did* feel ready to take on those two creatures, that would be proof that you were not. But by being a willing learner, you show your wisdom. You will be ready when the moment comes. And if you really aren't... well, your friends will make a fine meal for the Ogressi, and my friends and I will have to go back to wandering these hills and waiting for a *worthy* leader to come along."

A roar of laughter broke out around the campfire. Even Denny reluctantly joined in. *If Denny isn't concerned, he must not have seen anything alarming in his dreams. Surely his own death, or Arnem's, or mine would have prompted one of those visions of his.* Or so she thought—so she hoped.

⸻

THEY LEFT THEIR CAMP IN THE WOODS AFTER THE THIRD night.

"We have come across the Ogressi dozens of times over the last few years," Teyla explained, "yet they've never attacked us unless we were hunting the same pack of animals they were."

"That's happened?" Arnem asked.

"When you're cursed to walk the same lands over and over for years, it is bound to happen."

"And where do the Ogressi normally live?"

"Well, they're terrified of Ferathan, I can tell you that. Whatever spell the Witch of Ferathan cast over the town, it's done the job. We've seen the Ogressi most often up near Hightower."

Teyla pointed east, where the hills rose up into the towering Esteron Mountains. Even from that distance, Gemma could see that the hills grew much more rocky, their inclines more dramatic. Jutting out from the middle of the range was a particularly tall and narrow peak.

"The base of Hightower is full of deep tunnels and caves. Some say the tunnels lead to an underground city. Others claim they lead hundreds of miles east under the Esteron Mountains and end at the edge of the Great Eld Desert."

"Have you tried going through the tunnels?" Gemma asked.

"We can't go too far in—half a mile at most. Any farther

would take us out of the Fingers, which we are bound to by the curse."

They walked on throughout the day, but it didn't feel to Gemma like they were getting any nearer to Hightower. Its enormity made it appear closer than it really was. The path they were on started to descend into another forested valley, and the hour was getting late.

"Perhaps if we stay up here on the hill tonight, our campfire will be more visible to the Ogressi and draw them out of their cave," Gemma said. "They may not come right up to us, but at least they'll know we're getting nearer."

"So you want to eliminate any element of surprise?" Teyla asked. "I'm not questioning your plan, Gemma, but I want to make sure that's what you intend."

"I don't know," Gemma said. "What do you suggest?"

"Oh no," Teyla laughed. "You don't need to ask us. We're following your lead now. So lead us with wisdom, Gemma."

Gemma blushed. She looked around at Arnem and Denny, then at the other Nazseke warriors. She expected to see expressions of mocking distrust or nervousness. Instead, everyone seemed to be looking at her with respect. *What have I done to deserve this?* Gemma wondered.

"All right, then. Let us draw them in. The sooner we slay them, the sooner we can get back to Richard and make sure the Witch of Ferathan has stayed true to her word and healed him."

Gemma set her pack down where they stood, a somewhat flat spot partway down the hill that led into the forest below. She instructed some of the Nazseke to collect firewood and the others to catch game for their dinner. They all nodded obediently and set off on their tasks. Gemma sat and motioned for Arnem and Denny to do the same. She turned to Arnem, who had a big smile on his face.

"You're really enjoying this, aren't you?" Arnem asked.

"No! No way. It's so weird. These are accomplished warriors, and I have no business telling them what to do. I can't lead!"

"You can lead, and you are leading," Denny said. "Just like in my dream. They will follow you through all of this, and you will lead them to freedom."

"Better you than me, Gemma," Arnem said.

"But you have more experience out here than I do!" Gemma said.

"Sure, as a follower and companion to better men than me. I've never had the qualities of a leader in me. And you are a true warrior. The way you slaughtered that creature back in town. The way you can shoot arrows with such precision. And have you seen the way those ladies look at you when you're swinging your machete around? Total respect. They see you as one of them, I'm sure of it."

Gemma's cheeks were pure crimson by that point. Leader? Warrior? She'd never thought of herself as either of those things. And the monster she'd killed in Ferathan... that was only to protect Richard and avenge Walker. Anyone would have done the same.

The wood collectors returned a few minutes later, and the group got a nice-size fire going. Another few minutes passed before Teyla and the other hunters returned with fish impaled on the tips of their spears.

"There's a nice stream just through the trees," Teyla reported. "Water clear as glass. We should fill the waterskins tomorrow morning."

They ate a good dinner and started to turn in, but Gemma wasn't satisfied. She walked over to Arnem and Denny, who had separated themselves from the women to set up their sleeping spots for the night. They had their own fire going, along with a third on the other side of the camp, in hopes of catching the attention of the Ogressi.

"What's troubling you, Gemma?" Arnem asked.

"It's just that every day and night that pass feel like wasted time. I can't help but think how worried my family must be back home. And who knows what has become of Richard? Can the Witch of Ferathan even be trusted?"

"Don't rush things. You are being trained by the best warriors in the north. The best in all of Aepistelle, even. It feels strange to say this, but I do believe Richard is in better hands with Naliah than he would have been with us after what happened to him. We are doing the right thing. Your family will be so proud of you, Gemma."

Gemma turned to face the women settling down around their own firepit. She walked back over to them, and they stayed up for several more hours, detailing their adventures from their years in the wilderness.

CHAPTER 27
GEMMA

Gemma wasn't sure if it was the snores of the other women or the insufferable stones and pebbles under her back that kept her awake, but she was done tossing and turning for the time being. The moon was starting to fall in the western sky, and she knew the first rays of morning light were only a couple of hours away. Gemma rose as silently as she could manage, picked up her empty waterskin, and crept around the fading embers of the firepit. On second thought, she went back for her machete, then made her way down the hill to the forested area below.

After relieving herself under the cover of the trees, Gemma continued into the woods, following the sound of the stream. Slivers of moonlight punctured the canopy above so that she didn't trip over any protruding roots or oversize rocks. She found the steady flow of water and began to fill her waterskin. She sat on a large rock as the skin expanded with the cool liquid.

Perhaps we should have camped in here, Gemma thought. *It's just as rocky as the hillside, but at least the sound of the stream is relaxing.* She rested one elbow on her thigh, balled her hand into a fist, and leaned her forehead against it. The sleep that had evaded her that night finally allowed itself to be caught, and her eyes drifted closed.

Whether it was five seconds or five minutes later, Gemma wasn't sure, but she did know that something had stirred her awake.

An animal passing through the trees? Or one of the Nazseke women coming down to look for her? Gemma realized she had let go of her waterskin during her brief slumber, but she found it wedged between two rocks just a couple of feet downstream. As she crouched down to grab it, she heard another noise. The steps seemed too heavy to be a deer or one of her traveling companions.

Fifty feet east of the stream, Gemma saw the silhouettes of the trees parting. Her intuition was correct; something much, much larger than a deer or a Nazseke warrior was indeed coming her way. Gemma had never been much of a climber—though at least she wasn't afraid of spiders in the trees the way George was—but this was a journey of firsts, and she didn't see why that night should be any different. She made her way up the closest tree, using knots in the trunk as footholds until she was able to scale the branches. She heard a splash below; the newcomer had reached the stream. Gemma stopped climbing and slowly turned in the direction of the water.

She was face-to-face with a giant.

The Ogressi. Definitely the male. Gemma considered her current position at the beast's eye level. *What was I thinking, climbing this tree?*

The Ogressi's eyes widened as he noticed Gemma a few

feet in front of his face. He backed up two steps as he focused on the potential late-night snack, but then seemed to hesitate. Gemma looked the Ogressi over and realized how old and frail he appeared. Despite his immense height, his legs and torso seemed crooked, and he was wavering from side to side a bit. *Is he sick? Is he starved?* Gemma didn't know anything about the average lifespan of an Ogressi, but she knew from the Witch of Ferathan that this one and his companion had been in the area for many decades.

Gemma and the Ogressi continued to stare at each other, each waiting for the other to make the first move. Except for the stream below and the Ogressi's labored breathing, there was no other sound in the vicinity.

Nobody is coming for me, Gemma thought. *Nobody will save me tonight.*

Gemma's mind flashed back to the ambush in the Forest of Despair, when she'd hidden in the tent as Richard fought off Walker and the Aepistelle soldiers. She recalled the last hours of the journey through that wretched forest, when one of the dark trees had attacked her and she'd done nothing to save herself. When Walker's body had been torn to shreds by the monster in Ferathan, Richard had been at the brink of death before Gemma had finally acted. But this time, there was nobody there to save her.

The Ogressi seemed to notice the change in Gemma's demeanor. At the same moment that Gemma unsheathed her machete, the Ogressi shrieked out an odd sound and moved his arms into a defensive position. Gemma managed to run forward a few steps along a thick branch before leaping into the air.

The machete plunged into the giant's bare right shoulder. With strength she didn't even realize she had, Gemma kept hold of the handle and dangled in the air. The blade started to slowly tear down the torso of the Ogressi. Blood squirted out of the fresh wound, and Gemma took the bulk of it in her face and hair.

The Ogressi grabbed Gemma, his massive fingers wrapping around her legs and midsection. Her arms were free, and she maintained her grip on the machete as it pulled out of the Ogressi's flesh. More blood showered onto Gemma. With both of her hands around the hilt, she swept the machete through the air and hacked at her captor's thumb. His screech was nearly deafening, and he swung his hand through the air, but Gemma drove the machete into his thumb again and again, each blow digging deeper into the bone than the last. When half of his thumb had detached, the giant dropped Gemma.

She finally released the machete and used her hands to catch herself on a protruding branch. It gave way under her weight, and she dropped fifteen feet to the ground in front of the giant. He was too busy clutching his injured hand to notice that Gemma had survived the fall relatively unharmed. His blood spewed out of the wounds and rained down on Gemma. She scrambled for the machete nearby and crawled away. A moment later, the Ogressi turned and headed back to wherever he had come from.

Gemma sheathed her machete and located her abandoned waterskin. She walked back up the hill, passing her Nazseke companions as they looked on in shock, apparently awoken by the Ogressi's shrieks but too late to come to her aid.

She didn't need them. Gemma had taken control of the situation. She had saved herself. And now she would rest. Under the incredulous stares of Teyla and the others, and drenched in the blood of the giant male Ogressi, Gemma climbed into her blankets and drifted off into a deep sleep.

MORNING ARRIVED, AND STILL GEMMA SLEPT. EVERYONE stayed near her, whispering about what must have happened in the night, but they didn't dare to wake her.

When Gemma did arise, itchy from the dried blood that covered her, everyone scrambled to pack up their blankets. The warriors started to discuss catching some breakfast and began to build up the fire, but Gemma wouldn't have it.

"We move now, not later," she commanded. She felt all eyes on her, and it didn't feel good. But then she met one particular set of eyes. Teyla was clearly impressed, even proud, of Gemma's big moment. She nodded with approval.

"You heard her, warriors!" Teyla called out. "Up and out, come on!"

And so they walked down into the woods, made their way to the stream, where Gemma washed off the filth and the others filled their waterskins, and headed east toward the imposing cliffs ahead. They followed the tracks of blood and crooked footprints. By noon, it was clear that they would make it to their destination before nightfall.

When the sun was on the wane, Gemma and her companions arrived. The deep footprints that decorated the ground led to what appeared to be the largest cave opening at the base of the cliffs. There were patches of trees spread out in the valley that lay before Hightower. Gemma had the warriors split up and gather as much kindling as they were able. They spread out in a large half circle, each of the fifteen of them building their own fire. Gemma's was even with the opening of the Ogressi cave, with Teyla to her immediate left and Arnem and Denny to her right.

"Light them up!" Gemma called.

"Light them up!" Teyla repeated to the left flank, and Arnem to the right flank.

Within a few minutes, all fifteen fires were burning strong. Gemma didn't know what else to do at first, so everyone stood and waited, staring hard at the cave opening.

"Should we have made sure they're even in there?" Denny called out to Arnem.

"They come out at night, so we should see them any time now," Arnem said. "The sun is nearly down."

"I wasn't kidding about using you two as bait," Teyla chimed in. Gemma could see the smirk on her face, but it wasn't visible to Arnem and Denny in the dusk. Denny made a shocked grunt and then sat down next to his fire.

An hour passed, then another. The companions continued to feed their fires with excess branches, but it didn't seem to have any effect on the beasts hiding under the mountain. Finally, Gemma had enough of waiting. She lit a makeshift torch, picked up her machete, and began walking toward the cave a couple hundred feet in front of her.

"Ogressi!" Gemma yelled. "Face us! Come out of hiding and meet your fate!"

There was still no movement in the dark cave. Teyla and five other Nazseke warriors followed Gemma with their own torches and spears. Arnem, Denny, and the other half of the warriors remained at their posts, feeding the fires.

Gemma continued walking until she arrived at the mouth of the cave. When she got there, an overwhelming stench filled her nostrils. She jumped back and lifted one arm to cover her nose.

"I forgot to warn you of their smell," Teyla said, laughing. "As enormous as their size."

Gemma scrunched her face in disgust and then let out her own laugh. She backed up a few steps to get farther from the reeking air that seemed to be pouring out of the opening. They stood in silence for several minutes, listening for any sign of life. Then a sign came.

One of the Ogressi emitted a low and painful groan somewhere deep inside the cave.

"Reveal yourselves," Gemma called in, and her voice echoed.

As she heard her voice amplified and repeated by the rounded cave walls, Gemma almost could not believe the absurdity of the situation. Only days before, she'd been a researcher and writer for the University Press, hoping for her big break, barely confident enough to present her proposals to her editor and her peers. Now she was leading a dozen women warriors from a tribe thought to have been dead for decades, attempting to face off against two giant beasts in order to free a town full of people from the grasp of a witch. If she didn't know better, she would have thought this was only a very elaborate dream.

Gemma called out again. The only answer was another groan.

"Do you think it's a trap?" Gemma asked Teyla as she narrowed her eyes in confusion.

"There's only one way to find out. I can take the front, if you'd prefer."

Gemma nodded with relief. Teyla pointed her spear tip forward as she walked into the foul-smelling tunnel. Gemma followed her, with the other five Nazseke behind them, spears at the ready. Gemma was surprised by how spacious the entrance to the cave felt. The tunnel was so vast, she thought her family's entire home could have been placed inside and stacked twice before hitting the ceiling. She understood then why the giant Ogressi pair would want to make their homes in there.

As they walked farther in, the smell got stronger. Growing up in the city, Gemma had never been around much wildlife except for the horses that were used for transportation. She could only imagine that this was what it would smell like if several animals died and rotted in a pile of their own feces in some forgotten barn on a scorching summer day. She turned to the side and vomited. Embarrassed, she avoided eye contact with her companions and continued walking, doing her best to take only small breaths.

Another moan carried through the tunnel from the direction they were heading, much nearer this time. Up ahead, Teyla motioned for the group to hold still. They all stopped immediately and lifted their spears, except Gemma. Silently, she crept to where Teyla was standing, where another cavern opened up off to the side of the main tunnel. She peaked around the corner and was shocked to find the two Ogressi lying on the ground in the middle of the cavern.

The combined light from their torches gave Gemma a better view of the creatures than she'd had in the dark woods the previous night. As Teyla and Arnem had described them, the Ogressi were a dark gray with scattered white hair. Even lying down, they appeared to be the height of a few men combined, but as Gemma had noticed the previous night, they were both relatively thin, even brittle. The female lay in a fetal position with her head on the chest of the male, facing away from where Gemma and Teyla stood. She was shivering despite the moderate temperature. There was no sign of life from the male, and maggots and flies crept all over his newly deceased body.

Gemma's heart dropped. Here were two creatures who had lived in companionship—maybe even love—for so many decades, torn apart by Gemma's actions hours earlier. The pride she had felt about defending herself was suddenly gone, replaced by a profound sense of guilt.

Gemma motioned for the others to join her and Teyla at the intersection of the two caverns so that they could all see what they had come for. The warriors slightly lowered their spears as they looked on with relief.

"Hello," Gemma called, not knowing what else to say. The surviving Ogressi let out another pained moan but did not turn to face them.

"So much for the surprise kill," Teyla said.

"I can't kill what is already dead, nor can I go through with hurting his companion." Gemma turned to Teyla with sad eyes. "Could you?"

"Well, I suppose it would only make the smell worse if we killed the other one," Teyla said, eliciting wild laughter from her warriors. "What about your mission for the witch?"

Instead of answering, Gemma turned and walked back out of the cave. She crossed the clearing to Arnem and Denny.

"What happened?" Arnem asked.

"One was already dead, the other is close enough to it," Gemma said. "I can't bring myself to finish the other one off. She doesn't even seem like a threat."

"The last of her kind," Denny said. "I think I know the feeling."

"The witch will expect proof of their deaths, whether it was by our hands or not," Arnem said.

"So then it seems we must kill her after all," Gemma said. She wasn't looking forward to it, but she knew she had to if she wanted to maintain her position as a leader. It was what was expected of her.

I've always done what was expected of me, she thought. *Did that ever make me a leader in anyone's eyes?*

There was silence for a moment. Gemma could feel all

eyes on her, including those of Teyla and the other Nazseke warriors who had followed her out of the cave.

Gemma shook her head, stood tall, and spoke again, this time with full confidence.

"No. We don't have to slay the giant. If the witch wants evidence of the downfall of the Ogressi, we can provide it. That is, if the survivor is able to walk."

CHAPTER 28
MARZELE

The overnight train from Pinedrop arrived in Capital City not long after sunrise. A man with a considerable mustache was among the first to step onto the station platform. In other towns he had visited in the past few days, he'd stood out in his dapper suit, but among those arriving in the country's center of business and political power, Marzele blended right in with many of the morning commuters.

As he passed through the crowd waiting to board the southbound train, Marzele looked beyond the gates of the station toward the sprawling city. He stared in disgust. This was a place that reeked of corruption and evil, one that lifted up Aepistelle's richest while walking over its poorest. The haves and the have-nots, crammed together in one place.

"It's not quite home," said a voice behind him, "but it's where we're meant to be right now."

Marzele turned to face a man just ten years his senior, though the man's hunched shape as he leaned over his cane made the gap in their age feel far larger.

"Bertram," Marzele said as he patted the man gently on the back. "You've shrunk, my old friend."

"As will you, when you reach seventy-five years old. As will you."

"If only I could have even half your wisdom at that age, Bert." They started walking away from the crowds and took a seat on a nearby bench. "It's wonderful to see you, though I wish the circumstances were more pleasant."

"I can't think of a more noble effort than this. Nothing is guaranteed to be pleasant in this life, but our Lord Solendaron has given us this calling."

Marzele looked around to make sure nobody was within earshot. He didn't think there were any spies around, but he had been wrong before. He lowered his own voice to a near whisper and hoped that would remind Bert to speak their god's name more quietly.

"I can't help but feel that we'd be of more use assisting in the north. The Protector is the only fighter among them, and he's grown nearly as old as the two of us."

"Don't underestimate the younger ones. Even the heroes of the Great Journey were soft and inexperienced when they started out, and look what they were capable of. I have faith that Solendaron will guide the Inquisitive One and the Dreamer in their own journeys. We've received all the signs."

"We've been wrong before, Bert."

Bertram reluctantly nodded in agreement. They stood up and walked into the city to meet with the others.

***

By noon, Marzele and Bertram had arrived on the west side of Capital City. They declined to hail a cab, in case the cart driver should suspect anything and report them to the Committee. In Capital City, no one could be trusted, especially when reward money was worth more than a month's salary for service workers. Marzele wouldn't have had it any other way, though. He didn't know how much more time he would have to catch up with his old friend and mentor, and it had been nearly twenty years since they had parted ways. Especially at the height of the Royal Mystic Committee's great purge, it had been too dangerous for men or women of the cloth to be seen together without being accused of conspiracy against the state. They had often exchanged notes through couriers, but even those were limited to brief cyphered messages inside shallow letters. Marzele had gotten a job as a banker, putting to use his skills from his time as the southern district treasurer of the Order of Priests of Solendaron. He had lived a life of solitude outside of his menial job, not willing to put others at risk should his true identity ever be revealed. The priests of Solendaron were allowed to marry and have families, but Marzele had never met the right woman, even if he hadn't been living a double life.

But now he was here with Bertram, and they were finally able to catch up, so the long walk across the city was worth it. He learned about how Bertram was living with a large family on a farm southeast of the Great Centeron Lake. He assisted with taking care of the livestock and tilling the fields, picking during the harvest, and even taking a grandfatherly role with the family's children. Bert's eyes shone bright when he talked of the children, as he would never have any of his own, just like Marzele.

Bertram led Marzele through a set of iron gates and up a pathway to a maroon door of an impressively large and well-kept house.

"How did Horace even afford this place?" Marzele asked.

"He did come from old money, you know," Bert said. "His family disowned him when he began to follow Solendaron, but they welcomed him back with open arms when things turned bad for our type."

Bertram rapped on the door with his cane. A moment later, it opened slightly as an eye peered out at the men on the porch, then was flung the rest of the way open. There stood a very well-fed man with long, curly hair, wearing an elaborate light blue suit with white trim. He nodded with approval, and his chins wobbled along.

"Mr. Marzele, you've arrived just in time," Horace said. He stepped aside to let them in. "Down the hall, you can't miss it."

Marzele looked around at the elaborately decorated foyer filled with marble statues and framed paintings. He walked down an arched hallway and into a large sitting room.

"This is it?" Marzele asked. "This is everyone?"

The room could have held Marzele's entire apartment three times over, but all the visitors were concentrated in one corner on a selection of couches and chairs. They all stood to greet Marzele and to welcome back Bertram. That is, all who were able to stand did so. There were a man and a woman who were older and in worse shape than Bertram, and they understandably remained seated.

"There are seventeen of us, Marzele," Bertram said.

"Seventeen? Seventeen... It will have to do," Marzele muttered. Horace walked up behind him and gave him a heavy pat on the back.

"We can do all things with the blessing of Solendaron," Horace said.

Marzele walked over to sit with the rest of Horace's guests. *The Order of Geriatrics of Solendaron*, he thought. He couldn't help but let out a laugh.

"So we can," Marzele said. In that moment, he recalled why he was there. He regained his confidence. He stood tall and spoke. "We have all spent our lifetimes studying the Holy Scriptures. We've spent the last twenty years in our own minds, living in the memories of what we read before our books were destroyed by King Davin. Daily have we sought the signs that the prophets swore would come. A second Great Journey. The Inquisitive One. The Dreamer. The Protector. The Loyal One. Those who would tear aside the veil of darkness, who would loosen the clutch of evil magic, who would prevent the fall of mankind. The Lord Solendaron has spoken of these things, the scribes have recorded them, and we have taught them to our people for generations. And now the time has come—the time for us to emerge from our hiding places."

The old woman raised her voice. "As our Lord Solendaron has spoken it, we will live it."

"Aye," everyone called out in agreement, all except for one man who was slightly younger than Marzele. He stood, a confused frown on his weary face.

"Then what are we doing here in Capital City?"

"Gregory," Bertram said, "we cannot be there to fight alongside these foretold heroes. We were not called to do so. Half of us can hardly even fight our way to the bathroom in the middle of the night." This got a round of laughs, and even the defiant Gregory cracked a smile.

"While these heroes fight for the future of humankind, we must fight for the past," Marzele said. "We must reclaim our freedom and find what is left of our Holy Word, should there be anything that was not destroyed. We must show the people of Aepistelle that we are still here, that Solendaron is Lord and Protector, faithful to the end. We must overthrow King Davin while he is vulnerable, not just for the sake of the followers of Solendaron, but for people of all faiths. Everyone deserves the freedom to worship their gods. And our heroes deserve to come back to a country that will welcome them home, not imprison them, as King Davin would do. The end of the reign of King Davin and his Royal Mystic Committee is upon us. We will see to it—all of us, young and old—that persecution is ended for the people of Aepistelle."

CHAPTER 29

GEMMA

They left as three but returned as fifteen.

Well, sixteen, if one counted the giant they pulled along with them.

The last remaining Ogressi would have been twenty feet tall had it—*she*—been able to stand straight, but due to malnourishment, she was hunched over dramatically. She fell several times during the three-day hike back to Ferathan, and she was bruised and bloodied. None of the falls had even been that rough, but her entire body was weak, her skin dried and cracked, her thin hairs blowing off in the slightest wind. One tumble into a low boulder even caused a tooth to fall out. To Gemma's horror, Teyla picked up the tooth and pocketed it, saying she'd make a necklace out of it once she and her warriors were free of the curse that held them in the Fingers.

The curse itself presented a dramatic moment for some of Teyla's warriors on the last morning of their trek. Gemma had fallen back from the lead, choosing instead to walk alongside the Ogressi and the three warriors who held the ropes attached to her arms and neck. The Ogressi seemed calmer when Gemma was around, as if she knew that Gemma had spared her life and meant her no harm. Whether the giant suspected that Gemma was responsible for murdering her companion, Gemma couldn't tell. The whole group was shocked at how resigned the Ogressi seemed. She certainly didn't seem like a dangerous man-eating monster. Gemma didn't doubt that this Ogressi and her deceased partner had once been forces to be reckoned with, but starvation and loss had tamed her.

After climbing one last peak, Teyla and the three women who walked alongside her caught sight of Ferathan below them to the west. They got so excited, they began to run. This seemed to frighten the captive, who rose nearly to her full height, causing the ropes to pull taut. All three of the Nazseke warriors who held the ends of the ropes were launched up into the air, where they lost their grips on the ropes and fell back down to the ground. The Ogressi spun around, left and right and left again, causing the rope around her neck to swing rapidly. The end of it caught Gemma's left cheek, tearing open the skin. Gemma screamed in shock, then touched her cheek. She pulled her hand away and saw that it was covered in blood. The Ogressi stopped flailing and turned to Gemma, towering over her. Before she knew what was happening, five more warriors nearby jumped into attack positions with their spears aimed at the Ogressi.

"No!" Gemma shouted. "Leave her alone!"

The Nazseke stood and looked at each other, not knowing what to do. Denny grabbed on to Arnem's arm in fear. Nobody said a word or made a move for a few seconds. Then the three fallen warriors got back to their feet and wiped the dirt off themselves. The Ogressi looked at Gemma for a moment longer, then slowly reached out a hand and rubbed the blood off of her cheek with the back of a finger. Then she turned back in the direction they had been walking, held her arms out so that the ropes dangled down, and allowed the three Nazseke warriors to resume their grip on them. They made it to the peak and looked down. Teyla and her three companions were much farther down the slope to Ferathan, unaware of what had just taken place.

Near the bottom of that final hill, Teyla hit what seemed to be an invisible wall and flew backward as if blown back by a massive explosion. She slammed into one of her companions, and they both tumbled to the ground. The other two ran over to them in confusion. Gemma, Arnem, Denny, and the others witnessed it from farther up the hill.

"The curse still holds them captive," Denny said.

Arnem carefully but quickly jogged down the hill to help Teyla up, but she was on her feet by the time he arrived, and he was sweating and out of breath.

"You need Gemma to lead you through," Arnem said.

"You think so, Weeping One?" Teyla asked, then let out a laugh that surprised Arnem. She reached over and slapped him hard on the back. The other Nazseke joined in the laughter as the rest of the party caught up to them. Teyla turned to Gemma. "Lead us through, my lady."

Gemma looked at her hesitantly. Her cheek stung from being whipped with the rope. Her feet were blistered and sore from the days of hiking. Her hair was wild from the wind in the hills. She hadn't changed her clothes in longer than she could remember, and the ones she wore were stained with the blood of the male Ogressi she had slaughtered in self-defense. She certainly didn't feel much like a leader.

She turned and met Arnem's eyes. It was his look that inspired her. Arnem must have looked at Maachel, the leader of the Great Journey, with that same expression full of admiration and respect. She didn't know that she deserved it, but it gave her confidence nevertheless. Arnem nodded to her, and she nodded back and smiled despite her pain and discomfort. She shifted her eyes to Denny, who shot her a look of hope and faith. She looked around at the twelve women who had been trapped in these hills for years, prisoners of dark magic and an invisible barrier.

They looked back at her not as just a young woman, not as just a novice, but as a leader.

The one who would deliver them to freedom.

Gemma stood tall and led the way. She walked right through the unseen force field that had stopped Teyla from proceeding just moments before. Arnem and Denny followed. The Nazseke warriors looked at each other with some uncertainty, but then Teyla walked past the spot with no hesitation and continued on her way. The others walked through after her, leading the Ogressi gently with no issues. They followed Gemma across the fields toward Ferathan Manor.

"It is here that we must part ways with your company," Teyla said.

They had arrived at the gates of Ferathan Manor. Gemma could see the grotesque statues that lined the path to the porch up ahead. The three Nazseke warriors who gripped the Ogressi's ropes held them out to Gemma, Arnem, and Denny. Arnem and Denny looked to Gemma, who shrugged.

"Will you not finish the journey with us?" she asked.

"For all those years, we were imprisoned in the mountains by a sorcerer's curse," Teyla said. "We are free now and would have no dealings with another sorcerer or sorceress. The Witch of Ferathan holds all the people of this town captive. She is the last person we wish to see."

"And where will you go?" Arnem asked.

"Most of our people may still be at home, or in the hidden retreat that the Nazseke have long maintained for emergency situations. Not long ago, we came across a group of our kin who had cut through the Fingers on their way south, fed up with the rudderless leadership of those who remained. These traitors declined to lead us out of our curse, unlike the brave Gemma Calvertson. I don't know if they made it through the dark forest. I don't know if I care. Our people need direction. They need strength. We aim to return home, make things right, and provide them with protection and leadership."

Teyla sank down on one knee and bowed low to Gemma. The other eleven Nazseke warriors did the same. Gemma awkwardly looked around.

"I understand," she said. "Please, rise and be free."

They rose in unison. Teyla smiled warmly at Gemma.

"Thank you, my lady. You have what it takes to be a great leader, as you have displayed on this journey. Some may consider compassion a sign of weakness, but you have proven otherwise. I admit that on the night we met, I did not think you a warrior who could free us. You were merely the first woman we had crossed paths with in all our years out here who wasn't a cowardly Nazseke or an Ogressi. But your friends had faith in you, and so I pretended to. Now that I have seen your true character, I know that I was wrong in my initial assessment of you. I have never been more happy to be wrong."

Teyla then turned to Arnem and Denny.

"You two are also caring souls who will lift your friends into the positions they were destined for. Weeping One—Arnem, I mean—you are not just a follower anymore. You never were just a follower. You have true worth of your own. You inspire greatness in others. And Denny, though you are just a young man, your gift of foresight will help you accomplish much greatness once you learn how to wield it. Goodbye, my friends."

Teyla turned and headed northeast. Her eleven companions followed without looking back. Gemma held the rope that was tied around the Ogressi's neck, while Arnem and Denny held the ones attached to her arms. Gemma led them up the pathway and onto the porch. The Ogressi hunched even more dramatically to avoid slamming her head on the arched porch ceiling. The doors opened in front of them, and there stood Naliah Lunarra alongside Richard the Elusive, flanked on both sides by several of the children of Ferathan.

"Richard!" Gemma called out in surprise. She let go of the rope and ran the rest of the distance to the door. She threw her arms around Richard. "I'm so glad you're okay!"

"I had a great healer," Richard said, glancing over at Naliah.

"And we had a deal, girl," the witch said. "You were to kill the beasts, not bring them here."

"This one is not dangerous," Denny said.

"Not dangerous? Did you cut open its stomach and count the human remains inside? Did you ask it how many people of Ferathan it has eaten in its lifetime? How many animals from the farms it consumed?"

"Just look at the creature," Arnem said. He glanced at Gemma, who didn't appear willing to talk about killing the male Ogressi, so Arnem skipped over the details. "Her companion was dead when we found her. She was mourning his death. She is malnourished and near the end of her days. She did not fight us when we put the ropes around her, nor did she give us trouble on our journey back."

"That cut on the girl's face," Naliah replied. "Did it do that?"

Gemma brought her hand up to her cheek, remembering suddenly that it still stung from the whipping of the rope. It was a pain she felt she deserved for taking a life.

"She was just frightened by something this morning," Gemma said. "It was not intentional. She really has been gentle the entire three days we've been with her. If she was an actual threat to you or to this town, your protection spell would have barred her from entering."

Naliah shot an inquisitive glance at Gemma, then looked at the Ogressi.

"The very last of her kind," Naliah said. "I suppose there are some interesting uses for that. Very well. I'll have the children lead her around to the barn out back. Children?"

Three of the older children stepped forward and took the ropes. They led the Ogressi back down the steps and out of sight. She didn't fight them but instead crouched even lower, resigned to whatever fate awaited her.

"Come in, travelers," said the witch. "I'm sure you'll want to catch up with Richard here while you recover from your little adventure."

THE WITCH OF FERATHAN LED ARNEM, DENNY, RICHARD, and Gemma upstairs to a large suite in which Richard had been recovering for the last few days. The bed appeared to be well broken in from having Richard's large body resting on it. Beyond the bed, there was a sitting area with two sofas facing each other next to a fireplace. The four sat down as Naliah shut the door behind them to go about her business in the manor.

Arnem immediately got back up and hugged his old friend.

"Richard, it's been so long. I'm so sorry for making you set off on this journey all alone. Well, not alone, but you know what I mean. You were in good company with this one." Arnem gestured to Gemma. "She really has what it takes, Richard. A lot like Maachel, she is."

"I'm glad you are here, Arnem the Loyal. Even if you did not respond to my letters. I understand the danger I put your family in by sending them, and for that I beg your forgiveness."

Arnem began to weep. *Now I understand the pet name Teyla had for him*, Gemma thought.

"That was precisely why I did not reply, but it was so selfish of me. You had no one else to turn to."

"Well, I did try to contact Jestan as well—he doesn't have as much to lose as you—but it was only silence from his end. Alas, we are here now without him. Perhaps that speaks to your own character, Arnem. You should not doubt yourself. You truly are a loyal friend."

"And I'm Denny," the youngest in the room said. Everyone looked at him suddenly and laughed together.

"Yes, sorry, this is Denny," Arnem said. "He is the reason I came here. He receives visions in his sleep, and he saw that you were in trouble, and eventually he saw Gemma as well. Denny, meet Richard the Elusive."

Denny bravely stood, stepped over to where Richard sat, and shook Richard's massive hand with his own small one.

"It's an honor, sir. I've read all about you for my whole life."

"The honor is mine, Denny," Richard said. "Thank you for what you have done to reunite me with my old friend."

"Richard, did the witch give you your books back?" Gemma asked.

Richard pointed to stacks on the other side of the bed,

reminding Gemma of the volumes that filled up his home back in Pinedrop. "I've been studying them every moment I've been awake these last few days," Richard replied. He reached for a particularly well-worn book on the top of a pile. "And this is a journal my father wrote in, the last of his writings that I'm aware of."

"And what have you learned?" Arnem asked.

"Exactly what I expected. The prophecies all line up with what I've found in other ancient texts back home. My father had it all pieced together, but there was nobody to assist him back then." Richard paused for a few moments as he fought back tears. He took a deep breath and spoke again. "The time to fight for the lives of all the men, women, and children in Aepistelle is now. Right now. I've learned more about who my father thought the Tzakabya were. Where they came from. What they've done in the past. What they have been working toward just north of here in Emyhrsen. All the signs from prophets and philosophers throughout the history of Aepistelle's tribes point to one thing, but my father was the first to put it together. The Tzakabya have been creating a force of sorts to conquer the rest of Aepistelle. They must be defeated."

"Defeated?" Arnem cried out. "Defeated by what army?"

Richard gestured to the four of them. A teenage boy. A young woman. Two middle-aged men. They were merely four souls, but they would have to take on forces of darkness with no other army to back them up.

THEY WERE OUTFITTED WITH NEW SHIRTS OF MAIL, FRESHLY sharpened swords and machete, and a quiver full of arrows and restrung bow, as well as a newly recovered man and a newly confident and empowered woman. The group walked out of the towering front doors of Ferathan Manor, across the covered porch, and down the steps into the sunlight. Naliah, the Witch of Ferathan, followed them to the edge of the porch, where she stayed in the shade to see them off. The children crowded the tunneled porch and looked on.

"How will we know that you've freed these people now that the Ogressi are no longer a threat?" Gemma asked. Richard turned to her, stunned, and put a hand on her shoulder as if to tell her to back down before Naliah changed her mind about letting them go. Instead of showing anger, though, the witch chuckled.

"My girl, you have grown up these last few days, haven't you?" Naliah observed. "But you can trust me. If there's one thing you can count on, it's that my people always keep our word, for better or worse. You may pass through this town on your way back home, should you survive whatever it is you seek to do next. You will find it a changed place. I promise you that. I began my time here under a full moon, and so will I end it under one. We are only a few short days away from that. And then I can finally rest."

"And what of the Ogressi?" Denny asked. Gemma and Arnem both turned to him, stunned that he'd spoken with such boldness. They remembered how terrified and speechless Denny had been when they'd arrived at Ferathan Manor the first time and met Naliah.

"No harm will come to that one by my hand, nor by anyone else's here. Again, I make a promise to you."

"Thank you for healing my friend," Arnem said. "For all that is said about you, you have treated us with true hospitality, and you have kept your word to us. May you find the rest you seek."

Richard looked at Naliah and nodded without saying

anything. Naliah gave him a smile that Gemma felt was motherly, caring, even loving, but not in a romantic way. Then they turned and made their way down the statue-lined path and out the gates where they had parted ways with the Nazseke the previous day and set off to the northwest. Gemma lamented that it was not the same direction that the Nazseke warriors had gone; she regretted that they would not run into Teyla and her companions again.

CHAPTER 30
GEORGE

They waited for help to arrive, but it didn't come.

George wasn't sure how long Jestan intended to wait, and he also didn't have faith that the light of the tower's hearth could reach more than a few miles in any direction, no matter how big the flames or how high the tower. Jestan kept reassuring George that the magic of the Ancient Ones allowed the flame to be much more visible than logic could explain.

For several days, they waited. George grew anxious and irritable. Jestan, on the other hand, seemed calm and patient. He spent his days exploring the rooms on each level of the tower, shuffling through wardrobes and chests, trying on lush robes that had been left behind by previous inhabitants, admiring the fine details on all of the abandoned antiquated furniture. He particularly enjoyed spending time in the armory on the second floor. George had to admit that the metalwork on the swords was beyond even his own skills. He wasn't in the business of making weaponry, nor had his mentor been, but he knew all about the art of smithing, and he'd never seen anything that could compare to these swords, shields, and suits of armor.

On one rainy afternoon, George decided he had wasted enough time lying awake in bed. He wandered down from the fourth floor, where he had taken up residence. As he came down the stairs just beyond the third floor, he could hear Jestan talking. *They've come at last!* George thought. He ran down the rest of the stairs to the ground floor, expecting to see the Ancient Ones in full military attire, ready to take on their enemies and rescue Gemma.

Instead, what George walked in on was Jestan, wearing pieces of a much-too-small suit of armor from the armory, swinging a sword around in midair, making battle sounds and talking to unseen companions.

"Um, Jestan?" George said. Jestan quickly turned, lowered the sword in his right hand, and swallowed down his embarrassment. "What are you doing? I heard you talking and thought someone had arrived."

"Oh, hey, George," Jestan said. "Just practicing for the next run of my show. You know, doing some reenactments of the Great Journey and such. A lot of great props here."

"Right. Well, carry on, I suppose." George turned and started to walk back up the stairs. After two steps, he stopped and turned back. "No, you know what? Don't carry on. We shouldn't be sitting here this long. I came to you in a time of need, and that time is not over, but all we're doing is waiting. For *days*. We can't act like help is going to just show up, because it's not. Your friend Maachel and all his Ancient Ones left this country behind years ago, and they are not coming back."

"Georgie, please have faith in them. I know it's been longer than we expected, but they *will* come. They will."

George waved him off, went back up to his room, and

slammed his door, the way he used to when he was a teenager and Gemma was a kid who loved to make a mess of his room.

—

By that night, George was at his wit's end. He didn't join Jestan for dinner or a chat with him at the campfire they normally started outside the tower in the evenings. He stayed in his room until the sun went down, then walked to the armory, grabbed one of the fancy swords and a shirt of mail, and headed outside. Jestan was out checking the hunting traps they had set, which had been left in the tower by the Ancient Ones who had once lived there. George began making his way down the side of the mountain. He was only a few minutes into his descent before he realized how stupid he was being. It was difficult enough to make the climb *up* the mountain *in the daylight*, yet there he was, not bothering to act sensibly.

Gemma could be captured, even dead, he thought. *I can't keep waiting around, and Jestan apparently has no intention of conceding that the Ancient Ones are not coming back to help us.*

And then he slipped.

George lost his balance as he tried to lower himself down onto a ledge that was covered in unexpectedly loose gravel. As he fell, he tried to grab on to the ledge he'd slipped on, but he couldn't get a good grip. He fell fifteen feet and landed hard on another ledge that fortunately protruded farther. The wind was knocked out of him for several seconds, and then he tried moving his hands, his arms, his feet, his legs, his neck. Blessedly, nothing appeared to be broken.

"Oh," he groaned. He tried to yell, but the air hadn't yet filled his lungs enough. He stayed there for another minute or so, not moving. Finally, he drew a deep breath and yelled, "Jestan! Help me!"

He tried a few more times. It was dark now, and he didn't know if he was going to be able to find a safe place to climb back up the side of the cliff. And then the rain came.

A short time later, he heard Jestan.

"George! Where are you?"

"Jestan! I fell off a ledge. Help me!"

A minute later, he felt pebbles falling down on him. Either he was about to get crushed by a rockslide, or Jestan was above him. Fortunately, it was the latter.

"You down there, buddy?" Jestan yelled. "It's a bit wet and dark. I don't know if this is the best idea you've had."

George couldn't help but laugh at the ridiculous situation he had gotten himself into, and at Jestan's humor, which never seemed to fade.

"Just had to get away from you, you big dumb oaf," George yelled out in jest, and Jestan roared with laughter from above.

"Hang tight. I saw some ropes in the lower storage room."

It was another half an hour of rain and mud on the cliff-side before Jestan was able to rappel down the side and find George. They were slow and cautious climbing back to the top, but George was relieved once they made it back up to the tower, out of the rain.

"You didn't learn to climb from all of those little kittens of yours?" Jestan quipped.

"I'm sorry, Jestan. Thank you for risking your neck to save me. I just can't sit here and wait while my sister might be dying out there."

"I get it, man, I do. No need to explain. Tomorrow morning, we'll gather up all the supplies we can use, and then we're gone. That is, if you're able to walk." Jestan burst into laughter again, and George joined him.

TRUE TO HIS WORD, JESTAN WAS UP AT SUNRISE THE NEXT morning to select weapons, mail, and barely edible dry foods for the journey. They found some durable yet portable bedding and warm coats in case of more inclement weather. Jestan grabbed as much rope as the two of them could carry and some metal spikes for scaling the steep sides of the mountain. After eating what they thought could be their last good breakfast in quite some time, they headed out.

"You know, I found an easier way down the mountain," Jestan said. "I'm sure falling all the way down would be fast and all, but you're going to want to be able to walk after you get there."

"You didn't," George said with a look of disbelief. "Did you?"

Jestan led George a few hundred feet east along the ledge and pointed it out.

"You did!"

"I did."

To George's surprise, there was a narrow staircase carved into the cliff's edge. It blended right in, but sure enough, it was there.

"I'll take the lead as long as you promise not to fall on me from behind and take us both out," Jestan said, slapping George hard on the shoulder.

"For all that is holy, *please* take the lead, and I promise I will not fall again. I don't think my bones will be so lucky if I take another spill like that."

It took hours, and there were some difficult portions where they had to use their ropes and spikes, but they made it to the bottom by late that afternoon. George nearly collapsed with a mix of exhaustion and overwhelming relief. After a breather in the shade of a tree, they resumed their journey. The Amassa River was just a quarter mile south, and from there they would head east for as many days as it took.

They were miles away from the tower on the mountaintop when they set up their camp that night. As he set out his bedding, George looked to the west and tried to identify their home from the last several nights. He found himself pleasantly surprised when he spotted it—the fire was still burning, perfectly visible from where he lay.

It filled him with hope.

PART III
TRANSCENDENCE

CHAPTER 31
MARZELE

It was in a filthy, damp alleyway not far from King Davin's castle that Marzele gave a woman hope.

He didn't have the luxury of stalking her for several days to know which route she took on her way to work early in the mornings, just as the sun was starting to peek out from the east. He didn't ask her coworkers questions about her routine, as if they knew anything about this woman who labored hard, then went home to labor even more over her perpetually ill husband. Marzele didn't need to do any of that. The Lord Solendaron was on his side. Solendaron would give him wisdom.

He set out the night before. He knew he wouldn't be able to sleep anyway, not given what was planned for the day that followed. So he walked, speaking in a low voice, praising his Lord, pleading for wisdom, foresight, strength, and honor. Solendaron gave him all he needed, and he would give himself for Solendaron.

In one particularly rough neighborhood, two men walked up to him from either side—tall, yet not as tall as him, and bearded, though their mustaches were not as impressive as his own.

"A man in a fancy little suit comes walking down our street, he must be ready to pay the price," the one with long hair said.

"The price is money or blood," the one with no hair said. "Money or blood. Which will it be, fancy man?"

Marzele took a step to the side so he could see both of them at once. He knew better than to leave both sides undefended. He did it with a smoothness and confidence that threw off both men. The hairy one shot a glance at the bald one. Then they both turned their gazes to Marzele.

"You heard my friend," Hairy One said. "Which will it be?"

"Gentlemen, have you ever heard of Solendaron?" Marzele asked. There was not a hint of fear in his voice. "The Great and Merciful Lord. The Creator of the Ever-Giving Sun. The Bringer of Light and Creator of Life. Have you heard of him?"

The follicly-challenged man's eyes narrowed in confusion. He took a step closer to Marzele.

"What are you on about, fancy man?"

"Gentlemen, you seek meaning in your lives, clearly. You seek it through intimidation. Through roughness. Through altercations. Through your adorable companionship—you clearly care deeply for one another. But there is a deeper meaning to life that can only be found through understanding of the true power, the true love, the true reality that is Solendaron." Marzele held up both his hands, palms facing his intimidators. "As you can see, there is nothing in my hands. And yet there is something beyond the vision of man. Something divine."

In that moment, as the two men stared at Marzele's hands in confusion, a brilliant light flashed. It lit up not only the street where they stood but the darkest corners of the sleeping neighborhood, shining through the blacked-out windows of the shuttered stores and apartments. It shone most directly into the eyes of the two men. They screamed in shock and pain. They both bent down quickly, slammed heads, and then fell to the ground. Marzele's hands faded back to their normal pasty white, and he stepped over the men and continued on his way.

An hour before sunrise, he stepped into an alleyway between a branch of the Royal Bank of Aepistelle and a Southern Reaches food importer. There was no sign that indicated this was the place. There were no telltale footprints to give him a clue. The Lord Solendaron put it in his heart and in his mind, and he was sure of it. He stood in the alley and waited.

Nearly an hour later, he heard footsteps. Though the sky had changed from deep purple to hazy pink and orange, it was still quite dim between the buildings. The woman didn't notice him until she was halfway down the alley. When she finally did see Marzele only a few feet from her, she jumped and let out a brief cry.

"Please, Mrs. Calvertson," he said. "Please be calm."

"How do you know my name?" she asked.

"I know your children. Or I know of them, I should say. I know what they are doing right now."

Serena Calvertson looked at Marzele untrustingly. In the dim but incrementally brightening morning light, she didn't see any hint of threat or malice on his face. She relaxed her posture a little bit, and Marzele knew that the Lord Solendaron was at play. Ever faithful, the Lord was.

"I know that your son went off without warning. He is safe, though, for now. He set out to find your daughter. She has faced unimaginable challenges in the last several days, but she has come out of them stronger. She is a new woman. No longer a fearful girl but a brave woman. A hero, even."

"How could you know this? Who are you?"

"I am Marzele of Southplains. I am a priest of the Order of Solendaron. My Lord has led me here to you. He has great plans for Gemma and George. Their names will be celebrated for generations to come. I wanted to bring you this good news as encouragement, even though I cannot say any more about it."

He took in her speechless, open-mouthed stare, and he was proud of himself. He decided he'd take it just one step further.

"I know you do important work, serving King Davin and the royal family and advisors in the castle. Please, I must warn you about today. If the castle is under duress, you need to get to safety. We will let you and the other servants leave unharmed. You can keep everyone calm and lead them out. It is King Davin we are coming for."

"You cannot be telling me that friends of my children will be attacking my king, can you?" Serena was beyond confused, and that was when Marzele realized he had made a mistake.

"Please, for the mission of your children to be completed, you must do as I say. Remain calm, and you will be unharmed. Do not say anything about this, lest your children be endangered." He reached out a hand and laid it on her shoulder. "The Lord of Solendaron wills this day to be as it is. All will be made right. The path has already been set, and your children will be heroes. They will restore Aepistelle to its former glory. They will save us all, as He wills it."

"As He wills it," Serena said. Her gaze looked distant. Her speech was slow. There was a thrumming from Marzele's hand as it rested on her shoulder, which did the trick. "Yes. As He wills it. Yes." She started to walk back the way she'd come in a dazed stupor.

"Wrong way, Mrs. Calvertson. I do wish I could send you home instead, but we don't want any suspicion from King Davin or any of his companions. But you will remain safe. And you will be the mother of heroes."

"Wrong... way... mother... heroes..." Serena corrected her course and continued on her way to work. She would snap out of the trance by the time she arrived, and she wouldn't remember what had occurred. She would only be filled with a strong sense of hope.

Marzele was proud of himself, at least until he returned to Horace's home, where he and his coconspirators were preparing to make their move to overthrow King Davin. Until he told his companions about what he had done.

"You careless, no-good fool!"

Horace was livid. All of the priests of Solendaron were livid, but Horace was the most vocal about it.

"You may have jeopardized all of us. All of the planning we've done since the downfall of our order. All because you are a careless, no-good fool."

"Please, Horace, calm down," Bertram interjected. "We must collect ourselves. Now, Marzele said that Mrs. Calvertson walked away from their encounter filled with a sense of hope and pride for her children. Would she really give that up in support of the tyrant King Davin?"

"As I said, she was filled with relief when we parted ways," Marzele promised. "She will not betray us. I am confident of that. I just felt I had to let her know that she need not panic when we begin our operation. And I truly believe I did as the

Lord willed. He led me right to her this morning. That was no happenstance."

"We better hope so," Horace growled. "Now, we have work to do. Let us begin our mission. Everyone grab a lantern and follow me."

Horace led them down into the cellar. This wasn't a damp, dirty, dark root cellar, but rather a lower floor of the luxurious home that Horace had procured with his family's old money through no hard work of his own. There were spare chairs and tables and fine serving dishes for the fancy galas Horace threw for his wealthy Capital City companions. They passed all of these and went into another room beyond. Here, Horace opened a closet door. In the back of the closet, he revealed a false rear wall. It opened on unseen hinges, and behind it, another staircase led even lower under the house.

Down the stairs they went, into the darkness and dampness reserved for spiders and other creeping, crawling things. At the bottom of the stairs, they turned to find a series of wardrobes. Horace opened the nearest one and pulled out a white frock with an elaborately stitched sun. The Ever-Giving Sun. The symbol of their faith.

"It has been two decades since we have adorned ourselves in the robes of our order," Horace said. "As the scriptures tell of our Lord: *In the deepest cavern He awoke. He arose. He adorned Himself in light. And out from the darkness, He revealed Himself and made all men bow down to Him.* So too shall we, the last surviving priests of the Order of Solendaron, rise up from darkness and make King Davin bow down before us. We will restore freedom to all the oppressed people of Aepistelle. We have lived our lives for this moment, friends. We will be victorious, as the Lord Solendaron foretold. Our Lord wills it."

The old men and women in the room began to cheer, to weep, to embrace each other. Then they donned the holy robes that had long been forbidden in Aepistelle. They ascended from the cellar, ready to fulfill their mission.

—

As they walked through Capital City in their robes, they drew the attention of a few people, then dozens, then hundreds. By the time they arrived at the gates of King Davin's castle, they had a massive crowd of witnesses made up of common city folk who assumed this odd collection of elderly people were about to get arrested, or worse. They had broken the decrees of the Royal Mystic Committee and King Davin, which banned the wearing of religious garb, public congregation for worship, proselytizing, and practicing of mysticism, magic, or prayer.

The seventeen remaining holy men and women of the Solendaron faith spaced themselves out as evenly as they could around the walls that encircled King Davin's castle. The walls were thirty feet tall, with even larger towers every block or so. The castle complex was at the center of the city and was several blocks wide on every side, so even with seventeen people, Marzele and his companions could barely see one another. It would be difficult to know if one of them had been arrested or killed by the guards, so they would have to keep going with faith that their invisible bond would not be broken.

As the crowd looked on, Bertram held out a mallet and bell. He started to ring the bell, and they began to pray in unison after the fifth chime. The words spoken by the seventeen were not in the common tongue of Aepistelle, but rather an ancient language kept alive throughout the centuries by the followers of Solendaron. Even in the days of religious freedom, it had been fully understood only by the priests of

Solendaron, and it had been almost fully snuffed out by the religious purge over the past two decades.

"Holiest Lord Solendaron, crafter of these lands, true founder of Aepistelle, bringer of light, creator of life and of the Ever-Giving Sun, highest is Your name. Your lowly servants stand here today in Your honor to enact Your will. Here we restore the faith of the people in Your divine name. Here we present ourselves as a sacrifice to You by bringing an end to the evil rule of the oppressive King Davin, who seeks to drive us into darkness, to extinguish our flame. We call on You, Lord, to deliver us to victory. We call on You, Lord, to push down these walls, to bring us into the inner courtyards of this palace of evil. We are Your loyal hands and feet, Lord."

The prayers continued in that strange tongue. The castle guards stood on the wall overlooking the oddly dressed elderly men and women who raised their hands and spoke what sounded like gibberish. The guards turned to look at each other, unsure what to do.

The ground shook.

Being near the west coast of Aepistelle, Capital City had its fair share of shakes from the shifting tectonic plates under the Western Sea, but the guards could tell immediately that this was something different. With horror on their faces, they looked back down at the priests of Solendaron. A commander of the guards began to yell orders for the bowmen to fire at will, but before he could finish the command, the walls impossibly crumbled. The commander and his men did not live to see what happened next.

Even as the outer walls fell, Marzele and his companions continued their prayers. Their confidence grew after this first display of power, and Marzele found himself nearly yelling the words. In the corner of his vision, he saw the crowds beginning to swell, but despite their numbers, they stood in stunned silence, taking in the strange words being uttered by the strange people wearing strange white robes emblazoned with golden suns.

Marzele and the other priests walked forward. They climbed over the mounds of stone debris and entered the inner courtyard of the castle grounds. To Marzele's amazement and delight, the common folk of Capital City followed them. This was the first time many of them had stepped foot into the center of power, despite having lived their entire lives close to the castle. This was also the first time in twenty-five years that these onlookers had seen a public display of not just the Solendaron faith, but of any religion. If he could have stood any taller with pride, Marzele would have.

They continued their prayers to their Lord Solendaron. They spoke the words over and over, now calling for the entire castle to come crumbling down. As they spoke, a figure appeared high on a balcony of the castle's central tower. Even from below, in the shadow of the structure, Marzele knew who it was. King Davin stood on high, looking down at the swift destruction of his castle's defenses. Marzele, Horace, Bertram, and the other priests began to yell their prayers to ensure that they were heard by their enemy above. The king stood there, scowling down at them.

Marzele turned his attention to the inner gates of the castle. He expected guards to come pouring out, but none came. *Surely there must be a small army in there that could defeat us,* he thought. It was then that he found himself forgetting the words to his prayers. The chain of unity among the seventeen was now broken. He tried as best he could to catch up to the others' words, but he struggled to maintain focus. Far to his right, he saw Bertram glancing over to him, knowing that something was wrong with Marzele. Then Marzele noticed a man walking up behind Bertram. Quickly, Marzele shot a glance to his left, where the priestess Shenesa stood. A man was walking up behind her as well.

Marzele whirled around, knowing he would find someone approaching him, too. It was a large man dressed in what looked to be common townsfolk garb, but he was carrying one of the gold daggers decorated with rubies that the Royal Mystic Committee's enforcers were known to use. He saw his fellow priests on either side of him fall, their throats cut open by their unseen attackers. The man in front of Marzele lowered his dagger, sheathed it, and tackled Marzele to the ground. As he fell, Marzele thought for a split second that he saw Mrs. Calvertson up on the balcony above, stepping out next to King Davin and the king's personal guards, pointing down to identify Marzele.

I have been betrayed, he thought. *I have failed my Lord. Our rebellion has come to an end.*

Marzele's head slammed against the cobblestones, and the last thing he saw before he fell into unconsciousness was an explosion of light against the darkness of his eyelids.

CHAPTER 32
GEORGE

George and Jestan's course was easy as they headed due east along the northern edge of the Amassa River. The canopy of the ancient forest along the path provided all the shade they needed at the height of the afternoon sun. The lush river lands were full of edible wild berries, easily hunted game, and fresh water to drink and bathe in.

It was the morning of the fourth day since they had set out from the foot of the mountain that housed the ancient Western Watch. Jestan was sprawled out on a soft patch of grass, his arms folded behind his neck, propped up against a fallen tree trunk. The breeze was just cool enough to keep them from breaking a sweat in the morning sun.

"Here we go," George said, pulling a large skewer away from the fire. "Fish was definitely not on the breakfast menu back at home, but it doesn't get any better than this out here, does it?"

Jestan laughed joyously and sat up. They split up the morning's catch and ate it right up.

"I'm glad to see you're really getting into the spirit of adventure, George. You were sure about to crack when we were camped out in that old tower, weren't you?"

"It was no good, just sitting there and waiting for nothing. Not when my sister is out there in danger. But this is something else. We're moving. We're making things happen. We'll find them somehow. I know it."

Jestan stood and began gathering up their things for another day of hiking.

"Not much farther, I hope." he said. "I don't fully recognize these lands from this side of the river. When last I was here, we were on the south side. Once we see the Bowl, I may get a better feel for how far we've come."

"The Bowl?" George asked.

"The mountains that surround the castle of the Vheisenia. Their stronghold is enclosed on all sides except the north, which faces the river. We may see what's left of their castle from this side of the river. It should be in good shape if King Harold and the Tzakabya didn't destroy it."

"Ah, okay. I know what you speak of. My father used to tell us about how he arrived at those mountains overlooking their castle. That's where he was when the forest was destroyed around them."

"I wish I remembered which one your father was," Jestan said. "His company was in shock when they arrived, as were we. We were expecting hundreds or even thousands of soldiers, but there were fewer than a hundred. Fought hard, they did. Arnem, Richard, Maachel, and I get called the heroes, but let's be honest—we would have been dead men if not for the assistance of your father and his company. Things moved so fast from that point, though, that we didn't get to learn their names. They went off to approach the enemies from a different side."

"They did fight hard, but they also paid a big price," George said. "They came home damaged, my father maybe the worst of all. I've been thinking that maybe this whole thing with Gemma, her running off with Richard on whatever adventure they think they're on, is about her trying to find a way to help my father."

"She sounds as brave as your father was," Jestan said. "Now, come on, let's continue on our way."

They put in another full day of walking. George kept an eye on the south bank of the river, hoping to see the spires of the castle of the Ancient Ones or the high peaks of what Jestan referred to as the Bowl. He never saw either, though. *Perhaps this journey east into Emyhrsen will take longer than we expected*, he thought.

By evening, the forest to their left began to thin out. Jestan stopped just ahead of George and turned around.

"Do you smell that?" Jestan asked.

George stopped as well. He took a deep breath in through his nose, and his eyebrows shot up. "Someone's cooking," he said. "We must be close to civilization. Maybe we'll get to sleep in a real bed tonight!"

Jestan shook his head slowly.

"George, I don't think that's an animal being cooked. The smell of human flesh burning is a distinct odor, one that I'll never forget."

"What? But..." Before George could continue, the westward breeze brought with it the distant sound of screaming. Of pain. Of agony. "We have to get away from here!"

George turned and started to go back the way they came, but Jestan grabbed him by his pack and stopped him.

"We can't run. The only way to go if you want to get to Gemma and Richard is the way we were headed, in the direction of those screams. We've come this far; we can't run away when things get tough. Your father certainly didn't run, George Calvertson."

"I... we... you're right. That could be Gemma and Richard in danger. Or it could be one of the Tzakabya. Maybe there's a rebellion, King Harold's men overthrowing the oppressors."

"Maybe," Jestan said. "Only one way to find out. Are you ready to be a hero yourself?"

"Is anyone ever ready for such a thing? I certainly don't feel ready."

They prepared their armor and swords that they had taken from the tower's armory. Jestan stayed in the lead, and he was proud of George for not falling considerably behind out of fear of what they were about to face.

They left the clear path on the river's edge and made their way into the cover of what remained of the forest. They headed northeast, the smell growing stronger, the evening getting darker, until they reached the edge of the forest, which lined a farm full of well-tended rows of vegetables.

"There it is." George pointed to a large barn, outside of which a fire burned in a pit. They could see the silhouettes of dozens of people around the fire. Even from that distance, George could tell that most of them were frail and malnour-ished despite the plethora of vegetables that were growing in the fields. Dotted throughout the crowd were what appeared to be guards, some of whom carried swords or whips. "What do we do?"

"We wait. It's dark, so they're going to go inside soon. Then we get a closer look and assess the situation."

At Jestan's insistence, they crouched at the tree line and observed. After a few minutes, one of the guards barked orders that George could not quite hear, and the crowd around the fire broke up into organized groups. They were led into nearby barracks. The guards locked the doors from the outside, and then most went into a house just beyond the barn. One guard stayed outside, apparently on night duty. He began making rounds, slowly circling the series of barracks. After the candles went out in the main house, the guard sat down in a chair outside one of the barracks.

"I think he's asleep," George whispered. Jestan nodded.

"Leave your pack here and take only your sword," Jestan commanded quietly.

They left the protection of the forest behind them, creeping slowly through the crops, crouching low. George tripped on a shovel that had been left out. He fell to the ground and let out an involuntary grunt. Jestan dropped to the ground next to him, holding a finger in front of pursed lips. The guard stood up and looked around, but he saw nothing and soon resumed his catnap in the chair.

They were both afraid to move, so they remained in the dirt for several more minutes. They watched as the fire slowly died down. The guard didn't move, and they soon heard him snoring loudly. Jestan stood, motioned for George to do the same, and then continued to move toward the barracks.

They reached the building farthest from the main house. It was a long, low structure with a flat roof. It was severely weathered from the harsh winter storms that plagued the northern country. Many of the windowpanes were cracked, and George noticed that there was one hole big enough to fit his hand through. They got closer to the door and confirmed that it was locked. George lifted his hands as if to ask Jestan what to do. Jestan pushed a hand through the air to signal for him to calm down. George watched him creep past the next barrack, on the far side of which the guard rested.

With his sword out, Jestan came within six feet of the guard before stepping on a large shard of a broken bottle. It crunched under his boot, and the guard jerked awake. He turned toward Jestan, who leapt forward, swung his sword, and lobbed off the guard's head before he had a chance to yell out. George gasped with shock, then ran over to Jestan. In the light of the fire's fading embers, George got his first close glimpse of a Tzakabyan man.

The severed head rested on the ground before him. The skin looked rough—scaly, even. The yellow teeth ended in sharp points, reminding George of the skeletal remains of sharks he'd seen in shops around the docks near Capital City. The eyes were still open, and even those did not look human. They were a pale yellow where human eyes would be white. Even in death, they looked to be filled with hatred and contempt.

George looked up at the body, which was leaning to one side on the chair, blood gushing down from the stump of neck that remained. More blood soaked into the wall behind the chair. The hands were covered in the same scaly skin, and the fingernails were as yellowed and pointed as the teeth.

Jestan searched through the corpse's pockets until he found the ring of keys. They walked up to the door of the closer of the two barracks. Jestan tried three keys before finding the right one. The click of the lock was a relief to them both. They pushed the door open, and a smell immediately hit them. It was dark inside the room, so George ran over to what was left of the fire, found a stick, lit it, and followed Jestan inside the barracks.

There were lanterns hanging on hooks next to the door, so George used his stick to light them. They walked deeper into the filthy room. All around, men were asleep in their ragged clothes, some on bundles of hay, others on mattresses, and a few on top of blankets on the floor. Their hair was shaggy, their beards unkempt. From a distance, their silhouettes had looked thin, but their frailness was even more striking up close.

One man stirred, opened his eyes, and sat up. He shielded his eyes from the light of the lanterns.

"Oh, sorry," George said. He used a hand to partially block the brilliance of the lantern. "Don't be afraid. We're here to help you, men of Emyhrsen."

"Who are you?" the man asked weakly with a quiet, scratchy voice.

"We've come from Aepistelle," Jestan said. "We were heading inland from the coast and came upon this place. Please, let us lead you out of here."

More men started to open their eyes and look up at the two strangers in their room. Those who had initially slept through the introduction were shaken awake by their peers. Once they were all awake, Jestan spoke again.

"Come, we will wake the men in the other building, and then we can all leave this place."

Jestan and George led the men outside and over to the next barracks. Jestan used another key on the ring to unlock the door, getting it right on the first try this time. The scene inside that room was nearly identical. The other men followed them inside and woke their companions.

"I am Jestan, also known as Jestan the Just. This is my friend George Calvertson. We came here from near the capital of Aepistelle. There is danger that may be stemming from the castle of your King Harold. We have other friends whom we believe are headed there as well. We mean to free you and others like you, but we need you to stand and fight alongside us. To fight for your freedom from these monsters who have enslaved you."

"We can't fight like you," said one of the men. "Look at us. We're starved. Broken. Brittle. We aren't armed. We will die out there." Other men began speaking up in agreement, many sitting back down on their beds in protest.

Jestan was taken aback, even speechless. Then George spoke up.

"My sister will be the one to die out there," he said. Jestan turned to him, surprised. "She is still young. She had so much life ahead of her, had she stayed home instead of running off on a suicide mission. But she didn't. She didn't want to stay where things were comfortable, where things were safe. And she's up here somewhere now, probably facing death. Jestan and I were going to do this alone, but there is power in numbers. There is power in all of you, if you'll only stand and fight. How many more in these lands are enslaved by the Foreign Ones? How many women and children are also in need of rescue?"

"All of us," another man said. "All of our countrymen, our wives, our children. All except those in King Harold's castle."

"Nay, even King Harold is a slave to the Tzakabya," an older man called out. "He got more than he bargained for, teaming up with those monsters."

"Let us all be the judge of that," Jestan said. "If King Harold is still alive, let us see it with our own eyes, and let us punish him for letting this evil into your lands. But to do so, you must fight for your freedom."

"Aye," said the first man who had woken up in the other barrack. "I'll go with you!"

"As will I," the old one said, slowly standing with the support of a makeshift cane. He looked around, then spat on the floor. "To hell with all of you who won't stand with me."

The other men looked around at each other, and soon they all were on their feet. George and Jestan watched with relief, and then they led the forty-three men out of the barracks and into the barn to gather pitchforks, shovels, and axes to use as weapons. They marched over to the main house, where Jestan unlocked the door with another of the keys. There, the formerly enslaved men picked off their captors one by one as they slept.

They gathered what food, clothing, and supplies they could and set off on their way. There would be more farms, more households, more towns full of oppressed northerners to rescue from their evil captors. Jestan and George led another three hundred men, women, and children of Emyhrsen to freedom over the next two days.

CHAPTER 33
GEMMA

In a lush patch of land at the intersection of the Amassa River, a feeder stream, and the Amassa Lake, Gemma got her first glimpse of King Harold's Keep. It was the castle that housed the man who had once ruled fairly and lovingly over the thriving kingdom north of Aepistelle. The castle of a king who had once employed Richard's father as an advisor. A castle he had willingly surrendered to foreign invaders after a dark period of obsession and paranoia.

The journey from Ferathan Manor to the edge of the great northern river had been a surprisingly pleasant one. They had avoided entering the dark forest on their left as they headed up around the massive lake. Near the water, there were plenty of smaller animals and edible plants, wild herbs, vegetables, and berries, once they were outside of the still-enchanted region of Ferathan.

"Will the witch keep her promise and free Ferathan from her spell?" Denny had asked the previous evening as the group sat around what would be their last fire before they got too close to King Harold's Keep.

"I sure hope so, or else she'll have to deal with us when we come back through here on our way home," Arnem said. They all looked at him, surprised by his bold statement, and laughed.

"She will keep her word," Richard said. "The fairy tales that are told in Aepistelle aren't all that truthful in their depictions of witches and warlocks. They truly do stick to their promises; it's the people who request favors from them who often don't fully think through what they're doing. That's the case in Ferathan. That's the case with King Harold and the Tzakabya. Naliah Lunarra has her own code of ethics, and she will act accordingly."

Gemma sat and wrote as she listened. When she'd set out on her assignment from Capital City, she had intended to write about the past, the great events of recent history. Now, she wasn't so sure she could write about such things neutrally, as she was living in an adventure of her own. So, while she continued to take notes about things Richard and Arnem revealed about the Great Journey and the history of the northern lands, she also meticulously detailed the events of the last few weeks. She didn't know what the outcome would be; she only knew that it was important to document the situation she was in with her extraordinary companions. As everyone else drifted off to sleep, Gemma wrote deep into the night until there was no light remaining from the fire.

THE NEXT AFTERNOON, WHEN THEY MADE IT TO THE overlook in the river lands, they spotted a small abandoned fishing village. Perhaps *village* was too generous a word. There were a few rotting shacks, a boathouse, and the skeletal remains of a dock that had once held the boats of local fishermen, travelers from the villages around King Harold's Keep, and folks from Ferathan who had crossed the Amassa Lake and made their way up along the feeder stream.

"I believe my father used to land here when he traveled south from Emyhrsen and down into Aepistelle," Richard said. "He called it Frogstown. I don't know if it even had a real name."

"Denny and I will search the buildings for supplies," Gemma said. "You two check the boathouse for a vessel we can use to cross the river. We should go at nightfall."

She saw a slightly stunned look pass over Richard's face, but it was quickly replaced by a half smile of respect.

"Aye," Arnem said. Richard nodded in agreement. The men made their way down to the structure by the dock. As Gemma led Denny toward the other decaying buildings, she turned to her young companion.

"You're quiet, Denny," she observed. "More than usual, I mean. What did you dream about?"

Denny looked at her with a worried expression. He shook his head, refusing to answer.

Gemma stopped in front of him. "Denny, please. If we're walking to our deaths, if we're making the wrong choices, you need to tell us."

"It's not that I don't want to, it's just not clear. I saw..." Denny pointed across the river to the castle in the distance. "*Them*. The people in that castle. They were surrounding us. But I don't know if it was a bad thing. I didn't feel dread in the dream. It felt like it was meant to be. I do think things will work out for us, Gemma, but it won't be easy, and it won't be pleasant."

"Then I'm glad we're in this together," Gemma said as she reached out and patted Denny on the shoulder.

They continued toward what must once have been a few

small houses and shops. The door of the first shop was in poor shape, and not just from inclement weather over the years—it had been forced open at some point with some sort of heavy object or battering ram. Inside, a large piece of furniture that had been used to block the door from the inside had been knocked over during the forced entry. The skeletal remains of several people were sprawled around the room. Gemma turned, wanting to cover Denny's eyes, but it was too late.

"I've seen worse things in my visions, Gemma," he said.

"The Tzakabya must have done this."

Everything inside was destroyed. There was nothing of use to them there. They went on to the next shop and the next, all equally ransacked, all filled with nothing but death and decay. Gemma hoped Richard and Arnem were having better luck in the boathouse. She led Denny out of the last building and across to the waterfront.

"They found something!" Denny shouted with excitement. On the remaining stretch of dock, Richard was pulling a rope attached to the front of a small rowboat. Arnem was sitting in the boat, using a pair of oars to propel it toward the dock. Richard tied the boat to a post as Denny and Gemma approached.

"It'll be a tight fit, but I think it should hold all of us," Arnem said. He was breathing heavily from the short time he'd spent rowing. He realized everyone was staring at him and laughed. "Of course, I'm out of shape, so if anyone else wants to volunteer to row this thing, we may move more quickly."

"It will be a little tough to get across to the other side of the river," Richard said. "The water flows west more rapidly than I expected, and it's a lot wider than the River of Giants back home. The flow may take us a couple of miles downriver.

It won't be a bad thing, though, landing a bit farther from the castle. There will be fewer guards that way, and we'll have the cover of darkness."

Gemma looked at Denny, wondering if they'd be taken by the Tzakabya when they landed. She wouldn't have to wait long to find out. Nightfall was coming, and then they would make their way into the fallen kingdom of Emyhrsen.

———

As Richard expected, they landed on the opposite bank of the river about two miles due west of King Harold's Keep. They could have come ashore a little closer, but that night's full moon eliminated much of the darkness they had hoped to use as cover.

They pulled the boat up onto the rocky shore. There were wildly overgrown shrubs nearby, so they tucked the boat under them as best they could.

"If it wasn't so rocky, I'd say we should stay by the river as we make our way east," Richard said. "But as rough as this is, we'll have a broken ankle or two before we make it there. Let's go up by the road and keep our ears peeled for any approaching riders. We'll dive into the bushes if needed."

"Have your weapons accessible as well," Gemma added. She repositioned the machete on her belt so that it was within easy reach. She looked over at Denny and smiled as she watched him pull out his dirk. He was a bit too scrawny for the swords in Ferathan Manor's armory, and the oversized dagger had seemed like the best option. He'd been a bit embarrassed at first, but now he wielded it proudly. Richard carried a great sword that matched his own large size, while Arnem brandished a single-handed sword that, in truth, didn't make Denny's look all that small. Gemma had grown attached to the machete that had been used to threaten her, then to kill the creature that had murdered Walker and nearly crushed the life out of Richard. Now, she wondered if she would have to use it against any of the Tzakabya. It seemed very likely.

A wind began to pick up, and low clouds moved in. Before long, the moon was blessedly covered and they had the protection of darkness. Soon after, they spied the castle and moved back down to the uneven ground along the edge of the river. Up ahead were the castle's docks, though no boats were tied up there, and no guards appeared to be patrolling them.

"When I was a child, I used to sneak out of my family's apartment on the castle grounds and slip through a drainage system that let out in between the nearest two docks," Richard whispered. "If we can make it over there, we may find the entrance still accessible."

"And what do we do when we get inside the castle?" Arnem asked.

"We must get to King Harold, assuming he is still alive. Those are his banners still flying." Richard pointed up at one of the towers, where a banner sporting a sigil of a castle on a river flapped in the midnight wind. "He must be pushing eighty-five or ninety years old by now."

"Kept alive by dark magic, no doubt," Denny said.

The river widened a great deal near the castle and formed a lagoon directly in front of the docks. The current didn't seem as strong there, and Richard hoped that was actually the case, as they were about to hop in. He tucked his pack under a shrub, and the others did the same.

"You all ready?" Richard asked.

"To go in the water?" Denny asked. "But I can't swim! I can't go in there!"

"We'll help you," Arnem reassured him. "The important

thing is to stay calm. Keep your arms and legs moving to stay afloat."

"You can hold on to me, Denny," Richard said. "We'll take care of you."

Denny nodded, but it was clear to Gemma that he was still terrified. She gave him an understanding smile and stepped into the water, then jumped right back out from the shock of how cold it was. Everyone laughed, but they were just as taken aback by the frigid river once they made their way in.

When they'd swum about halfway to where the docks jutted out from the castle walls, they spotted a guard carrying a lantern. The man paced out to the end of one of the empty docks and sat down on the edge. He lit a pipe and smoked. Gemma and her companions held as still as they could, lightly waving their arms and cycling their legs to stay afloat, but they were losing ground against the current, even with how calm it was there. Then, from up on the wall, they heard a shout.

"Not sitting down while on patrol again, are you, Gressal?" the guard on the wall goaded.

The smoking guard, Gressal, stood up, turned to his shift-mate up on the wall, and made an obscene gesture. Then he pouted his way back up the dock and through the castle's gate. The guard up top disappeared as well. Gemma turned to Denny, who was shivering in the water next to her and turning pale.

"Okay, let's get over there quickly," Gemma said. She put one arm around Denny to get him started and began to paddle toward the docks. At one point, she turned to check on Denny. Instead of being white from fear, he had blushed red, apparently flattered by Gemma's touch. She turned forward again and gave a silent laugh, then removed her arm and increased her distance from him slightly. "I think you've got this, Denny."

They were within ten feet of the dock when they heard the sound of a boat approaching, several paddles dipping in and out of the water in unison. Gemma looked over at Richard in a panic. He pointed under the docks, then took a deep breath and put his head under the water as he swam. Arnem followed suit.

"No, no, I can't," Denny whispered.

Gemma reached back and took his hand. She gave him a reassuring smile and counted down from three with her other hand. On one, she took a breath and ducked under the water, pulling Denny with her. He flailed at first, but then calmed and followed Gemma's lead. They made it under the dock, but Gemma ascended into a mess of spiderwebs. She wanted to scream—she was almost certain she felt something crawling on the back of her neck—but she caught sight of Arnem's alarmed face and kept quiet. From above, they could hear one of the sailors jumping off the boat and onto the dock, where he tied the boat up. Five others got out of the boat as well and began making their way down the dock toward the castle. They were right above Gemma and her friends when one of them stopped. He called out to the others in a foreign tongue Gemma did not recognize. She looked up to see the bottoms of his boots just inches above her head.

Denny gasped.

Gemma quickly turned to him. He wasn't looking up at the figures above them; he was looking at Gemma. Then she felt it. She violently shook her head, trying to throw off whatever was crawling in her hair. She took a breath and ducked underwater. When she came back up, she opened her eyes to see a black-and-white-striped spider nearly the size of her hand floating off down the river. She looked up again to see that the sailor was making his way toward the castle to catch up with his peers.

After they heard the gates slam shut, Richard led them to the drainage grate he'd mentioned. Gemma thought it looked just big enough to fit Denny and her, but she didn't believe Richard and Arnem would be able to squeeze through. Arnem caught the look on her face and gave a knowing chuckle.

"Perhaps I should have skipped those last few meals, huh?" he quipped quietly.

Richard shot a worried glance back at him. Then he reached for the bars and tried to force the grate open. It didn't budge. Arnem rose up next to him and added his strength. The metal let out a squeal as the grate scraped against the pipe, and then it opened on hinges. Richard and Arnem moved to either side as they carefully lowered the heavy grate. Filthy, dark sludge began dripping out of the drainage pipe. It stank.

"No..." Denny whined. Gemma didn't feel like she was in any position to console him this time; she agreed that crawling through that muck would be repulsive.

And repulsive it was. They made their way through what felt like hundreds of feet of dark and slimy pipe. *Perhaps the sliminess is what helped Richard and Arnem to fit*, Gemma thought, and she prayed they wouldn't get stuck somewhere along the way. On at least two occasions, her hands and knees slipped out from under her and she went chin-first into the mess. Denny did the same, then turned and vomited. It just blended in with the rest of the filth. At another point, they heard a steady stream of liquid coming down from a smaller pipe that flowed into the main artery. When Gemma felt a tinge of warmth, she realized they must be near the guards' latrines. They all moved as fast as they could, but the two larger men couldn't quite help their slow speed in that claustrophobe's hell.

Finally, the pipe they were crawling through opened up into a larger pool. Off in one corner was a ladder built into the sewer system. Richard made his way over and began to climb. He motioned for them to wait below while he figured out if they would be able to exit. Richard made it to the top, where he slowly pushed up one side of a round manhole. He listened, then pushed it up more and peaked around. When he realized the coast was clear, Richard motioned for everyone to follow.

They sent Denny up, then Gemma, and finally Arnem. As glad as they were to be out of the mess, Gemma regretted it instantly.

Surrounding the four of them were four guards and six rough-skinned creatures.

They were caught.

CHAPTER 34
GEMMA

The smell of their cell under King Harold's castle was absolutely wretched, and that was *before* they were locked up in the dark, damp room. Once Gemma and her companions were thrown in together, still soaked to the bone with river water and sewage, it became an unimaginable stench that would make a warthog vomit in disgust.

And yet, there they were, crammed into the brick-walled, stone-floored room with no light except a torch that hung on the corridor wall, just out of reach of the steel-barred door. The cell had no furniture, just piles of rough and filthy hay and a rusted chamber pot that may or may not have also reeked—nobody in the cell could tell, given their own olfactory offenses.

They all sat down in their own dripping filth, shivering and downtrodden. Nobody spoke a word. Somehow, they found themselves drifting off to sleep one by one, first Denny, then Arnem, followed by Richard. Before Gemma joined them in slumber, she heard Denny muttering more nonsense in his sleep.

Tsechev ni-fellen szoren al-zar.

Gemma glanced in his direction, unsure if she should wake him, then decided against it. He may have been having one of his divine visions, which she did not want to interrupt in case it revealed something about their fates.

Pylen far-wellen zal ul-goetz nohar.

To her horror, she could see the whites of Denny's eyes as they rolled back between his slightly open eyelids. She shuddered in fear, but it didn't keep her from eventually letting go of her consciousness for what remained of that night.

A HEAVY DOOR SLAMMED SHUT DOWN THE CORRIDOR, waking the four companions. As Gemma shook herself back to reality, half a dozen flies hopped off of her and flew away. She didn't know what time it was, since there were no windows in the subterranean dungeon. Had they slept an hour? Five? She had no way of knowing. She glanced over at Richard, who was rubbing his sore neck. She spotted a look of concern on Arnem's face. Denny appeared to be deep in thought, perhaps reflecting on whatever he had seen in his prophetic dream. She was relieved to see that he didn't look scared.

"Denny, last night, did you—"

Gemma broke off as heavy footsteps approached. Their only source of light was suddenly blocked by an obese, well-dressed man who stopped in front of the door to their cell. He did not look like a guard or a soldier. The man took a breath, about to speak, and caught a whiff of the smell from their cell. He coughed in disgust and covered his nose.

"The Lord of Emyhrsen has requested your presence," he said as several more sets of footsteps approached. "Once you are clean, we will lead you to His Majesty's audience chamber."

Four guards crowded into the corridor behind the large messenger. "On your feet, you despicable vermin," growled one of them.

Gemma, Richard, Arnem, and Denny all stood up, though they all found it difficult considering the postures they had slept in. Gemma realized parts of her clothing had dried in stiff, crusty clumps. She wanted to cry out of disgust and discomfort. In that moment, she would have given anything to be back home with her family, or sitting in the first-class dining car on the train to Pinedrop, or even in that eerie black forest. But they had come this far. There was no turning back.

One of the guards, a muscular man with a wild beard, opened the cell door and waved for them to follow. Gemma looked at her friends with uncertainty, but Richard nodded to her, indicating that she should follow the orders. She shot another glance at Denny as she turned to leave the cell. She still didn't think he looked worried at all, which was completely unlike the boy she'd known for a very long week.

The guards led them down the corridor, through a heavy door, up some curved stairs, and out into the sunlight. Gemma couldn't help but cover her eyes from the shock after spending the last several hours in the nearly dark dungeon. They were back in the courtyard where they had been caught the night before, but she didn't see any of the strange-looking Foreign Ones who had encircled them. The four companions were corralled toward a small gate in one wall. When it opened, Gemma recognized the docks from the previous night, though the boat that had nearly blown their cover was no longer there.

"Undress and throw those filthy rags into the water," Wild Beard yelled. "Don't even think about trying to swim away. I don't want to get wet, but I'll do it, and I'll drag you straight back to that cell."

Gemma's companions turned to her. She didn't feel like she had a choice in the matter, and she was desperate to get out of the crusted clothing she wore, so she began to loosen her belt.

"Not you, little miss," Hairy Face said with a laugh. "We ain't all uncivilized here." He turned toward the gates they had walked through as a plump, elderly woman approached. She held a large folded sheet and several towels.

"Come with me, my dear," the woman said. She dropped a few of the towels at the foot of the docks, then led Gemma around the corner, away from the docks and out of view of the men. At the river's edge, she set the remaining towel down and shook the sheet open. She spread her arms wide and held the sheet up to shield Gemma from any prying eyes. "Now, I know the water will be uncomfortably frigid, but please remove your clothing and wash the muck off of yourself."

Gemma did as she was told. The first step into the river sent a shock through her body, but she did not want to show discomfort. She took a deep breath and walked in until the water was up to her waist. She knelt down to get the rest of her body wet and dipped her head under. When she came back up for air, she saw the woman pull a lump of soap from an unseen pocket in her frock. The woman tossed the soap to Gemma.

After getting as clean as she was able to, Gemma shivered

her way back out of the water. The woman quickly dropped the sheet and wrapped a towel around Gemma.

"Now, that should be the last ice-cold bath you will take here, young lady. Our good king will surely see to it that you and your friends are treated well as long as you assure him that you don't mean any harm to the kingdom."

"Thank you," Gemma said in a quiet, shaky voice.

She followed the woman back around to the docks, but it wasn't easy. She'd left her soiled shoes at the edge of the river along with the rest of her clothing. The rocky trail was painful to walk on, but she didn't want to show any weakness. As motherly as the woman seemed, Gemma didn't know if she could be trusted. As she approached the docks, Gemma found that Richard, Arnem, and Denny were wrapped in towels as well. Denny looked over at Gemma in her towel and blushed. Arnem caught sight of it and put his hand on Denny's shoulder, turning him away from Gemma wordlessly.

They were led by the guards and the woman back through the gates. The cobblestones of the courtyard were already heating up in the morning sun, but they were a relief to walk on after the rough gravel outside the castle walls. Gemma felt even better when they made their way past the door that led down into the dungeon. They crossed the courtyard toward the castle, though they entered through a side door meant for servants rather than the primary entrance. *This is the kind of door Mother uses when she arrives at King Davin's castle for work every morning*, she thought.

They walked down a cramped hall, then up a narrow staircase. Several times, they pressed against the walls to let busy maids and footmen pass them by, with all parties looking a bit embarrassed about the prisoners' state of undress. Finally, on the third floor of the service wing, they arrived at the servants' quarters. The guards led the men through a door on one end of the hall while Gemma followed the woman to a room at the other end. There was a bed on one side and all kinds of mannequins, linens, needles, threads, and clothing scraps on the opposite side.

"This is my own apartment and workspace as His Lordship's royal seamstress," the woman said proudly. "My name is Adelina Forester, but you can call me Addy. Now, let's get you dressed."

"I'm Gemma Calvertson. Thank you for your kindness, Addy."

The seamstress pulled open the door to a large closet. A window on one end provided a great deal of light. She searched through a number of dresses, but from Addy's mumbling, it didn't seem like any of them were near Gemma's size.

"I'm sorry, dear, but you'll never fit into any of my dresses, and I won't have time to make you one of your own before you're called in to meet His Lordship."

"The slacks and shirts hanging behind you look close enough to my size," Gemma said. "I would prefer to be dressed in those clothes, anyway. Don't get me wrong, your dresses are beautiful, but I'm not here for presentation."

"Is that how they do things down south these days?" Addy asked disapprovingly. She turned toward the clothes Gemma had referred to and nodded reluctantly. "Very well, then."

Gemma dressed in slacks and a shirt and was relieved to be in neither soiled rags nor a wet towel. A knock came at the door. Addy opened it and admitted a maid carrying a cup of tea and some breads, cheeses, and meats on a platter. Addy helped the maid set the meal on a small table before dismissing her.

"Come and sit, Miss Calvertson. I'm afraid you've missed

breakfast, but an early tea might just hit the spot. We'll have a more formal luncheon before you know it."

Gemma ate the food right up. It was the first bread she'd had that wasn't hard as a rock in as long as she could remember. The tea was a welcome change from the lukewarm water from a skin that she'd become accustomed to during her adventures. As soon as she was finished with her snack, a bell rang out from somewhere down the hall.

"It's time, Miss Calvertson. Let's go find your friends."

Addy led Gemma back down the hall, where she spotted Denny, Arnem, and Richard in their new attire. All four friends looked nearly identical, though where Denny's and Gemma's clothing was slightly too baggy, Arnem's was stretched to its full capacity over his considerable belly, and Richard's shirt and pants were far too short and snug for his big-boned frame. They looked at each other and gave out nervous laughs. Denny still looked more relaxed than Gemma would have expected.

As they walked down a flight of stairs, Gemma sped ahead to be next to him. "What did you dream last night, Denny?" she asked quietly.

"I think you're about to see for yourself," Denny said with a hopeful smile.

They walked on in silence through a set of doors that led deeper into the castle. Here, even the hallway was wider and more gaudily decorated. The carpet was plush, and the smell was pleasant. The guards led them to large double doors where two additional guards stood. They eyed the prisoners with contempt but opened both doors and stepped aside to let them enter.

Gemma and her friends walked into a huge audience hall adorned with large windows, inviting furniture, several chandeliers holding dozens of burning candles, and a magnificent throne up on a dais on the far end of the room.

"Guards, please leave us," a weak, scratchy voice called out before dissolving into a fit of phlegmy coughing. The guards and Addy all bowed toward the throne, then turned, walked out, and closed the doors behind them. Gemma realized then that a thin, frail man was slouched upon the throne. He beckoned for them to approach. "Please, entertain an old king and step this way. My eyes aren't what they once were."

When they came within ten feet of the dais, King Harold's eyes swept over the four companions, but he seemed interested in only one of them. A look of recognition turned into an expression of immense sorrow. He looked down at his own lap as if in shame.

"My dear young Richard," Harold started, "how you have grown up. I suppose it really has been a long time since I lost control of these lands. Lost my people. Lost my most loyal friend and most trusted advisor. Lost your father."

Gemma looked over at Richard, who seemed to be growing uncomfortable at the mention of his father, but she turned back to the throne when she heard the sound of weeping. Harold was crying into his gnarled hands. It was then that Richard knelt. Arnem, Denny, and Gemma remained standing, not sure what the protocol should be for a man who did not deserve their respect. Even Harold appeared shocked by Richard's act of fealty.

"I do not deserve such a thing, my good boy," Harold stated in an even shakier voice. "Please rise."

Richard lifted his head toward the crumpled man on the throne but did not get off his knees. He spoke with confidence.

"Even in dark times, you are the king who commanded my

mother and father, the one for whom they lived their lives. You are the king of Emyhrsen, the land of my birth."

Richard rose back to his feet, and Harold began to lower his own feet to the floor below the throne. He reached to the side and took hold of a cane that Gemma hadn't noticed.

"In absence of my guards, will you please help an old man down these steps?" Harold asked. Arnem and Richard stepped forward, climbed the two stairs to the dais, and supported King Harold on either side. "Thank you, gentlemen. Now, behind that curtain is my dining room. We will have a private luncheon. I hope you've brought an appetite."

Gemma and Denny followed the three men down the hall and into a small dining room with large windows. It was clearly not a room that a king would normally host guests in except on the most intimate of occasions, but it was still grander than any place she'd dined in her life. The food was already set out, with lids over platters to keep some of the dishes warm. They dined on duck confit, dates, root vegetables, luscious fruits, and fresh breads. Fine crystal glasses were filled with delicious red wine. Denny looked at Arnem, who gestured that it was okay to drink the wine, though he was not old enough back home in Aepistelle to partake of such a beverage. Gemma laughed at the silent exchange, then even more when Denny promptly spit out his first sip of the bitter drink. She reached for a pitcher of blissfully cold water and poured it into one of the glasses for the boy.

"Richard, I have much to talk to you about," said the king. "I assume I can trust your companions, and I apologize to all of you for any mistreatment you endured in the prison below the castle. If I had known the little boy whose birth I was present for would be visiting, I assure you that you would've had a much more welcoming arrival."

"Is it safe to talk here?" Richard asked. "Are we safe from *them*?"

"The Tzakabya maintain a small presence within the walls of the castle, but they mostly let me be. I don't believe they will interrupt us, and no spies listen for treasonous conversations here."

"I thought there would be more of them around here," Richard said. "We only saw a handful last night."

"At my age, and with this broken body of mine, I am not much of a threat to them. Even if I were to rally the dozen guards who serve me, we would not be enough to rebel. The leader, Tseledon Ni-Alwen, and his advisors have moved into the abandoned castle of the Vheisenia down the river a ways. The others are scattered throughout what was once my kingdom, enslaving my people on the farms and in the mines. The villages are all but abandoned. I am a figurehead, but I have no say in what happens here. The kingdom is all but lost."

"But it isn't lost," Denny said. Everyone turned to him, surprised that he had spoken up. "I saw it in a vision last night. There is some kind of army on their way here now, ready to fight."

"Who, Denny?" Arnem asked.

"I don't know. It wasn't clear to me. I couldn't make out the colors or their sigils. But there is no way they could be coming to fight *against* us, right?"

Everyone looked at him, not so sure that he was right. For the first time that day, Denny's assuredness seemed to fade.

"Richard, tell King Harold why you're here," Gemma said. "About the prophecies."

"I'm not so sure His Lordship is interested in hearing about the prophecies," Richard said with a hint of fear in his voice.

"And why not?" Harold asked. "You assume I have not

learned from my downfall, but I assure you that is incorrect. What prophecies does the girl speak of, Richard?"

Richard appeared to be shocked, but not offended. Gemma recalled the stories of Harold's earlier obsession with —and then outright rejection of—prophecies that had led to the downfall of his kingdom. She was sure that the same stories were running through Richard's mind at that moment.

"Well," Richard began, "all of them. *All* the prophecies point to this moment. Much like my father, I've spent years reading the texts of dozens of the ancient religions. I've learned many forgotten and forbidden tongues in an attempt to translate them myself. I believe that people of all different tribes in all different parts of Aepistelle received the same visions, from farther north than this to the Nazseke in the Esteron Mountains to the dwellers of the deserts beyond to the inhabitants of Central Aepistelle and the Southern Reaches. They all saw what would come to pass thousands of years in the future. There were warnings of strange foreign visitors from distant, dark lands who would sail in on black vessels. These beings would take over the lands—not just the people, but the land itself would fall under their powers. They would start small while they built up their resources, but within fifty years, they would amass enough power to launch an attack on the rest of Aepistelle. And they wouldn't act alone. They would have allies here who would support them when it was time."

"Like me." King Harold looked into his cup in a deep, regretful daze. "I let them in. I am responsible for the coming destruction."

"Not you, my lord," Richard said. "Your regret shows me that you are not the one who will help them achieve the remainder of their dark deeds. I speak of another king."

"King Davin?" Gemma asked in shock.

Richard turned to her. "I believe he has already struck a deal with the Tzakabya."

"But what about the army Denny speaks of?" Arnem asked. He patted Denny on the shoulder.

"Denny said himself that he only saw the army, not who they have come to fight for," Gemma said. "I think we need to prepare ourselves for the very good chance that King Davin has sent his soldiers to eradicate us and what remains of King Harold's defenses."

They sat in stunned silence for a moment before a door opened and a nervous guard ran into the dining room.

"Your Majesty," the soldier said with a rushed kneel, "the dark ships are approaching upriver. Our scouts claim there are men with them. Not *our* men, my lord."

"Thank you, Captain Malik," King Harold said. "We don't have the ability to fight back, so we'll see what they want. Let us get our guests into hiding before these ships arrive."

Gemma stood up. "No, sir," she said. "We did not come all this way to hide from danger. I believe I speak for all my companions when I say that we will stand up to these forces or die trying."

She looked around at her friends. They stared back at her with a mixture of fear and pride. Then they joined her on their feet. It was Richard who spoke next.

"We will fight for the people of your kingdom in Emyhrsen. We will fight for the survival of all of Aepistelle."

CHAPTER 35
GEMMA

"Full defensive lockdown!"

There were about a dozen trained guards who protected the king, as well as double that number of footmen, butlers, advisors, and laborers who resided within the walls of the castle. They all were provided with armor from days past, back when there was a full army stationed in and around the castle in the event of a foreign invasion. King Harold also had Captain Malik outfit Richard, Arnem, Denny, Gemma, and even the king himself in that old armor. The swords and shields that were passed around had rusted in the damp unattended armory, but they would have to do, if only to help the makeshift soldiers look more imposing and less like a bunch of broken and frail old men and women in a defenseless castle.

Gemma didn't feel broken and frail, nor rusted and makeshift. She delighted in knowing that she was taking a stand for something she believed in. She wondered if this was how her father had felt when he'd marched north with his unit a quarter century ago and arrived at the castle of the

Ancient Ones, not far down the river from where Gemma now found herself.

It also helped that King Harold had sent out some men to gather the belongings the travelers hid in the bushes near the river, so Gemma was reunited with her bow and machete, and the rest of her companions had their familiar weapons as well. Gemma and three of the guards who were also archers stood on the rampart above the river gates as the black ships approached the docks. They would split up to cover the main gate if needed, but Gemma prayed it would not come to that.

There were four ships, each with what looked to be around thirty people onboard, not counting the unseen rowers belowdecks. About two-thirds of the visible occupants on each ship were soldiers from the Aepistelle Royal Army, carrying the banners of King Davin. Each ship carried long, bulky objects Gemma couldn't identify, covered in large tarpaulins. She assumed they were supplies for the troops.

So it's true, she thought. *Richard understood the prophecies after all. It really is King Davin who's partnering with the Foreign Ones to take control of our people.*

Behind her, King Harold and four of his guards climbed the steps to the platform overlooking the docks. They watched as an elaborately dressed Tzakabyan man descended a ramp from one of the ships onto the dock, followed by one of the soldiers. As Gemma squinted to see the man who was in league with the Tzakabya, she realized who it was: Sir Marin Allemon, Secretary of the Royal Mystic Committee. Allemon turned his attention to the people on the wall, taking each of them in with a glare, and then stopped on Gemma. They had never officially met, though Gemma had seen him around the Capital University Press office when he visited with Hannon. She assumed that Walker must have pointed her out to Allemon when they'd set up her assignment to ensnare Richard the Elusive. Now it was clear that he recognized her. After giving her a knowing stare, Allemon continued to study the others on the wall.

He's looking for Walker, she thought. *He'll realize Walker failed his mission to arrest Richard before he could make it here.*

"Harold!" Allemon yelled up. "It is time to surrender. On the authority of King Davin of Aepistelle, I hereby pronounce you an enemy of the people. These lands that were once your kingdom have fallen into neglect under your shameful rule. The five other kings of Aepistelle bowed to King Davin and ceded their powers, and you must do the same now. The northern kingdom of Emyhrsen will henceforth be rightfully governed by Tseledon Ni-Alwen of the Foreign Lands, who has been overseeing your kingdom for many decades due to your incompetence.

"Additionally, you are harboring a criminal, Richard the Elusive, who has committed murder in the town of Pinedrop and who has violated King Davin's laws regarding the study and practice of magic and religious arts. You will hand over the traitor and his companions, and you will give up your castle without incident, and His Majesty may spare you from a painful and drawn-out execution."

King Harold stood taller and straighter than Gemma would have thought possible. Either he was not intimidated by the army below, or he did a great job of hiding it. He started to clear his throat but choked and fell into a coughing spell. Finally, he regained his breath.

"You must be Davin's lackey," he yelled back down. "Well, hear me now. I have made grievous errors in my time as King of the Northern Keep—I grant you that. But let it be known that it is Davin who is the real enemy of the people. It is Davin who will bring about the downfall of humanity, along with those repulsive creatures from the Foreign Lands. I will not give up my kingdom again, and I vow to win back the freedom of my people from the clutches of the Tzakabyan invaders."

As King Harold spoke, most of Allemon's soldiers and the Foreign Ones descended the ramps of the boats and crowded onto both docks. On the wall, the lead archer motioned for Gemma and the other two archers to nock their arrows. They took aim at Allemon and those who flanked him, presumably the highest-ranking Tzakabya present as well as Allemon's two top lieutenants.

"Have your guards stand down, Harold," Allemon called up calmly. "We'd hate to start killing when that can be prevented. You just have to come down here and surrender yourself. Simple as that. Well, you and Richard the Elusive. Where is that old boy, anyway?"

Gemma swallowed nervously. She turned back to see Richard climb the stairs and stop next to Harold. Like the old king, Richard stood tall and imposing, looking much more like she imagined he had on the Great Journey in his younger days.

"Your fall will hurt the most, Richard," Allemon yelled. "We will find a way to spin it so people aren't too crushed to see the decline of one of their longtime heroes."

Richard stood in silence. Suddenly, Arnem darted up the stairs and took his place next to him.

"You'll have to do the same to me, Sir Allemon," Arnem called out. "I'm in this with my old friend. Go ahead and try to explain to the people of Aepistelle how I, too, was some evil threat to their safety. I think your story will start to unravel quickly."

"And who are you again?" Allemon taunted. "Ah, yes, the fat one. I remember now. You can be sure your family will also suffer for your unlawful resistance, Mr. Wynstone. I seem to recall you have a wife and two daughters. This is your last chance to spare them. Surrender yourself now."

Both sides stood in silence. Gemma and her fellow archers waited for the order to fire their arrows, but it did not come. Then the Tzakabyan man next to Allemon raised his right arm, lifted his pointer finger, and flicked his wrist toward the castle. Gemma watched in shock as Tzakabyan soldiers on each of the four boats tore away the tarpaulins to reveal large barrel-shaped iron contraptions that appeared to have open ends pointed toward the castle walls. The soldiers grabbed burning torches and lit some kind of fuse on each contraption before stepping back.

A moment later, deafening booming sounds rang out. Gemma thought she noticed brief flashes of light from each of the contraptions, but she didn't have time to think more about it. In a fraction of a second, something came crashing through the castle walls in four different places. Shrapnel flew up, but not before Gemma was able to fire off an arrow. She hadn't waited for the order to come, but she didn't care. The head archer, standing a mere three feet to Gemma's right, was knocked down by a hail of debris from the explosions. As Gemma dove down, she caught a quick glimpse of Allemon's nearest lieutenant, who had taken the arrow to the chest.

Once she hit the ground, Gemma looked over toward Richard, Arnem, and King Harold. They had dropped down for cover about fifteen feet to Gemma's left.

"What kind of dark magic are they using?" Arnem cried out, his arms folded over the back of his head for protection.

"The Foreign Ones call them *cannons*," one of the surviving archers yelled. "Even our castle walls are no match for them."

Gemma lifted her head just enough to peek over the walls. She noticed that the Tzakabyan soldiers were stuffing something heavy into the openings of the cannons. She reached for another arrow and nocked it, but by the time she aimed, all four cannons were loaded and lit again. She dove back to the ground and covered her head as another loud *boom* rang out and another few sections of the castle's fortification were blown to bits.

"They blasted through the gate this time," Richard yelled. "They'll storm the courtyard now."

"Denny!" Arnem yelled. He shot to his feet and turned toward the stairs that led down to the courtyard. Two of King Harold's guards followed Arnem partway down, intent on stopping any enemies from making their way up to the king.

Gemma turned to the two remaining archers on the wall with her and waved for their attention. "You two, aim for the Tzakabya that are firing those things. You can do this!"

Gemma turned and ran to the interior ledge. She watched as Arnem rushed down the stairs. When he was only a few steps from the ground, the Aepistelle soldiers beginning to pour in through the destroyed gate. One of them saw Arnem heading down the stairs and turned toward him. *He probably thinks he'll be rewarded for capturing one of the traitors of the Great Journey,* Gemma thought. She pulled back her bowstring and fired off an arrow. It hit its mark, and the soldier fell to the ground. Arnem shot a quick glance up and nodded to Gemma, then continued running toward where he'd last left Denny and a few of the makeshift castle guards.

Gemma turned to see Richard leading old King Harold to the nearest tower entrance. Then she checked on the two archers. A satisfied look on each of their faces told her what she needed to know, and they were reaching for additional arrows. She confirmed that two of the creatures on the ships below had fallen next to their death devices. That left two more. She nocked another arrow and fired at the same target as one of the other archers. Hers was the one that connected with the rough-skinned being who was loading another round into a cannon. The final cannon was already loaded and turning toward their section of the wall. Its operator evaded an arrow that sailed several feet over his head and splashed into the water. Gemma fired another arrow at him and missed as well. The wind was suddenly picking up over the river, making it more difficult to aim. The Tzakabyan soldier reached for his torch, brought it up to the cannon, and lit the fuse.

"Run!" Gemma called out to the other archers. She turned to her left and ran in the same direction as Richard and King Harold, but after only a few steps, she heard the foreboding *boom* of the cannon, quickly followed by the explosion of masonry from where she'd just been standing. As she fell to the ground, she caught a glimpse of both archers getting pulverized by the pieces of bricks that flew up from the impact. One tumbled off the inner edge of the wall and into the courtyard below, while the other lay still, covered by a pile of debris.

"Gemma, come on!" Richard yelled from across the wall. She thought about sprinting in his direction, then realized she needed to finish her mission to take out the last cannon operator. She reached for the bow on the ground next to her, pulled another arrow from her quiver, nocked it, took a deep breath, and rose to her feet. She took aim at the Tzakabyan as he finished reloading the cannon and shifting it in her direction. She took note of the wind and compensated in her aim. Gemma pulled back the bowstring and let go.

The arrow flew down over the pathway below where the soldiers continued to climb through the opening at the gate and over the dock where Allemon, his surviving guard, and the lead Tzakabyan stood. It continued over the deck of the ship toward the last cannon. It sailed inches from the cannon operator's head and made contact with the torch just behind him. The flame went out as the tip of the torch cracked right off.

Gemma reached back to grab another arrow, intent on stopping the creature before he could relight the torch and ignite the cannon's fuse. Her hand made contact with an empty quiver instead. *The surplus arrows are over in a bucket*, she realized. She had taken only enough to get off a few shots before refilling, just as the other archers had been commanded to do. She looked over toward where she'd been standing, but the arrows were nowhere to be seen. In the meantime, the Tzakabyan soldier on the boat had darted several feet away to fetch another torch. He grabbed it and turned.

He neared the cannon. He held the torch out, moving it toward the fuse. He was ten feet away. When the fire connected with the fuse, it would send another blast toward the wall, toward Gemma, killing her. In the space of a moment, her own great journey flashed through her mind. The train ride. The market at Pinedrop. Meeting Richard the Elusive. The dark storm. The vagrant who had attempted to kill Richard and take Gemma. The tunnel. The black forest. Walker. Ferathan. The monster. The witch. The Nazseke. The Ogressi. The river. The sewer. The dungeon. The disgraced king. And now this. Gemma had started her journey as a scared and inexperienced historian setting out on her first big assignment, and now it appeared that she would end it as a proud warrior.

The Tzakabyan's torch was now mere inches from the cannon's fuse.

At the rear of the black boat that faced the river, something caught Gemma's eye. A massive creature climbed up out of the water. Dripping, it reached for the cannon operator. The Tzakabyan turned his head just quick enough to catch a brief glimpse of the thing that stood next to him. And then the new arrival reached out her gigantic hands, laid one on the Tzakabyan's shoulders and the other around the back of his head. She separated his head from his body and tossed it overboard.

The last Ogressi had arrived to help Gemma.

Gemma turned back to the slaughter in the courtyard below as Aepistelle and Tzakabyan soldiers alike struck down untrained and defenseless men and women. She didn't know if Denny and Arnem had found each other, if they had found a place to hide or a way to escape. She turned toward the boats again to see what the Ogressi would do next. Allemon ordered the soldiers who had not yet made it through the wall to attack the giant who stood on the black ship. Allemon and the Tzakabyan leader stepped aside to allow the soldiers to pass. As they ran down the dock toward the ramp at the end, the dock itself suddenly exploded from below. The soldiers flew up into the air in a hail of splintered wood and landed in the water.

Gemma looked farther up the river and caught sight of several smaller vessels rowing toward the castle. An old woman stood at the front of one of the boats. Her arms were outstretched, her palms facing up. The glowing light in her hand extinguished in a final wisp of colored smoke.

Naliah Lunarra, the Witch of Ferathan, was approaching along with dozens of children adorned in shining golden armor that appeared to have been crafted specifically to fit their small bodies.

Suddenly, things didn't look quite as dreadful.

CHAPTER 36

MARZELE | LE'NELLE NIGHTSTAR

Marzele's slumber was lengthy, but not at all peaceful.

Metaphors for failure cycled through his dark dreams, penance for his sins. Each cycle ended with scenes of his peers dying, daggers piercing through the necks of Bertram, Horace, Shenesa, and the others. Each ended with Marzele falling, catching a split-second glimpse of Mrs. Calvertson pointing out Marzele to King Davin up in the castle.

That man is the one who warned me, she might have said, or *he is the traitor to his people*, or *he knows what happened to my Gemma, please spare him for now.*

Between each dream, Marzele struggled to climb out of the blackness of his mind. There was a strong pain in his head that pushed him back down. There was a regret that held him there.

The Lord Solendaron misled me, Marzele thought. *He has forsaken me. He brought me to the mother of the Inquisitive One, told me to warn her, and yet that seems to have been our downfall.*

They were ready for us.

They stopped us.

Now, I am all that is left of the Order of Solendaron, and apparently only to die in some torturous manner.

And so, when the fog of unconsciousness finally began to dissipate, Marzele was unsure whether he was actually still dreaming. When his eyes opened, he was staring at water. Waves were crashing against wood twenty feet below him. The pain in his head was stronger than ever. His mouth was completely parched. His lips felt as if they had dried up and cracked off in flakes, leaving raw flesh exposed. His clothes were soiled, and only partially with his own fluids. The roughness of rope had cut its way through his cheeks, his forehead, his arms, his legs. Yet he continued to lie there in a daze for several more minutes, waiting for some other dismal scene to play out, another reenactment of his friends' deaths.

Their deaths didn't come, though, and that was when he knew that he must be back in the land of the living. It took all of his strength to simply lift his head. Pain shot down his neck and through his spine. He groaned loudly, and more pain came, this time from his dried-out throat. He lifted his head again and turned it to look around.

Marzele of Southplains was hanging in a net off the side of a ship, dangling high above the water. Neither his hands nor his feet were bound, but he was a prisoner nonetheless. As he struggled to move his body, the net began to swing. Looking back down, he could see the waves growing larger, lifting and dropping the ship violently. The net swung out, then slammed back into the ship's side. His arms were so numb, his hands so blue from lack of blood flow, that he hardly felt it when his limbs were crushed against the ship. Still, he took as deep a breath as he was able and called out.

"Help!" He attempted over and over again to be heard. He

couldn't turn far enough to look up at the deck, so he didn't know if he was being watched. "Please, help me up from here!"

Cruel laughter sounded from somewhere above him. He heard some shouting but couldn't make out what was being said. It was then that the dehydration really hit him, and he could yell no more. Just as he started to drift back into an unwanted sleep, he felt an upward jolt. He was being lifted.

The net was brought up onto the deck. He saw only boots as he was dropped face down on the solid surface. Someone grabbed the net and flipped it over. Marzele looked up to see a mix of men dressed in Royal Navy uniforms and men in white-and-gold King's Guard attire. They all looked at him with a blend of hatred and scorn, as if he were a rabid dog they were ready to kick to death in a dank alley in Capital City.

"You must be thirsty," one of the guards said before he cleared his throat loudly and spat a wad of phlegm down onto Marzele. All of the men followed suit. Marzele couldn't move. He couldn't do anything but take it.

This is what you want for me, Lord Solendaron, he thought. Marzele didn't know if he was crying. He certainly felt liquid dripping down his face, but he didn't think it was his own.

"Back off, boys," a voice called. The faces of Marzele's tormentors grew worried. They opened up their circle and faced the speaker, standing straighter, as if at attention. "Goodness, this man disgusts me. Private Alwood, clean him up for me, would you?"

"Aye, my lord," Private Alwood said.

Marzele grunted in pain as his net was lifted again. He was pushed overboard once more and flipped violently down. As he looked at the ocean, he noticed it was rapidly getting closer to him. When he crashed into the water, it felt as hard as concrete. The waves drifted over him. He couldn't help but take in a mouthful of salt water. Then he was lifted out. As he coughed the sea out of his lungs and struggled to breathe, he realized he was far above the water again. Private Alwood pulled the net back up to the level of the deck. A man reached over, grabbed the net near Marzele's face, and turned it toward him. The burning salt water cleared from Marzele's eyes, and that's when he found himself face-to-face with King Davin.

"I expected there to be more hatred in the eyes of a man who helped lead a rebellion against me," Davin said. "I suppose two days of hanging over the side of this ship would take the spark out of even the strongest-willed, though. Now that you're all cleaned up, let's bring you inside. You could use some drinkable water and good food, I'm sure."

Davin stepped aside as one of the guards pulled out a sword and cut open the net that entangled Marzele's numb body. Two other men forced Marzele to his feet. After several tries that ended in him collapsing under his own weight, they carried him across the deck, following their king into a cabin. Inside, they dropped Marzele into a chair, where he struggled to stay upright.

"Leave us," Davin said to his guards. They obeyed, shutting the door as they went. Davin poured water from a silver pitcher into a glass. He walked up to Marzele and held the glass to his lips.

"Th-thank you," Marzele managed to say. Davin stepped back and gave him a look of pity.

"You and your friends didn't accomplish what I'm sure was your primary goal—killing me—but you sure caused a lot of destruction regardless. That show of magic in front of all those onlookers was really something. But you also damaged your own cause. When you knocked down the walls to my castle, you also crushed many people in the debris. Servants. Gardeners. Visitors on a tour of the grounds. Sure, I knew you were coming, and I could have kept the area clear, but why not help you fail?"

"You knew..." Marzele forced out. "You knew because I told the woman?"

"Not the wisest choice you could have made, my friend. But then, she didn't tell me of her own free will. The seers could tell something was off with Mrs. Calvertson. They warned me, and I got it out of her."

"Seers?"

"I have an army of them—many in my palace, many more in the prisons run by my Royal Mystic Committee," Davin said with pride. "You didn't think I had them all killed, did you? Not when they could be of so much use to me, as proven by the thwarting of your attempted coup."

"And why... why didn't you kill me?"

King Davin laughed.

"Kill you? No, not yet. I believe you thought your god sent you on a mission, one in which you would be victorious. You thought running into Mrs. Calvertson that morning was a sign that it would go as planned. But I believe in the supernatural as well, Mr. Marzele. I believe that meeting was a sign that *I* will be victorious. You see, it told me that there really is something substantial going on here, that you believe the young Calvertson girl and Richard the Elusive will achieve something big in the north. I initially thought Sir Allemon could take care of it with the small army I gave him, but perhaps I needed to send more soldiers. And what good is a victory if I am not there to see it? I have a vested interest in the north. I need the Foreign Ones to retain their power there. If they fall to a rebellion, what kind of message would that send the other former kingdoms of Aepistelle? I'd have uprisings all over the place."

"You're in league with the Foreign Ones? The Tzakabya? They enslaved an entire country. How could you?"

"How could I not? My father was king of what was once West Aepistelle, just one of seven kingdoms on this continent. I didn't want to be just one of seven. How ordinary that would have been. Everyone could see that King Harold of Emyhrsen was cracking, and what better opportunity would I have? I boarded a ship with those loyal to me, and we sailed across the Western Sea for months. We made our way to a land we didn't have on our maps: the land of the Tzakabya. It was their temporary home, but it was no better than a wasteland. They were ecstatic at my offer. And once they made their way back across the sea to King Harold's castle and took control, it was only a matter of time before the other kings of Aepistelle realized we needed to join together under a single ruler to protect our freedom."

"You speak of freedom," Marzele said, "yet you take our freedoms away. The freedom of the people of Emyhrsen. The freedom of religion. The freedom to use the powers given to us by the gods."

"Again, it's all about control. I have a team of practitioners who did away with Harold's sanity. Why do you think he went from being the most respected of the seven kings to being the one who cracked? Had I let him continue on as he was, he would have been the one the kingdoms turned to in the difficult times that were to come. I did what I had to do to get where I am today."

"You will not be able to regain control. By now, Richard the Elusive and Gemma Calvertson have surely inspired the people of the north to rebel against the Foreign Ones. The Lord Solendaron assured me of their victory."

"I wouldn't be so sure of that," Davin said. "In fact, I think I will have some leverage over the girl, and then she can be used as leverage over Richard."

"What do you mean?" Marzele asked.

King Davin rose from his seat and motioned for the priest to follow him. "Come," he said.

He led Marzele across the cabin to an interior door, picking up a lantern on the way. He procured a key from his pocket, unlocked the door, and opened it. Marzele saw stairs that led deeper into the ship. He followed Davin down. At the bottom of the stairs was a small hallway and another door. Davin used another key to unlock this one. He pushed the door open and stepped aside for Marzele to see.

"Mrs. Calvertson!" Marzele called out. The woman didn't appear to be in the decrepit condition Marzele was in, but she looked sad and confused. Sitting across the room and was a man; he was not much older than Marzele, yet he looked quite unwell. Marzele turned to Davin. "Why have you locked them up? What did they do to violate your laws?"

"Mr. and Mrs. Calvertson were very concerned for their daughter," Davin said. "They jumped at the chance to come see her and to talk some sense into her. They are not prisoners on my ship. As long as they do as they're asked and convince young Gemma to come home with them, neither they nor Gemma will be imprisoned."

Geoffrey Calvertson stood and looked at Marzele, but the priest couldn't decipher the look in his eyes. It was as if he didn't know he was on a ship, in the presence of a king and a terrorist. A crooked smile broke out on his face.

"Georgie boy, I don't remember you having such a silly, stupid mustache on your face," Geoffrey said to Marzele. Serena Calvertson walked over and grabbed her husband by the shoulders, directing him back to the chair he'd been sitting in. Geoffrey's expression changed quickly to anger. He began to flail his arms and legs in a childlike manner. "I don't want to be here! I don't want to be inside when the fight is out there! Did you see the trees burn? Did you?"

Geoffrey then jumped to his feet, turned, and kicked his chair against the wall. Davin quickly led Marzele back out of the room and closed the door while Serena did her best to calm down her husband. From behind the thick wood, Marzele could still hear the man yelling and banging things around. He hoped Serena would be okay.

"I expect that the sight of her parents will lead Gemma Calvertson back to her senses. But if not, there are four more ships trailing ours. Five hundred soldiers in total, not to mention the rowers we have onboard to get our ships upriver and the rest of the crews, plus the men Sir Allemon brought with him, around a hundred more soldiers. You see, Mr. Marzele? You have failed. Even if Richard and Gemma have managed to rally a few poor souls to their cause, they are doomed to fail."

King Davin led Marzele farther down the hall and motioned toward a small, dark room.

"I know you have the power to melt this knob with your hands and get out of here, but you will not be able to fight your way off this ship. I trust you'll behave because you know it's your only means of survival for now. I'll have a nice meal and some more water delivered to you shortly."

Marzele stepped inside the room. He settled onto a chair and looked out the small porthole, the one source of light. King Davin shut and locked the door behind him.

As Marzele sat and stared toward the west, he thought he caught the slightest glimpse of a far-off ship. It was too distant to be one of the four ships King Davin had said were accompanying them. Most sane people in his position wouldn't have found hope in such a sight, but Marzele wasn't like most others. He was a priest of the Lord Solendaron, the god who had led him this far. He was certain now that it was not all for nothing.

THE SIGHTING OF FIVE MILITARY SHIPS SO FAR NORTH OF the mouth of the River of Giants wasn't just strange—it was unheard of in the days of King Davin's rule. The captain of the civilian ship wasn't sure if they'd been spotted, but it didn't seem likely, as none of the naval vessels bothered to change course. But those weren't just any royal ships. They were capable of rowing. They wouldn't need such capabilities on the open seas, not unless they were planning on turning into a river and making their way against the flow, or unless they were smugglers hoping to make their way into a guarded port under the cover of darkness, like this captain's own crew. These ships clearly weren't part of a smuggling job, and the only river in the direction they were headed was the Amassa River... the same river where two passengers had been dropped off days earlier.

"I knew we'd stayed around here for a reason," the captain said, raising an overflowing tankard and chugging its contents. Actually, that wasn't the reason they stayed around so long. The real reason was that they had spotted an old shipwreck on their way back to the south, a curiously black ship that had crashed onto a particularly rocky shore a few miles south of the mouth of the Amassa River. The decaying ship had turned out to have an entire hull full of weapons, including a number of massive cannons, which the captain had never seen before and had no name for. It didn't take long before Captain Le'Nelle Nightstar and her crew figured out how to use those, and they were perhaps the first people of Aepistelle who had ever done such a thing. Loading the weapons onto her ship had turned out to be an ordeal that took a few days.

But that was all beside the point. A belch erupted from her as she turned toward her inebriated crew. "Ladies, prepare to reverse course! We're heading back north!"

The crew of the *Ales and Sails* looked up from their cups and murmured in disbelief. The captain had already kept them circling in these waters for an extra couple of days with their newfound cargo, fishing and avoiding the naval patrols that would be near the shore once they headed south. Her crew was more than ready to get back to port.

"You heard me right," Captain Le'Nelle called out. She didn't know why Jestan the Just had been catapulted back into her life in the raucous tavern in Portsville, but deep down, she was a true believer in destiny. She'd been raised on the concept in the temple her parents took her to as a child, the one she'd pretended to forget as she grew up in a world that burned down houses of worship and the books they preached from.

Everything happens for a reason, Captain Le'Nelle thought. *Even running into that miserable lump Jestan.*

"Jestan paid us well to bring him and his friend into the north," she told her crew. "So I imagine he'll pay us double if we save his skin."

The *Ales and Sails* adjusted its course and began to make its way back north toward Jestan the Just and his mismatched companion, George Calvertson. Captain Le'Nelle had grown bored with her life on the seas. Perhaps her true destiny was calling.

CHAPTER 37
GEMMA

Gemma watched from the wall as the Ogressi cleared the shore, assuring that the Ferathan children and their sorceress leader were able to make a safe landing in their small boats.

Allemon's men poured back out of the walls of King Harold's castle, swinging their swords at the Ogressi and finding themselves getting lobbed back several feet. The Ogressi had torn the mast off one of the black ships, and she was using it as a massive club to knock down all of her would-be attackers.

"Gemma, watch out!" a voice called from somewhere in the castle courtyard. When she turned, Gemma saw half a dozen Tzakabyan soldiers rushing up the stairs, swords in hand. They had apparently taken out the castle guards who'd been protecting the bottom of the staircase while Richard and King Harold retreated to the upper level of the castle.

Gemma knew she couldn't take on these horrifyingly strange men on her own with only her machete, and it didn't appear that there was anyone around to help. She turned and looked toward where the Ogressi was still battling the Aepistelle soldiers down below the outer wall. It was her only option.

"Ogressi!" Gemma yelled out. The Ogressi didn't seem to hear her. Gemma ran along the wall, careful not to trip over debris or fall into any of the massive holes the cannon blasts had made all around her. When she got near enough, she yelled out one more time as she made a flying leap off the edge of the castle wall toward the outer perimeter. "Ogressi!"

This time, the Ogressi turned and saw Gemma sailing toward her. *Please remember who I am*, Gemma thought. *Please don't swat me away like a fly.*

Gemma took a deep breath, held it, and closed her eyes as she fell. She didn't think she'd die from the fall itself, but the broken bones would end her in a battle like this. Fortunately, she didn't have to worry. The giant took one more swing with the mast at the last of the approaching attackers, then reached out with one hand and caught Gemma.

Gemma opened her eyes and released her breath. She looked down and saw Naliah and the children jumping off the boats and running toward her. The Ogressi set her down safely.

"You came," Gemma said to Naliah, tears forming in her eyes. "But why?"

"Child, the full moon rose, and my bond to Ferathan was complete," the witch said. "I outstayed my welcome in that place, so it was time to find a new home. I thought perhaps if I could help Richard and his friends free Harold's kingdom, they may just allow me to stay."

"But what about the children?" Gemma asked. "Their parents must be relieved to finally see them go free."

Naliah lowered her face sadly. She looked back at the children, then at Gemma, though she did not meet her eyes.

"My actions were not all noble. When I took power over Ferathan, I kept the people from aging for decades. I have not released the children from my grasp just yet, though I did release their parents."

"Why have you not released the children? Wasn't that part of the agreement?"

"I care about them too much," Naliah cried out, tears now dripping down her cheeks. "They've become my family. I couldn't let it happen to them."

"Let what happen?" Gemma asked.

"When my bond was lifted from the townsfolk, the Spirit of Time rolled over them, reclaiming what was taken from it. In mere seconds, men and women went from thirty years old to a hundred. Buildings went from pristine to crumbling. The fields of plenty became fields of famine. I never intended to help them forever, only to help myself for as long as I wanted to be there. It was never going to end well. Yet I've grown to love these children, and I'm sorry for the mess I made for their families."

"So what will happen to the children when you free them?" Gemma asked with genuine concern.

The children were all close enough to hear the conversation. They looked at Gemma and Naliah with full understanding. Rabia, the little girl who had guided Gemma the first time she'd met the Witch of Ferathan, stepped forward and grabbed her hand.

"It's okay, friend," Rabia said. "We know what will happen to us, just as we know what happened to our parents. Young as we may look, we have lived for decades. We're tired. We'll be ready for eternal rest when our time comes."

"It is the curse of the Azhelda," Naliah said. "My people can live forever by stealing time away from others. We're a dreadful group."

Before Gemma could reply, movement from up on the wall caught her eye. Where she had been standing just moments earlier were Sir Allemon and Tseledon Ni-Alwen, the leader of the Tzakabya, accompanied by several Aepistelle and Tzakabyan soldiers. They were looking back and forth between the inner courtyard, where most of King Harold's guards and staff were likely being slaughtered, and the place where Gemma stood with the Ogressi, the witch, and the children of Ferathan.

"It's over for you all," Allemon yelled out. "Your little revolt has failed. Wherever you are hiding, Harold, it is time to come out. The same goes for you, Richard. We have your friends Arnem and the boy as our captives. We've captured some of your maids, cooks, and servants and killed the rest. We will do the same to your remaining friends if you do not reveal yourselves and lay down your arms."

Gemma turned toward the tower she had witnessed Richard and King Harold running into several minutes earlier. With the walls damaged all over from the cannon blasts, she was able to see the doorway that led from the tower to the walkway on the wall. Sir Allemon followed Gemma's gaze and watched as the door opened. Richard walked out slowly, clearly ready to surrender. He dropped his sword and held his hands up. Behind him, King Harold drooped, looking more like the old, frail man Gemma had met earlier that day. Sir Allemon laughed, reveling in his victory. The soldiers of Aepistelle down in the courtyard began a chant in unison.

"For King Davin! May his reign be long! For King Davin! May his people prosper!" They repeated these words, and Sir Allemon joined in.

His victory was short-lived, however.

From somewhere around the corner, a spear flew through the air toward the group of men on top of the wall. It pierced

Sir Allemon's left shoulder from the rear as he faced his soldiers in the courtyard below. As he turned in pained surprise, Gemma could see that the sharp end protruded all the way through the front of his shoulder. The guards jumped in front of him to protect him from any more projectiles, and they took spears in the chest, groin, and face. Tseledon Ni-Alwen and two of his guards darted away, heading toward the tower door that Richard and Harold were still standing in front of.

Gemma looked in the direction from which the spears had come, and there she saw Teyla-te-Anya, her eleven warrior companions, and a host of other Nazseke people on horses. They were all yelling out battle cries in a language Gemma did not understand, and she wouldn't have been able to decipher most of the cries even if she had known the language. With the exception of the twelve warriors Gemma knew and a few boys and girls close to Denny's age, the last of the Nazseke adults screamed out despite having their tongues removed years earlier by the forces of evil they were now here to fight.

From atop her galloping horse, Teyla nodded toward Gemma with a proud smile. She turned toward the open gate and sped through. Her fellow warriors and the rest of their people followed suit. They didn't slow down as they passed through the narrow opening, unafraid of being ambushed. They entered the courtyard and faced down the hundred stunned soldiers of Aepistelle. Gemma, Naliah, the Ogressi, and the children of Ferathan followed behind them and joined in.

Gemma glanced back up at the top of the wall. Sir Allemon wriggled around on his side, the spear still skewered through his shoulder. Richard was up there as well. He had reclaimed the sword he'd surrendered minutes earlier and was using it to defend old King Harold from the soldiers who had made their way up the stairs. Gemma didn't see Tseledon Ni-Alwen anywhere, though his two guards were dead at Richard's feet. *He must have made it into the tower*, she thought, *and Richard made the choice not to abandon the man he recognizes as his king.*

A young Aepistelle soldier rushed toward Gemma and stopped about six feet away from her, sword drawn. He looked terrified. He was maybe four or five years younger than she was, and when he spoke, Gemma recognized his distinct Capital City accent.

"Listen, girl, I don't want to hurt you," the young man said. He was trembling. She held her machete up, ready to clash with him if she had to. He spoke again. "Please, put down your weapon and surrender."

"You should be the one to surrender," Gemma said with authority. "You are in the wrong here. Your commander has partnered with a foreign enemy who has enslaved an entire nation of people. You and I both come from Capital City, I can tell. Let us fight for freedom together."

"I..." The soldier stood in front of Gemma, conflicted between integrity and duty. "I can't. You are a traitor to the crown of Aepistelle and an enemy of the people. I'm sorry I must do this."

The soldier raised his sword in a dramatic arc. He must not have received proper combat training, or perhaps he thought Gemma would just stand there and take the hit. Instead, she gave him a quick slice with her machete. The blade dug into the soldier's right armpit through a gap between the armor protecting his arm and the chain mail over his chest. He cried out and dropped his sword. Gemma removed the machete and swung for his neck. It connected, slicing right through. Though she'd killed a monster in

Ferathan, a giant in the foothills, and a few more soldiers from a distance with her bow, she was still fully unprepared for killing a human enemy up close with a blade.

A fellow Capital City native.

Barely a man.

Gemma didn't have time to dwell on it. Seeing one of their own fall, two more soldiers rushed toward Gemma, screaming with rage. She turned toward them. The first one swung his sword wildly, and she jumped back quickly enough to evade his first two attempts.

As he swung again, Gemma darted to her left, unsure if she'd make it out of the way this time. She heard galloping and then a scream of pain. Gemma turned just in time to see Teyla crushing the first attacker under her horse's hooves. It gave Gemma just enough time to defend herself against the other soldier's first blow with his sword.

Like the soldier she had just killed, this was another young man on his first tour of duty, perhaps not even done with basic training. She clashed blades with him three, four, five times. His sixth swing sliced Gemma's right thigh as she tried to jump back. The soldier hesitated, seemingly shocked to have drawn a woman's blood, and that was all Gemma needed. She lunged forward and put the machete right through the young man's throat.

She looked over and caught Teyla watching the action. She met Teyla's eyes, and an unstated respect passed between them, warrior to warrior. Despite all the guilt and disgust Gemma felt over shedding blood, and even through the pain in her leg, she smiled. Teyla returned the smile, then turned away to continue fighting.

Gemma looked down at her wound. It wasn't as bad as it could have been. No arteries had been severed, and the cut didn't seem to go down to the bone. It would leave a mark, surely, but it was a mark Gemma thought she could be proud of. And yet the thought of taking another human's life still made her sick. She didn't know how to reconcile her feelings.

"Gemma!" Richard yelled from up on the wall. She looked up and was momentarily blinded by the bright afternoon sun, but her vision cleared quick enough to see Richard pulling his sword out of a fallen Tzakabyan soldier. "Have you seen Arnem and Denny?"

Gemma turned to Teyla, who sped over to her and extended an arm. Gemma grabbed hold, and Teyla pulled her up onto the horse.

"Let's find them together," Teyla said. "I won't let the Weeping One die on my watch, nor that sweet little boy."

They rode through the courtyard, careful to avoid the Nazseke and the children of Ferathan. Teyla stopped her horse a few feet from a door to the castle. They dismounted and ran toward it. Two Aepistelle soldiers were there to defend the castle. With Sir Allemon lying injured on the wall, Gemma assumed these men must be guarding either Tseledon Ni-Alwen or a group of prisoners. Teyla took down one guard, and Gemma slayed the other easily enough. Teyla kicked open the door and rushed inside. Gemma followed her down a hallway to two grand doors she recognized.

"That's King Harold's audience chamber," Gemma said. No one was guarding the entrance now; every able-bodied man and woman had joined the battle, and many had perished when the enemy breached the outer walls.

Gemma turned the crystal-adorned knobs and pushed the doors open. She walked alongside Teyla into the cavernous chamber. Right away, Gemma spotted the prisoners up on the dais. She recognized Adelina Forester, the king's seamstress who'd come to Gemma's aid that morning and dressed her. There were seven other women, along with a few young children who belonged to King Harold's staff. Behind them, Gemma spotted Arnem with his arm around Denny. The boy appeared the most shaken of the whole group of prisoners. When Arnem saw Gemma and Teyla enter the room, he patted Denny and pointed them out. Denny met Gemma's eyes, and his demeanor immediately changed.

Four Aepistelle soldiers stood in front of the dais to keep watch over their prisoners. They turned to face the two women and drew their swords.

"Well, two little girls have come to join the party," said a tall soldier with long, curly hair. He began to make his way toward them with a conceited smile on his face. The others kept their swords out but did not bother to follow their brazen companion. "Lay down those weapons, and perhaps I'll let you come lie with me. I'm sure we can find a clean room somewhere in this crumbling mess of a castle."

Gemma and Teyla exchanged glances, both rolling their eyes in annoyance. In unison, they swung their blades at the approaching soldier. Curly was clearly shocked. He started to lift his sword, but his grip was weak. Teyla's sword connected with his, and he dropped it. Gemma's machete met his chest, but his armor deflected the blow. Immediately, she swung for his neck, but she didn't account for his height and struck his armor again. Teyla laughed as she cut a lock of the man's long hair that hung in front of his shoulders. The curly brown locks fell to the ground, and he looked down in dismay. While his attention was elsewhere, Gemma swung a third time, and her machete connected with his face, slicing his cheek open from lip to ear. He screamed for a moment before Teyla put an end to him.

As their companion fell, the other three soldiers looked at each other in shock, then slowly began to make their way toward Teyla and Gemma. The two female warriors followed suit, intending to meet the men in the middle, when a long, guttural cry sounded behind the men. The Aepistelle soldiers turned around to find Addy the seamstress charging at them with a five-foot-tall candle holder with a heavy base. Addy swung it at the smallest of the soldiers, and the base connected with his temple, sending him tumbling to the ground with a pained groan.

Arnem followed Addy's brave example and leapt off the dais. He reached for another tall candle holder and lunged at the two remaining soldiers. One of them swung his sword and knocked the object out of Arnem's hands while the other was tackled unexpectedly by young Denny. Adelina slammed the base of her candle holder into the face of the soldier who came inches from slicing off Arnem's head. The bones in the soldier's nose were shattered—he'd never breathe right again if he walked away from this battle. If that wasn't bad enough, Arnem swung a fist into the man's face and knocked him the rest of the way down. Before he could come to Denny's assistance, the seamstress warrior smashed in the face of the soldier Denny had brought down as well.

"It looks like he found a few others to lie with instead of you, my dear," Adelina said with a laugh, nodding toward the curly-haired soldier on the ground. Gemma walked over to Adelina and threw her arms around the brave, kindhearted woman. Denny and Arnem waited their turns to hug Gemma. Then Arnem turned to Teyla, who looked upon him with respect. She nodded slowly to him, almost bowing.

"Not just the Weeping One any longer," Teyla said. "Arnem the Candle Wielder. No, that doesn't have the right ring to it."

Teyla and Arnem embraced and laughed together. Adelina picked up one of the swords dropped by a fallen soldier. She waved over another woman and handed the sword to her.

"Enough of this cowering. We're all capable of being warriors," Addy said to the rescued captives. "Let us protect ourselves and our children here while these ones get on with their battle. And Gemma, please send any injured folks in so we may care for them."

Gemma nodded and headed for the doors. Teyla, Arnem, and Denny followed. Arnem and Denny each picked up a sword that had belonged to a fallen guard outside of the door to the courtyard. As they surveyed the scene, the four friends smiled in relief. All around them, the children of Ferathan, their witch, the Nazseke warriors, the giant Ogressi, and King Harold's surviving palace guards stood in apparent victory. Nearly thirty Aepistelle soldiers and a small handful of Tzakabyan fighters were being tied up, kept alive as captives.

The calm lasted for only a few moments.

In seconds, the sky darkened, a far cry from the blinding afternoon sun. Gemma had seen this happen before, so she wasn't entirely shocked. She followed the upturned gazes of many of the soldiers. There was something up on a balcony of the tallest tower. Gemma realized it was Tseledon Ni-Alwen, the leader of the Tzakabya.

Tseledon was speaking in his strange tongue, not to the men and women below in the courtyard but to the sky, waving his arms around as he did. Gemma thought she felt a slight rumble in the cobblestones beneath her feet. She looked up at the wall where Richard still stood with King Harold. The king pointed to something in the direction of the river, and Richard turned to follow his gaze. Gemma raced across the courtyard and took the stairs two at a time to see what had captured their attention.

Across the river, the dark, horrible trees of the Forest of Despair were swaying in the wind.

No, not swaying.

Moving.

Actually *moving.*

Gemma watched as the trees uprooted themselves and slithered toward the southern shore of the Amassa River. The water didn't stop them. They entered the rushing river, making their way across like serpents swimming toward the north shore and the castle.

Not tens of trees.

Not hundreds.

There were *thousands* of them.

Tseledon Ni-Alwen was directing the monstrous trees to attack the survivors of the battle of King Harold's Keep.

CHAPTER 38
ARNEM

Wars involve two or more rival forces battling for some tangible or idealistic cause. A leader believes he holds some moral claim or divine duty worth sending his people to their deaths.

Those people, typically of an age when they would otherwise be experiencing love and childbirth and employment and independence for the first time, are sent out against their will or are coerced into believing that what they're doing is best for the common good.

Many don't actually hold a strong opinion either way. They don't know their enemies personally and thus can't hate them on a real, individual level. Under any other circumstances, they wouldn't see the equally young men and women of the other side as villains, as evildoers, as deserving of violent deaths. Perhaps in another situation, they'd even be friends or classmates, taking care of each other's children, going out for drinks, celebrating joyous occasions together.

But in a world where war is normalized, it takes

extraordinary circumstances to overcome the hatred formed on the battlefield.

Extraordinary circumstances such as an enemy that is not a different nationality or political party but a completely different species. One that may well be the prophesied unnatural army that will bring the complete destruction of humanity.

Extraordinary circumstances such as these.

"Untie us!" The captured soldiers of Aepistelle begged for their freedom out of fear, out of self-preservation, out of a sense of duty to their fellow man. "Untie us, please!"

Arnem looked over at a group of his countrymen who were chained to a large overturned cart in the middle of the courtyard. These men, wearing the same uniform as those who had captured Denny and him after storming the castle less than an hour earlier, who'd fully intended to tear down the castle and murder every northerner in it, now didn't look so intimidating. Arnem even felt bad for them. Given what was crossing the Amassa River at that moment to destroy all the humans in the castle and beyond, Arnem didn't think it was fair to leave these soldiers tied up.

"Do it," Denny said.

Arnem turned to him and saw in the wise boy's eyes that Denny was of the same frame of mind as he was. Arnem gripped his sword and faced the captive soldiers.

"Death is approaching us, men of Aepistelle," Arnem said. "I aim to return home to Plentimore Valley and raise my daughters and love my wife. Many of you also have family back home, or ladies you plan to make your wives, or careers you hope to have when your military service ends, or rest you long to take. We may have met as misguided enemies in someone else's war this afternoon, but now let us be brothers, fellow humans, fighting a common enemy for the sake of all those in these lands and all those back home.

"Let us fight as one!"

They raised a battle cry as Arnem brought the sword down on the chains that kept the soldiers in bondage. His aim was true, his arm was strong, and the chains gave way. Arnem led Denny and the soldiers of Aepistelle across the courtyard, leaving the few Tzakabyan survivors tied up. They followed the Nazseke, the children of Ferathan, and the other survivors near the gates.

As they passed through, Arnem looked up to see Gemma, Richard, King Harold, and Naliah taking in the view beyond. Even from down below, Arnem could see the fear on all of their faces. Outside the crumbling castle walls, Arnem stopped alongside Teyla and watched as the slithering black trees made their way across the river.

"Will those things have the ability to fight?" Denny asked aloud. "Will it take cutting off branches to stop them?"

"Are you not the seer, child?" Teyla asked.

"I wish I could control the visions. I don't know why they come to me at all if they don't prepare me for things like this. I'm sorry I'm of no use."

Denny looked as if he was about to cry, and he may have were it not for all the soldiers standing around him. Arnem put an arm around his shoulders, then gave a resigned frown to Teyla.

"Denny, perhaps we each have a role to play in situations like the ones we've been in over the last couple of weeks," Arnem said. "When I journeyed with my friends years ago, I felt just like you do now, and I didn't even have the powers that you have. I was convinced I was deadweight compared to the bravery of Jestan, the strength of Richard, the wisdom of Maachel. But when they needed me most, I was there, loyal to the end, and what sounded like a worthless trait became vital to our party's survival.

"And had you not told me of your visions, I wouldn't be here to assist Richard and Gemma. They may not have made it this far. The people of Ferathan may not have been freed from the curse of the witch. Teyla and her companions might still be wandering throughout the Fingers. King Harold might still be a slave to the Foreign Ones. You've helped bring us all here, Denny. Stand proud, my young friend."

Denny did stand proud, noticeably taller, with a large grin on his face.

"Oh, and perhaps you should stand with them," Arnem said, pointing to Rabia and some of the other children from Ferathan. "They look like they could use a protector such as yourself."

Denny took another look at the approaching enemies and didn't need to be told twice. As the boy ran over to the children, Teyla smiled at Arnem.

"You truly have come a long way, old friend," she said. "Maachel would be proud."

"Perhaps," Arnem said. "Let's finish this fight before we reflect on any more old times." He tightened his grip on his sword and walked through the ranks of men, women, and children who stood between him and the river.

He made it to the front lines just in time to see a serpentine limb shoot out of the water and grab one of Teyla's eleven companions by the ankle. It wrapped around her like a snake and pulled her into the river. She screamed, thrusting her spear into the dark water that surrounded her, but she couldn't catch her attacker with the sharp point.

Her head went below the surface, and all was silent. Nobody knew what to do. In their shock, they didn't back away from the river. Five seconds passed, but it felt to Arnem like five minutes. Then the Nazseke warrior's head came back up and she gasped desperately for air.

She lifted her spear again and plunged it back down into the unknown. It appeared to find its mark that time, and she was able to make her way back to shore. She started to run toward the crowd of onlookers, a mixture of victory and terror on her face.

The black vine shot out of the depths of the river again, reaching higher this time. It wrapped around her neck with the speed of a whip cracking around a pole. Her spear dropped as she lost the ability to breathe. The creature yanked her back into the water, and when her head emerged again, it was floating on its own, no body to weigh it down.

"Sybelle!" Teyla screamed in despair. "No!"

The rest of the Nazseke looked to Teyla, who used their confidence in her to regain her composure.

"Spears at the ready!" Teyla ordered. "Release at first sight of these monsters! Kill them all!"

Arnem turned and looked up at the figures on the wall. Richard stood stoically, perhaps reflecting upon the prophecies he had spent most of the last twenty years studying, all of them leading up to this moment. Gemma had been reunited with her bow and a spare set of arrows. She had an arrow nocked and ready to fire. Arnem turned back to the river and readied for a fight. He thought back to what Teyla had said minutes before.

If Maachel could only see me now, he thought.

The *thwang* of a bowstring rang out, and an arrow sailed over the heads of the army on the shore. It found its target just an inch or two below the water, and one of the serpentine trees flailed about, suddenly revealing its upper half. In a rage, it sent more of its vine tentacles out to attack those on shore. One of the boys from Ferathan who was near Denny's age was struck by a swinging tentacle. His helmet flew off, but that was the only thing the tree was able to grip, as the boy sliced the tip of the tentacle clean off. Two younger girls dashed toward the injured appendage and stabbed it. Dark, gooey liquid sprayed out of the injury, causing the children to dart back and cover their eyes. A few drops landed on Arnem's chest. He rubbed it with his bare hands. It was something between sap and blood, deep purple and sticky.

More of the creatures were approaching the shore, making the river look to be moving unnaturally. There were so many of them in the water that the current seemed to calm, more of a swirl than a rush. Across the river, an endless line of trees entered the water.

Is it truly the entire Forest of Despair come to life?

The trees were making it to the north shore. As each one reared its top half out of the water, the Nazseke sent spears flying at them, hitting their marks nearly every time, but the spears would soon run out. The tentacles that lashed out of the water toward dry land were met with the slashing swords of the Ferathan children and the Aepistelle soldiers. The strength and might of the lone Ogressi giant with her ship mast club helped keep the monsters at bay, though her range of motion was quite limited, as she had to be very careful not to trample any of the humans. Arnem got a few good hits in with his sword, and he couldn't help but wish that his wife and daughters could somehow be there to witness his bravery from a safe distance.

All these elements worked well together, but it wasn't enough.

Farther down the river, where there were no defenses, the trees came to shore by the dozens and slithered their way toward the battle.

They would soon be overtaken.

CHAPTER 39

GEMMA

"**R**ichard, we have to help them. They're getting slaughtered down there!"

Gemma had only three arrows left out of the two dozen she'd been able to scrounge up from the rubble on the wall. So far, she hadn't wasted a single one, and she knew that Walker would have been proud of her skill had he been here to see this. Then again, she wasn't certain which side Walker would have been fighting on before the leader of the Tzakabya had called upon the monstrous trees.

Richard and Naliah just stood there as if they were merely spectators while their friends risked death below. The two of them exchanged words in hushed tones, too low for Gemma to hear, except for when Richard ordered King Harold to carefully make his way down the steps and into the audience chamber with the elderly, the children, and the injured. King Harold gladly complied.

"Richard, Tseledon is still up on the tower chanting spells," Gemma said. "What can we do to stop him? I may be able to hit him from here, but I don't have many arrows to spare."

Richard finally looked over at Gemma. She pointed up at the tower high above the courtyard. The leader of the Tzakabya was on the balcony, shouting his strange words, moving his arms wildly, and swaying his body.

"He'll have put a protection spell on himself," Naliah said. "He's safe from projectiles and physical confrontation. Save your arrows, girl."

"You're the witch here—why don't you do something?" Gemma asked. It came out harsher than she meant it to, but there was no time for subtlety.

"It's not so easy," Naliah said. "I may be able to conjure an offensive spell against his creations in the river, but not against him directly. His words must be broken by others who speak his tongue. I may be powerful, but only over the Azhelda or over the willing. I can take power from those who know my language or those who know no enchanted tongue at all. But just as the Tzakabya weren't able to come into Ferathan while I protected it, I can't penetrate his field of protection up on that tower."

"That's ridiculous! How were the Tzakabya able to take power in these lands all those years ago? King Harold had every text from every known religion on the continent. He had practitioners of many of them to protect him, but the Tzakabya were still able to break through it all."

"I've thought a lot about that," Richard said. "I grew up believing that King Harold let them in willingly, that he gave in to their control. But that doesn't seem like the man to whom my father dedicated his life or the man who welcomed us here this morning. I think someone else was able to gain control over him and trick him into letting the Tzakabya in."

Richard turned his head, and Gemma followed his gaze to

where Sir Allemon was still sprawled, bleeding out all over the rubble on the wall. His breathing was heavy, but he was still somewhat conscious. He was gesturing for their attention. They walked over to him and knelt close enough to hear his raspy whispering.

"I know now... I know... my mistake in f-following King D-Davin. He set all of th-this up. Harold's downfall... p-planned. Sorry... I'm... Sorry... Never should have followed him..."

Allemon's eyes closed for the last time, and his labored breathing ceased. None of the witnesses to his death shed tears. This was a man who had blindly followed a cruel leader's orders to imprison or even kill thousands of men and women around Aepistelle for continuing to practice their religions. He had destroyed sacred texts, historical buildings, and cultures that were hundreds or even thousands of years old.

Perhaps he got off too easily, Gemma thought, but she quickly regretted it. Having taken the lives of a few men herself that day, she didn't know if she had the right to judge others any longer.

A scream of pain below the walls broke Gemma out of her thoughts—an elderly Nazseke man had met his death between the tentacles of another evil tree serpent.

"Richard, so many more people are going to die down there. We need to go and help them, now!"

Gemma didn't wait for a response. She dropped her bow and quiver, pulled out her machete, and started to make her way down the steps to the courtyard. She turned to see if Richard was following her.

Richard unsheathed his sword. As he took a step toward the stairs, Naliah reached out and grabbed his shoulder.

"You do not need to use your sword, Richard," Naliah

said. "You've prepared for this day with a different kind of weapon. Use it to protect your friends."

"It was magic that brought all of this upon us," Richard said. "It was a mistake to think I could use magic to end it, too. No, Witch. Those creatures will die by my *sword* instead."

He rushed down the stairs behind Gemma. She nodded to him as they passed through the gates.

Gemma surveyed the scene. All around her, the children of Ferathan fought as valiantly as the Nazseke warriors, who were wielding the swords of fallen Aepistelle soldiers now that their spears were spent. The rest of the Nazseke people held their own in the fight as well; Gemma was sure they were making Teyla and her crew proud. The Ogressi was having perhaps the largest impact, sweeping away three or four of the attackers with each swing of the mast she still held. Even the few Aepistelle soldiers who remained were fighting along-side those they had originally come to slaughter.

A few hundred feet to the west, Gemma spotted Arnem, Denny, and Teyla, all battling a cluster of trees that had made it to shore. As Gemma watched, she realized the trees were cleverly beginning to surround her three friends. She looked over at Richard and could tell he was thinking the same thing. They ran toward the group.

One of the trees sensed their approach. It turned and shot a long, slimy tentacle at Gemma. She slashed at it just before it could slam into her. The severed tip spewed sticky purple blood. She gave the flailing appendage another slice farther up and thought she heard the tree squeal with pain.

"You have to cut it open at the trunk," Denny yelled when he noticed their arrival.

Gemma rushed at the creature she had injured. Another of its branches-turned-tentacles caught her left ankle, wrapped quickly around it, and flung her up into the air. She fell back down, slamming into the rocky ground. An explosion of white-and-yellow lights took over her vision for a few seconds, long enough that she didn't realize the creature was reaching for her ankle again. This time, it picked her up and dangled her right in front of its trunk. Gemma used the close proximity to slash at it with her machete, right on the trunk, like Denny had said. She was surprised that it felt more like cutting open an animal than slicing through tree bark. And like an animal whose belly has been sliced open, foul-smelling guts and more of the thick purple blood spilled out of the creature. Its grip on Gemma immediately loosened, and she fell into the pile of innards below.

Naliah ran over and helped Gemma to her feet. She was covered in filth from the creature, but there was little time to dwell on it.

"I need you to protect me, girl," Naliah said. "I've no sword, only my tongue as a weapon."

"But you said your magic won't work to counteract theirs!"

"It won't allow me to hurt Tseledon directly, but that doesn't mean I can't use it to take down his repulsive abominations."

Gemma followed Naliah away from the shore until they were out of reach of the tree monsters. The Witch of Ferathan began to speak rapidly in the Azheldan tongue, her eyes rolling back in her head. As she repeated the verses of the spell in a rhythmic pattern, Naliah's voice dropped more than a full octave. It was a bassy sound Gemma never would've expected could come out of the woman. Then she began shaking as if she were having a seizure. She kept repeating the words as her voice shot up to a warbling high pitch.

As Naliah continued to recite the spell, the sound of footsteps rushing toward them snapped Gemma out of the trance she seemed to have fallen into. She turned to find three Tzak-abyan men running in her direction. They carried axes, but the weapons were not raised in attack position. Their faces were full of fear. It wasn't until she raised her machete that they seemed to notice her. The lead runner lifted his axe to strike Gemma, but she put her own blade through his chest before he could take a swing. As she pulled it out of him, his two companions halted and dropped their weapons.

"Please, spare our lives," one of them said. His voice was a growl that shook with fear. The two men were panting, and they bent over with fatigue.

They've been running from something, but what? Gemma looked in the direction they had come from, but she could not see anyone pursuing them.

Naliah's voice rose to a near yell as she continued her incantation. The ground shook, and suddenly, Gemma heard the sound of rushing waves. She turned just in time to see the river rise several feet above the shoreline, yet it kept its normal course as if there were an unseen wall that stopped it from spilling over. It moved as quickly as a herd of running horses, knocking hundreds of the trees farther downriver. While there were still dozens of the creatures on the shore, it gave just enough relief for the warriors and the children to fight them one-on-one or even two-on-one.

This reinvigorated the fighters. Many let out victorious battle cries as they finished off their opponents.

The celebration didn't last.

As soon as Naliah released the water back to its natural flow, Tseledon's voice echoed over the castle and beyond the walls. He was calling out a new spell of his own. A silence cut through the air from the direction of the river.

The water's flow had completely stopped.

Now that the rocky riverbed was exposed, hundreds more trees crossed the missing Amassa River with ease. Fish floundered around on the muddy ground until they were trampled by the beasts.

While Tseledon held the water at bay with his looping incantation, Naliah scrambled to come up with another idea. She started and then abandoned several spells in her native language, but none of them seemed to counter the one that allowed the trees safe passage to the north shore. They approached and began pummeling the shocked warriors. Cries of pain and death rang out from all over. Gemma ran to help her friends.

It appeared to be the last stand for all of them.

And then, it wasn't.

Tseledon's voice cut out as he took notice of something in the distance. His sudden silence allowed the river to resume its flow. The water crashed back into place with the power of a tsunami, and a thousand more tree monsters were washed away.

Gemma turned back in the direction from which the Tzakabyan men had approached. Coming over the hill and down the road were several hundred men, women, and children—newly freed northerners. Many of them held ropes or chains that bound their former Tzakabyan captors. As they got closer, Gemma heard the last voice she ever expected.

"Gem, you're alive!"

She spotted the man who'd spoken.

"George?" She ran toward him with a mix of hope and confusion.

A boisterous laugh sounded from her brother's companion. He was a tall, muscular, middle-aged man, not unlike Richard, but far more handsome and spry.

"Calvertson, you never said your sister was a brilliant warrior!"

Gemma had never met the man before, but she knew it was the voice of Jestan the Just. He bowed to Gemma.

"Pardon me, dear, but it appears I have some friends to help."

Jestan ran past Gemma, pulled out his sword, and began slaying the beastly trees that surrounded Denny, Arnem, Richard, and Teyla. He moved with a swiftness that was lacking in Richard's stiff body, and he had no trouble taking down several of the monsters. Half of the men who accompanied George and Jestan followed suit, giving relief to the fatigued children of Ferathan, the Aepistelle soldiers, and the Nazseke fighters.

Gemma and George embraced.

"But what are you doing here?" Gemma asked. "How did you know to look for us in the north country?"

"It's a long story. I'd say you would never believe it, but look at you. My sister, a war hero in the making!" They hugged again, then ran down to join their friends in battle.

Gemma realized that Denny, Arnem, and Richard had mastered the timing of the trees' branch-tentacle strikes, and they kept a perfect distance that allowed them to avoid being entangled and suffocated. She followed suit as she reentered the battle. Gemma was close enough to hear Denny muttering under his breath with every swing of his sword. They were the same words she'd heard him say while he slept and when he thought no one was listening.

"Tsechev... ni... fellen..."

"Denny," Gemma interrupted, "what are those words? Are they from your visions?"

"Words?" Denny was embarrassed. "I'm sorry, it's just gibberish. Sometimes I wake up and they're on my mind. I think it's some kind of dream-speak. It doesn't really make sense, just like most dreams."

"What if it's something more, though? What if it does mean something? It could be that the—"

"More ships incoming!" Teyla yelled.

Gemma sliced a large incision in another tree and watched it fall. As it hit the ground, she looked downriver to find five Aepistelle Royal Navy ships rowing against the current. A flag flew on the first of the ships with the seal of King Davin.

"The real beast is here now," Arnem said. "King Davin himself."

Since the docks had been destroyed by Naliah during her grand entrance earlier that afternoon, the king's ship dropped anchor just off of a stretch of riverbank that wasn't overly rocky. Everyone who wasn't in the midst of a duel with one of the trees stopped to look.

King Davin and three of his guards stepped onto the deck of the ship in full view of the warriors on the bank. He took in the view before him, and then he spoke.

"People of Aepistelle! People of the northern lands! Those from the Foreign Lands, and the beasts they've created! It is time for this madness to come to a close. Look across the river; the number of trees ready to cross and join the battle is nearly endless. There is no victory for you rebels. Let us go back to the way things were, and your lives can continue on their old paths."

"No," one of the northmen yelled. "We will not go back to a life in chains. We do not recognize the rule of the Foreign Ones any longer!"

Hundreds of others cried out in agreement. Jestan stepped in front of them and raised his sword toward Davin's ship.

"Your time is over, Davin," he shouted. One of the serpentine branches shot out of the water, and Jestan cut right through it without even turning his head. "We will continue fighting, and we will be victorious. All the people of Aepistelle will soon know the truth of what you have done here, what you have allowed to happen. You are finished."

Davin broke into laughter, then waved a finger behind him. More guards walked up to the railing of the deck, escorting prisoners.

"Mother!" Gemma yelled out. "Father!"

George walked over to Gemma and put an arm around her shoulders to calm her, but she could see the distress on his face as well.

"Ah, the Calvertsons are all here," Davin said. "I suppose they will be the first to surrender to me, unless they want to see their mother and father slaughtered before their eyes. I'll even do it myself."

Davin pulled out a jeweled sword and displayed it.

"Wait, please!" Gemma yelled, but it was the last time she begged to King Davin.

A loud *kaboom* rang out, and then four more in quick succession. Wood and soldiers flew off the ships in all directions. The men and women on the riverbank began to cheer, but everyone was confused. Then the sails of another ship came into view behind the five naval ships. A flag featuring a sigil of a large mug of ale flew high on the mast.

"Captain Le'Nelle!" Jestan yelled out, and George laughed loudly. Gemma looked at her brother with confusion.

More cannon blasts came from that ship. On the king's ship, a mustachioed prisoner ran up onto the deck and knocked over one of the guards who stood next to Gemma's parents. The guard lost his balance and fell over the railing. The other guards pulled out their swords, but the man and both elder Calvertsons jumped overboard.

"They're going to drown!" Gemma screamed as she watched them fall into the rushing river with their hands still bound. She ran down the river's edge, and George followed.

Their mother's head went under and then bobbed back up as she struggled to catch her breath.

Loud footsteps pounded next to Gemma. She turned to see the Ogressi darting down the riverbank. The giant waded into the river and grabbed Gemma's parents and the third captive. The current had already carried them several hundred feet, far beyond where any of the warriors had gone to fight off the trees. The Ogressi pulled Gemma's parents and the strange man close to her chest, like babies at a mother's breast. She walked back toward the shore, but the area was swarming with the tree monsters. As the Ogressi stepped onto the riverbank, Gemma saw that several tentacles were wrapped around the giant's ankles. The Ogressi used a massive amount of force to try and yank the tentacles right off of the trees they stemmed from, but she lost her balance. As she fell onto the riverbank, she twisted her upper body so that she did not crush the people she carried.

The Ogressi hit the ground, and the trees on the shore didn't hold back. Several more slithering tentacles wrapped around her neck. She let out a deafening scream, but another tree seized the opportunity and shot its serpent branches down her throat.

"No!" Gemma screamed. She ran toward the Ogressi, machete in hand, not thinking about the odds. George followed her, determined to help their parents to safety. Gemma glanced back and realized that Richard, Arnem, Denny, Jestan, and Teyla had all followed suit.

The Ogressi's face had gone blue by the time they arrived, but she was still moving around in pain. Her legs kicked weakly in the water, but the grasp of the trees in the unseen depths was strong. She still had her arms around those she'd rescued, protecting them from the monsters rather than using her hands to pry the branches off of her. Gemma struck at the first tree she came to, and it flailed its free branches wildly, trying to knock her back. Gemma managed to cut a deep slice into the trunk, and it spewed its filth, tipped over, and pulled its vines out of the Ogressi's mouth. George swung his sword at one of the trees that was choking the Ogressi, but he didn't get as lucky. That tree's appendages knocked him down and started to wrap around his torso.

"Not today, despicable creature," Jestan called out as he leapt over George and swung his sword at the tree. He hit his mark in one swoop, and the tree loosened its grasp on George's body and the Ogressi's neck. Richard and Teyla took on a few more of the trees that had wrapped their branches around the Ogressi's throat while Gemma defended the Ogressi's vulnerable head from more attackers.

Arnem and Denny climbed up onto the Ogressi's shoulder, trying to get to Gemma's parents and the other man. Denny muttered the odd words as he made his way up. "Szoren... al... zar..."

Arnem reached out for Serena Calvertson. She had worked her hands free from the rope that bound them. One free arm dangled outside of the Ogressi's grip. Arnem took her hand and helped to pull her out. When her other arm was available, Denny took her right hand, and together they got her free. The Ogressi realized that these were friends freeing those she had rescued, and she loosened her grip on the two men as well. Gemma ran over and helped her mother down while Arnem pulled Geoffrey Calvertson to safety. Denny reached for the remaining man and then stopped as he recognized him.

"It's you," Denny said. "I saw you at the train station in

Plentimore Valley, and again walking around Pinedrop. You're one of Davin's spies!"

The man with the notable mustache laughed and shook his head.

"My dear boy, I am no spy. I am a man of faith who spared no expense to see that a prophecy came true. You are the Dreamer, and you are quite an observer." He held his hand out to Denny. "I am Marzele of Southplains."

Denny hesitated for a moment, but seeing only kindness in the man's eyes, shook his hand.

"Denny of Esteron City," the boy said.

The moment didn't last long. The Ogressi was being pulled back into the water. Denny and Marzele jumped down to join their friends. With no people left in her arms, the Ogressi was free to use her hands again. She reached up to her neck, where one tree stubbornly held on, two slimy branches closing tight. She was wheezing furiously, trying her best to breathe. She grabbed the tree with her large right hand and squeezed. The beast burst open like a cockroach squashed under a heavy boot. Its guts squirted all over the Ogressi's face, but she seemed relieved to breathe again. It was clear, though, that her breath didn't flow as easily as it should have. She turned and spat out gallons of blood, careful not to drench any of her companions. Then she let out a pained scream as she realized she was being pulled into the water by the creatures still attacking her feet.

Gemma, Denny, Arnem, and George all grabbed on to the Ogressi's left hand while Jestan, Richard, and Teyla took the right. They pulled with their full combined strength, but it wasn't enough. The unseen trees in the river continued to pull the Ogressi's body in deeper. In seconds, only her sliced-up neck, frightened face, and outstretched arms were visible above the water. Her friends were being dragged along, unable to plant their feet and pull her back up.

The water went up over her chin.

Her mouth.

Her nose.

Her head went completely under.

Gemma and the others grunted as they pulled with all their remaining strength. Bubbles rose from where they assumed the Ogressi's mouth and nose were in the murky river.

"Hang on," a voice shouted.

Gemma looked upriver and saw the same vessel that had blown the king's ships out of the water with cannons. Several women jumped overboard with spears and harpoons. Gemma thought she could hear them laughing, as if this were entertaining for them. Then she heard Jestan laughing as well in his boisterous manner, and she was really confused.

When they hit the water, the women unrelentingly stabbed their weapons down into the unseen depths. Innards of trees started to float up to the surface. The Ogressi's feet kicked up out of the water. Her hands flicked away Gemma and the others as the giant pulled herself up. She sat up, coughing out gallons of blood and water and struggling for breath, but she was alive. She reached down toward her feet and allowed the women to grab on to her hands, and then transported them to shore. She stood up and limped her way off the battlefield, toward the hills George and Jestan and the freed northmen had come over not long before.

Jestan ran over to one of the women from the boat and threw his arms around her. The two laughed and embraced for half a minute before Jestan spoke.

"Le'Nelle, I knew you couldn't resist seeing me again so soon!"

"That's *Captain* Le'Nelle, I already told you! And you're right, I couldn't resist you and the fee I know you're good for because I came back to rescue you, you old lug."

The group worked together to fight off the trees that crowded the riverbank. Gemma's parents and Marzele kept close to Gemma, George, Denny, and Arnem. As he swung his sword at the trees, Denny continued to mutter his strange words.

"Pylen... far... wellen..."

"Zal... ul-goetz... nohar..."

Gemma turned.

The last three words had not been spoken by Denny.

They had come from her father.

Gemma looked at Denny, who also was staring in confusion at Geoffrey Calvertson.

"Dad, what was that?" Gemma asked. "What did you say?"

"It's that thing he's been mumbling for years, Gem," her mother said. "You know how he gets."

"No, Mother, it's something else. Denny has been saying the same words, but he doesn't know what they mean. Dad, what is it?"

"It's... I... Vheisenia... Ancient Ones..." Her father struggled to get the words out cohesively, but Gemma was accustomed to that. She let him continue talking while Arnem and some of the women from the ship protected them from the trees nearby. "At their... castle... I learned... the verse..."

"Please, Dad. Close your eyes and think back." She walked over to him and rubbed the back of his head. When he was calm and had his eyes closed, he sometimes regained some of his memories and was able to think and speak more clearly.

If ever there was a time for you to remember, Daddy, this is surely it.

"It's... not sure of the meaning... but..." He seemed to

relax. "Tsechev yezets knowlen al-zar, pylen far-wellen tsech nor goetz nohar."

Denny's mouth dropped in amazement. Then he joined in.

"Tsechev ni-fellen szoren al-zar, pylen far-wellen zal ul-goetz nohar."

Geoffrey opened his eyes and turned to meet Denny's. He smiled and giggled liked a child. He reached over and patted Denny on the shoulder so unexpectedly hard that the boy fell right over, but Denny was laughing, too.

"That's it. There must be a reason that the dreams gave those words to Denny. There must be a purpose." Gemma looked around. The Ogressi was resting away from the battle, Richard and the others had cleared away most of the nearby trees, and up near the castle, the other combatants continued to defend the riverbank from the endless flow of new trees popping out of the water. Even a great deal of Aepistelle soldiers that had accompanied King Davin had fled the ships and were defending themselves against the trees, as the beasts did not care which side they were on. Several of the freed northmen remained near Naliah in the same place Gemma had left her minutes earlier. "Richard, we have to go back into the courtyard! Denny, Dad, you guys need to come as well. We'll get Naliah on the way."

The group turned and ran back toward King Harold's castle, where Tseledon Ni-Alwen continued to spew out his dark incantations from a balcony at the top of the highest tower.

CHAPTER 40

GEMMA

"**W**hat's this about?"

Naliah was shocked when Gemma ran up to her and grabbed her hand in the middle of an incantation, cutting off the words the witch was using to set up an area of protection for the injured fighters to rest in.

"I think I know how to break through Tseledon's defenses," Gemma said. "There's no time to discuss this as a committee, just trust me."

They arrived at the riverside gate, but it had caved in. The cannon blasts from the Tzakabyan ships had severely damaged the structural integrity of the castle walls.

I'm just glad we weren't still standing on top of the wall when it finally caved in, Gemma thought.

"The front gate," Teyla said. They changed course, running past a large group of the children of Ferathan, who were resting after fighting relentlessly. They looked on as their caretaker and former captor, Naliah, ran faster than they'd ever seen the old woman move in their decades of knowing her.

They arrived at the large gate along the main road, but it had been lowered. Even with the whole group pulling up, they couldn't get it to budge.

"Tseledon must know we're coming," Naliah said. "There's no use. It is over for us."

"Step aside, please."

Gemma turned to see the mustachioed man, Marzele, walking up to the gate. He wore leather gloves that were wet from the river, but he peeled them off as he approached and dropped them into the gravel at his feet.

"And what are you going to do, knock the gate down with your gloriously groomed facial hair?" Jestan asked. He, George, and Le'Nelle all burst into laughter. The rest of the group just looked at them in disbelief. Jestan noticed their dour looks and apologized. "Just playing, my new friend. Go on."

Marzele laid his hands on the bars. He closed his eyes, bowed his head, and began speaking in a low voice. It was yet another language Gemma did not recognize. She gasped when the man's hands began to glow, a brilliant light emanating from them. Then, like Gemma had seen in the forge in George's shop, the metal heated up, turning red and malleable. The entire gate, large enough for two carts to pass through side by side, burst into a million pieces. The man took a step back and spoke again, this time in the common tongue.

"The great and merciful Lord Solendaron has allowed us to pass. His favor is with us in this noble quest."

Jestan reached his hand out to shake Marzele's, but the priest of Solendaron pulled his own hands back.

"Sorry, my friend, I don't want you to go the way of that gate," Marzele said. He winked at Jestan, who laughed and patted Marzele's back instead.

They walked into the courtyard. It was full of rubble. On one end, the staircase Gemma had used to reach the top of the wall had crumbled. Gemma spotted her bow and the remaining arrows, miraculously spared by the debris. All around, dead soldiers and civilians still lay on the ground where they'd fallen.

Crows and pigeons scavenged throughout the lifeless area. Marzele clicked his tongue and called out in his language. The crows continued about their business, but the pigeons immediately stood at attention, looking in the direction of the group. They dropped whatever was in their beaks and walked toward Marzele. He continued his incantation, and the birds somehow understood him, a flock heeding the words of their shepherd.

In unison, the pigeons flew off, hundreds of them. They circled the tall tower as they gained altitude. When they neared the highest balcony where Tseledon was standing, they seemed to bump into an invisible barrier. They flew out of sight.

"Okay, Gemma, we're here," Richard said. "What would you have us all do?"

Everyone turned to look at Gemma. She looked back at her family and all the friends she had met on this journey. They didn't look at her like some child out of her element. They stood attentively, ready for her to lead them through her plan.

"Between Denny and my father, I think we've figured out the spell that will break Tseledon's own. The more of us who speak the words, I think, the more likely we'll be to succeed. Dad, Denny, will you recite the lines so we may learn them?"

"It's... I..." Geoffrey Calvertson tried to speak, but his mind had clouded again. He looked down in shame.

Naliah walked over to him and softly placed her hand on

his cheek. He looked up at her, meeting her eyes. Naliah whispered an incantation. Gemma's father's far-off gaze turned into a knowing one, clear for the first time in years.

"Tsechev yezets knowlen al-zar, pylen far-wellen tsech nor goetz nohar."

Denny joined in for the second half.

"Tsechev ni-fellen szoren al-zar, pylen far-wellen zal ul-goetz nohar."

The two of them repeated the lines once, twice, three times. Each time they spoke, a couple of the others joined in, learning the strange words as they went. Geoffrey began yelling the words, a smile breaking out over his face. Gemma turned to her mother and saw tears streaming down her cheeks. It had been years since Serena had seen the man she loved speaking with confidence and clarity, even if she didn't know what he was actually saying. Gemma looked to Richard, who stood behind the group. His mouth wasn't moving. He wasn't joining in with the rest of them.

"Tsechev yezets knowlen al-zar, pylen far-wellen tsech nor goetz nohar.

"Tsechev ni-fellen szoren al-zar, pylen far-wellen zal ul-goetz nohar.

"Tsechev yezets knowlen al-zar, pylen far-wellen tsech nor goetz nohar.

"Tsechev ni-fellen szoren al-zar, pylen far-wellen zal ul-goetz nohar.

"Tsechev yezets knowlen al-zar, pylen far-wellen tsech nor goetz nohar.

"Tsechev ni-fellen szoren al-zar, pylen far-wellen zal ul-goetz nohar."

Over and over, they spoke the words. Far above them, Tseledon Ni-Alwen's own spell was reaching a crescendo. He was fighting hard to retain his power, and he was losing.

Gemma saw the flock of pigeons returning, flying high above the courtyard. Again, they circled the balcony at the top of the tower and seemed to bounce off.

"It's not enough," Gemma called out. "Keep going!"

"Tsechev yezets knowlen al-zar, pylen far-wellen tsech nor goetz nohar.

"Tsechev ni-fellen szoren al-zar, pylen far-wellen zal ul-goetz nohar."

The pigeons returned for another pass. This time, Gemma thought she saw Tseledon flinch. *He felt the flutter of their wings* she thought.

The group continued to recite the verse. Gemma turned and ran toward the fallen stairs.

"Aaaaah!" Tseledon yelled from high above them. He changed his own verses, no longer repeating the incantations that kept the tree monsters moving. The remaining walls and structures around the courtyard began to shake.

"Get away from the walls!" Gemma shouted from across the courtyard. They quickly moved toward the center, carefully avoiding the bodies sprawled out among them. The arch where the main gate had recently stood suddenly collapsed. The debris missed Richard and Serena by mere inches. Gemma reached what had once been the foot of the stairs and found what she was looking for.

The pigeons made another pass around Tseledon Ni-Alwen as debris rained down upon Gemma's friends. They were hit by pieces of stone and brick, but nobody appeared to be severely hurt. They continued their incantation in unison. The pigeons circled around the balcony once more, and this time, they ran directly into the Tzakabyan leader. He swayed, losing his balance. He nearly toppled over the waist-high railing, but he held tight, regaining his stance.

Gemma picked up her bow and shook the dust from it.

She reached for an arrow, but it had snapped in half under the weight of a large chunk of stone that had landed on it. She grabbed a second arrow, but the tip was broken off.

Only one chance to do this; get it right, Gemma thought to herself as she surveyed the final arrow. It looked straight, undamaged.

She nocked it.

Aimed up.

It was a nearly impossible shot. But then Gemma remembered the last few weeks. She'd seen a lot of things that she would have once called impossible. A man with magic hands that could melt an iron gate. A giant crying in a cave. A witch who'd kept children young for seventy years. A forest of trees come to life. Nothing about her journey fit into the worldview she'd held just a month earlier.

She checked her aim again, compensated for the wind.

Gemma pulled back her bowstring.

Took one more breath.

Released.

Her friends continued to recite the incantation. Tseledon continued to send debris down on them with his own strange words. The pigeons circled the tower yet again. Richard looked on silently.

Gemma's arrow sailed upward.

It struck its mark.

Tseledon Ni-Alwen took the arrow through his heart. His voice cut off as he slumped forward. He tried to grab the rail to support himself, but the pigeons arrived just at that moment. Tseledon tried to swat them away and missed his chance to steady himself. He toppled over the railing, fell through the air, and slammed into an overturned cart in the middle of the courtyard.

Tseledon Ni-Alwen's reign of terror over King Harold's kingdom was at its end.

It was finished.

CHAPTER 41
ARNEM

All eyes were suddenly on Gemma.

All except Richard, they'd been so focused on repeating the strange words that they hadn't even noticed she'd walked away. Then, the twang of the bowstring had sounded out, followed by the flapping of wings. Arnem looked up to find the leader of the Tzakabya tumbling over the balcony to his death below.

They ceased their incantation when the evil being hit the ground, then turned and caught sight of Gemma, bow still in her left hand. She stood in shock at her own skill. Half a century of oppression had finally ceased with that shot.

Denny was the first to run to her, followed by Gemma's mother. Arnem watched as, one by one, most of their party made their way over to her. She had begun to cry, and Arnem wasn't sure whether it was due to shock or joy, but he soon found himself in tears as well at the thought of the danger he had been in all this time while his wife and daughters were at home, worrying over him. As Arnem looked at the crowd gathered around Gemma, he realized he wasn't alone in holding back.

Arnem turned to find Richard the Elusive crouched on his haunches, his right hand keeping him balanced, his sword resting on the ground in front of him. Arnem stepped over to his old friend.

"Richard, it's over. We've done it." Arnem looked at the large man, but Richard didn't look back. "Are you upset about something?"

"It's just..." Richard stood up, though there appeared to be a weight on his shoulders that kept him from rising to his full height. He looked up at the tower where Tseledon Ni-Alwen had been standing just minutes ago.

"You thought you'd be the one to finish him off. To save the kingdom." Arnem stepped closer and put his hand on his friend's shoulder.

"I wanted to do my father proud. Maybe it was revenge I wanted for the way my father was displaced and disgraced by the Foreign Ones."

"Richard, we've had our time. We've had our own journeys, our own victories. Look at them." Arnem pointed at Denny and Gemma, who were embracing among all the others. "It's their time now. They've earned it. We helped them along, but this is their victory."

"You're right," Richard said. A proud smile broke over his gruff face. "Gemma had it in her all along. And Denny..."

One of the castle doors opened, and Adelina Forester stepped out, shaking hysterically.

"The king is dead," the royal seamstress said. "King Harold, Lord of Emyhrsen, is dead."

Richard rushed over and embraced her as she let out her tears on his shoulder. The others walked over, eager to find out what had happened.

"He was sitting upon his throne in the audience chamber, telling us stories about the kingdom's past, and then, in the middle of a sentence, he put his hands to his chest, breathed his last, and slumped forward."

"His fate was tied with the Tzakabyan's," Naliah said. "It's a common power spell in some cultures. He died without pain, at least."

Richard joined Addy in mourning for the king of his childhood country. The big man shook uncontrollably as he sobbed.

King Harold was the closest person left to Richard's father, Arnem thought, *and now he's lost to time.*

THEY WANDERED OVER THE RUBBLE OF THE ARCHWAY AND out of the courtyard, eager to see how the battle had progressed outside the castle walls. When they turned the corner and faced the riverbank, everyone was staring in awe.

Thousands of trees stood as still as statues along the edge of the river or jutting out of the water, and thousands more had frozen in place while waiting to cross the Amassa River from the other side. Many of them had their long, twisted branches outstretched, frozen at odd angles in the midst of flailing about to kill their human combatants. Now that the spell that had given them life was broken, they were like grotesque statues of krakens and beasts, not unlike those that adorned the walkway of Ferathan Manor.

In the river, the five royal ships bobbed in disrepair, the cannons having blasted entire chunks of the siding away. Masts were bowled over, sails tattered and flapping wildly. Le'Nelle's crew had captured the surviving Aepistelle sailors and soldiers from the ships, as well as King Davin himself.

Dozens of the northerners helped keep the prisoners contained on the riverbank. The children of Ferathan and the other survivors sat together, laughing joyously as they took in the sights of their victory. The Nazseke people had developed their own sign language in the years since their tongues had been mercilessly cut off by agents of the Tzakabya, and they were presently signing wildly about their battles against the monstrous trees.

The Ogressi was sprawled out atop the hill, alone and unmoving.

She has breathed her last, Arnem thought, *a hero in the end*.

Vigils were held for the Ogressi and all the others who had been lost, but it was not all dour. The sounds of celebration rang through the night. Bonfires were started—miraculously, the black trees burned easily now that the cursed life had been removed from them—and the victors were provided food, wine, and ale from the castle stores. Songs were sung, stories were told, laughs were had, and tears were shed. Eventually, most everybody fell asleep under the starlight. The morning would bring its own excitement.

"INCOMING SHIP! PREPARE THE DEFENSES!"

The champions of the previous day's battle had hoped to sleep in later; they had earned it after all the fighting they had done to defend Emyhrsen against true evil. But it didn't seem to be in the cards for them.

"White-and-green sails," Denny said as he looked down-river. Arnem's eyes weren't good enough to see the ship yet, but Denny had youth on his side.

"White and green? I've seen such sails before when I said goodbye to..." Arnem trailed off, deep in memory.

"A ship of the Ancient Ones," Richard said. "But why have they returned?"

A laugh broke out, then a second one. Arnem turned to see George and Jestan embracing, clearly celebrating something.

"Do you two have something to do with this?" Arnem asked.

"I can't believe it really worked," George said. "I thought Jestan was just full of hot air!"

"Well, he definitely is full of something," Le'Nelle quipped.

"I told you the signal would work, Georgie boy," Jestan said. "I just thought it would work a little faster. Thank the gods we didn't sit and wait for them longer than we did."

By the time the ship landed—which wasn't an easy task, considering that the river was full of lifeless trees and the docks had been destroyed—the entirety of the castle and the surrounding camps had emptied out to watch. The Vheisenia —the Ancient Ones—did indeed look different from the people of Aepistelle, closer to the Tzakabya people, but smaller, less imposing, more graceful. Many of the elders of the northern kingdom and of the Nazseke had seen them before, as had the survivors of the Great Journey, but those of the younger generation had not.

Arnem saw the surprise on Gemma's face as her father ran over to greet them ahead of anyone else. Richard followed with Teyla behind him. Arnem, Denny, Gemma, Le'Nelle, Naliah, Jestan, and George made their way over shortly after.

One of the Vheisenia was dressed slightly more ornately than the others; they all wore flowing white robes with gold trim and embroidered green sigils, but this particular one also wore a jeweled crown on his head. Like the rest of them, he looked centuries old and as young as Denny at the same time. It was almost as if, depending on the angle and the lighting, one could see wrinkled skin or flawless skin, flowing blond hair or white hair, eyes of youth or eyes that had seen centuries of change on the same individual. Arnem had met this man before.

"Hello, my friends," said Verellion Sal-Vheisenia, Emperor of the Ancient Ones. "We came as soon as we saw the signal, but it appears we are too late. Victory is yours and yours alone."

Mr. Calvertson dropped down at the emperor's feet in a display of reverence. Gemma reached for her father, guiding him back a few steps to give the emperor space.

"Geoffrey Calvertson, loyal soldier of Aepistelle, my people and I remember you fondly. You fought valiantly many years ago, and you were instrumental in our success."

"It... I... th-thank you, my lord," Gemma's father said. He turned to Gemma and George with a proud smile, one that revealed years of hope that his children could know of his bravery in the old war even though he was unable to tell them about it himself. Gemma hugged her father and cried into his shoulder.

Arnem looked beyond the leader of the Vheisenia to those making their way off of the ship. There, among those who had once resided in the castle not far to the west, was one man who stood out. He was wider than the others. His hair was shorter. His skin was more like Arnem's own. His movements were clunky compared to the others. He was a man of Aepistelle. Of Plentimore Valley, more specifically. It was Maachel.

When Maachel spotted Arnem, he smiled widely. He looked just like the boy Arnem had grown up with, only a bit grayer. Maachel raced down the gangplank onto solid ground and threw his arms around Arnem. The two men laughed and spun around in circles joyously.

"You came back," Arnem said. "Please tell me you've come back for good, Maachel. Please tell me so."

Maachel pulled back and looked at Arnem with more seriousness than before. Sadness, even.

"I can't tell you that, old friend. I wish I could, but there was an agreement when I went with the Vheisenia that I wouldn't be able to come back."

"But you're here now, are you not? Surely you're not just a specter."

"Yes, of course I'm here now, but it's an exception. I don't fully understand it. Something about unfinished business being like a curse. The Vheisenia couldn't rest until the curse of the Tzakabya was lifted, so we returned when the signal came, but we must go back when it has been resolved."

"When it has been resolved?" Arnem asked. "We defeated them last night. It is finished."

"No, Arnem," Emperor Verellion said. He walked over to Maachel and Arnem. "Back at what was once our castle, there are hundreds more Tzakabyan people. A few more men, but mostly women and children. We left two ships behind to ensure they couldn't come here and attack you. As long as they remain in this land, we cannot rest."

"Will you slaughter them?" Gemma asked.

"No, young Calvertson. We will not slaughter them. That is not something our people have ever been able to do. We are bound to them and have been for many generations. Tens of thousands of years ago, we came from the same lands far from here. Our two races lived together in harmony until civil war ripped us apart. They learned a system of dark magic from someplace we have no record of, some other evil people. They irreparably damaged our lands; they can no longer produce fruits or vegetables. Wildlife does not roam in those lands, nor do flowers grow there. We fled to what is now the north of Aepistelle, and we made our home here for several centuries. But there is still kinship between us, no matter how ancient it is."

"Then they must return to your island of paradise with you," Richard said.

"They cannot. They renounced their birthright for all generations to come when they began to practice those dark arts. If they tried to step foot on the island, they would catch fire and burn to ashes immediately. Since we cannot kill them and we cannot bring them with us, we must ask that the people of Aepistelle take revenge on them and finish what has been started."

The freed men of the north cheered. They held a deep hatred for the Tzakabya, who had been their captors for the last few decades. Arnem understood why these men were eager to draw blood, but it didn't feel right to him. He looked to his friends and could see that they felt the same way.

"Why do we need more death?" Gemma asked. She stepped forward. "I hold much hatred for those creatures—perhaps not to the same extent as the people of Emyhrsen, but I've seen enough death to last a lifetime in these last few days. We all have. Why can't we figure out another solution?"

"What do you propose, young Calvertson?"

Gemma looked around, clearly hoping that someone had an idea. It was the Witch of Ferathan, of all people, who met her eyes. Naliah walked over and stood next to her.

"I will help them resettle," Naliah said. "I may be an old hag, but I'm a powerful old hag, as many here will tell you. I will take them back to these ancient lands you speak of. I will use my powers to make the lands fertile and plentiful again. I will protect them as much as is necessary. It's the one thing I'm good at, my lot in this life."

"It is quite a distance, and we did not bring enough ships, but we will help you transport them there if this is truly what you want," the Ancient One said.

"I have a ship!" It was Captain Le'Nelle. Her crew looked at each other with confusion for a moment, and then erupted in cheers. "I ask only that these northerners provide us with barrels of ale as payment and some other food and supplies for sustenance, and we will take the Foreign Ones back home with the witch."

"I cannot think of a reason to deny you permission if this is truly what you wish to do." The Ancient One turned to Jestan. "And you, Jestan the Just, look as if you have something to say. I've never known you to be the silent type."

"Aye, my lord," Jestan said with a bow. It was more deference than Arnem could remember ever seeing from his old pal. "I could use another adventure. More tales to tell means more books to sell. I will happily go with them."

"And I!" Gemma's eyes widened in shock; her brother, George, had just volunteered to go. "If this adventure has taught me anything, it's that I want to see the world. I've only ever known Capital City. Jestan has shown me that there is more than that, and I want to see it with my own eyes. Plus, Captain Le'Nelle's cats are just so precious!"

"Uh, George, are you sure?" Gemma asked. George shot a smile at Jestan, which was returned, and then nodded to his sister. She gave him a hug, proud of her brother.

"That settles it, unless any others want to chime in." There was silence at Emperor Verellion's prompt. "We will meet you travelers back at our former castle when you are ready and discuss the location of our ancestral home. We must return to our island as soon as possible, though, so please make haste."

With that, the Ancient Ones returned to their ship. Maachel was given leave to stay with his old friends and return with Captain Le'Nelle's ship in the coming days.

That evening, Richard, Arnem, Jestan, and Maachel hiked away from the castle, heading east along the river. They caught up on their years apart. They reminded one another of old stories from the Great Journey. Maachel was quiet about his life with the Vheisenia. He seemed distant, even though it was clear he was glad to be among his old friends. As the sun was setting, he turned to the group.

"There is room for all of you among the Vheisenia. You all deserve eternal rest. You earned it with the first journey, and now again with this latest one. I would be most honored to present this plan to the emperor."

Jestan let out his rowdy laugh and slapped Maachel on the back. "I'm all set up for adventure and riches, my old pal. I would visit if I could leave, but I know that's not an option, so I'll have to pass. I mean, can you imagine the crowds that will be on the edge of their seats when I tell stories about fighting those serpent tree monsters? Or sailing with the evil Tzakabya and the old Witch of Ferathan to a far-off land? Not to mention being at sea with Captain Le'Nelle and her crew—that will be a story of its own!"

"Maachel," Arnem said, "you are my oldest, dearest friend. I've always dreamed about what it would have been like if I had taken you up on that offer the first time, or if you had stayed behind. You would have been like an uncle to my children. But for their sake, and for my wife's sake, and for

Denny's sake, I must decline. I miss my family so. I'm miserable without them. I will forever mourn the lack of your presence in our lives, but I cannot go with you. I will take Denny with me; he could use a good home. And I need to salvage what remains of my business, Wynstone and Sons—no, Wynstone *and Family*."

"And you, Richard?" Maachel asked.

Richard had been quiet, even distant, for most of the evening. Arnem thought he was still upset over the loss of King Harold, and it was affecting him deeply.

"I've been wondering if you would ask this question," Richard said at last. "I know that it would be a true honor, one no other man of Aepistelle will ever receive. But for once, here in the north, I feel that I am at home. In Emyhrsen. My father's land. This is where I will remain."

And so he did.

CHAPTER 42

GEMMA

It was some time before Gemma could get away from her parents.

Adelina had procured them an apartment within the castle, one big enough for all four Calvertsons. Gemma's mother had been traumatized by the events of the last several days, and she spent most of the night crying on Gemma's shoulder. At the same time, she was happy to see her little girl again and didn't want to let go of Gemma. Shortly before sunrise, her mother finally fell asleep. Gemma tiptoed out of the apartment and walked down to the audience chamber, where Naliah and the children of Ferathan were sleeping on cots.

When Gemma entered the chamber, Naliah was already standing in the middle of the room, facing the door. Somehow, she had been expecting Gemma. Gemma motioned for her to follow her out the door so as to not wake the children. They made their way into the ruins of the courtyard, not far from where Tseledon Ni-Alwen had crashed to his death the day before.

"I felt your presence all night, girl. You were waiting to talk to me. Your mother needed you more, though. It was good of you to stay with her. A great leader you are at such a young age."

"Thank you, Naliah." Gemma paced slowly around the courtyard, her head lowered in sadness.

"I fear I know what you mean to ask, but I need to hear it from you directly."

"It's just... yesterday, you laid your hands on my father. You said something in your tongue to him, and his eyes cleared. His mind began to work like it always should have. When I looked at him in that moment, I saw the man I always knew was trapped behind his troubled exterior. It was like the gray clouds drifted away from him for the first time in my lifetime and the sun was shining on him.

"When I set off on my journey, one thing I hoped to learn was what happened to my father during the war. What made him lose his mind. I thought perhaps I'd learn something about it from Richard. He seems to have trouble with his emotions, but it's nothing compared to what my father suffers. Yet my father became his old self again after Tseledon was killed. Your spell wore off."

"You'd like to know the spell? So you can keep bringing back pieces of him that aren't really there anymore? It won't work, I'm afraid. It won't last, and the more you try, the less effective it will be. Eventually, it will start to damage his mind instead, even more than it already is."

"But you made a spell last for seventy years over the entire population of Ferathan. Why would a spell over one man be more difficult?"

"Child, if you think I didn't fatally damage every man, woman, and child in Ferathan with my selfishness, you have learned nothing. Please just enjoy the time you have left with your father. Accept him for who he is and be there for him. Perhaps the journey back home will be good for him; it'll keep him away from the crowded city he's been trapped in for years. That may be the best elixir for him, but he will never return to the man he once was. I'm sorry."

Gemma looked at Naliah with deep disappointment. *It's not fair*, she thought. *I'm not being fair to her, expecting a miracle.*

Gemma began to cry. She reached for the old witch and embraced her.

"I'm the one who should be sorry," Gemma said. "You are right, of course. I will love my father for who he is, not for who he was. Thank you, Naliah. Thank you for everything."

———

By late afternoon, the *Ales and Sails* was stocked with the requisite drinks, food, and more drinks. The few Tzakabyan soldiers who were being held captive in King Harold's castle were brought aboard. Captain Le'Nelle and her crew, along with Jestan, George, Maachel, and Naliah, would soon sail downriver to meet up with the Vheisenia at their former castle. There they would split the crew, with one half taking control of a remaining black ship that had belonged to the Tzakabya. The Vheisenia would bring the Foreign Ones out and split them between the two ships, give instructions on how to find their ancestral lands, and take Maachel back with them to their own island of paradise.

Gemma knew it was time to say goodbye to those she had met over the course of her journey. Everyone gathered on the riverbank. Gemma's mother was crying hysterically on George's shoulder, and Gemma was relieved her own shoulder was free of tears for that short time. Finally, George pulled away and gave his sister a hug.

"I am so proud of you, Gem. You've always accomplished anything and everything you wanted to, ever since we were little. You've saved an entire kingdom this time."

"And you, George—you came out of your shell! You'd never left Capital City before, and now you're heading across the seas! This is crazy. Are you sure we're not dreaming?"

"Best dream we could have come up with, if we are actually dreaming. Take care of Mom and Dad for me. I'm sorry I won't be there to help, but I guess that's not much different than it's been. Thank you for being there for them. And don't forget to take care of my cats! Give them lots of kisses for me!"

"And Wellyn?" Gemma asked.

George's eyebrows shot up. Gemma was sure he hadn't even thought of Wellyn during his entire journey.

"Please, tell her goodbye for me. I think she'll understand. It's been a long time coming, and I think I've finally found myself." As he spoke, George shot a glance up the riverbank at Jestan, who was boarding the *Ales and Sails*.

Mrs. Calvertson began weeping loudly again, so George allowed her to throw her arms around him once more. Even their father looked emotional, and he joined in on the hug. Gemma used the opportunity to escape for a few minutes. She knew Richard had been looking over at her, waiting for an opportunity to speak with her. She walked up to him.

"Richard, that day back in Pinedrop when you caught me following you, did you ever think the two of us would end up doing something as enormous as what we've done?"

Richard the Elusive's usual look of seriousness was broken by a laugh. His stiffness softened.

"I truly thought you were a spy then. Even as we fled through those tunnels under the forest, I wasn't convinced that you weren't one. We did well, though. *You* did well. Even in spite of what happened to Walker. I'm sorry I didn't do more to save him. And I'm sorry I didn't do more in the battle."

"Richard, we defeated the enemy, and we did it together. You, me, and everyone else here. What more could you want?"

A wave of guilt washed over Richard's face. He slumped his shoulders in shame.

"For twenty years, I stayed holed up in my home, frantically searching for answers. I knew there was danger, and I thought that if I kept studying, I'd figure out how to stop it. I lost out on any chance of friendship, of fellowship, of love. I pushed away my old friends, even endangered them with the paranoid letters I sent them. And when it all came down to it, I didn't have the answer. I didn't know how to stop the Foreign Ones. I stood in shame as you came up with the solution. You encouraged the group to recite those words. It was you who shot down that evil despot in the tower. All along, Gemma, it was you. You were the solution all the ancient texts of all the religions of Aepistelle pointed to. It was you this whole time. I'm sorry I didn't recognize it sooner."

"I'm not something special," Gemma said. "I'm not a chosen one. I was just in the right place at the right time. I had a great set of teachers and companions to guide me. We all did this together."

Richard wept. And then he laughed. Gemma was confused, but she broke into laughter, too.

"You know, for everything we achieved, there sure has been a lot of crying around here. It's not like this is goodbye forever or anything."

"It is, Gemma. I'm staying here. I will help this kingdom rebuild, and I will live among these people for the rest of my days. Aepistelle is not my home; it never was. It was merely a hiding place. It was the place my parents hid me away in my youth, and it was the place I hid myself away for the last twenty-five years. I'm done hiding. I'm ready to live among my own people now in Emyhrsen. So yes, it is goodbye. Farewell, Gemma Calvertson, and thank you for all you've taught me on this great journey we've been on together."

They embraced one final time.

GEMMA AND HER PARENTS SET OFF FROM KING HAROLD'S castle the next morning.

Arnem, Denny, Marzele, the captive King Davin, and the defeated soldiers of Aepistelle would all make their way south once the royal ships were repaired. The Calvertsons had been invited to sail with them. However, Gemma and her parents had declined. Gemma had requested enough supplies to allow them to take their time rather than heading directly home.

She said farewell to Arnem, who made her promise that she would come visit Plentimore Valley someday to meet his family. She then threw her arms around Denny. He was bashful at first but then tightened his arms around her. She gave him a kiss on the cheek, and when she stepped back a moment later, he was as bright red as a fresh tomato. Arnem laughed and rubbed his hand over the boy's head, ruffling his hair like a playful father with his son.

Gemma guided her parents across the river and then west to the former castle of the Ancient Ones. It was vacant by the time they arrived, so they spent two full days and nights there. Geoffrey seemed to remember the place, and he brightened up immensely. It wasn't quite the same as when Naliah had put the temporary spell on him, but it was as close as Gemma could have dreamed of.

By the time they left, Geoffrey was able to lead them up into the mountains that overlooked the castle to the north and what was once the forest in every other direction. It was there that a younger Geoffrey Calvertson and a small company of his fellow soldiers had witnessed the flash that had destroyed the forest and killed an army of thousands. This time, however, it was a place of new beginnings. They set up camp and watched the sunset.

Across the campfire that night, Gemma met her father's eyes. In them, she saw neither trauma nor confusion, neither sadness nor disappointment.

She saw a person who had sacrificed his well-being to help save a kingdom. That man looked into Gemma's eyes and saw the same thing.

The eyes of a hero.

***

GEMMA'S STORY CONTINUES IN *THE ISLE OF ABANDON-MENT*. PLEASE VISIT MACHETEANDQUILL.COM OR YOUR FAVORITE BOOKSTORE TO ORDER A COPY.

NEWSLETTER

Please join the author's email newsletter at https://www.MacheteAndQuill.com for exclusive updates, behind-the-scenes content, and more.

If you enjoyed this story, please leave a review on Goodreads, BookBub, and your favorite online retailer so others can hear about it. Please tell your friends and librarians about the book as well!

Thank you.

AUTHOR'S NOTE

This is the second version of the book released. The original release of this book was in November 2021.

Though the text of the actual story remains the same, the cover and series name were updated in 2024, and I retitled this book from *Gemma Calvertson and the Forest of Despair* to simply *The Forest of Despair*. The series was previously titled *The Aepistelle Chronicles*. The original cover art was by Natalia Junqueira of Dawn Book Design.

I updated the series name because I felt the original name was confusing. Those who haven't read the books yet won't have any connection the the name *Aepistelle*, and even those who have read the books may not know how to pronounce it. As the series progressed, the theme of Gemma and her friends fighting for truth in a nation shrouded in dark lies really became more apparent to me. Likewise, Marzele's journey in his faith also matched the new name. Thus, *The Pierced Shadow Archive* was born, and while *The Aepistelle Chronicles* name is no more, you may just see it pop up in the final book of the series, *The Realm Beyond*, in a very special way.

I loved the original covers, but I also had to change those. I attempted to rehire the original designer of *The Forest of Despair* and *The Isle of Abandonment* to make changes on those covers, but the designer appears to have stopped communicating with clients in late 2023. Unfortunately, I had to move on with a new designer and pay to have all new covers designed. The silver lining was that even though I loved the cover of *The Witch of Ferathan* as well, it never matched the other books as it had a different designer. By starting over, I was able to get a design theme that matched across all of the books in the series.

If you happen to have the older covers of any of these books, think of it as a limited edition cover. I hope you'll cherish it, as I love those original covers and they'll always be important parts of my publishing journey. Thank you for your support.

We Are Not Alone in the Dark

A high school bully, quarreling friends, and an abusive father are the least of Bryan's worries. When night comes, so do the visitors, and he can't fight back. Who will rescue Bryan if nobody believes him? A coming-of-age alien horror novel.

Ditch of the Damned and Other Tales

A collection of five short stories by Ryan Hoyt.

Senior Class: A Raventree Hollow Story

Pearl and Rosemary are the last of their kind. At 90 years old, death calls for them. Who will be the left standing? A short story chapbook set in the town of Raventree Hollow, this can be read as a standalone tale or enjoyed along with *Raventree Hollow*.

Butterscotch: A Raventree Hollow Story

A family moves into an old home to find the previous owner has left behind a hutch with a candy dish. Aggressive neighbors, a trio of cats, and a hidden purple bag lead the family to seek out answers. "Butterscotch" is a short story chapbook set in the town of Raventree Hollow.

Ditch of the Damned

While traveling with her family across the American frontier, Eudora is pulled off the wagon trail by a sensation deep within her bones. She ignores a warning sign and proceeds toward a hole in the earth in the middle of the wilderness. "Ditch of the Damned" is a short story set in 1847.

The Hoarder's House

Erica's sister went missing in her own home. As Erica and her husband search for the lost woman, they find something luring in the depths of depravity.

Freddy Goodman (Ain't No Good Man)

His coming-of-age story was *so* twenty years ago. So why do the words of that old witch still haunt him? A short story of contemporary fiction with elements of magical realism.

ACKNOWLEDGMENTS

Thank you, reader, for going on this journey with these characters and with me. I've been dreaming about this world for years now, and I have so many more stories to tell in it. I hope you'll come along with me for more adventures with Gemma Calvertson and her friends in Aepistelle.

I couldn't have completed this without the support of my wife, Marsha, and our daughters, Natalie and Daisy. They've allowed me the time and space in between my day job and making family dinners, or little bits of a break from hanging out on the weekends. I may have replaced a few of their bedtime reading sessions with drafts of this story, hoping to get some feedback outside of my target audience.

I am also indebted to my friends and fellow writers Muriel Tronc and Dave Howard. They each read an early draft of this manuscript and provided invaluable feedback and encouragement that helped to shape future drafts and edits. Please seek out their works and consider showing your support; Muriel has a pair of YA novels, *Five More Pixs* and *Call Me, Gwapo*, while Dave has written *Death Before Life (The Wall Book 1)* and its forthcoming sequel. Thank you also to my other beta readers, including Marsha and the fine folks at The Spun Yarn.

Gratitude is also owed to my mom for instilling the love of books in me and always taking me to the bookstore and the library. From R.L. Stine in the fourth grade to Stephen

King and Richard Matheson in middle school, my mom always let me pick out new worlds to explore.

Finally, this book wouldn't be half as sleek without the copy and line editing talents of Alison Cherry and the design skills of MiblArt. Please consider their services if you are working on a book of your own. The original release of this book had cover art by Natalia Junqueira of Dawn Book Design.

Thank you all for your support, and I look forward to sharing more stories with you very soon. Please follow me at MacheteAndQuill.com, where you can find links to my mailing list and social media sites.